PREVAILING WIND

A NOVEL BY

THOMAS DOLBY

ARCHWAY
PUBLISHING

Archway Publishing books may be ordered through booksellers or by contacting:

Archway Publishing
1663 Liberty Drive
Bloomington, IN 47403
www.archwaypublishing.com
844-669-3957

Cover Illustration and internal sketches by Russ Kramer. www.russkramer.com

ISBN: 978-1-6657-5831-4 (sc)
ISBN: 978-1-6657-5833-8 (hc)
ISBN: 978-1-6657-5832-1 (e)

Library of Congress Control Number: 2024905464

Print information available on the last page.

Archway Publishing rev. date: 05/20/2024

For Kathleen, my compass and my North Star.

"A ship snatches remote voices from the air in its wires, and serves as a sounding board for wind and waves. But a foghorn speaks of the menace that lies at the edge of land, calling up thoughts of heroism or penetrating the night to disturb our dreams."

(Frank Graham, Jr.)

PART I

CHAPTER ONE

SHORTLY before his seventeenth birthday, Davey Haskell caught his first glimpse of unimaginable wealth. Not just the fancy clothes and automobiles, but the sick-making, absolute, Astor-Rockefeller-Vanderbilt sort of wealth.

It happened on a warm evening in the late summer of 1913. The Atlantic horizon was dotted with sails. With a fading sea breeze behind them, the shabby Deer Isle fishing fleet were heading back in to Stonington Harbor from rocky coves and inlets all around Penobscot Bay. It had been another dreadful day for Davey and his brother—the latest of many. Their lobster pots were empty. A few pathetic flounders and one or two sardines flapped in the bilges of their leaky fishing sloop[1].

Davey sat cross-legged in the bows, sifting through his gill nets, humming to himself. To hide the acne on his forehead, he'd let his tousled fair hair grow until he could hardly see out. His skinny forearms were criss-crossed with scars from hauling up the barnacle-covered traps. His brother Jacob, at twenty-one, was more rugged, with deep-set eyes and a square chin. Jake was perched on the sloop's stern, a rolled-up smoke between his lips, trimming the mainsheet with one leathery hand and steering with the other.

Jacob grunted: "Here's trouble."

A gaff-rigged catboat was rounding the iron marker buoy off Sam

---

[1] There is a Glossary of Sailing Terms and sail plan diagrams at the end of this book

Stick Ledge. It wasn't hard to make out Bill Otley at the tiller, with his lank black hair and weathered sea coat. He was from the West Bay fleet—their sworn enemies.

Jacob said under his breath: "The other lot ain't fared much better, by the look of things."

"Who's the ginger bloke with the sour puss?" Davey whispered.

"I'll tell you later."

Otley's mate on the foredeck was a grisly older lobsterman with a high, sun-baked forehead, and stringy reddish hair pushed back into a wool cap. He tipped a bucket of undersized lobsters off the bow with a plop. When he spotted the brothers watching him, he scowled and spat a gob of sputum over the side.

"Billy Otley!" Jacob shouted across the water, "anything feedin'?"

Otley just fixed his gaze straight ahead, his arm draped over the tiller.

Jacob steered a little closer, close enough to see the pockmarks on Otley's craggy face, and hailed him again. "Hey Bill, race you back to the harbor? I'll wager your catch against ours."

Bad idea, Davey thought. Otley's hull number was DW63—his catboat was nearly new. Their own clinker sloop, DE14, was twenty years older, with a mainsail like a yellowing tearag. Their Pa built her by hand before Davey was born.

But they'd got Otley's attention. He flicked a glance their way. "What've you got there, Haskell?"

Jacob reached down into the bottom of the boat and rattled an empty lobster pot. "Five red fatties," he said, with a sly wink to Davey, "couple of keepers, and a bucket of cod. You up for it?"

Davey was trying to stifle a laugh. "You're a lying sod, Jake," he muttered through the side of his mouth. "What happens when he susses us out?"

They were only a boat-length apart now, and Otley's mate leaned forward, his grizzled hands gripping the gunwale. He had a grating, adenoidal whine: "We could lick you sailing *backwards*, Jake Haskell— you and that weird little brother of yours."

Jacob shrugged. "Come on then, you old buggers! We'll race you *backwards*."

"—and we'll beat the shite out of you, an' all!" Davey yelped, pulling himself up to his full height. He wished his voice was deeper, more like his brother's.

The freckled one bared a single gold tooth, hissing with laughter. "Backwards, eh?" He grinned at Otley who nodded his head. "You're on. But you fuckers ain't got no chance. Last boat to Powder House Island hands over the whole day's catch." Otley threw the tiller over, and the catboat jibed away in a sheet of foam.

Both crews jumped to it. It was a routine they were used to—they often had to sail backwards to pick up a string of lobster traps. "You steer, titch," Jacob said, and he made his way forward shoving pots, oars, anchor and tarpaulin into the bows. Then he planted his feet with his back to the mast. "Bring her up nice and slow."

Taking the helm, Davey hauled in the mainsheet and carved a smooth turn into the eye of the wind. The sloop came to a near standstill, sail flapping, bobbing in the chop. Jacob leaned his broad muscular arms back against the boom, forcing it steadily out until it touched the shroud. At first the sail just acted as a brake; but as it filled with wind from the wrong side, their sloop started to move through the water in reverse, slowly at first, then picking up speed. Davey could feel the fragile balance of forces acting on his rudder. It took a few moments to find the sweet spot; he leaned his weight one way or the other to help steer, careful not to over-correct. It came naturally to him. It was just physics.

Otley's catboat was on a parallel course, fifty feet away. The two fishing boats were neck-and-neck now, ploughing stern first through the foamy water. The West Bay boat should have been faster, with her newer sail and cleaner bottom; but Bill yanked awkwardly on the tiller, and his freckly mate at the boom was slighter and punier than Jacob. A stone's throw from Powder House Island, it was plain that Davey and Jacob were in the lead. Pulling away, they led past the tip of the island by three clear boat-lengths. Jacob was grinning ear to ear; he started singing *Spanish Ladies,* as if to rub salt in the wound. The West Bay pair looked dejected.

Davey spun the little sloop beam-on and let his mainsail flog. When

Bill Otley pulled the catboat alongside with a bump, his face was grave. "Reckon you've earned this, you lads, fair and square," his ginger-haired mate said, and he dumped the entire contents of a metal bait pail over the side of the brothers' sloop: herring heads, fish guts in seawater, and a few anemic-looking black eels.

Cackling, Otley hauled in his sail and took off towards the western harbor. Davey was left staring down into the pool of fish guts around his bare ankles. The red-haired one hung back off a shroud, gave them the finger, and rasped: "Apple don't fall far from the tree, eh lads?"

Davey plucked a string of cod viscera out of his rolled-up pant leg. He stared after the catboat, a foul taste in his mouth. "You know him, that ginger geezer?"

"Ayuh, his name's Gardie Greene. Nasty piece of work. I'd give that sod a wide berth next time, kid."

By the time the brothers reached the breakwater, the breeze had died to a balmy nothing. It was already half-dark, and spectral patches of fog settled on the water. They dropped the sail and took took to their oars, slipping between a couple of rusty dredgers at anchor. The tide was out, and the sloop's wake rippled along mudbanks that burped bad gases. The cranes and warehouses were deserted, with nets spread to dry on empty crates. A stench hung in the air. It was a Deer Isle evening, just like any other.

Davey Haskell had smelled that stench every day of his life. He was born here on the island, and he'd seldom ventured beyond the Penobscot Bay fishing grounds. He never had money or prospects. He wasn't swarthy, or good at sweet-talking the ladies like his brother. The local Catholic school didn't amount to much—Father Michael was more of a toucher than a teacher. But Stonington had a small public library, with all twenty-nine volumes of the Encyclopedia Britannica. He pored over them, any chance he could get, and made copious notes and drawings in his sketchbook. He mainly liked geography, boatbuilding, and navigation. Anything else he needed to know of the world, he could read in mystery magazines like *Argosy*, *The Thrill Book*, and *Top Notch*.

Plus he'd been to the motion picture house in Bangor—twice!

Ma said he had his Pa's eyes, pale like the dawn sky. But he could thread a course through that harbor in pitch darkness, or eyes closed. With his scrawny arms and narrow shoulders, he kept his oar in precise step with the sound of Jacob's, matching him stroke for stroke.

Jacob took a hand off his oar to squish a black-fly on the back of his neck. His dark hair was tied back with string, and he'd unbuttoned his checkered shirt to the belt. Jake didn't talk much when he was working, especially on a day like today, when the catch was crap. It really had been a day to forget. But that was all about to change.

Davey was the first to spot it. He stopped rowing and motioned with his chin. Jacob caught the line of his stare and swiveled round. There was a strange silhouette on the wharf that didn't belong.

Deer Isle's lowly fishing harbor had an unexpected visitor.

A white motor yacht lay alongside the landing pier, a trickle of steam still rising from her funnel. The glow from her oil lamps was mirrored in the slack water, showing her to be eighty, maybe ninety feet at the waterline. Even docked as she was now, her sleek lines gave a powerful impression of speed.

Davey mouthed the name emblazoned on the motor yacht's stern: *Nemesis*. She was the most luxurious vessel he'd ever seen. The mahogany wheelhouse had a spinning observation window in its windscreen, and some sort of radio antenna mounted above. At her mast's peak, lit by the anchor light, hung a single ensign, with a white star in the center of two red stripes. Her low afterdeck encircled a wide cockpit and canopy. The plump silk cushions on her bench seats were monogrammed with the letters *N.Y.Y.C.*

The fog seemed to close in, deadening all sound. A flounder's tail flopped in the bilges. He was about to speak, but Jacob shushed him with a finger to his lips.

They glided through the oily water with their oars dripping. No one was on deck, but the yacht's interior shone with light. The angle blocked their view into the engine room, but he could make out several crewmen in their undershirts, playing cards around a table, smoking and laughing.

They let the sloop's momentum carry them on past the galley, where a dark-skinned man in a chef's hat was scrubbing pots; and beneath the picture windows of the brightly lit saloon. Inside, scratchy music was playing from a gramophone record. The curtains were tied back, and the beveled glass was steamed up, giving off an electric glow like the movie screen at the Gaumont.

Davey brushed the hair out of his eyes and stepped up onto the sloop's thwart. Balancing on tiptoes with a hand on the mast, he was just able to see in to the saloon, where a curious scenario was unfolding. Dinner was over, and a servant girl was scraping crumbs off the tablecloth. She cut a slender figure in her uniform, lace apron and cap. She poured two cups of coffee from a silver pot, and brought the tray to the gentlemen at the far end of the table.

He could see the two men's lips moving, but it was hard to make out their words. Were they quarreling? The older one had coiffed black hair and a Kaiser mustache that turned up at the tips, and his necktie was undone. He leaned heavily on the arm of his chair, swilling brandy in a crystal glass; with his free hand he made wild shapes in the air. His companion wore a quilted smoking jacket. In his mid to late twenties, he gave off a noble, well-bred air. He clutched a wooden pipe to his lips. Davey caught the faint aroma of his tobacco.

They drifted past the second window. Behind the gentlemen, on a stool facing the bar, a woman in a shimmering evening dress was touching up her lipstick in the mirror of her compact. The maid offered her coffee, but she waved it away. A jeweled necklace glinted green in the gaslight.

Mustache seemed upset. He stood up, red in the face, gesticulating as if to drive home a point. Pipe sat across the table from him, listening intently, occasionally shaking his head. He blew smoke and gave a curt response, which only seemed to make Mustache more flustered.

Lipstick swiveled on her bar stool. Her voice was shrill, and Davey was able to make out a few words: "Oh, do shut *up*, Cochran. Both of you! You're such a *bore*."

Davey turned to his brother in the stern of the sloop to see if he was getting this too. Jacob just tossed his head back, and pouted his lips, pretending to fiddle with a precious necklace.

Mustache slumped back down like a spoiled child. He took a sip of brandy, wrinkling his nose. Lipstick reached into a cigarette box, fixed one in her holder and lit it. She flashed Mustache a superior look. Then she slinked off the bar stool and across the saloon. There was a curious electrical apparatus on the bulkhead. She lifted its receiver to her ear, wound the handle a few times, and shouted into the horn.

"Hello? *Hello?*" After a few seconds, she wedged the earpiece back on its hook. "Still nothing! Damn and *bother.*" She had a trace of a foreign accent that Davey couldn't place.

The servant girl had her back to the gentlemen, stacking dishes on a tray. Mustache, his face flushed with drink, was eyeing her hindquarters. Glancing back to make sure Lipstick wouldn't see, he reached a hairy hand up inside the hem of the maid's apron to the fleshy part between stocking top and buttock. The girl recoiled at first, but checked herself, then turned and shuffled off towards the double doors with her tray.

There was a crawling sensation under Davey's skin. He caught a fleeting glimpse of the poor girl's face as she passed close to the window. Her eyes had misted over, and her bottom lip was quivering. She couldn't have been more than eighteen—only a year or two older than him. With her blonde hair tucked up into the lace cap, and her milky complexion, she was simply the most angelic creature he'd ever laid eyes on. He imagined her profile framed in a vignette, the kind they sold on the boardwalk in Camden; he could almost smell the candy apples.

His chest tightened. He longed to rescue her, like they did in the movies; but he was helpless. He turned to see if his brother felt the same way. Jacob only stuck out his tongue, panting like a dog.

Just then a heavy wheelhouse door clanged open twenty feet above them, snapping Davey out of his rêverie. He flopped down and pretended to busy himself with his nets. A bearded figure in a peaked cap staggered to the rail and leaned over. Swaying precariously, the man spat a glob of tobacco juice into the harbor, reached in his coat for a slim flask, and fumbled it open. When he caught sight of the boys in their fishing boat, he stiffened and cleared his throat.

Jacob touched his knuckle to his forehead. "Evenin', Skippah."

The big man grunted.

"Whose barky is this, then?" Jacob asked, eyeing the elegant sweep of the yacht.

The big man spat again, narrowly missing their sloop. "That's nae concern o' yours, laddie. Not 'til tomorrow morning, anyroad." The light of the oil lamps etched deep suspicious lines on his face. He leaned farther over the railing, locking eyes with Jacob's. Then his glare shifted to Davey.

"Would you lads happen to be Haskells, at all?" the Scot barked. Davey froze.

Jacob's eyes narrowed. "Who's asking?"

The Scot flashed Jacob a knowing look. "*Aye*. That figures. Haskells, eh. I heard about your old dad—Ernie, isn't it? You two're the spit image. How is he bearin' up?"

"That's no concern o' yours, neither," Jacob said with a sneer.

Davey whispered through the side of his mouth, "Tell him to fuck off, Jake."

The big man scowled. "Well now. Why don't you lads spread the word among your fisherman mateys. We're up here to talk business with the best sailors among you—if there be any." He laughed and turned away from the rail, calling over his shoulder: "We'll be in the back room of the Oddfellows Hall tomorrow, after church." The word *church* was more of a belch. The wheelhouse door slammed behind him.

The brothers rowed on all the way into the shallows without a word. Barefooted, they hauled their sloop up the muddy beach in front of their shed, and made it fast to the mooring chains. Jacob went to fetch a lantern, and by its light they began to work together to flake their nets over the side of the sloop, throwing the day's paltry catch into a flat wooden crate they could barely fill.

Davey loosened the handkerchief around his neck. "What was that all about, then?"

"Use your loaf, shorty." Jacob faced the distant glow from the yacht.

"It's happening all over again. Remember Pa used to tell us about when the rich men came to Deer Isle? Nah, you wouldn't, you were too young."

"Nobody never tells you stuff when you're the littlest," Davey mumbled.

"You know, how he raced on the *Defender*, in the old days? In the America's Cup?"

"Ayuh. I like them stories. Tell me again."

Jacob leaned an elbow on the sloop's transom and made shapes in the night air. "Big topsail cutters. *Defender*, in '95, and *Vigilant* before that. There was this rich gent, came here from New York to pick up a crew from Stonington sailors—Iselin, that was his name, Ollie Iselin. Sail racing legend, he was. Won the Cup four times, or something."

"Why here?"

"Because Deer Islers are the best seamen on the coast, that's why."

Davey nodded. He felt a warm pang of pride.

"And it was Deer Islers as won it for him, too." Jacob dipped into his tobacco tin and rolled himself a smoke. "You know that ring Pa's got, in the box by his bed? When they scrapped *Defender* and melted down her topsides, Iselin gave each man an aluminum ring for a keepsake. Even though Pa was mostly stuck down below-decks."

"That who we saw in the saloon, then? Ollie Iselin?"

"No, numbass. He'll be an old man by now. These fellas are younger by far. But they're from the same club, see—the New York Yacht Club, I remember their flag. They'll be up here looking for a new crew, out of the best sailors on Deer Isle." He untangled a big mess of seaweed from the net and threw it aside on the mud. "Which rules you out for a start, bub, 'cos you're just a fart in a mitten." He jabbed Davey the ribs.

Davey made to play along. He was actually two inches taller than his brother. Since his sixteenth birthday, he'd fairly exploded out of his shoes. He was over six foot now, but whereas his brother had a broad burly chest and square jaw, Davey was more gangly, with his mop of sandy hair and his dimple. Ma said not to worry, his shoulders would fill out soon enough. Like his brother, he'd sailed since he could walk. By the time they were ten, they knew where and when to fish, how to bait and lay traps, how to read the messages in the different colors of the marker buoys. Jacob got the knowledge from their Pa. Davey had to learn it from Coo Bray and the other lobstermen in the East Bay fleet. He only faintly remembered going to sea with Pa, years ago when Pa was still well enough to work.

That previous spring, Jacob had got lucky. In the lean years, local men were forced to take jobs on the big commercial freighters, up and down the east coast, to Nova Scotia and New Haven and New Jersey, down to the Chesapeake Bay and as far as Charleston, with cargos of granite from Deer Isle's quarries, or holds filled with seal pelts and furs from the Bay of Fundy. Jake and half a dozen mates had picked up a few weeks' work in New York Harbor on the coal barges that plied the Hudson and the East River. He was a topmastman, and topmastmen got two dollars extra a week, for the risk. He came home from New York with his wages from the coal barges in his pocket, and wild stories that kept Davey up long into the night: the massive buildings with their tops in the clouds, and the gleaming ironworks of the Brooklyn Bridge. The awful immigrant slums of lower Manhattan. The women of the night who peddled their wares to the longshoremen and dockhands. And, of course, the yacht racing.

"We seen them toffs heading out to Sandy Hook every weekend, in their money-buckets," Jacob went on. "Big honkin' topsail racers, some almost as tall as the skyscrapers. Canvas enough to cover a cow pasture." He tossed a couple of undersized sardines onto the rocks for the seagulls.

Davey gazed out across the darkened waters and tried to imagine those immaculate sailboats criss-crossing their own Penobscot Bay.

"I bet they were quick as lightning?" he said.

"Wicked quick, mate, but flimsy. Useless for anything but racing and wagering. After a couple of seasons they was too beat up to be worth anything."

"Jeezum. Imagine having that kind of dough. And these toffs, were they any good ?"

"Nah. Most had professional skippers to steer for 'em, and big crews, all decked out in their personal colors. Sometimes the toffs weren't even on board, I reckon; they'd just watch from their steam yachts, lordin' it with their rich friends. Pa said, at the big regattas, they'd lose hundreds on a race and laugh about it all the way back to the clubhouse."

Davey stuck out the tip of his tongue. "What about when it came to racing against the Brits?"

"Well, that's the America's Cup, ain't it? It only comes round every few years, and when it does it's front-page news. Half of New York turns out to watch. There's some *serious* bettin' money changes hands. It's bigger than boxing—bigger'n the horses, even. Good wages for the crews, too, but wicked hard sailin', for weeks on end. Workin' those big cutters takes top seamen, as can pull together. And us Mainers fit the ticket, 'cos we're church men."

"Why do the toffs even care?"

"'Cos at night we read the Holy Bible in our hammocks, 'stead of going out drinking. Well, most do, anyhow," Jake laughed. "So, years ago, they started coming up here to pick out their crews, with one of the paid skippers, Uriah Rhodes. He knew what he was about on a race boat, all right. Pa said he never liked him though—Scots bastard, ran the barky like a proper slave driver."

Jacob grabbed a moribund black eel that was tangled in the purse of the net. He whacked its head on the gunwale and handed it, stunned, to Davey. "You give that to Ma, titch. She'll salt it up and make you a nice pie."

Eels made Davey queasy, but he stuffed it in his inside pocket anyway. It wasn't much to bring home. As for the rest of the meager catch, it would only fetch a buck and a half, maybe two at market in the morning. But Ma needed the cash, with one son moved out, and Pa upstairs in bed, unable to speak.

There were gaps in the clouds now, and patches of dappled moonlight on the water. They finished putting the old sloop to bed, and let her float off the beach on her weighted mooring rope. The usual row of cormorants had settled for the night on the exposed pilings to dry their skeletal wings. Black flies were out in force.

Davey scratched his ribs inside his shirt. It was easy to picture Jake up the topmast of some huge racing cutter, swinging about in the rigging like an orangutan. But for his own part, Davey had never sailed anything bigger than their clinker-built sloop. He didn't know if he could cut it on a real racer, a Cup contender at that.

"So what do you know about this tea fella, then?" Davey asked.

"Who… Lipton?"

"That's the gent. Sir Thomas Lipton."

"Well, he's quite a rig. British geezer, stinkin' rich. He's come over here to race for the Cup three times, and lost it three times. The papers love him though, so he keeps coming back."

"He must be selling loads of tea."

"Ugh. Tea." Jacob pretended to stick his finger down his throat, and they both cracked up. They headed up the beach towards the ice house with the crate between them. Davey threw a glance back over his shoulder at the *Nemesis*, rocking gently on the rising tide. He said, "You really think they'll be hiring us for a new Cup crew?"

"Must be. Whoever this Cochran fella is, he ain't come to Deer Isle for a vacation. There'll probably be tryouts. And I'm going up for it, kid! I'll be first in line at the Oddfellows tomorrow. Doubt they'll take a gawmy little shortass like you, though," he said, ducking and jabbing at Davey with his free hand.

"Ayuh." Davey put up his guard, a bit late. "It's worth a shot, I reckon."

"You're sixteen. You have to finish school. Ma'd never let you sign up."

"No harm in stoppin' down to the Oddfellows tomorrow, though—just to show my face?"

"Ah, I wouldn't do that, Dave. It'll only upset her."

A new thought occurred to him, but he stored it away, changing the subject. "So that Scots geezer with the beard on the foredeck, that must have been—"

"Uriah bloody Rhodes, mate. Here to give us peasants a good bollockin'."

Jacob dropped to his haunches, flipped up the collar of his coat, and struck a match to relight the butt of his smoke. Sucking it deep in to his lungs, he peered out across the Bay at the darkened horizon.

"Never thought I'd get a real shot at a Cup ring, me. They ain't run it in, I dunno, more'n ten years. Might be my one chance to get out of this pisshole for good, titch, and have a real life."

Nothing stayed a secret for long in Stonington. The next morning there was a palpable buzz in the town. The moment mass was over, the doors of St. Mary's burst open and a stream of men poured out. They hurried the five blocks down Main Street to the Oddfellows meeting hall. A few pulled hunks of bread out of their handkerchiefs, or legs of cold chicken, and ate while they walked. Davey was carried along with the crowd, in his Sunday best, such as it was: a pair of dark blue trousers that were too short, his only good shirt, and a wool jacket. But at the crossroads he broke away from the mob. He peeled off down the side lane behind the telegraph office, and squeezed through the hole in Rollie Staples' chicken wire fence, right by the harbor. He skipped over the detritus at the high water line, and bolted round the beach.

It was good to run. He felt wild, and free. Father Michael's sermon went on forever. It was all about loving thy brother—so how come on days like these he felt nothing in his heart but loathing for his? This was just the way Jake was. He never missed a chance to sail closest to the wind or be first to pick up a crab pot, or beat the fleet back to harbor by a couple of boat lengths. Always had to know the shortest route home, have the cleanest bottom. Had to net the biggest catch, get the best price at market; flashing his money around for the girls to see. Jake was a rat. Davey tried not to let the rat gnaw at him—for Ma's sake, really. It made her so low when the two of them fought.

He reached the back of Oddfellows Hall, and snuck in along the fence that stank of urine and seaweed. It was a single-story building with a leaky saltbox roof, and a windowless main room, built back in the days when the whole town's population was tiny. It was never designed for the hundred and fifty men now filing in through the double doors. Some were still clutching their family prayer books, milling around in small groups or standing on the wooden benches along the side walls.

There was no sign of Jacob yet. Davey wriggled his way through the crowd. He'd always had the knack of making himself invisible. He climbed along the back of a bench and hauled himself up into the rafters, and settled on a splintery beam, where he had a perfect view of the hall as it filled up.

Despite their Sunday attire, these were the same plain fishermen he saw every day on the water. He recognized most of the faces. As usual, the islanders gravitated to one or other side of the room, according to the generations-old division of the six original families, and their lobster grounds in the East or West Bay. Not much love was lost between the factions. "There's ancient scores to be settled," Jacob was fond of reminding him. Davey never took it that seriously; he got on with pretty much anybody.

He'd almost forgotten the brown paper bag of plums in the pocket of his coat. They were squashed to a pulp, and dripped through his fingers, but one was still edible. He sucked on it and surveyed the hall. There was Jake now, clowning around with a bunch of his pals from McGinty's Pub.

The air was already thick with dust and tobacco smoke. A campaign table had been set up on the low platform, with the Maine state flag as a backdrop. Fred Weed, the retired skipper of the Stonington trawler fleet, sat propped up in a chair with a blanket over his legs, flanked by his doting wife. A couple of the older fishermen went over to pay their respects. The hall was packed, buzzing with laughter and eager conversation.

Then he saw three strangers enter the room from the side door. Chatter died down, and their heavy footfalls echoed on the worn floorboards. The crowd parted for them. They seated themselves behind the table alongside Weed. Davey's pulse quickened: they were the men he'd seen on the *Nemesis* the night before. The one with the mustache, that the woman had called Cochran, was got up in a tweed riding jacket, boots, and plus-fours. His younger, taller male companion with the pipe sat next to him, in a khaki suit and a spotted brown silk neck scarf. At the far end was the bearded and severe-looking Scot—all six and a half feet of him, and sober now, apparently—with his knee-length sea coat and peaked cap. Someone below pointed, whispering his name: Uriah Rhodes.

Fred Weed banged his stick twice on the floorboards, and the room fell completely silent. His wife helped him to his feet. He began to speak, with slow, measured words:

"Friends, we are honored to have in our presence two gentlemen from the New York Yacht Club: Mr. Alexander Cochran and Mr. Harold S. Vanderbilt; and Captain Uriah Rhodes. They have come to our town to recruit a crew..." he raised a crooked finger on the handle of his stick, "...for the defense of the 14th America's Cup."

Cheers and applause rang around the packed room. Fred Weed's wife tucked the blanket back over his legs, and Alexander Cochran rose to speak. Davey shielded his eyes to get a better look at him: imperious and aloof, he was a man that looked like he'd rather be somewhere else. He threw his shoulders back, waiting for silence.

"Thank you, Captain Weed. And good day to you, men of Stonington." How wrong his Yale-educated accent sounded in a place like the Oddfellows! He cleared his throat: "It has been over ten years since the last America's Cup challenge. In 1893 and '95, you Deer Isle sailors proved your worth. Some of you men served in those campaigns. With your help, the United States retained the greatest trophy in sport, against an old enemy."

The older sailors nodded their heads knowingly.

"Now, is it true that we build faster vessels than our British counterparts? Yes. Do we also have the advantage of sailing in home waters? Certainly. But what truly sets us apart is the superior seamanship of our sailors—men like yourselves, and the fine skippers that command them." He gestured towards Rhodes, who shifted his weight to the other buttock. "Some here may remember Charles Oliver Iselin, the greatest of them all, winner of four America's Cups. Well, Ollie is godfather to my children, and a good friend. At the end of his racing career, he manned his crews with Scandinavians and Bostonians..." A hiss spread around the room, giving way to a hearty laugh. "But for my part—and this view is shared by my esteemed colleagues—I believe we have the means to assemble the finest racing crew in the world, right here in this room!"

"We're wicked cheap, an' all, mister," whined a familiar, adenoidal voice that was drowned out by the explosion of hoots and clapping filled the hall.

It was hot and humid now, up in the rafters. Davey noticed how intently Harold S. Vanderbilt had been studying the sailors' faces. He looked about twenty-seven, twenty-eight—not much older than Jake, but he had to be worth millions. Amazing—a real live Vanderbilt, in their town, sucking on his pipe, and the same calm demeanor Davey noted in the *Nemesis'* saloon.

The grim Uriah Rhodes was buffing the buttons of his coat with the back of his sleeve. Cochran raised both arms like some sort of preacher, hushing the crowd.

"A week ago, Sir Thomas Lipton of the Royal Ulster Yacht Club laid down a challenge with his latest vessel, *Shamrock IV,* that the New York Yacht Club has duly accepted. The Cup racing series itself will take place in New York next August. The honor of defending the Cup will be contested, over the summer, between two American yachts: the topsail cutter *Resolute,* and my own newly commissioned *Vanitie.*" Here he took his voice up a proud notch. "Now, I aim to win the trials with the fastest boat and the best crew. And I expect to go on and crush Sir Thomas Lipton, and lift the Cup once again for the United States of America! Who among you Deer Isle men will join me?"

A blast of cheering and stomping shook the hall. The crowd below waved their caps and clapped each other on the back. Cochran sat down, visibly pleased with himself, and leaned over to shake hands with Vanderbilt and Rhodes. There was that hairy hand again, that he'd stuck up the pretty servant's skirt. Davey gagged at the thought of it.

After a beat, Frank Weed banged his stick, rattling the floorboards. Condensed sweat dripped from the ceiling tiles above Davey's head. The big Scot rose to his feet, and his voice boomed out across the room. "All right, listen, you rabble. My name is Captain Uriah Rhodes, and when you hear my voice, that's when you know it's time tae *pipe doon!*"

A hush fell. Rhodes took a few measured paces across the platform, fixing his stony stare on each face in turn. "Now then. We need thirty-five men to race the *Vanitie,* and a few spare," he began. "We'll be tryin' out the best of you on the water this Tuesday, on Mr. Cochran's *Westward*. If you've never heard o' the *Westward,* you're in for a treat. She's the finest American two-masted schooner ever built. This is her final stop before Cowes, in England, where last season Mr. Cochran scooped every major trophy. Come high tide this Tuesday, the *Westward*'ll be anchored outside Powder House Island, and we'll be taking a measure o' you, and your sail handlin' skills, such as they are."

Harold Vanderbilt pulled on a pair of little round spectacles, and took a notebook from his briefcase. Rhodes continued:

"In a while, we'll be fillin' the roster. To those of you as make it on to the crew, Mr. Cochran is offering six months' continuous employment from April to September, at a rate of…" Vanderbilt slid the open book across the table: "…of $45 a man per month, plus a bonus if you stay the season; and $5 for every race won. This—as you know—is more than a merchant seaman takes home. And a load more'n you'll make from your lobster pots, things bein' the way they are."

Some of the men turned to each other, nodding gravely. Davey's jaw went slack. He had never in his life made $45 in a single month, or even in a year. Given his family's current means, it sounded like a fortune. But a few West Bay men at the far wall seemed unmoved.

"Now, there'll be sewing, rigging and tuning to do. You'll be eatin' and sleepin' aboard our tender, down at City Island in New York. I don't need to tell you that every man jack will be expected to work his fingers to the bone, and stay sober, at that! You'll be months away from your wives and sweethearts, but all of you—even the young bucks—you'll nae succumb to the sins o' the flesh, not on my watch. Do I make myself understood? New York's an evil city, rife with temptation."

A lone "Hooray!" rang out, triggering a round of titters and guffaws. It was Jacob, of course. He'd know his brother's voice anywhere.

The Scot raised a single bushy eyebrow, silencing the room. "Now, listen. I know there's men here as have captained their own sloops and smacks. There's men as have served as mates on freighters. There's even them as have raced on a fine gentleman's yacht like the *Westward*. But I'll only say this once: on a ship o' mine, you're all just ordinary seamen, got it? You obey the commands o' the skipper, and that's *me*." He thumped his chest twice, loud enough to make Davey blink. "All right noo, let's be having ye."

Rhodes sat back down and opened the ledger, dipping his quill in an inkwell. The hush became a murmur as a queue started to form. Davey dropped down off the beam to the bench, and from the bench to the floor. He pushed his way into the line of sailors, making sure Jacob hadn't seen him.

They all knew Fred Weed, and he knew them. The older seamen had worked under him, and he could vouch for the younger ones by the reputations of their families. Rhodes was taking their names in the ledger. He had an unusual way of writing: he had to contort his sinewy left hand, angling his cursive script in the wrong direction.

Davey got closer to the table, with a pit in his stomach. His palms were sticky from the plum juice. He craned his neck to hear the older men ahead of him in line: Cyrus Thompson, Bill Otley, Coo Bray, Robbie Sellars... they were all experienced racers. Some made sure to flash their aluminum rings, melted down from *Defender's* topsides. But he had never set foot on a big racing yacht in his life. It would be a bit different from a sixteen foot fishing sloop with one ratty sail.

When it was Jacob's turn, he sprang up the steps.

"Name?"

"Jacob Haskell, sir, twenty-one years of age." He beamed from ear to ear. "Topmastman, sir. Been sailing all my life, and I can trim, haul and hand with the best of 'em. And I've worked aloft on the big New York coal freighters."

Fred Weed had known generations of Haskells. He muttered something to Cochran and Vanderbilt, and motioned at Jacob's strong physique.

Rhodes said, "Masthead man, eh?" and wrote it in his book. "Thank ye. Next."

As the line dwindled, Davey got increasingly twitchy. His moment finally came and he stepped up onto the platform, cap in hand. "David Haskell, sir, nineteen. My father raced on *Defender* and *Vigilant* both."

Jacob, in a huddle with his mates, spun around in surprise. Davey flashed him a cheeky look.

"Another Haskell?" said Cochran, already bored.

"Yes, sir. And I can do anything my brother can do—plus I can read and write." A lot of people heard it and laughed.

Weed, who was close to dozing off, snorted awake. "Nineteen, are we, Davey?"

"I'm old enough, skippah, you know that."

"Ah, he's okay," Weed said. "He's a clever lad. Knows the wind and the tides."

Davey grinned at Rhodes, and glanced down at the ledger. "Foredeck'd suit me nicely, cap'n! Or mainsheet..."

Rhodes looked him up and down doubtfully. Davey tried to puff out his sunken chest, but he felt thin as a twig. He blew his hair out of his eyes. "Or a deck hand on the tender?" he added quietly.

Harold Vanderbilt—who to this point had said little—peered over his spectacles and spoke in Rhodes' ear. Rhodes hesitated, then wrote Davey's name in the ledger with his squeaky quill.

"You can try out with the rest of 'em, laddie, but don't hold your breath."

The brothers sprinted the length of the beach all the way back to the landing, howling like wildcats. "You're a jammy sod, Dave!" yelled Jacob. "What're you going to tell Ma? Huh?"

Davey felt a smack between the shoulder blades, sending him sprawling on his hands and knees in the oily sand. He picked himself up, and they raced along the wharf, their boots clattering on the cobble stones, skidding round the corner of the cannery. There they stopped short, panting, face to face with the beautiful servant girl from the *Nemesis*.

CHAPTER TWO

She was laden with loaves of fresh bread in one basket, and four quarts of milk in another, but when the boys tore around the corner she nearly dropped the whole lot. They were tall and wild, panting in her face like feral beasts. Davey tried to catch his breath. Had he used his tooth powder this morning?

He brushed off his knees and elbows, searching for some words, any words. *That's a lot of bread…*

Jacob beat him to it. "Pardon us, miss—we didn't mean to startle you." Jake pulled himself up to his full height. His shirt was open, and his wide chest was glistening with sweat. The girl blushed and stared straight past him.

"The name's Jacob Haskell, and this is my little brother Davey." Jake flashed her his fine set of teeth. "Can we help with your groceries? We seen you, last night, in the saloon of the barky there. She's a nice shiny one, that. We was just at the Oddfellows, listenin' to your boss talking, Mr. Cochran."

"Mr. Cochran is *not* my employer," the girl said. "That would be Mr. Harold S. Vanderbilt, the owner of the *Nemesis*. And thank you, but I can manage perfectly well." She made to pass them to the other side, but Jacob cut her off and reached for one of her baskets.

"Seriously, it ain't no trouble at all," Jacob said, taking the handle. "We insist. Here, Davey, you get the other."

Davey took the basket of milk from her, and the two of them flanked her, leaving her little choice but to walk between them towards the end of the pier.

"Aren't you going to tell us your name?" Davey managed to get some words out, but his voice sounded squeaky compared to Jacob's. The girl glanced sideways at him. He hoped she'd notice the thin line of down on his upper lip, and the dimple in his chin, and not his acne.

"I'm Edith Armitage," she said, adjusting her cap. "I'm maid on the *Nemesis*, and my father is chief steward. He'll be expecting me now."

"It's nice to make your acquaintance." He tried to sound calm, though his arteries were still thumping. "How long d'you expect to be here in Deer Isle?"

"I'm told we're due to return to Newport on Wednesday, or Thursday if the tryouts go a second day…"

Jacob cut in. "There'll be two whole days of tryouts, you're sayin'?"

She hesitated. "I don't know what I'm allowed to say."

"Well, I hope you'll be stickin' around a bit," said Jacob. "It ain't often a hick fishin' town like ours gets a lovely visitor like yourself. Maybe you'll let me row you round the harbor one evening and show you the sights? Such as they are," he laughed. "It'd be grand to see you again… Edith."

Davey shuffled on his too-big feet, and cast his eyes across the harbor, rubbing his forearm for no particular reason.

"Well, I'm not sure what Father would say to that. I have my duties to attend to, don't I?" She had the slightest hint of an accent. He tried to remember if he'd ever met an Irish girl before. He hadn't. There was that hard-drinking sailor, O'Duff, that worked the Nova Scotia smacks. He had the Blarney patter all right—the *gift o' the gab*—but Edith's lilt was milder, more sonorous. It matched her beautiful face.

Jacob lengthened his stride and swung his broad frame around to face her, striding effortlessly backwards on the uneven planks of the pier.

"Aw, c'mon Edith, you should get out and live a bit!" He did a mock-waltz with the shopping basket. The corner of her mouth broke into a little smile.

At that moment, a silver-haired man in a white uniform emerged from the companionway on the deck of the *Nemesis*. Davey whistled through his teeth. Jacob spun on his heels. Edith put a hand to her mouth and giggled. They reached the foot of the gangway, and the brothers handed her back her groceries, tipping their caps to her disapproving father.

For an instant, Jacob held on to the handle of the basket, and seemed to lock his deep brown eyes with hers. "Be seein' you around then... Edith Armitage," he said quietly, and he brushed past her. She turned to climb the gangway, and Davey snatched a last glimpse of her slender calves. Then he hurried to catch up with his brother along the pier.

He had to do an occasional split-step to avoid the invisible lines. Since he was a small child Davey had seen imaginary forty-five degree angles on the ground or in the air, clear as day—made by the intersecting corners of paving stones, or the wide planks of the pier. He was obsessed with them. They intruded on his thoughts, and irritated him so much he had to step over them as if they were trip-wires. Once when he was small he tried to explain the invisible lines to Jacob. But Jake told him it was rubbish, and he was making it up. He never mentioned them again to anyone.

When they were out of earshot he turned to Jacob and said: "A bit frosty, that steward geezer, eh? The girl seemed nice though."

"They never fuck, her kind," said Jake, without breaking stride. "Too stuck up by half. I'll be giving Missy a wide berth, unless she comes beggin' for it."

"Ayuh. Me too, I guess. Guess I'll be giving Missy a wide berth, an' all."

"'Course you will, Dave," Jacob said with a scoff.

Davey's lip curled. It stung him when Jake talked like that. He felt bad that he'd never had a sweetheart himself. Jake got a head start when he was only fifteen.

When they reached the ice house, a new thought hit him, and he said more brightly, "Hey, you wanna help me fix the gill nets before lunch?"

"Nah, I have to see this fella about a circular saw. Tell Ma to save me some grub, though. I might stop by for a bite later." Jacob took off towards the back door of McGinty's pub—which was supposed to be closed.

Right then, a voice pealed out. "Young man!" It echoed round the harbor. Davey spun around. It was the elderly steward, Edith's father, at the top of the *Nemesis'* gangplank. Davey touched a finger to his chest, and mouthed the word, *me?*

Mr. Armitage nodded and beckoned him over. He took a few cautious steps back along the pier. Armitage was a proper-looking man, with streaks of platinum hair carefully combed back across his temples. His white uniform was immaculate, and his patent leather shoes shone like mirrors. His accent was stronger than his daughter's, but as he got closer his tone softened—much to Davey's relief.

"I need to ask you a question. Is there a public telephone in the town?"

"Yes sir. There's a phone booth in the telegraph office."

"I take it the office is closed on a S*o*nday, is it? Would you happen to know who *ro*ns it, now?" The man had a very strong accent, but beautiful clear enunciation.

"That'll be Mr. Dawson, sir. He's our cousin. Or uncle, or something."

"You *on*cle, is it? Or your *co*sin?"

"I'm not quite sure."

"You know where he lives?"

Davey shrugged. "Yep. He'll be round at ours for Sunday lunch, as it happens. Why?"

"Do you think he'd open the office for one of our guests? She needs to make a telephone call to California."

"He usually naps in the middle of the day. Maybe later?"

"Actually would you be a good fella, and run and ask him right away? We have a radio telephone on board, you see, but it seldom gets good reception in these remote harbors."

Deer Isle's first and only public telephone booth was in the back room of the U. S. Telegraph Office on Rhode Island Road. Davey helped her into the booth; it was awkward, with her heels. The woman smelled of expensive scent. Her hair was wrapped in a beaded scarf, and she'd draped a fox fur round her shoulders. She folded the double doors shut behind her, perched on the stool, and clicked the receiver several times to reach the exchange.

He flopped down on the bench. There was a hole in his canvas smock, and he explored it with his finger. It reminded him about those rips in his gill nets. He disliked the feeling of walking around town, knowing there were rips in his gill nets that needed fixing.

From across the counter, Jim Dawson started bending his ear off. Jim was Ma's boring brother. Davey had never liked him much, growing up, and wondered if they were really related. (Or if they were related more than one way, which was Jacob's theory.) He was a heavy-set man in his fifties, with straggly thinning hair. Ma said he'd never heard the call of the sea. Judging by his complexion, Davey believed it. Why would the sea call to a pasty old git like that? A desk job suited him well, licking stamps and taking down Morse. He was always harping on about something. "Your ma can barely cope on her own," he said, "with Ernie upstairs in bed sick, and the bills piling up…" blah blah blah. Davey wasn't even listening.

What was far more interesting was the muffled voice leaking through the doors of the booth. "Operator? Ah, *finally*. This is Rula Vanska. *V-A-N-S-K-A*. I need to place a trunk call to Los Angeles, California. Mr. Al Christie, at the Paramount Pictures Corporation," she shouted. "No, *Christie*. Allan Christie, he's my husband!… *Yes* I have a different last name, I'm a famous actress, you idiot."

A real movie star, in their town!

Uncle Jim, annoyingly, wouldn't stop talking in his other ear: "… And you should tell that brother of yours he's gotta to pull his finger out and bring in more money for the family. Either that, or give up that stupid room he rents at Mug Budro's, so Stella can have the extra dough for groceries…"

With a bang, the doors of the kiosk unfolded, and Mrs. Vanska stuck her head out, her head scarf rattling like a snake's tail. "You. What's the name of this place, already?"

He jumped to his feet, cap in hand. "This is Deer Isle, Maine, missus."

She slammed the folding doors and went back to her conversation; and now here was Uncle Jim, starting in on him again about money. Davey just crossed his eyes and sang "*la-la-la-la!*" with his fingers stuck in his ears. Jim finally got the message and shut up, so he could have a proper eavesdrop.

"In Maine, apparently… the back of beyond!" she was saying.

"I'm up here on Harold Vanderbilt's yacht, with Harold and few of his friends… *no*, certainly not!—I don't think Harold even *likes* women, darling… but spit it out, Allan, what's the latest with my two-reeler?… oh… oh Christ… well, *when* will you know?… it shouldn't take them five months to pick up an option… why can't I just come out there and *help* you with your brown-nosing?"

When Mrs. Vanska was done, he escorted her back along Main Street. People were stopping to stare. She had to take very rapid short steps on account of her tight velvet skirt and high heels, cursing at the unevenness of the pavement. He followed a few paces behind, trying to keep a straight face. He had to suppress an urge to giggle. When they reached the pier, within sight of the *Nemesis*, she spun in a little pirouette. "What was your name again—Jamie?"

"Davey. Davey Haskell, miss."

She unclipped a small pearl purse, reached in and pinched a silver half-dollar. "This is for your trouble, Jimmy." Her mouth briefly widened into an imitation of a smile, which cracked her face powder. He noticed the European accent had vanished. She sounded like she was from the mid-west. He took the coin, and knuckled his forehead.

The tide was all the way in now, and the fishing sloops were afloat in six feet of water. He hopped down onto the small strip of sand behind the ice house. Boats weren't going out today, it being Sunday. Further down the beach, Willie Bishop was caulking his skiff's upturned hull. A couple of other fishermen were hammering in their sheds, or on their sloops doing odd jobs. The crickets were chirruping, and the wavelets lapped gently on the mud; the stink of yesterday's catch hung over the harbor. Davey blew out a long breath. Would he ever get out of this dump?

He kicked off his shoes and socks and rolled his trouser legs above the knee. Yanking on the weedy mooring chain, he pulled Pa's clinker sloop to within wading depth and swung his legs over the side. He started sorting through his gill nets, going to work on the holes with a thick curved needle and a leather thimble, humming while he darned.

Rhodes' ledger was playing on his mind. Had he definitely made the short list for the *Westward* tryouts? His brother was a shoo-in, obviously, with his masthead experience. But Davey had never worked on a fancy yacht like that. The principles were the same as on any sailboat—and he was a *good* sailor. Maybe not as accomplished as Jacob, or as strong yet, but nimble. He knew the Bay, every eddy and inlet; but he had no concept of big topsail schooners, or the rules they raced by. Perhaps he'd stop by the public library in the morning. When he was tucked away in his little L-shaped alcove with its single armchair no springs, no one would bother him. It gave him a warm feeling, to fill up on ideas and knowledge. Splendid tales by Melville, and Jonathan Swift, Nathaniel Hawthorne and Mark Twain. He read them cover to cover. Ma told the neighbors his mind was like a sponge. Yes, he'd stop by tomorrow and read up on sailing theory, learn the names for all those queer racing sails and extra ropes.

The moored sloop began to swing around with the ebb, and it gave him a pretty good view of the *Nemesis*, half a cable's length away, the water lapping on her pristine white hull. He admired her rakish lines all over again, and her gleaming coachwork. Though the sun was high now, the yacht's afterdeck was shaded by an expansive canvas canopy. A portable luncheon table and chairs had been set out in its shade, along with a fold-down mahogany cocktail bar. And there was Mr. Armitage, in his cotton steward's coat and kid gloves, busying himself with the table setting; holding each piece of glassware or silverware up to the light with one eye closed.

The lovely Edith appeared in the companionway, with her little lace cap on her head, tying her apron behind her back. Davey ducked down below the gunwale. She was looking very prim and professional, the way she took a stack of napkins and folded one on each of three side plates, angling them precisely; then leaning over the table to fiddle with the centerpiece, an arrangement of white and purple orchids. Her arms were bare, and her skin was a milky white. Her skirt rode up above the knee. He let out a deep sigh.

She and her father were putting the finishing touches to the luncheon setting. The silver service and crystal wine glasses sparkled, and the striped yellow canopy cast pretty shadows on the table cloth. Just then he caught the first delicious whiff of seafood and roast beef, wafting across the water from the open port-light of *Nemesis'* galley.

The words were garbled, but the gentle brogue of their two voices drifted over the stillness of the Harbor.

"...A ladle for the Lobster bisque... the silver porringer... no, the *English* mustard, child..."

"And the '98 Lafitte... very well, Father. One bottle or two? I'll tell Jeb."

Manly laughter exploded from the interior of the saloon. Alexander Cochran and Harold Vanderbilt stepped out into the sunlight, sharing a joke, and crossed to the stern rail. The servants instantly switched modes. Mr. Armitage stepped behind the bar to mix drinks in a cocktail shaker, and Edith brought them their aperitifs on a tray, with a little curtsey. The gentlemen turned and leaned on the rail, gazing out across the water towards Powder House Island.

Davey sank a little lower in the bows, and slyly payed out the mooring rope so the sloop edged closer to the *Nemesis* on the ebb. He was only a stone's throw away, but his sloop was inconspicuous among all the other moored fishing vessels. He could hear the gentlemen's voices clearly now.

"I've given more thought to this timed start theory of yours, Vanderbilt."

"Aha?"

They had changed for luncheon, and Davey couldn't help admiring their spiffy attire. Cochran wore a striped sport coat, Panama hat, silk tie, and wingtip brogues, and his hair was combed like a polished boot. Harold Vanderbilt, the yacht's owner, cut a dashing figure in his white linen trousers, blazer, starched shirt, and a cravat that matched the steel blue of his eyes. He peered out from under the rim of his little round spectacles and packed his pipe from a leather pouch.

Cochran's brow was pinched in concentration. "The one flaw, as I see it, is that on a given day, your opponent might position his vessel to prevent you from tacking towards the line at the required moment..." He cut angles on the rail with the flats of his hands.

Vanderbilt lit his pipe and puffed thoughtfully. "I think you're missing the gist of it, old sport. It's not a rigid thing. The technique can be adjusted or abandoned at any point. If he tries to block me, I can opt to gybe instead of tacking, and begin the maneuver ten, twenty seconds earlier; the main thing is to cross the line at full velocity, right after the gun. Look…" He stepped to the carefully arranged lunch table, reached for a pair of napkins, and folded back a corner of the tablecloth, as if to illustrate his point.

The conversation continued like this for a bowl's worth of his tobacco. When he tapped the dregs into an ashtray, Edith slipped invisibly behind him and removed it, replacing it with a clean one.

Davey was stunned that this was sailing they were talking about. It wasn't sailing as he knew it. He tried to follow the choreography, visualizing two enormous, sleek topsail racers vying for position on an invisible start line. Vanderbilt explained it with quiet authority. Despite being at least ten years younger than Cochran, he was clearly the expert of the two.

"This," Vanderbilt concluded, "is why your tryouts this week are so vital. To execute maneuvers like these will take a crew of men accustomed to the precise co-ordination of movement, in all states of wind and sea, with a minimum of yelling from the skipper. And you must drill them over and over, until they are able to hoist, trim and douse with their eyes closed."

"Well, I'm still skeptical about your formulas," said Cochran. "I may be new to all this, but I'll tell you, when Charlie Barr was helming for my godfather, he never seemed to have a plan. He would feel the wind in his beard, and judge the trim of the sails by the weight of his helm. He'd reach down the line on starboard until the last minute, and by God if someone got in his way, he would just sail straight at 'em until they chickened out!"

"Ah yes, Charlie Barr. A law unto himself," Vanderbilt said. "Charlie was very adept at gambling with someone else's money. He made Lloyds of London nervous. You, on the other hand, Alex, have a huge pile of your own invested in this campaign, as do your partners. Would they really want you to take that sort of risk with half a million dollars' worth of steel and mahogany?"

"Look, Harold, I really wish you'd reconsider my invitation to join the Syndicate."

Vanderbilt laughed. "You need my advice and experience more than you need my cash, old chap."

Cochran took a deep breath and smoothed his mustache. "Show me the timings again, will you?"

"Certainly. It's really quite simple..." He took a ballpoint pen from his blazer's breast pocket and, looking around for something to write on, grabbed another napkin from the table, making a quick scribble which he angled to show Cochran.

"Here. The time T is let's say... three minutes and ten seconds..." They were speaking so quietly now that it was hard to make out the words.

Cochran picked up the napkin and shook his head incredulously. "I have to hand it to you, Vanderbilt. No one but you could distill the subtle art of sailing to a mathematical formula."

"Tell you what, old sport, we'll try a few practice starts in the *Westward* on Tuesday or Wednesday. You'll soon get the hang of it. Oh! here's your companion."

"Ah, Rula, there you are," said Cochran. The gentlemen bowed in unison.

The three steps up to the afterdeck must have been tricky in those heels. Mrs. Vanska's hair was still tied up in her fringed scarf. She had changed into a shoulderless dark red dress that was tight around the knees. She squinted in the sunlight, glanced at the lunch table, and wrapped her arms around her shoulders, shivering. "Do we have to be outside, Alex? It's bloody freezing. Can't we eat indoors? I'm not a polar bear, you know."

"I'm sure everything could be moved into the saloon, could it not, Armitage?" Vanderbilt said. "Why don't you bring Mrs. Vanska a sherry, then you and Edith can quickly set us up inside."

Cochran wrapped Rula in his blazer.

"Make that a whisky sour, steward," she rasped. "And I prefer 'Miss'

Vanska, Harold, if it's all the same to you." The three of them withdrew to the saloon.

The servants went into action, and the luncheon table was cleared and reset in only a few minutes. Armitage's face showed no trace of frustration. Edith was the last to leave. She looked a little put out, understandably, as she stacked plates and cutlery on a tray. Davey wished he could do something to help. He noticed her slip Vanderbilt's napkin diagram into her apron pocket.

She must have caught a brief glimpse of movement in Davey's sloop, and she did a double-take. He ducked down in the bilges and bit his tongue, but he had clearly been spotted. At first she pursed her lips, annoyed. Then her face softened. As she turned and left the afterdeck with the last of the crockery, she glanced over her shoulder at him once more, and flashed him a tiny, furtive smile.

CHAPTER THREE

The day of the tryouts dawned with a fresh nor'easter. Davey woke to the rattling of the corrugated iron roof on the outhouse. He dressed excitedly, pulling on his fawn duck trousers, a cotton shirt and a thick sweater. His sandy hair was a mess, and he had trouble finding a pair of matching socks, so he went without. He dabbed his toothbrush in a tin of powder, brushing his teeth with one hand and pulling on his boot with the other. All he could think about was the sea trials on the *Westward*—the longest and fastest boat he'd ever set foot on, and by far the most complicated.

But none of it mattered if Ma wouldn't let him go.

She had been up for a while, toiling in the kitchen. He grabbed a half-empty bottle of milk from the cupboard and chugged it down. Crouching by the stove, Ma took an oven cloth and flipped open the door of the furnace. She shoved another log in, closed the door, and stood up slowly, blowing air out through pursed lips, her hand pressed into the base of her spine.

"Aw, Ma, you should let me do that!"

She wrinkled her nose. "It's done now."

He cast an anxious glance out the kitchen window across the harbor, and took a deep breath.

"Right. I'll be off then, Ma."

"Bide a while, love. I'm goin' in to see your father, presently."

She slid the cast-iron soup pot onto the burner and stirred it with a wooden ladle. Could she go any slower? He looked at her lovingly—her little narrow shoulders, her sad face stooped over her chores, and the same faded floral apron, day in and day out. She was definitely shrinking. Her hair was entirely grey now. And even if she didn't let it show on her face, she really couldn't cope on her own.

He helped her up the narrow stairs and into the low attic bedroom, which smelled stale and musty. "Pray with me, Davey," she said. He took her hand dutifully. They knelt in silence by the bed. But he kept one eye open.

It was hard to tell how much Pa was really taking in, or what was just wishful thinking. His withered hands, scarred by rope burns from his nets, lay helpless in his lap. His face was twisted on one side; and though Ma had propped him up so he could see across the harbor, he sat there in his striped pyjamas and nothing seemed to register. His empty pale blue eyes reflected the sea. Who knew what he was really thinking? Perhaps all he could remember now was the lean times, the relentless Atlantic storms, the intense cold of the long winters. Sometimes a single tear would run down his face, but Ma said that was just involuntary, on account of the strokes, like his runny nose.

"...Amen."

Davey kissed Ma on the forehead, grabbed his lunch box and his oilskins, and headed out the door before she had a chance to say something. He sprinted the length of Shell Beach, up over the rocks to the coastal trail that led to his brother's place on the edge of town.

Jacob lived in a rented room above Mug Budro's bait shop. The shutters were open, and the racks had been freshly hosed down. Mug was already out front in his rubber dungarees, shoveling live maggots into a bucket.

"Morning, Mug," Davey said brightly. "Looks like another good one!"

"Good for *zome*," Mug grumbled. Mug was a leathery French Canadian with a voice like chalk. He'd left New Brunswick many winters ago during a big freeze, heading for Louisiana, but only made it as far as Maine.

"So everyone is going *yot-ting* today, ha, Davey? You won't be needing no live bait on zat fancy *schooneur*."

Jacob stuck his head out of the upstairs window.

"Give me two ticks, I'll be right down," he called. There was a loud fleshy slap, and a feminine giggle. Moments later Jacob appeared in the shop doorway, pulling a canvas smock over his broad shoulders. Davey cast a wary glance at the open upstairs window.

"Finest kind of horse flesh, that Mary Beth," said Jacob with a grin. He roughed up Davey's hair, striding past him down the cobbled steps towards the water, his seabag over his shoulder. Davey followed close behind.

Mary Beth was in his bible class. He'd watched in awe as his big brother courted girls from the town, one after another. Jacob stole that shy beauty Evelyn's heart, only to ditch her and seduce curvy Sarah Eaton, luring her to his love shack above the bait store. This month it was Mary Beth. But what about Edith, the angelic maid from the *Nemesis*? He'd surely have to have *her* as well, wouldn't he, despite what he said. Edith, who was so innocent and flawless, like a shining pearl. What did Jake have to prove? She was far too young for him anyway—but that wouldn't stop him.

"Ma made us both lunch," Davey said.

"Bless her cotton socks." Jake was staring off at the skyline across the bay. "Ayuh, it's a fine morning, kid. High tide's nine-thirty—we need to be on that first boat out to the *Westward*. I heard as Rollie Staples is doin' the ferrying."

Mug Budro watched the boys leave, hands on his hips. "You make sure Jacob don't get picked," he called after Davey, "or I lose a lodgeur *and* a customeur!"

"We're both gonna get picked, Mug," shouted Davey across his shoulder, loud enough to drown out the little voice that was niggling in his mind.

Crew names and positions were pinned on the notice board by the loading crane. A dozen men jostled to get close. The two brothers found a way through, and squinted at the list. Jacob ran his finger down the columns.

"Haskell, J.—Masthead, First Team. Eh, I'm going aloft! And here's you, shorty, on Runners. You know what that means?"

"I have to run errands for the captain?" Davey was amazed just to see his name on the list.

"Aww, you hear that, lads?" Jacob laughed, and clapped him on the back. "My little brother's gonna run errands for the skippah!"

A titter went around. Davey acted like he'd cracked a good joke.

"No, mate," said Coo Bray. "Running backstays, with me. Them as holds up the mast and topmast. You'll be all the way in the stern, takin' up the strain when we go about. Only, don't be lettin' off the wrong one at the wrong time, or you'll bring the whole blooming rig down."

"Piece of cake," Davey said, and he changed the subject. "Will you look at that? They've put most of the West Bay men belowdecks."

"Ayuh. That'll be Frank Weed's doing," said Jacob. "Keep us apart from Gardie Greene and his moldy lot."

"You shut yer yap, Jacob Haskell!"

It was the freckled seaman from Bill Otley's catboat. His red curls were pushed into a greasy wool cap, well back on his forehead. He was leaning on an upturned crate, scratching at a piece of whale bone with an antler-handled fishing knife. An aluminum ring glinted on his middle finger. The crowd was pushing and shoving, talking excitedly about the names on the list; but everyone gave Gardie Greene a lot of elbow room—even his West Bay 'mates.'

"Come on, shorty," Jake said, tugging on his jersey, "let's take a gander at this fancy schooner." He strode off towards the end of the stone pier. Davey followed, hands thrust in his pockets, feeling Gardie's eyes staring a hole in the back of his head.

At the end of the pier they each hopped up on a bollard. There, as promised, was the *Westward,* anchored off the south end of Powder House Island. They both let out a low whistle. She was magnificent, the longest and tallest sailboat Davey had ever dreamed of. She made the *Nemesis* seem small: from the tip of her noble bowsprit to the end of her main boom, she was nearly two hundred feet long—over half the length of a football field. He tried to picture her alongside the tallest thing he'd ever seen, the ancient white spruce in the Acadia forest, but even the shorter of her two towering masts had to be as tall as that spruce tree. Along her sleek white hull was a line of twenty bronze portholes, suggesting a luxurious interior. The massive main and foresails were draped over her booms, while the smaller sails were still flaked on her bowsprit. A huge American flag flew from the staff on her stern; but even from a good distance away, Davey could tell that the sailors on deck, nine or ten of them, were not Americans.

He was sorry he'd put on so many layers, because the day was already warming up. He took off his jersey and rolled his duck pants up to his calves.

Rollie Staples' tugboat chugged its way towards the steps at the end of the pier, where upwards of fifty men were milling around. In the bow stood the imposing figure of Uriah Rhodes with his long black sea coat flowing behind him, and Rollie's little yapping terrier at his heel. The tug came to a halt, rocking on her own wake.

Rhodes cupped his hands and called the men to the edge of the pier, where he could address them in his booming, gravelly voice.

"All right then, good morning. We're taking thirty men at a time. I'll only be having the first team from the list. The rest of youse can make yourselves scarce. It disnae mean you've not made the crew. Ye'll get your chance, later in the day."

The crowd divided, and the Scot started a roll call. Each man stepped forward as his name was called. Davey's was near the end. As he came down the steps, he avoided eye contact with Rhodes, half-expecting to be kicked off the tug.

"Haskell, minor, is it?"

"That's me sir. Davey Haskell."

"Come aboard, laddie."

He found himself a place in the stern among the coiled ropes and buckets of hardened tar. The tug smoked across the harbor towards the looming shape of the *Westward*, which was just beginning to swing with the tide, her brasswork glinting in the morning sunlight. The closer he got, the grander and more technical she looked. His tongue felt prickly and dry. Jacob whispered something in Coo Bray's ear; Coo turned to Davey and gave him a comforting smile and a nod.

"You all know your positions," boomed Uriah Rhodes over the thump of the tug's engine. "Soon as you're aboard, it'll be all hands to the mainsail. You'll meet the Swedish crewmen already aboard, but they're just here tae show you the ropes. I'll talk you through each maneuver, and we'll likely run it several times. Let's see what you're made of, eh? Remember, I'm lookin' for strength, teamwork, obedience—and above all, dinna fall *off* the barky!"

"Aye aye, skippah," they returned in unison, some laughing.

The men were packed into the tug's stern, and Davey was uncomfortably close to Gardie Greene. His sunburned lips crinkled as he chewed on a toothpick, revealing a flash of gold tooth. There was no mention of the fish guts incident, but those ice-cold eyes pierced him, and Davey felt young and useless.

As the tug drew alongside the *Westward*, he scanned the faces of a dozen very foreign-looking sailors at the rail, in their matching cotton uniforms with dark blue trim. They had milky complexions compared to the Deer Islers. Some were smoking or chewing tobacco, and one hung off a shroud. They gawped down their noses at the rookie tryouts. A pair of bare legs dangled over the side; Rhodes flashed their owner a poisonous look, and they were hastily withdrawn.

The sailors fended off with boathooks as the tug rocked in the swell. At the stern quarter stood *Westward*'s owner Alexander Cochran, hands thrust in the pockets of his dark blue blazer. His temples hardened as he leaned over the rail and eyed the waterline, as if to warn Rollie that the topsides of his precious racer were not to be scraped by the fat little tug with its oversized rope fenders.

The tryouts boarded in single file, thirty men in all. Some of the older Deer Islers, those that had worked on previous America's Cup boats, wore special boots with the leather soles torn off, so the soft inner soles would not scratch the pristine decks. Davey dropped his own boots in a basket. He hopped off the gang ladder, savoring the warmth of *Westward*'s spotless white pine planks under his bare feet. The blazing metal and varnished woodwork all around made him squint. He had to shade his eyes to gaze up into the rigging. It was a canopy of taut lines on two masts—a web of spreaders and stays. He tried to snap a mental picture, and match it to the diagrams he'd studied at the library. As Jacob came aboard, Davey was itching to point out each halyard and spar, to show he'd learned all the proper terms. Jake, of course, was acting like this was all in a day's work.

The huge main boom, eighty-five feet long and two feet thick, had already lifted off its crutches. Davey joined a line of twelve men at the peak halyard, clapping on to the thick rope, trying to get a firm footing with his bare feet. Across the deck, twelve more seamen were hauling on the main halyard.

"On three, all together," a skinny Swede shouted. "One... two... *heaf*! and... *hole*! and... *heaf*! and... HOLE!" They all joined in the chant—mimicking the Swede's thick accent, with a few guffaws—and put their backs into the task. Cyrus Thompson started singing, and they all joined him:

"Them Camden girls they have no combs..."
"HEAF! HOLE! HEAF! HOLE!"
"They comb their hair with codfish bones..."

The Deer Islers' strong calloused hands made easy work of the coarse ropes, and the massive wooden gaff spar rose higher with each heave. Davey soon fell in with the motion, which was more of a snatch than a steady pull. The mainsail began to take on its shape, as the breeze shivered its diagonal seams. It was gigantic. He flashed on the pictures of objects he'd marveled at in library books—the Eiffel Tower, the Half Dome, the Pyramids...

The sixty-foot gaff spar was well above the diagonal, with its rope spans tight as a drum. Davey thrust his hands in his pockets and gazed up at the shivering mainsail. It was over seven stories high. He'd barely seen buildings that tall, on a trip to Bangor. The lowest row of reef points was already higher than the tip of his little fishing sloop's mast.

"Look alive there, sonny!" Rhodes barked at him. "This isn't a bloody holiday." A flick of Rhodes' thumb sent him scurrying to his station on the afterdeck. As he hurried aft past the low saloon skylight, he hardly dared peek down, but he got a brief glimpse of its opulent interior: a cushioned seating area, a trophy cabinet, and shelves of leather-bound books. He caught up with Coo Bray and the other trimmers around the helming station.

They formed into a circle. Alexander Cochran was in the middle, in his peaked hat, blazer and club tie, studying a paper navigation chart. Davey caught the glint of his Patek Philippe watch, his matching *N.Y.Y.C.* tiepin and cufflinks. His mustache was carefully oiled and combed, and there was a whiff of cologne about him. He took his time before glancing up from his chart to scan their faces.

"Names?"

One by one, the seamen recited their names and positions. Davey knuckled his cap. "Haskell, sir, runners." He tried to deepen his voice and stop it from wavering. It didn't work.

Cochran folded the chart and stuck it under an arm, linking his hands behind his back to address them. They were not to talk to him directly while he was helming. They would take their orders from Uriah Rhodes as they handled the sheets and runners on different points of sail. "Very well, get to it," he said. He didn't wait for questions.

Coo Bray clapped a meaty hand on Davey's shoulder and led him to the afterdeck. He had to shout now, over the racket of the flapping sails. "All right, kid, just follow my lead. First up, when they hauls in the boom to the centerline, it's you and me as coils the falls o' the mainsheet and keeps her tidy..."

Davey's eyes bulged. The heavy mainsheet rope was wider than his wrist, and many, many yards long, fed through six free-swinging wooden blocks, each large enough to knock off a man's head.

"Now, here's your running backstays, one each side. All the way to the tip o' the topmast, see? Each time we tack or gybe, we've gotta slack off the old backstay and take up the strain on the new one. And we better time it right, 'cos Davey lad, we'll only have a few seconds to get 'em set, or it's... *timber!*" Coo did a little pantomime of the topmast and sails crashing onto the afterdeck. "Ayuh. You make a single mistake, mate, that bastard boom could crash against the other backstay and snap the mast like a twig. That's why we're called runners... you see that mast coming down, you *run!*"

Coo's down east humor did little to help calm Davey's nerves. There was a colony of butterflies in his stomach. The old lobsterman squeezed his shoulder, and said: "You'll do fine, lad. I'll see you right."

Just then, the companionway doors flew open and Harold Vanderbilt emerged, pipe in one hand, newspaper in the other. Davey carried on with his work, but he was close enough to listen.

"Did you see the *Times*, Alex? The *Resolute* syndicate has upped their campaign budget again. They've raised close to half a million now."

Cochran frowned. "Some of that's Boston money, I'll bet. Coolidge, Winthrop. Charlie Adams..."

"And they won't skimp on any gadget that'll make *Resolute* go half a knot faster."

"It means the world to the Brahmins. They've never won the Cup."

"Let's make 'em wait a little longer, eh?"

Cochran chortled. He was picking his back teeth. "I must say, Vanderbilt—that Negro chef of yours makes a cracking Châteaubriand. He's quite the treasure."

"Jeb's a clever chap, actually. He has a degree in fluid dynamics."

Vanderbilt had pulled a canvas jacket over his white cricket sweater, and his hair was combed flat. A stopwatch swung from his neck as he brushed past Davey to the aft rail. He scanned the horizon, and then the boat's rigging, then the horizon again, and took his place alongside Cochran at the helm. Leaning in close to his friend's ear, he said something Davey couldn't make out over the din of the flapping sails.

Cochran replied: "You'd think the buggers'd be happy to get out of this forsaken place for a few months and go racing. Well, they'll just have to make sure we win every damn race, and stick around to pick up their bonuses, is all I can say. This campaign is already costing over... too darn much, whether we're selected or not."

And win or lose, Davey thought, *Vanitie* will be good as worthless after the campaign. There'll be no other yachts fast enough to race against, and she'll be too stripped-down for comfortable cruising.

"Anchor's up and down, sir!" bellowed Rhodes from the bow. The schooner was lying with her head to the northeasterly wind, like a greyhound straining at the leash.

"Let's get cracking, then, eh?" Cochran grinned at Vanderbilt, flexing his hands. He took a firm grip on two spokes of the wheel, ready to reverse the rudder.

Rhodes shouted, "Back the foresail!"

Six men at the capstan cranked the anchor up off the bottom, click by click, until it broke the surface in a cloud of mud. The schooner slipped backwards and her bow payed off, and as the sails filled, the din subsided. She began to move forwards through the water, her bow wave gradually rising from a trickle to a flood.

Davey sighted up his now-rigid backstay all the way to the tip of the topmast, a hundred and sixty feet above the water. Far aloft on the outer forestay, the baby jibtopsail was still tied up with wool stops, like a sausage. When Rhodes yelled for it to be sheeted-to, it opened and set beautifully, and the broken stops fluttered down to the water. The windward shrouds and runners creaked, taking up the strain on the masts. As the schooner heeled and accelerated, the sails took on the smooth aerodynamic curves designed into them. *Westward* was a beautiful cloud of white Egyptian cotton. The power and sheer scale was like nothing Davey had ever seen: it was physics in motion. He had to remind himself to keep breathing.

"All hands to the weather rail!" bellowed Rhodes. "And look lively there!"

The experienced racers in the crew were used to this type of sailing, but Davey and the other novices were surprised by how rapidly—and how far—the white steel schooner heeled over. Men scrambled up her slanting deck, the first of them reaching the highest part as a foamy wash started to spew out from under her stern. Most of the Swedes were already up on the high side, lying back on their elbows and jeering at

Willie Bishop, who had tripped over a stray line and was now struggling to make it up the slant of the deck. Uriah Rhodes shook his head and tutted.

Davey felt the wind whistle through his shirt: the *true* wind, enhanced by the *apparent* wind generated by their forward motion. He'd boned up on the theory in technical books. *Apparent* wind was what made a race boat so quick—as fast as the wind speed, or even faster. It was hard to fathom. A modern racer would be capable of making eleven knots in a ten-knot breeze. He felt he had a grasp of the science that made it possible, but there was nothing like feeling the thrill of it firsthand.

Squatting on the highest part of the afterdeck, he gazed back at Westward's frothy wake. How quickly was the town moving away behind them? He calculated they were making eight, nine knots now, easy—more than twice as fast as he'd ever sailed in his life. He could already barely make out Ma's cottage, still in the shade of Staple Point. A pair of inquisitive seagulls that had been circling the boat had to work harder just to keep up.

Cochran stood at the helm, his silk scarf blowing behind him. Vanderbilt squinted at the chart, matching it to visual landmarks that Davey knew like the back of his hand: Two Bush Island, and Thurlow Head to the right; Scott, Flea and Green Island to the left; and five miles ahead in the haze, the low rocky shape of Isle Au Haut, the last dry land before the open Atlantic Ocean. Any moment now they would need to bear off and head south. Sure enough, Vanderbilt gave the new compass bearing, Cochran turned the wheel down a couple of spokes, Rhodes called for the sheets to be eased. Westward's bow moved powerfully away to starboard, driving into the light chop.

Gardie Greene slid down the deck and took a wrap off the staysail sheet, almost losing his grip. Several feet of the coarse rope slipped painfully through his leathery hands. Many of his mates saw it too—there was a sharp intake of breath through their teeth. Uriah Rhodes pursed his lips, but Gardie's craggy face showed no emotion.

Davey had sailed Penobscot Bay all his life—its shallow waters and deeper channels, its archipelago of low wooded islets and rocky coves—but he'd never seen it from quite this viewpoint, ten feet above the water on the polished rear deck of a luxurious racing schooner. He felt like a prince in state. The wind was slightly aft of *Westward*'s beam now, her fastest point of sail. Her velocity continued to pick up as she rode over the gentle swell. From this height it was easy to spot the darker patches on the water where catspaws of wind were forming and disappearing. Away from the shelter of the land, a few random whitecaps had started to appear on the crests of waves. The wind was picking up.

Harold Vanderbilt pointed out the course on the chart with the tip of his pipe. "If it were me, old sport, I'd come round George Head, you see? then head east up Merchant's Row where you'll have a clearer wind. The channel's pretty deep there, and the swells will be longer, more like you're used to in Long Island Sound. One eighty-five should do the trick."

Cochran nodded, and checked his compass.

But watch out for Sam Stick Ledge, gents! Davey thought.

"Look out for Sam Stick Ledge, mind you," said Vanderbilt, as if he'd read Davey's mind. "About a mile south of here. Nasty sandbank, a hundred yards long. At this state of the tide it's covered, but you'll probably see the white water. There's a green marker buoy to the west of it. You'll need to leave that well off to port." He took off his small round spectacles and folded away the chart. Cochran peered at the waters ahead.

Rhodes was amidships, barking orders into his brass speaking trumpet. "Hoist the club tops'l, port side—masthead men into the main tops!"

Cyrus and Jacob sprang on to the ratline ladders for the long climb to the top of the mainmast. They ran up the ratlines like squirrels up a tree. The last part was a wobbly overhang, ninety feet above the water; but both men had gone aloft in far trickier conditions aboard the big coastal freighters.

Four West Bay men wrestled the heavy topsail out of the hatch, with Anderssen bringing up the rear. Davey noticed Anderssen's muscular bare arms were covered with remarkably ornate depictions of naked Swedish women.

"Who's got the tops'l sheet?" Rhodes shouted.

The men looked from one to another. No one had been assigned the task. Rhodes cursed under his breath and shielded his eyes to sight up at the tip of the gaff, a hundred and forty feet above the deck. All he saw was an empty block flopping against the peak of the mainsail. A couple of the Swedes had a private snigger.

At the helm, Cochran leaned towards his companion. Davey heard him say, "All thumbs, these fishermen!"

Vanderbilt took the pipe out of his mouth. "One might even say, 'clewless'."

Rhodes cupped his hand and hailed aloft. "Masthead, there! You on the port side!" He turned to Bill Otley at his hip and said, "What's that man's name?"

"That's Thompson, skipper. The other's Jake Haskell."

He boomed into his speaking-trumpet. "Thompson! Hike up there and thread the sheet!" Rhodes pointed forcefully at the top of the gaff, taking several steps aft for a better view.

Cyrus Thompson cast a doubtful eye at the top of the thick gaff spar stretching diagonally above him, angled out over a sheer drop of a hundred and forty feet to the water. There were no ratlines here, or other means of support.

Rhodes muttered into his beard. "What the devil's keepin' you, you Yankee lily-liver?"

Jacob yelled down: "I've got it, skipper!" With one foot astride each spreader, he stretched round the full diameter of the mast and took the rope end from Cyrus. He tied it to his belt, rolled up his sleeves, and began the perilous hike up the taut spans of the peak halyard; then he started to traverse, like a mountaineer crossing a chasm. When he ran out of spans, he wrapped his arms and thighs round the gaff spar itself, and edged his muscular bulk, pound by pound, up the last ten feet towards the tip, where the boat's swaying motion was most extreme.

Davey watched from the stern with his eyebrows stitched together. The sailors on the foredeck, too, had stopped what they were doing, and the men working below had their heads out of the hatch. The entire crew fixed its gaze on Jacob. Shirt sleeves and pant legs flailing in the wind, Jake reached the very top of the gaff. He untied the rope, threaded it through the thick wooden block, and tied it back on to his belt. Then he began to shin back down, to loud cheers from the Deer Islers below.

"Sir! *Dead ahead!*" Davey screamed.

No one had been paying attention to the yacht's course—not even Cochran. Half a boat length from the *Westward*'s bow was the large rusty iron buoy marking Sam Stick Ledge, and beyond it a wide patch of white water. They were heading straight for it.

Cochran threw the helm down, and the *Westward* responded instantly, carving a tight circle to starboard and away from the buoy. The schooner heeled radically over and a great sheet of foam fanned across the water. The sudden turn almost brought her by the lee, with the wind blowing from the wrong side of her sails; her booms started to rise precariously. For a terrible second Davey thought she was going to do an accidental crash-gybe that would surely have catapulted Jacob into thin air. But Cochran swung the helm back to port, carving an S-turn with the boat's wake; and the sails filled with wind again as the booms settled.

The torque of the turn almost wrenched Jacob's grip free. There were gasps from some of the crew. He'd slipped halfway around the polished wooden spar, barely hanging on, but somehow hauled himself back on top. Then he glanced briefly down at the deck with a cheerful thumbs-up, and resumed his descent towards the throat of the gaff, to the sound of more hoots and applause, mainly from his mates in the East Bay contingent.

Davey whistled through pursed lips, but went back to busying himself with his work. This was typical Jake stuff—cranked up a notch for the big occasion. He and Coo went forward to help hoist the topsail.

Westward left the Sam Stick Ledge buoy in her wake. With the sand bar behind them, Cochran eased the schooner back on to a fast broad reach, and she leveled off. The new topsail filled the huge triangle between the gaff and the topmast. Davey felt the extra surge of power kick in as the *Westward*'s bow pressed down into the chop of the Bay.

"Nice catch, old man!" said Vanderbilt in the cockpit, a hand round Cochran's shoulder.

Cochran's face was set hard, and serious. "Can't afford mistakes like that in a race, Captain Rhodes," he grumbled. Rhodes just stared blankly away to the horizon, his jaw clenched.

Vanderbilt surveyed the trim of the sails, and made his way forward to the shelter of the companionway to refill his pipe. "Let me know when you need to take a break, Alex," he called over his shoulder.

Coo Bray and Davey exchanged a silent look, and joined the others on the windward rail. The pair of them, up to this point, had had little to do, other than tidying loose ropes. But soon the *Westward* would harden up for the beat through Merchant's Row, into the wind; and they would spring into action. Even a fine racing yacht could not sail directly into the wind. On a day like today, the passage would take at least a dozen zigzag tacks in his fishing sloop; he was intrigued to see how few the *Westward* could do it in, for she was a sleek, efficient sporting machine, not some homely Maine lugger with a bagged-out sail and a fat leaky hull loaded with lobster pots. A modern design like *Westward* could sail as little as thirty degrees off the true wind. But with her deep draft, she'd need to tack well clear of the shallows on either side. Already, the criss-cross pattern of angles was forming on the grid of Davey's mind: lines that glowed brightly to him, but were invisible to others.

Jacob hopped down off the ratlines at the base of the shrouds, to a muffled round of applause. Jerker, the freckled Dane, was sitting cross-legged, rolling a cigarette. He licked the paper, nodded somberly to Jacob, and stuck it in the corner of his mouth.

"Lucky for you dis was not de *jackyard* tops'l," he said.

Coo flashed a grin at Davey. "A jackyard topsail's the kind we'll likely use when racing *Vanitie*. Nearly twice the size of this one, with its own spars, an' all."

"Ayuh," spat a raspy voice from the rail. "That jacky's a sail with *murder* in its heart." It was Gardie Greene, and he was looking straight at Jacob.

"Why's that cunt staring at me, Coo?" said Jake.

46   CHAPTER THREE

Rhodes walked among the crew, booming over the roar of the boat's wash. "When we harden up, don't be caught down in the lee scuppers." He glared at Willie Bishop. "...or ye'll be washed away like a piece o' driftwood. We might need to tack in a hurry on a wind shift, just like in a race, so be on your guard. This is how it's going tae work…"

The *Westward* sliced a wide left-hand curve towards the eye of the wind. The trimmers hauled in the heavily loaded sheets in unison, and the schooner's bow pressed deeper into the Atlantic swell. The hum of the wind in her drum-tight stays rose half an octave.

Gripping the rail on the afterdeck, Davey felt an exhilaration he'd never felt. He knew a race boat was designed to heel way over like this, and sail as close as possible to the wind; still, it was an utter thrill to feel it for himself. The blurred spray shooting out from the bow looked almost like smoke—as if the *Westward* was on fire. He closed his eyes to savor the strong breeze, and tasted the wisps of spray on his face. A cauldron of cavitated water bubbled below him. Stretching far behind, the spume of *Westward*'s frothy wake was like a paddle steamer's, tracing the arc of their wide turn into the channel, under the clear blue sky.

With the weight of nearly thirty men pressing on her windward rail to counter the heel, it was plain to see how all the immense power from *Westward*'s sails was channeled into the forward thrust of the boat. It reminded him of the old 'sandbaggers'—the over-canvased oyster boats that needed their sailors to shift heavy bags of gravel from one side of the boat to the other to keep them upright. Mishandled, he had seen sandbaggers flip upside-down; but when they were balanced right, they were lightning fast.

He tried to tell his body to relax—like Cochran and Vanderbilt there. With their fine clothes and superior airs, they seemed to belong to a different species altogether. Upright and proud, knees slightly bent, riding easily at the helm: this was how these gents spent most of their days! Only the ruling classes could afford yachts like *Westward*. Yet, riding here behind them, he almost felt like a millionaire himself. He imagined steering this schooner—*owning* this schooner, commanding his own crew and personal staff, and a glamorous debutante waiting for him below in his cabin. For an instant he pictured Edith sprawled on his bed, in a sequined evening gown with a slit up the side. Then he scolded himself. Edith was far too pure for that.

Cochran's hands cradled the spokes of the wheel, while Vanderbilt alternated his gaze between the trim of the sails and the surface of the ocean, scanning the broken tops of the waves for any sign of a shift or a lull. They were at full speed now, pushing twelve knots, carving along the face of the wind as if on a razor's edge.

The wooded slopes of Merchant Island started to loom greener, and the surf broke white on its rocky beaches. Davey readied himself for the call to tack, wrapping his arm around the loose tail of the running backstay. But Coo Bray, squatting close to him, spat: "Psst! Not like that, Dave, you'll get yelled at! Or worse, you could lose an arm. Lay it across your back, mate, see…?" And he took up the corresponding slack on his side to show Davey how.

"Hey, Coo. You were on *Defender* when she won the Cup, right?"

"Yes, mate. *Defender* and *Vigilant*, both."

"How come you don't wear the ring, like the others?"

Coo looked hesitant. "That's a story for another time, kid."

Cochran twirled his hand above his head, signaling he was about to start the turn. Rhodes lifted his speaking-trumpet and shouted a rapid series of commands to the men, ending with: "Ready about… Lee-*ho*!!" In a few seconds the *Westward* slewed up into the wind, firing reams of frothy ocean from under her bow as her momentum carried her into the turn. For a few moments the sails flogged wildly. Men ran everywhere, shouting, cracking off one set of sheets and hauling in on the other.

Davey picked his moment. As soon as he felt the pressure come off his backstay, he whipped off the two remaining wraps, allowing the weight of the block to drop it to the deck. Then he scampered across the deck to help Coo take up the load on the new windward side.

It wasn't smooth. He felt like a beginner. He tried not to think about Uriah Rhodes' eyes that were surely fixed on him, judging his every move.

The schooner had slowed a little in the turn, pitching her head into the oncoming waves; but as her sails filled on the new side, she quickly regained her former momentum. Davey lay sideways on the white pine planks, bracing one foot against a strut. He was short of breath—more from his nerves than anything—but he and Coo must have done their job acceptably, since it drew no comment.

Westward's next tack was smoother, and Rhodes looked pleased. Vanderbilt jotted notes in his book. "When a maneuver is perfectly executed," he observed to Cochran, "you keep driving the sails all the way through the turn, and almost no speed is lost. It shouldn't cost you more than half a boat-length. But a couple of bad tacks—well! That could easily lose you the race."

He wondered how many races Vanderbilt had won in his career. Only six or seven years older than Jacob, he must have been sailing since he could walk. Same as Davey and his brother, in fact—only on a very different class of vessel. And it was a sure bet that a Vanderbilt never had to sail fast just so his family could eat.

Westward zigzagged up the channel, and the Deer Islers breathlessly hauled and belayed, hauled and belayed, scrambling more nimbly with each maneuver to their new positions on the windward rail. After three quarters of an hour the entire sequence was running like clockwork. Davey exchanged a contented smile with Coo Bray. Up ahead where Penobscot Bay was directly exposed to the Atlantic, the sea was piling up into a steep chop.

The bosses had evidently seen enough of the men's upwind work. "We're a little overpowered now, anyway, old sport," Vanderbilt said. "We should probably bear off and run back down the channel the way we came." He pointed out the course on the chart. "Wind's veered a bit, and we can practice some sail changes. It'll be a nice beam reach back up the Bay to Stonington. We'll be against the ebb tide, but we should be back in an hour and a half, hour and a quarter."

Under his breath, Davey said to himself: "Quicker to cut through Bare Island Reach…"

Vanderbilt heard this, and swiveled around. Davey shrank back, wishing he'd kept his thoughts to himself.

"What was that you said, there?"

He swallowed. "Bare Island Reach, sir," he repeated, more clearly now. "The ebb sets in later there, an' you could still catch the last o' the flood. It'd knock twenty minutes off your time to Stonington, easy."

Vanderbilt examined his chart. "Bear Island Reach, you say? I don't see it marked."

"May I?" Davey stepped forward and pointed to the chart. "Sir, it's *Bare* Island, it's right… here. See the way the back channel leads past McGathery Rock, inside No Man's Land, then Ram Island? You've got six fathoms at least between Camp and Little Camp. Leave Russ Island to the south, and you're in the main seaway all the way back to town."

Vanderbilt turned to Cochran, who nodded, and spun the wheel, making for a rocky islet that Davey confirmed was Little McGathery.

"That's a handy bit of local knowledge," said Vanderbilt. "What was your name again?"

"Haskell, sir. Davey Haskell."

"You're not even a racer, are you?"

Davey laughed. "Nope. But we like to sail fast too. When the fish are shoalin', you want to be first out there to cast your nets. The quickest boat back to town sets the market price for the whole catch. So it's our business to know all the shortcuts." He waved towards the many islets to the north; but he felt Vanderbilt's eyes were still on him.

"Tell me, what do you think the weather'll do this afternoon?" Vanderbilt asked.

Davey narrowed his gaze at the large cumulus clouds gathering over the higher ground of the distant mainland, and then at the horizon out to sea, and flared his nostrils. "I reckon it'll veer another two or three points by about two o'clock, and pick up to a fresh sou'wester," he said. "That ought to hold till about six or six-thirty, bein' as it's nearly September. Might be in for some real weather tomorrow, though."

"I see." Vanderbilt packed his pipe, and held open the neck of his jacket to relight it; then he took the pencil from behind his ear, returning his attention to the notes in his book.

CHAPTER FOUR

Davey put in a brief morning appearance at the school, dodging Father Michael's mean-spirited jibes about why he was absent all of Tuesday. At lunchtime he headed to the town pier, and sat with his legs dangling over the edge. He took his lunchbox from his open satchel. He couldn't manage the second half of his crab sandwich, so he started to doodle in the back cover of his math book. A massive school of sprats flashed back and forth, making silver streaks in the dark water. He tore off a crust and crumbled it into small pieces, watching the sprats devour it in short order between the thick oak planks. Then he did a quick sketch of *Westward*'s prow, her bowsprit and bobstay, and the steel stanchion Coo Bray had called the 'dolphin masher.'

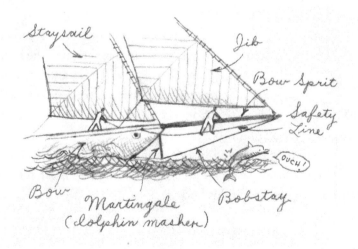

Far off in the distance, he could still see the top of *Westward*'s twin masts heading south across Penobscot Bay, manned now by the second team. She was heeled well over. The wind had veered and picked up, just as he expected. The West Bay boys were getting their crack at the precious places on the race team. But he knew he and Jacob and the East Bay sailors had given a good account of themselves.

To his left, tied up near the end of the pier, was the *Nemesis*. He glanced sideways at the beautiful stylish bow, with its polished bowsprit gleaming in the dull sunlight. He formed a mental picture of Edith, in her cap and apron, going about her daily tasks; stretching on tiptoes to reach a high ledge with a feather duster. He went back over his plan. He wondered if he really had the courage to go through with it. What if he couldn't get his mouth around the right words? What if she just said no? Or her old man shooed him away?

He rehearsed the scene in his head. He would show her the bag of shells, which had to all be exactly the same size, and if she seemed to like them, he'd say they were hers to keep. Girls loved that sort of thing. He knew a beach where there were lots more like them; he would be pleased to take her there some time and show her. He'd make small talk, and at just the right moment, he'd ask her back for tea and cake at his Ma's.

"They're yours to keep," he said quietly to himself. Then he cleared his throat and tried it again, half an octave lower. "They're yours to keep—you can keep them, they're for you… These are for you, Edith!"

Darn it. How would Jake do this?

The day was heating up, and the water in his canteen was lukewarm. He ran his fingers through his sandy hair. He was grateful for the apple slices; he didn't want crab breath. He sucked on the last of them, stood up, dusted himself off, and began to walk towards the end of the pier, trying to look casual.

The tide was halfway out. *Nemesis* was the only vessel docked there. Her portholes were level with the pier, and her gangplank sloped gently up to the deck. He could hear the sloshing of the water between her hull and the pilings, and the halyards slapping on her half-mast. At first he thought no one was around; then a delicious smell of baking reached him from the open port-light of the galley. Inside, there was movement. Davey just kept walking, as if he had somewhere else to be, but a loud voice came from the interior.

"You gonna pass right by me without sayin' morning? Where're your manners, little man?"

"Mornin'!" called Davey, squinting over his shoulder. "Afternoon, that is." He backed up half a step and tried again. "Hello?"

It was the cook, the one he'd seen the first night, in a white cotton hat. He came to the open port-light, wiping his hands on a tea towel. He was a tall enough that he had to stoop to avoid bumping his head.

"What's occurrin', little fisherman?" His voice was deep, with a rich Caribbean accent.

Davey was blinking rapidly. "Is Edith here, I wonder? Edith the maid? May I… converse with her?"

"Listen to you, talkin' all broughtupsy," laughed the cook, looking him up and down. "And who shall I say is calling, young sir?"

He could see the man's face clearly now. Vanderbilt had mentioned his name: Jeb. Handsome, around thirty, with large brown eyes, sideburns, and gold earrings.

"My name's Davey. I'm a friend of Edith's—well, not a friend, exactly."

Jeb's head tilted slightly.

Davey took a step nearer, and peeked into the galley. "It must be hard for you, working on a luxury yacht. Being as you're…" He stiffened a little. "So tall, I mean."

"Mmm-hmm,'" Jeb said. "Wait there, please… *Mister* Davey." He disappeared from view.

Davey tried to make out the muffled voices. A rash of nerves overcame him, and he started to re-run the lines in his head—but now they were a jumble. He fingered the bag of shells in his pocket.

A few seconds later, Edith appeared on deck. She looked like she'd been crying. She was in her uniform, but no cap or apron. She took one look at him and to his surprise, hurried straight down the gangplank. Without a word she took his upper arm and shuffled him back along the pier, glancing only briefly over her shoulder as if to make sure they were not being watched.

She spoke under her breath. "Davey! You have to help me. Come on, I'll explain."

When they reached the ice house, she steered him around the corner, out of sight from the yacht.

"What's wrong? What's going on?" he said, astonished.

Edith caught her breath and turned to face him. "Oh, Davey..."

"What happened to your arm?" Her left forearm was black and purple.

"Something bad happened last night. I did something stupid, and she saw it and now... she thinks she's got one over on me."

"Who does?"

"That woman, Mrs. Vanska. She's awful, absolutely horrible. She says she'll get me sacked."

"Sacked?"

"She says I've got to help her get away from here, without Mr. Cochran knowing, or she'll tell on me."

"Get away? Where to?"

Stop it! he thought. He was always echoing peoples' words back to them. Especially when it was a girl he liked. It was a reflex.

"To New York, or Boston, or somewhere. She's already married, Davey! She's an awful woman."

"Are you going to help her?"

"What choice have I got? I need this job. My father... Jesus and Mary, it would kill him. If the boss finds out, I'll be in worse trouble than I am now."

He looked into Edith's fragile blue eyes. She was so frightened, anxious. And so very beautiful.

He tried to make his voice reassuring. "All right, well... there's a steamer from Bar Harbor to Camden. It leaves twice a week, the *J.T.Morse*. It stops here overnight. The train station's in Camden; she can get to Boston from there."

"When's the next one?"

"6am tomorrow, from Greene's Landing." He pointed across the widest part of the harbor to the east.

Edith bit her lip. Then she reached into her breast pocket and pulled out some scrunched-up bills. She said: "Davey, I need you to book her on that steamer. Rula Vanska, *V-A-N-S-K-A*. Can you do that? How much is a single ticket to Camden? Will $10 cover it?"

"Yes of course, but—"

"All right, listen. Mr. Vanderbilt and the guests are going to Dr. Noyes' house in town for dinner and cards, and the crew has the evening off. Mrs. Vanska's got luggage, this heavy trunk—we'll need to get it off the *Nemesis* tonight, but it'll have to be after my father's asleep. I can get her round to the landing first thing. We'll cut through town, and get her on board the steamer before it gets light."

Davey glanced doubtfully in the direction of the *Nemesis*. "Won't the crew be still on board? How are we going to shift a big trunk without them knowing?"

"No no, they'll be in town drinking. Father's a light sleeper. His cabin's all the way forward, but if he hears footsteps on the dock…" Her expression became very focused. "Listen, Davey, can you get hold of a rowboat?"

"My brother's got a skiff. Why?"

Edith focused. "All right. It gets dark at nine. Bring the skiff to the end of the pier at nine-thirty, sharp. Keep your eye on the masthead. When you see the anchor light blink, that'll be my signal. Row under the stern. We'll get the trunk up on the afterdeck and into your skiff."

Davey imagined them trying to maneuver a heavy trunk into the flimsy wooden rowboat on their own. "We might need Jacob as well. I'll tell him."

The brothers stood on the porch at the back of Mug Budro's bait shop. The sun had nearly set over the granite quarry, and the tree hole mosquitos were starting to swarm.

Jacob leaned both hands on the railing. He was chewing on a matchstick.

"Let me get this straight, titch. You're gonna row to the yacht after dark, and take the actress woman's trunk round to the *J. T. Morse* without no one spotting you. Then what?"

"Then, first thing in the morning, Edith smuggles her off the yacht and gets her to Greene's Landing and on the steamer."

"But why's it all so hush-hush?"

"On account of she ain't supposed to be here. She's already married to some big movie type in Hollywood. The thing is, she's Cochran's lover—but he's engaged to someone else. He wants to break it off to be with her. She's worried her husband'll find out and be jealous, 'cos he's got a wicked temper."

Jacob was shaking his head incredulously. "And you're helping them why, exactly?"

"'Cos Edith's in a fix; she don't want to get fired. And the Vanska lady's got money. Edith gave me ten bucks to buy the ticket, and she reckons there's an extra fiver in it for me if I pull it off."

"Ah but Jeezum. Use your loaf, mate. If you get caught, you're risking your chance to race on *Vanitie*. Imagine if Rhodes found out! And it's my skiff—what if he thinks I was in on it?" Jacob's temples were tight as a drum.

"Well, you don't have to come, do you? Just lend me the skiff."

"Nah, I'm coming with you. You'll only mess it up, and get us both in trouble. But if anyone spots us..."

Davey smiled to himself. He knew how his brother's mind worked. It wasn't hard to talk Jacob into things. "Who's gonna spot us? The gents are going to dinner in town, at Doc Noyes' house. They'll be there all evening. And Edith's dad goes to bed early."

"What about Rhodes?"

"Bunkin' on board *Westward*, with the Swedes."

"And the crew?"

"Drinkin', at McGinty's."

Jacob was still unconvinced. "And this woman's got something on Edith, she's threatening her?"

"Something bad happened, and this woman saw it," he shrugged.

"She pinched something?"

"Dunno. But she's scared she'll lose her job if she don't do as she's told."

Jacob was silent for a while. Then he turned and scanned his brother's face. "You're soft on this girl, ain't you?"

Davey picked an imaginary splinter off a porch post. "She's just a nice girl, is all." For a second he thought of the downy hairs on the nape of Edith's neck, and how they would feel under his fingertips.

Jacob raised an eyebrow.

Finally Davey said, "All right, you tosser—yes. I'm soft on her. Happy now?"

Not long after sundown an orange three-quarter moon rose above the eastern horizon. It was a still August night, and the sky began to twinkle with stars. The tide was in. Water lapped on the rocks piled underneath the pier. Davey was balancing the skiff, hanging on to a rusty ladder. Jacob rolled himself a smoke, leaving the oars to flop in their rollocks. They could see the dimly lit stern of the *Nemesis* through the barnacle-encrusted stanchions of the pier.

"Bet you she don't show up," whispered Jacob.

"Shhh—"

At the top of the half-mast, the *Nemesis'* anchor light blinked twice. They both saw it.

Jacob scanned the deserted harbor, looking doubtful. But he took up his oars and started to pull, with short noiseless strokes, edging the skiff around the end of the pier. "Where's all the crew?" he whispered.

"In town, like I said. If any's left onboard, they'll be below in the engine room, playing cards."

"And it's five bucks each, right?"

"Shut up and row!" Davey was sitting on his hands.

Jacob made small hesitant dips, glancing over his shoulder. A couple of boat lengths away they heard the click of the sliding saloon door, and made out a shape. It was Edith, beckoning them towards the stern.

Jacob shipped his oars. When he caught hold of *Nemesis'* rudder post, Davey hauled himself up the stern and slid over the taffrail like a pirate, barefooted.

They didn't exchange a word. Edith led him down the companionway. The saloon was lit only by the bar lights. In the middle of the rug was a large leather-bound trunk with wooden struts.

They dragged the trunk up the steps to the afterdeck, and stood it on its end, rolling it cautiously over the rail. Davey hung on to most of the weight. Jacob, his feet straddling the skiff to keep it level, was able get one hand underneath the trunk, then the other. They inched it carefully down onto the skiff's cross-thwart. Jacob laid it flat in the bow and threw a fishing net over it.

Just then a look of shock came across Edith's face. She grabbed Davey's arm. Voices echoed across the water from the direction of the pier. A peal of laughter, footfalls—it was the dinner party returning.

He lowered himself swiftly over the gunwale. Now he could hear heavy footsteps on the *Nemesis'* gangplank. The skiff was in a blind spot behind the yacht's high stern, but Edith would be spotted the instant the guests entered the saloon. Davey felt his eyeballs bulge: he stuffed his hands under his armpits and he squeezed hard. Jacob, crouching in the skiff, motioned urgently for Edith to slip herself over the side. She seemed to hesitate; Jacob grimaced and motioned again. With a last glance over her shoulder, she swung her legs across the yacht's rail. Jacob reached up with both hands, caught her by her waist, and lowered her into the bottom of the skiff. She slumped next to Davey on a tarpaulin.

Jacob got his head down and began to pull away with long, firm strokes of the oars. Under the weight of the three of them and the heavy trunk, the skiff sat perilously low, only a few inches above the waterline; but Jacob's strokes were smooth and even. He pulled them into the shadows past the corner of the pier, just as the lights came on in *Nemesis'* saloon. There were snippets of conversation and laughter, the clinking of ice in glasses, music from a gramophone record. The sounds faded as they put distance between themselves and the *Nemesis,* leaving only the sloshing of water under the skiff with every dip of the oars.

Davey finally let out his breath. He noticed his hand was tightly gripping Edith's. He pulled it away, embarrassed. She looked up at him and smiled—but it was a kind, sisterly smile; not what he would have wanted. He mumbled something about needing to balance the boat, and shuffled aft to sit on an empty lobster trap.

"Thank you," she said, turning from him to Jacob. "Both of you! Thank you so much."

The moist night air cooled them. Jacob rowed the skiff across the wide harbor, his broad back making easy work of it despite the heavy payload. The oars dipped, and dipped again. The moon was higher now, more silver than orange. A flock of noisy Canadian geese crossed the dark sky overhead; the surface of the water reflected their passage like a pewter-stained mirror.

Edith leaned back on her elbows and closed her eyes. She pulled a pin out of her hair, and let her shining golden locks fall loose. Davey couldn't take his eyes off her pale neck, and the small bumps of her breasts under the lace apron. *When she opens her eyes again*, he thought, *she'll believe she's dreaming.*

Something otherworldly was happening to the dark waters of the harbor. The brothers had seen it before. Each time the tips of Jacob's oars dipped, they were illuminated by a bright green glow, a pool of brilliant flecks like a spotlight from the blackness beneath. The drips from the oars were made of the same sparkle.

"Psst, Edith! Look…" Jacob whispered.

She opened her eyes and gazed around; then she sat up, blinking in amazement. There was a long trail of bioluminescence in their wake, with pairs of wider green splotches wherever Jacob's oars had dipped. It was as if the skiff was floating above the dark expanse of the water on a cloud of glowing fireflies.

A corner of Jacob's mouth flicked into a smile. When he spoke, his voice was deep and guttural.

"I'm a magician, Edith."

His words seemed to hang in the air. The waters beyond their luminous green cocoon became darker and flatter still, so that Jacob's chiseled face was underlit by the soft glow. For a second, Davey saw him through Edith's eyes—the muscular arms, the calm expression, the shirt open to the waist—and he felt his stomach turn.

He said quietly, "You're pretty handy with your legs wrapped round a lump of wood too, aren't you, Jake?"

The spell was broken. Jacob fixed his black eyes on Davey's. "I could sail circles around you, little brother, and you know it."

"Except when we're sailing backwards, eh?" he said, grinning. Edith looked baffled. "Why don't you tell her yourself."

Jacob said nothing, so Davey carried on with the story. "We had a wager, see, against some West Bay buggers—first boat back to Powder House Island from the Ledge, sailing backwards. It ain't easy to do, Edith. You have to balance the rudder, and force the boom out to windward." He mimed the moves, as if the little rowing skiff had a sail. "Tell her what happened, mate! We licked 'em by a country mile, didn't we? And who was steering, eh?"

Jacob blew his hair away from his face and lengthened his stroke. "Ayuh, did you ever get the stink out of your toenails?"

Davey chuckled, feebly.

"Sailin' backwards is about the only way you'll ever beat me, tadpole," Jacob muttered.

"Aww, he's just sayin' that, Edith, cause he's never had the *feel* for it."

Greene's Landing was bathed in the fog from its electric floodlights as the *J. T. Morse* loaded up for her dawn departure. The big steamer, with its enormous central paddles, was moored alongside the dock. A trail of coal smoke drifted from the funnel. People were rushing everywhere— porters, seamen, the last few Stonington passengers. Crates of fresh fish and lobsters were stacked high on the cobblestones, packed in ice that only added to the haze.

Near the gangway, the uniformed harbormaster was checking off items on a clipboard. A pile of suitcases in thick netting swung from the hook of a crane. Most of the passengers were in transit, or had already embarked, and the light from the cabin portholes shone out in the night; there were sounds of music and jollity aboard.

The brothers tied up their skiff to an iron ring in the shadow of the dock. Between them they managed to haul Rula Vanska's trunk up the slimy stairway.

"Bloody hell, Edith, what's in this?" said Jacob.

Once on the dock, they blended in effortlessly. They set the trunk on its end with the other suitcases and tea crates, and Edith made her way through the crowd to see the portly harbormaster. Davey knew Mr. Wilkinson—he sat in front of them in church. Edith had to spell out the passenger's foreign name for him. He checked the reservation off his roster, took a piece of chalk and marked a large *C* on the side of the trunk, and ripped her a receipt from his pad. She handed him a generous tip, which he slipped into his breast pocket, with a knuckle to his cap.

Jacob saw the money and said, "I'll take my five bucks now while you're at it."

Edith peeled off a pair of $5 bills, and thanked them each again.

"Davey!" Mr. Wilkinson called. "Your ma was looking for you earlier. She wants you home."

Davey turned and gazed off across the harbor to Staple Point. "Is everything okay?" But Mr. Wilkinson had wandered off.

Jacob was rolling a cigarette. "Better get yourself home, titch, and check they're both all right. I'll get Edith back to the *Nemesis*."

With his pulse racing, Davey ran all the way around the harbor towards the cottage. Past the boarded-up fish shacks, the drying nets and traps, and the sloops pulled up on the mud. Over the rocks at Staple Point, and along the beach—Shell Beach, a silver-green crescent glistening in the moonlight where the small waves were breaking.

Shell Beach, where he'd hoped to bring Edith.

He slowed down, breathing hard, and took small backwards steps with his hands on his hips, straining his eyes towards the harbor. The surf lapped at his bare feet. He hadn't said goodnight to her, and now she was with Jacob. He felt in his trouser pocket, and his fingers closed around the bag of shells he'd meant for her. Clicking them together with his thumb, he pulled out the bag, undid the drawstring, and scattered them over the darkened beach. Then he spun around and sprinted home.

CHAPTER FIVE

He found Ma upstairs, in a state. Pa was having some sort of a fit. It had happened before once, when his pills ran out. She was tugging on her thin greying hair, fretting about how she was going to pay for this new medicine, this Phenobarbital. It stopped the fits all right, but it cost more than their family could afford—and Dr. Noyes couldn't keep giving them credit.

Late into the night, Pa was doubled up in convulsions, kicking off his bed sheets. Twice, he vomited on himself. Ma wouldn't leave his side, so Davey was back and forth to the kitchen for jugs of warm water and towels. He was finally able to catch some shut-eye on the mat, right before dawn. He would stop by the surgery later; perhaps Doc could spare them an expired bottle from his own supplies? Otherwise it was back to boiled willow bark, the traditional Deer Isle old wives' remedy.

The sun came up through the haze above the eastern horizon. Light poured into the upstairs bedroom. Pa was sleeping peacefully, and Ma had climbed up on the bed beside him, fully clothed. She smiled at Davey and and motioned for him to go, mouthing the words, "I love you." Feeling a little guilty, he left them like that and hurried down to the fish pier.

Coo Bray was there by the crowd at the notice board, running his finger down the new *Westward* crew list. From his sagging shoulders and long face, Davey could tell Coo didn't make the cut—which was worrying.

"'Morning, Davey. Looks like me and Willie Bishop are out, but you're in. You're on mainsheets, mate." He rested a hand on Davey's shoulder. "You done well. I knew they'd notice you, kid. They know brains when they sees 'em."

Coo was no spring chicken. His legs weren't too steady, and he was working on a paunch. He'd been sluggish getting about the deck. Davey made a mental note to keep it sprightly. Mainsheets would put him closer to the helm, where the tactics were decided; but it was a critical position, and today there'd be no Coo to look out for him. He looked down at his hands and frowned. They were still sore from yesterday's exertions on the backstays. He flexed his fingers and dug his thumbs into the sore muscles of his palms.

Coo squinted at the sky. "I reckon it'll get breezed up for you later." He stuffed his hands in his pockets and turned to leave.

"I need to ask you something, Coo," Davey said. "This feud between us and the West Bay boys—it's about more than just lobster pots, isn't it?"

"I don't get your drift, mate." He was avoiding Davey's eyes.

"Is it to do with the America's Cup? Something that happened on *Defender*?"

Coo's lips were pursed shut. Then he said: "You steer clear o' those bastards, Davey, is all I can tell you." He ruffled Davey's hair, and began the walk back towards town. "Look after yourself out there, kid."

He rode the tug out to the *Westward* and assembled around the mast with the others. The clouds gathering over Penobscot Bay were grey and unsettled, and the tails of distant Atlantic swells exploded among the rocks and inlets. One of the Swedes evacuated his nostril, right onto the deck.

Rhodes wasn't wasting any time. "Alright, ye lubbers, hear me *noo!*" he bellowed in his broad Scots. "It's down to the last forty of ye. If you're still here, it's because we think you've got the makings of a crack America's Cup crew. Come the spring, you could be livin' the high life in Manhattan wi' money in your pocket. But there's still half a dozen among ye as'll be stayin' home. Any dawdlers will be weeded out by the end o' the day. Let's get to sea."

Davey figured he still had a shot, so long as he pulled his weight today. But Coo and Willie were gone, and there were two new West Bay men on the backstays. Nothing was certain.

Jem Staples and Gardie Greene were on mainsheet with him. As they untethered the mainsail ready for the hoist, he found himself looking under the boom right into Gardie's deep-set, accusing eyes.

"What're you starin' at, sonny?" Greene said.

It was the first time he'd seen the man this close up. He was small and wiry, with a craggy, mistrustful face. The tips of two fingers were missing from his right hand.

"Nothin' much," said Davey.

Greene looked unsure if this was meant as an insult. "You Haskells better not fuck this one up," he hissed. His breath reeked of stale tobacco.

Davey hoped Jacob hadn't heard. Jake had a temper. He shrugged it off, and moved away along the boom. He took his time gathering up the sail ties, so he could stay well away from Greene, and close to the helm.

Alexander Cochran was by the wheel, dressed today in dun-yellow dungarees and a peaked leather yachting cap. He looked, if anything, even more aloof than yesterday. Harold Vanderbilt, with his steely blue eyes, was in sou'wester bottoms, sea boots, and a thick roll-neck sweater. He was focusing a pair of Abbe-König field glasses on the eastern horizon, where the Atlantic rollers were topped with white horses under a pale grey sky. "Should be quite a day! There's a nice wind line out there, and it's headed our way." He hung the binoculars on the binnacle and took a gulp from a large mug of coffee.

Cochran seemed preoccupied. "I still can't fathom it, Vanderbilt. D'you think it was something I said at dinner? Was she angry at me? To just up and leave like that, without a word…"

"Women, old boy. No end of grief. What can you do?"

"I mean, what girl wouldn't say yes to a free trip to Europe—an ocean crossing on the finest schooner afloat—casinos, Paris fashions, royalty? I don't get it."

The anchor came up over the side, and the big yacht picked up speed on an easy reach. Davey squatted by the mainsheet, sniffing the salty air.

The breeze in the Bay was already stronger than yesterday, and the wind line was closer inshore, with agitated breakers beyond. Cochran, steering with just his fingertips, pulled a slim silver flask from his inside pocket and flipped open the top. He offered it to his companion, who shook his head. He took a deep draft for himself. "It must be that ridiculous husband of hers; he's got her under his thumb. I kept telling her to walk away..."

Vanderbilt sucked on his pipe, and the thick tobacco smoke blew away across the deck. "The curious thing is, she left half her belongings strewn around the cabin. Wardrobe was full of her evening dresses."

"I know, I know," sputtered Cochran. He took a deep breath. "Well, she must've needed to take off in a hurry, I s'pose—"

"A spur-of-the-moment thing?"

"Still found time to pack that necklace I gave her, mind you. Diamonds and emeralds! It was my mother's. Worth a small fortune."

Davey gazed up at the set of the mainsail. He was intrigued by this new piece of the puzzle, and longing to relay what he'd overheard to Edith. With the mainsheet made fast, he moved forward and took his place alongside Jacob, lying on his elbow by the rail.

The *Westward* was close-reaching powerfully down the Bay with all sails set. Captain Rhodes cut an imposing figure by the foremast shrouds, with his long wispy beard and his black sea-coat billowing in the wind. He surveyed the expanse of the *Westward*'s canvas, then raised his speaking-trumpet. "Sir! What d'ye say to a balloon jib?"

Davey whispered in Jake's ear, "I give up, old boy—what *do* you say to a balloon jib?"

Cochran stroked his mustache. "Splendid."

Jacob jabbed his elbow in Davey's ribs. "That'll be you and me out on the bowsprit, titch. It's a big bugger."

The balloon jib was a bulbous whale of a sail. It would take a dozen men to rig the thing, edging their way along the twenty-six foot bowsprit on a single safety footrope; handing along the stoppered sail, then hanking its luff onto the outer forestay, clip by clip. Davey dashed ahead, eager to be first onto the 'sprit. But Jacob caught him with a firm hand on his wrist.

"You wanna check that footrope's lashed good and solid first." He leaned over the bow and pointed to a shackle where the safety rope was made fast. "That's all there is to hold the weight of the whole lot of us. Always check it yourself—" he leaned close to his brother's ear "—'specially with these West Bay buggers about." His eyes were fixed on Gardie Greene. "And clap on tight, 'cause we're sure to get a ducking!"

Davey checked the footrope for chafing, and gave it a hard kick with his heel. Stepping on, he began to shin sideways along the bowsprit. His feet were bare, so he could wrap his toes around and keep a grip on the thick rope. Some of the older sailors were wearing their sole-less boots. Below him, the yacht's sharp bow porpoised into each successive swell. Ahead was nothing but open ocean.

Jacob pointed out a thick stanchion, bolted vertically downwards from the underside of the bowsprit, supporting a high-tension steel bobstay. It alternately plunged and rose on the oncoming swells. "See that? That there's the *martingale,*" he grinned.

"But we calls it the *dolphin masher,* ain't it?" Davey was riding the tip of the bowsprit with both hands behind him on the forestay to steady himself. High above the water, with his salty hair matted to his forehead, he felt like a ship's figurehead. The rigging had a high-pitched musical hum, matching the vibration in the drum-tight forestay. He turned his back to the strong breeze, to take in the regal sweep of the *Westward*'s white pine deck, and the sheets of spray that soaked her planks and ran off down the scuppers. As the balloon jib hoisted and filled, he could feel the extra power of its enormous acreage pressing down on the bow of the boat.

The sun had briefly broken through the clouds—the last time they were likely to see it that day—and he shielded his eyes to gaze up at the *Westward*'s magnificent tower of canvas. The schooner was thundering down the channel at over twelve knots, into the last of the flood tide. The sailors were working well together now, East and West Bay men side by side. He made his way back to join his brother and crouched at the rail, taking a moment to catch his breath.

Jacob said, "What did she want, last night?"

"Who?"

He raised his voice a notch. "Ma. When you got back to the house."

"Oh. Pa had a fit. She thought it was another stroke, like last winter. He was all pekid and shaking, and he threw up his soup all over the bedsheets."

"He what?" Jacob cupped a hand to his ear.

"*Pa threw up.* All over the bed," shouted Davey.

"Christ. What did you do?"

"I offered to go for Dr Noyes for more of those pills, but Ma said no. She just wanted me home, in case…"

But he could see Jacob's attention was straying. Davey edged closer, and pressed a heel into his instep.

"So come on then, Jake," he said, "what did I miss?"

"Eh?"

"With Edith, numbass."

"I just rowed her back to the yacht, and she snuck back on board."

Davey scanned his brother's face. "What time would that have been then, about?"

"Oh—" Jacob checked himself. "Not long after you left us, round about eleven, I reckon."

Davey nodded sarcastically. They both knew it was closer to midnight. He'd seen them row off in the general direction of Mug Budro's shack. And at one in the morning, the lamp was still lit in Jacob's bedroom window. The bastard was obviously lying through his teeth, as usual.

"No really, that was all." Jacob gazed off blankly at the horizon, but Davey could see he was barely suppressing a smirk. He knew that smirk all too well. Jake never boasted about his conquests—he just left it to Davey's imagination to fill in the blanks, because he loved how inadequate it made him feel.

The *Westward* pitched and rolled in the growing swell. Davey peered back towards the town, barely visible now in the haze. He couldn't erase the previous night's images from his mind: the phosphorescent harbor—Jake's cozy room above the bait shack—the oil lamp behind the curtain, burning late into the night—the collection of animals carved from whale bone—Jake's soft feather bed… he felt a sickening emptiness in his stomach, and wished he hadn't skipped breakfast.

"Mate," said Jacob, "you're scratching your forearms again."

Most lobstemen's forearms were heavily scarred from pulling up the barnacle-covered pots—it was like a badge of honor. But Davey had a habit of scratching at his, whenever he was anxious. He abruptly rolled down his sleeves. It humiliated him when Jacob caught him at it.

He noticed Uriah Rhodes scanning the faces of the Deer Isle sailors. Was his mind was already made up? Jake was presumably a dead cert, after his skylarking antics aloft yesterday. Some of the foredeck and pit men, too. But most hadn't been pushed to their limits yet. With this Atlantic squall blowing in, it might be his chance to show Rhodes what he could really do.

The wind had moved aft and picked up, blowing the tops off the crests of the waves, like suds off a glass of beer. Cochran went below to relieve himself, giving Vanderbilt the helm. When he came back on deck, he had half a sandwich in his hand and an open bottle of pale ale in his pocket.

Vanderbilt called Rhodes to join them in the cockpit. "We really ought to practice some starts today. Many races are won or lost even before the gun, Alex. Let's see if these chaps can pull off the key maneuvers under pressure. It will give you the chance to try out my formula."

The image of Vanderbilt's 'formula' formed instantly in Davey's mind. He recalled it in perfect detail from the conversation he'd overheard during the gentlemen's luncheon on *Nemesis*, and he'd already diagrammed it in his sketchbook:

Start Line

Committee Boat

t = time to gun

Vanderbilt Start

Turn at $(t/2)$ +20 seconds

Vanderbilt pulled a folded chart from the rack at the side of the wheel and pointed to the broad tree-lined island a couple of miles ahead of them. "See the higher land? That's Isle au Haut. It's about five miles long. The water will be smoother on its lee side... here. We can set an imaginary start line as an extension of two visible landmarks—it's called a *transit*. We'll use the stopwatch and run the starting sequence a few times. What do you say?"

Davey had memorized everything he'd read about yacht racing, from boat speed to tactics. Strange to think your chances of winning depended so much on getting the perfect start, and crossing the line at top speed right at the gun. A start line was not something you could visibly see on the water: but he was born with the gift of seeing lines no-one else could. He'd often had to imagine how his row of lobster traps lay on the sea bed, using a pair of visual points on the land for reference. That must be what Vanderbilt was calling a "transit." It made perfect sense.

Vanderbilt rested his free hand on Cochran's shoulder. "Shall I do the first one, and you can watch?"

"Be my guest." Cochran took a bite from his sandwich and gulped his ale. "Nothing like learning from the master."

"All right. The final turn before the start is probably the key maneuver in the whole race. For the timing to work, you need to stay fully powered up. So, Captain Rhodes, we'll need the sails handled with *precision*."

"Aye, sir. Just watch the cross-currents between the islands here, will ye? There's strange eddies in these waters at the top of the tide. And it may start to get gusty, with this lowering sky."

Rhodes strutted around the deck with his speaking trumpet, talking the men through the maneuvers. When they were all set, Cochran marked the time, Vanderbilt initiated the turn, and *Westward* sliced through the water in a wide arc, with the crew heaving in the sheets to keep the sails drawing. Davey was amazed how the energy flowed from *Westward*'s stern to her stem like a slingshot. Vanderbilt managed it all with a quiet, competent authority, conserving every knot of the boat's momentum.

The schooner came smoothly through the eye of the wind, and the sails shivered momentarily and flopped across the deck. The yacht's keel bit as she settled on her new tack, and she sped back towards the line, water streaming along the port rail. As a single unit, the crew scrambled up to the starboard side, with Davey wedged in among the thirty-man human ballast. He glanced along the line of his mates' faces and grinned. It was all so much slicker than the previous day. He squinted at the water's surface a hundred yards ahead, where a glowing red line appeared in his mind's eye; they were approaching it at full speed. Cochran, stopwatch around his neck, counted down the last few seconds: "three... two... one... GUN!" At that instant he, Vanderbilt, and Rhodes swiveled as one, sighting back over their starboard quarter to the east—just in time to see Kimball Point align perfectly with the Isle au Haut lighthouse. They had hit their "transit" mere seconds after the imaginary gun: it was a yard-perfect start.

Cochran shook his head in disbelief. "Amazing—the 'Vanderbilt Start'! I get it now—I had no idea it was so simple." His dark glasses were coated with ocean spray. He was clearly enjoying himself immensely.

"Okay, Alex, why don't you try one?"

Cochran took over the wheel, and jibed back onto a broad reach. This time Vanderbilt called out the seconds on the stopwatch, while Cochran applied himself to the mental math.

Davey recalled the formula he overheard during their Sunday luncheon: *T over two, plus twenty, so... One forty-seven, or... Two minutes and twenty-seven seconds!*

"So we tack at...?" Cochran was still confused.

"2:27," said Vanderbilt. "Just don't turn any faster than they can haul in the sails. It's vital to conserve your speed. And remember to keep an eye on the compass. You must straighten out before you're dead due north."

Cochran's face was hard, his knuckles white on the spokes of the wheel.

Vanderbilt glanced at the stopwatch. "And... *go*."

"Ready about!" blurted Cochran, winding his wheel several spokes to the left. "I mean..."

"Helm's a-lee!" Rhodes corrected the errant order through his speaking-trumpet. Men scampered and slid around the deck to reach their stations. Turning sharply, the *Westward* carved a foamy trough in the ocean.

But the boat heeled too far over, and the trimmers struggled to keep up. The rudder almost seemed to skid sideways. The schooner lost momentum, stalled out, and heaved upright. For several seconds she was pointing aimlessly into the wind, her bow bouncing in the confusion of her own wake, sails flapping violently.

Jacob had the presence of mind to back the staysail. He grabbed the lashing sheet, and with the help of Siggi and Cyrus Thompson, hauled it back in on the starboard side, forcing her head round to the new tack. The rest of the sails filled, barely, and *Westward* began to gather way again, until she steadied on her new northerly course. The slingshot energy had dissipated.

Vanderbilt called out cheerfully: "Bang! there's the gun..."

They were still well short of their "transit". Some of the foredeck crew looked back in Cochran's direction, disappointment plain on their faces. In a real race they would have been a good half-minute late to the start line, and certainly not up to full speed. Davey knew it; everyone knew it.

"Not bad, old man, not bad at all..." Vanderbilt said in a reassuring tone.

Cochran was visibly flushed. "It was rubbish. Let's do another." Thick strands of his black hair had fallen across his face. "Rhodes!" he shouted. "We're going to try that again. And for goodness' sake, let's smarten up our sail handling!" He reached into his jacket for his liquor flask and took another slug.

"Aye aye, sir," muttered Rhodes. With a curt sideways glance at Vanderbilt, he made his way forward as if to reprimand his men.

Cochran's jaw was clenched, his brow set in a frown. He steered the course as before, sailing away from the start line. Vanderbilt reset the stopwatch and began the new countdown.

But something was not right with the boat. Many of the men felt it. Her movement through the water had changed. The bow wave had taken on a new shape. There was a sluggishness to her motion that had not been there before. Cochran was even having a hard time turning the wheel.

"What's going on, Rhodes?" he shouted.

Rhodes stepped onto the windward rail, grabbing the ratlines. He leaned far out over the water, craning to see down towards the keel. Then he turned and stared up into the tops, shielding his eyes with his free hand.

It was Jerker, the gangly Dane, who spotted it first. "Skipper!" he screamed, pointing aft. "*Dere!*"

Dragging through the disturbed water of *Westward*'s wake was a row of a half-dozen lobster traps, in a perfect line a hundred feet long.

All along the deck, the Deer Isle men stretched to their full height to catch a glimpse. There were a few titters at first, swelling into a torrent of laughter.

"Them's East Bay traps!" shouted Gardie Greene gleefully. "Never where they oughta be!"

Gardie's cohorts hooted and howled. Bill Otley gave Jacob a poke in the arm. Rhodes, a furious look on his face, skidded across to the leeward rail, then ran forward. He traced the direction of the rope below the yacht's waterline all the way to the bows, where he came to an abrupt halt.

"We've snagged a cussid lobster trap in the bobstay!" he yelled. "Must be a whole string of 'em, jammed under the keel."

Davey hurried to the foredeck, where a group of men had gathered, leaning over the rail to see. The lobster trap's marker buoy, a rusty brown metal float, was jammed solid in the angle between the taut wire bobstay and the martingale—the steel stanchion that Jake had called the 'dolphin masher.' Dragging behind it was a row of barnacle-covered lobster pots, two hundred feet long.

Rhodes' face reddened. "Siggi! Run back and tell Mr. Cochran to come head to wind! Otley—you come here. Take a knife and get down below the bowsprit, and cut that marker away, ye hear me?"

Gardie Greene took a step forward and pointed a bony finger at the marker. In his jarring whine, he said: "That's an East Bay marker, Cap'n.

You oughta send an East Bay man down to cut it out!" This triggered guffaws from Gardie's pals.

Jacob snapped back: "Yeah, an' if there's a mess o' bugs in them traps, your missus'll boil 'em up for my supper when I see her tonight."

Gardie Greene bared his rotten gums and made a lurch towards Jacob, but his mates held him back.

"*Bollocks* to your fuckin' lobsterman shite!" yelled Rhodes, out of earshot of the gentlemen. "Otley, I'll nae tell you again…"

Gardie half-turned to Jacob and grinned, making no attempt to hide that his hand was resting on the leather sheath on the back of his belt.

That was when Davey saw his chance. He sprang forward towards the bow.

"Davey, *no!*" screamed Jacob, and tore after him. The cluster of sailors parted.

With his arms out for balance, and the cork handle of his fish knife in his teeth, Davey leapt pigeon-toed onto the bowsprit and trotted ten feet along it, high above nothing but rushing water. He dropped to his hands, straddling the bowsprit's full width, then swung his legs down onto the safety line. From there he reached his right foot all the way to the bobstay, just ahead of the 'dolphin masher', followed by his left. His weight was now supported only by the steel wire of the bobstay itself, and he was gripping the safety rope with one upstretched hand. With each dip of the bows, he sank up to his knees in the foaming water. He hoped Rhodes was watching.

He heard Jacob's voice behind him as he edged sideways along the safety line. "Davey!" Jacob cried out, "I'm right here. Hang on tight!" But he was determined to do this himself.

The metal float was jammed hard between the bobstay and the dolphin masher, which was pounding down into each successive wave. With every dip of the bows, the metal float disappeared under the water. Davey reached down for it, but the force of the waves rushing past meant he didn't have the strength to pull it loose with his one free hand, never mind reaching the rope with his knife. He had to crouch lower.

"Grab the back of his collar!" yelled Rhodes, leaning over the rail. The boat was still moving swiftly through the water. In the confusion, the baby jib was let go, and the flapping overhead was deafening as its long sheets lashed about on the deck. "What's he playin' at?" Rhodes roared, spinning his head towards the distant helmsman. "Why the hell aren't we head-to-wind?"

Jacob was directly above Davey now, with both feet on the safety line and an arm gripping the bowsprit as best he could, trying to reach down and grab a good fistful of his collar. Davey bent lower to get both hands on the lobster float, the spray jetting up around his torso. He was just able to get enough purchase on the rope to make a loop of it, which he started to saw through with the serrated side of his fishing knife.

Then Siggi yelled at the top of his lungs: "He's *putting her about,* Captain!"

"Nooo-ooo-*oo!*" the Scot screamed.

Davey saw the fearful reality flash across Jacob's face like an electric bolt. This was the worst possible moment to tack the yacht through the eye of the wind. In another instant the sails and spars would crash violently over to the opposite side, and the bow could be pulled completely under.

Just as the *Westward* began the hard turn through the wind, a powerful gust hit her sails from a new direction. The trimmers were unprepared, and the foresail and jib, with their sheets still cleated hard, backed awkwardly, plunging the yacht's head down into the rolling swell.

Westward's bow bucked wildly in the chop. At first Davey thought he could hold on. But in the maelstrom of broken water, the safety line seemed to slacken. He lost his grip, dropped the knife, and fell backwards. He would have been washed clear into the boat's wake, but his right foot jammed in the angle between the bobstay and the boat's hull. As the schooner accelerated on the new tack, the sheer force of the water pinned his head and shoulders under the hull. He flailed his arms, struggling to free his ankle; but with each ducking his nostrils filled with water, making breathing impossible.

A blind panic overtook him. Blood was pumping behind his eyes. There was the blurred outline of his brother above him, yelling, trying to grab onto any part of his clothing. Then he felt something give in his leg, and a searing pain shot right through him. He knew he couldn't hold his breath any longer—his ribcage was ready to burst apart. He saw his hair float upwards like a weed, and the daylight seemed to get further away. For an instant he wondered what actually happens when you breathe in a whole lungful of the Atlantic Ocean.

Then, nothing but whiteness.

The whiteness was like a cloud, and when it cleared, he was staring down at the *Westward* as if from the tip of her mast. She was in full bloom, a sumptuous array of white cotton. He could see her entire sail plan laid out like the diagrams in the library books, with the name of each rope and sail labeled in Latin. Her white hull was a scimitar, carving a foamy groove in the dark seas. He floated effortlessly on the vortex of her sails, gravity-free. Men were running like frightened mice around the schooner's deck; yet up here it was all tranquility and silence, with only the soothing hum of the wind in his ears, and the occasional seabird's cry. He smiled when he saw Cochran, rigid at the wheel, his legs wide apart to brace himself against the boat's heel, and a wild, intense look on his face. Mr. Vanderbilt had been thrown to his elbows and knees, pipe in teeth, spectacles askew, still clutching his chart and the stopwatch. He spied his brother hanging off the bowsprit, drenched through, hair matted, reaching into the water, reaching again. The faint yellow of his own oilskin jacket was just under the surface. He saw Jacob drop like a rapier to the lowest part of the bobstay and grab desperately at the yellow splotch with both hands, yanking with all his might. And there now was his own water-logged body, with the foot jammed unnaturally in the martingale. Jacob screamed noiselessly for help, gulping air and spray; men were lying on the rail above, trying to stretch down an arm—a hand—anything, but unable to reach them. Davey wanted to call out, *Hey Jake, I'm actually not bothered! Let it go!*

He wafted downwards, closer to the foredeck. From somewhere, his brother found a superhuman burst of strength, and hauled the sodden torso up above the surface. He got the body wrapped in his arms, and turned to scream something. Davey read his lips: "Pass me a line! A *line!*" Someone loosened a coil of rope from its cleat. Jacob looped it under the cadaver's armpits, and half a dozen men were able to haul the lifeless lump of flesh over the bow, reaching down to grab any part of it, or its clothes, and lay it out on the planks. He hovered a few yards above them, watching with detached interest. The headsails were shivering, loose sheets cracking noiselessly on the deck: the racket should have been tremendous, but there was only silence and peace. The men just stood staring at the flaccid body in a stunned circle. Uriah Rhodes pushed through the crowd, and knelt to loosen the cadaver's collar. Its eyes were open, but unseeing. Rhodes slapped its face. No response. Slapped it again; then thumped its chest with both fists, while others helped Jacob clamber back onto the deck.

Jacob fell to his knees next to the body, and turned to Rhodes in desperation. Closer now, Davey could hear his voice; but it was many octaves too deep, and the sound didn't match the shape of his lips: "Is he alive? *Tell me he's alive!*"

For a few seconds the nothingness lingered, yet now the white mists were dispersing. He was gliding downwards, sucked towards the buckled corpse, until he was staring right into its lifeless eyes; then with a sickening crunch he was back inside the body, fused again to his own skeleton, his own blood and skin. He was choking and sputtering; his lungs burned like lava. The pain hit him like a bombshell and jerked his eyes open.

He heard Rhodes say, "He's alive, all right, Haskell. But he'll soon be wishin' he wasn't. Look at his leg."

Jacob's face which was sick with horror, as if his stomach had fallen out through his throat. Davey managed to lift his head a few inches off the deck, and he soon saw why. It was as if his foot was on backwards. A jagged six inches of bone poked through a large flap of skin above his ankle. The gaping wound gushed with his blood, pulsing in spurts. It mingled with the cold salt water in a pool on the deck; and soon after, with the vile retch of his own vomit.

CHAPTER SIX

Inches above his face, a yellow moth was trying to fry itself on the glass of a lantern swinging from the creaky beam. The reek of coal burned his nostrils. He was in the boiler room of Rollie's tug, with the engine throbbing beneath his spine. His neck was bathed in sweat, his whole body tense and contorted. Barely moving his head, he scanned the circle of worried faces in the half-light: Jacob kneeling beside him, holding his hand tightly. Cyrus Thompson, clutching a nearly empty brandy bottle. Other anxious sailors, caps in hand. And Dr. Noyes, leaning over him with a gold pocket watch, taking his pulse.

And then the pain hit. He tried to loosen the phlegm in his throat, but all that emerged was a low croak. It was beyond agony—his brain had *become* the pain. It erupted from his leg, spurting up through his skull. His eyelids felt sewn open, and his facial muscles had atrophied, frozen in some sort of death mask.

Doc Noyes lifted a corner of the blanket from his leg and rolled it back above the knee. It was a foul sight. There was a sodden tourniquet at the top of the calf; the knee was like a balloon, and the leg was purple and swollen, clamped with bandages between two strips of wood. A vicious V-shaped gash barely closed over the boney protrusion. Most of the blood around the wound was dried, but in places the gash was still oozing red.

"Jeezum," he rasped. "Jeezum fucking Crow!"

He started to shake uncontrollably. Hands reached forward from the shadows to hold him down. Jacob shushed him, stroking his face, his hair, until his breathing slowed.

Dr. Noyes cupped his shoulders. "Now then, David. I'm going to give you something for the pain, but we need to move you ashore, where we can take better care of you, do you understand? Your brother's here by you. You're in good hands, I promise."

He was unable to nod, as his chin was already buried in his neck. He blinked rapidly, just wanting the pain gone. Doc Noyes unrolled a canvas strap. He saw the flash of a glass vial, the gentle squeeze of a plunger. A drip squirted from the tip of a long needle. He felt the coldness of an alcohol swab on his haunch.

The sharp prick was like a kiss. Almost instantly, a soft glazed veil descended behind his eyes. The drug coursed through his veins, and his muscles turned to jelly. His lower leg began to feel less like it had a red hot poker jammed in it.

Doc Noyes backed away to the low doorway. Through his blurred eyes, Davey was aware of another man there, bent in silhouette. They spoke in low tones. He caught a few words over the throb of the engine: "...he's in traumatic shock... compound fractures of the tibia and fibula, and the main artery may be damaged... with proper care, yes... not on the island, obviously... vital we get him to the mainland within the next few hours—"

He was able to turn his face to catch what they were saying.

"—where on the mainland?"

"Belfast. There's an orthopedic unit at the Waldo County Hospital, I know the chief surgeon. With luck, he can save the limb, at least some of it. But my concern is the pain level, and the risk of sepsis. There's an argument for early amputation."

Jacob gripped Davey's hand tighter.

"Sepsis?" the stooping man said.

"Septicemia—toxic infection of the wound." The Doc's voice was a near-whisper. "With an open fracture, it can be fatal. But I have a lot of faith in Waldo, it's the best in the state."

"How far's Belfast, by water?"

"About thirty-five miles. It's pretty grim out there, mind you. The glass has been dropping all day. Could be a nasty gale blowing in."

Another shape came thumping around the corner and leaned in the doorway. "Bloody hell," he barked. "Will he die?"

"Shush!—he'll be okay, but he has to get to the mainland, tonight."

"Is there a steamer?"

"Not till the end of the week. And it'd take too long to drive all the way around. We'll have to chance it across the Bay in the storm."

"We should let him rest now."

Davey's eyelids were heavy, but he heard the three men leave, followed by most of the other sailors aside from his brother and Cyrus.

A muffled voice in the corridor said, "I'll do it."

Jacob was crouching close to his face. "Hold tight, kid. I'm here, alright? I'm not going to leave your side."

"Ma—" he said.

"All in good time. I'll tell her what's up, she'll come."

He motioned for Jacob to bring his ear closer to his lips. "No. You gotta stay with Ma and Pa! I'll be alright..." He was barely able to whisper.

"Mate, I'm coming with you to the hospital—"

"*Jacob!* I want you to stay with Ma and take care of her. Promise me?"

Jacob bit his lip. "Whatever you like, titch. 'Course I ain't gonna come if you don't want me. You call it, Davey, you're the boss. You'll be back home in no time, mind."

"You swear?"

"I swear."

Davey's eyes rolled back in his head, and his breathing slowed as he fell into a narcotic slumber.

Lamps blurred the ceiling of the hospital corridor. Nurses bumped the gurney round corners, scraping it through swing doors. He wanted to scream, but his mouth was smothered with an oxygen device. Then, hushed voices, the stifling whiff of ammonia; the blinding operating theatre light; a masked surgeon adjusting a steel rod, tips crisscrossed with nails. A rubber diaphragm, rising and falling with his breath. A dull prick. The anesthetist's green cap and craggy face, close to his, telling him to count backwards from ten.

He knew that poisonous grin from somewhere. He recognized the adenoidal voice:

"Apple don't fall far from the tree, Davey boy."

Then the shriveled hands pushed him down into darkness.

PART II

CHAPTER SEVEN

ON the morning of his seventeenth birthday, three weeks after the surgery, he was discharged from Waldo County Hospital. The orderlies wheeled him outside onto the forecourt with a blanket over him. A shiny white motor ambulance was waiting, emblazoned with a large red cross, and the words *Vanderbilt Rehabilitation Center*. As they spun him around to roll him backwards up the ramp, he watched the very first snowflake of winter fall slowly from the clouds and land on his cheek. He couldn't feel it melt. He felt nothing at all.

9th of November 1913

Dear Ma

I am writing to you from Newport. They moved me to another state cos they say this is a better place for me. I wanted to (write) before, but after the operation I wasn't feeling right, I kept throwing up and my eye sight was askew. That was a while back, this is one of my better days and now they got me so I can sit up in bed. Yesterday I got in a wheelchair for the first time, and they took me outside in the gardens for some fresh air. I asked for this paper and a pen. There is a brown thrasher in the shrubs singing away and it made me think of our house and that cheered me up a lot as I thought how you love that brown thrasher as sings in the oak tree up behind our house.

It still hurts a lot, specially at night but it comes and goes. I don't know if they told you what happened. Well, last thing I remember I was on the foredeck of the Westward and we snagged a string of traps and I had an accident. After that it's a blur. I can't remember nothing about coming to the mainland on Rollie's tug, or the operating room. They told me later my right leg was fractured so bad the bone was sticking out the skin, they would of had it off right then but these days they got new methods. Mr. Lehmann the surgeon explained how they do it, they go in through the knee with a steel rod down the middle of the leg bone, and that holds it together, then they bang nails through to keep it in place. Gory eh? They will know in a few more weeks if I can keep the leg, or if it is a goner. Even if I do (keep it) I will have a metal rod in me for ever Ma. Sounds weird don't it! Mr. Lehmann is famous in Switzerland and he hopes I will be able to walk again. I think I will, maybe even run around on a barky one day. He said I am very lucky cause if it got infected it would have been curtains for sure.

The nurses here are nice but I can't say a single good thing about the food. It comes on a trolley along with my linctus which tastes foul but takes the edge off. I miss your cooking Ma! And Pa as well. I am very sad specially at night and my thoughts are a muddle but the doc says that's very common after operations.

I hope Jacob has got the logs in for you from the woodshed, with winter coming on and all. It is a comfort to know he is there with you. I bet he told you, how I made him swear he would take good care of you and Pa, whatever happens. I am tired now so I'll stop but, don't worry about me Ma, don't worry about me one bit, or

*coming here to see me neither if it is hard. I will be fine
and I will be home with you and Pa and Jacob as soon as
I'm mended. I love you,*

*From, your adoring son
Davey*

He'd already rung, twice. Still no sign of the nurses.

Ever since they took the cast off, the aching had returned with a vengeance, even worse than right after the surgery. And it itched, too. He hiked up his right pajama leg and peeked at his ankle. The bandage had come loose. It still looked paler and skinnier than the other, like the last chicken on the shelf. And his shin hurt like a bastard.

He could hear music from somewhere. It was a beautiful, scratchy recording of a Chopin prelude that reminded him of piano recitals at the Oddfellows. He swiveled his wheelchair and rang again. Where were those bloody nurses?

Finally one of the staff showed up with a cup of ice chips and fresh bandages. It was Miss Ortiz, to change his dressings. She spoke near-perfect English, with a heavily inflected accent.

"How you feeling today, *mijo*?" she said. "Fed up?"

"Yep, I'd say so."

"You want to come and eat some lunch?"

"Not really."

He spun the wheels of his chair so he could see past her to the gardens. He knew his forehead was knotted in an ugly frown, but he didn't care. "You want to help me?" he said. "Get me some more of that tincture—that laudanum stuff."

She perched herself on the windowsill, right in the middle of his view, and took a deep breath. "I know it hurts, my friend, but you're already at the highest dose. If you want to get better, let me do what I do.

I have *especial* methods. You'll like it." She stood, grinning, and walked past him to the door.

"Tomorrow, Davey!" she called over her shoulder. "Tomorrow morning, we go to work."

"Yeah, I don't think so."

December 19ᵗʰ 1913

Dearest Davey

I was so excited to get your note and all the news. I read it out loud to Pa twice. Not sure how much he took in but everyone at home is rooting for you. I hadent heard what was up since your operation, I wanted to come visit but Dr. Noyes told us you might still be confused and they were moving you. I hope it is not hurting too much, love. How I wish I could cook you fish stew and ginger cake and all your favorite stuff for you.

It is funny what you said about the brown thresher, that was in the oak tree at the old house up on Post Street, I am amazed you remember it cause we moved from there to the cottage when you were only five! Oh and also it was not Rollie Staples as took you to the mainland that night in the storm, you was on that posh motor yacht of the New York gent's, but it's no surprise you don't remember. You are a very brave boy.

It is getting colder here with winter setting in. The neighbors have been so kind, and Father Michael comes by often to say a prayer with me for Pa. I been boiling willow bark for him as that fenobarb medicine is too dear. He still has his fits at night but he seems to be holding steady.

My love, you asked about Jacob but I have to tell you. Jacob left on the Westward, right after your accident. He got a job sailing to Europe. It is for the best and please don't be angry with your brother, darling.

*I am just sad we won't be all together for Christmas
and New Years but maybe Lent? I will pray for you every
night my darling, for your safe recovery and coming home
to us in one piece.*

Your loving Ma

The ribs of the conservatory roof were a web of cast iron with
hundreds of panes of glass, all steamed up by the balmy air. Water
trickled from an unseen hose, soaking the beds of orchids and toad lilies.
He studied the tall crowns of the palms, the curious succulent plants
with their fleshy fronds, and the ornamental finials atop the columns,
while Miss Ortiz arranged her instruments of torture on a steel trolley.

"I love it here in the early mornings," she said, tying back the silky
mane of her hair. "Later, the sun, it is too much."

"You a doctor?" Davey said.

"I'm a R.N."

"What's that mean?"

"Refreshments and Narcotics," she chuckled, and moved her trolley
closer. "No, a registered nurse. I'm Dr. Austin's... *lackayo.* If you like, you
can call me Lucía. We're going to be good friends. I'm the best chance
you got to keep the leg."

"Not much use if I'm dragging it around like a cripple, is it?"

"*Mijo*, you are lucky just to be alive. You were under the water a long
time. Too long." She tilted back his wicker chaise.

He tipped his head to the side. A large marble bust of Hippocrates
scowled down at him from its plinth.

"Who *built* this place?" he asked. "We don't have anything like this
in Deer Isle, I gotta say."

"A very rich Newport lady. Her husband left her a fortune. She
donated this annex in his name, *gracias Dios.* It's the top rehab facility
in all of New England."

"So how come they let riff-raff like me in?"

Lucía shrugged. "The doctors are interested in your case. And, you've got a secret admirer, is what I heard. Lucky!"

"A secret admirer? Who?"

She looked coy. "Then it would no be a secret."

"Huh." He took a moment to scan Lucía's face. It was the first time he'd really looked at her. She was nearing thirty, he guessed, with longish hair and a dark complexion, and a mole on one cheek. Her white scrubs were spotless. She had a watch pinned to her breast pocket, and a matching tortoiseshell fountain pen and propelling pencil, clipped to her lapel.

He realized he was staring at her chest. "Where are you from?" he asked.

"San Juan, in Puerto Rico. You know where this is?"

He was proud of his geography. He pictured the street grid of the old walled city and its natural harbor, the many bridges across the Seine, and the proud Acropolis on the hill. But thinking gave him a dull ache behind the eyes.

She'd rolled up the right leg of his pajamas. Everything below the knee was scrawny and yellow, still showing signs of bruising at the edge of the bandages. The black stitch marks of the exposed horizontal scar were oozing pus. Not a pretty sight. Lucía had probably seen worse.

Pulling over a low stool, she said: "Okay, listen, *corazòn*. You have a compound fracture of the tibia and fibula. This is the main bone, your tibia, and *this*—" she ran her palm down the outside of his leg "—is the fibula. It stabilizes the muscles that support your ankle and foot. The surgeon gave you an internal fixation, which means you have a vertical steel rod inside the main bone, and nails to keep it in place. *Suave*, no?"

"I don't get why they transferred me here," he muttered. "I'll only be wasting your time."

"You wanna keep the leg, yes?" Lucía cupped his calf softly in one hand. "With modern techniques, you may be able to walk again. But we don't want you limping all your life, or has to use a stick."

He sighed, and shuffled his weight on the chaise.

She was bathing his ankle with a warm washcloth from a bowl. *"Bueno.* Let me take the weight. It's been six weeks, so the bones, they will be start to glue themselves together. But your legs, Davey, they are losing their muscle mass. They can no support the new bone. We has to build your strength, and flexibility."

Grimacing, he let her lift his foot a few inches off the chaise. She pointed the toes by a few degrees and gently flexed the foot, repeating the movement, increasing the angle by a degree or two each time.

He squinted up at the condensation on the struts of the glass roof panes. "So what are you?" he said, "a nice girl from a good family? I mean, how many Porto Rican women get to land a proper job in the U.S.?"

Lucía froze, for a moment. Then she switched to a circular motion, and said quietly, "You don't know nothing about me, *mijo.* I grew up poor, like you. But one thing I learned is, no to judge people from the first time you meet them."

"Yeah well, you don't know nothing about me, neither." He feigned interest in one of the statues.

She placed a hand at the back of his right knee, and the other under his lower calf. "You seem to be in a dark place, Davey. Something else is on your mind? It's more than just the leg, isn't it?"

"Oh, you're a mind reader now?"

She let out a long breath. "Listen, you should be nice to me, *mijo.* I'm the one that stops the doctors from *keeling* you!"

"Reckon it'd be better if I'd a died."

"Of course you feel that way now. But take it a day at a time. Some of the patients here—" she lowered her voice— "they'll never leave, unless it's in a box."

"Sooner the better."

"Aww, Davey—"

He felt a jolt of pain as she bent his leg. She watched his face until it subsided.

"I can feel new tissue growing around your rod," she said, beaming. "Bet you never thought you'd hear a pretty girl say that?"

He forced a smile.

"With a tibial nailing, there's a possibility of malrotation. So each day, we flex a little bit more. Later we add a rubber tube for resistance. Is called dorsiflexion."

"Maybe I could take a bit more... dorsiflexion... if you gave me some of that linctus stuff first, the morphine?"

Lucía's eyebrow shot up. "Sure. What form you prefer it in? A bolus, perhaps? An injection into the cerebrospinal fluid? Or rectal suppositories, every hour?"

None of those options sounded very appealing.

"No, Davey. Your pain medication is... *muy adequado* for now. We will reduce the dose over the next couple of weeks, till you can make do with just aspirin. Then you brain won't be so foggy—and maybe you won't be such a *chayote*."

"What's a *chayote*?"

"He is a green hanging vegetable that looks like an *escrotum*."

He surveyed Lucía's face and wondered if he would prefer it without the mole. No, he decided, the mole could stay.

Some nights, the morphine didn't seem to help much any more. Were they messing around with his dose? And why did they always have the darn radiators turned up so high? He tossed and turned in his bed, kicking the sheet off then dragging back on. He clutched the pillow to his head to block out the noise of the pipes. His oozing scars itched his skin like crazy, and the bone ached from deep inside.

In the small hours, the bad dreams came again to taunt him, as they did every night:

Shell Beach, bathed in moonlight. No pretty shells, just black sand and a few silvery driftwood logs, and wavelets lapping at the high tide line. The punctured white hull of the *Westward* was high and dry on the rocks. Jacob sat cross-legged on the sand, mending a net, humming the sad melody from the Chopin. The swell was a deep dark burgundy, and the whole Bay was steaming, as if something was lurking underneath. Suddenly Jacob was right in his face, sneering, eyeballs popping, hair all wild. "Still hobnobbing it with the rich fucks, eh peewee?" He was missing most of his teeth, like Gardie Greene. Davey made a furious lunge; but Jacob wrapped him in a bear hug, picked him up by his skinny shoulders and shook him like a rag doll. His leg flopped around uselessly, a boneless bag of skin. The sea was beginning to boil now, bubbling like a vat of tar.

He forced himself awake. The hissing of the pipes was deafening. A blood-red moon was rising behind the poplar trees. He tried to roll over, but his sodden pajamas seemed to glue him to his mattress.

He was strapped to the table in *Nemesis'* saloon. The louvered screen door banged open and closed, open and closed. The yacht was lurching violently. A momentary sheet of lightning lit the ocean outside. It framed the blown crests of the Penobscot waves like a flash bulb, burning the scene onto the back of his retinae: Jeb Livingstone, the chef, on all fours, bleeding from the mouth. Mr. Armitage, clutching his rosary beads, reciting the Catechism. Edith, sobbing, flattened against a bulkhead. His teeth were chattering uncontrollably. Then, a sudden, searing pain split the back of his skull where his head had hit the floor. The trophy cabinet burst open, and silver cups and shields flew across the saloon in a spray of shattered glass. He had landed in a crumpled heap, rolling in broken glass. It scrunched under his bare back, the shards piercing his skin. He couldn't feel his leg at all—was it still there? He tore the blanket off. A sickening sight met his eyes: his right lower leg was screwed into a bizarre iron traction device, bristling with bolts and wires, but it had buckled, and the bandages hung off it, soaked with dark blood. A reek of chloroform mingled with the taste of vomit in his throat. He swallowed it back down, and when his voice finally came to him, he screamed at the top of his lungs for someone to help. The yacht was rolling and yawing, broadside on to the waves. Who was steering this thing? A porthole blew open, and a horizontal wave burst in and slapped across the saloon floor. Jeb clawed his way to the porthole and slammed it closed against the force of the storm. Jeb, Edith and her father manhandled his crumpled body back onto the table, lifting his fractured leg at an agonizing angle. He banged his fist on his thigh over and over, his eyes screwed in pain. He began to hyperventilate, grabbing hold of her wrist and squeezing until it stung her. The leather mask pressed to his face, and Edith twisted a faucet on the brass cylinder. A pungent chemical smarted in his nostrils; he sucked the powerful gas into his lungs. He tried to yank the mask away, but his eyes glazed over with a silky mist, rolling back in their sockets. The vapor flowed through his body and seeped all the way to the tips of his fingers and toes. She sealed the mask tight over his face again, clicked the dial twice, and...

He had never noticed Edith's halo before! It made perfect sense that she was a saint. She smiled, and her halo shone in a rim around her golden hair. Her loving blue eyes were the eyes of the Holy Virgin, bathing him in her sacred light. The smell of her lavender soap was like incense—and ah, here was Jeb Livingstone now!—Pope Jeb, with his mitre and robes, swinging the jeweled thurible, sanctifying him with the holy incense, mumbling a blessing in Latin. He made the mark of the cross on Davey's forehead—a martyr to crippled sailors everywhere.

Another sudden flash of lightning in the skylight above made him twist his face to the side. There was Rula's steamer trunk, on its end, her red blood seeping out of it in a widening pool on the Persian rug. He gagged, his throat paralyzed. Below his knee was a cluster of eel heads, chewing their way out of the flap in his leg, gorging on the fungus that grew from his stump. Their egg cocoons were hatching out as larvae, in a gushing phosphorescent jelly, sloshing around the floor of the saloon.

Then he threw up, every last drop of bile left in his stomach, and he felt it soak his neck and cool on his skin. All was quiet in the ward aside from his own sobbing. The moon had risen now, and fingers of frost crept across the windows.

Ice floe, frozen in time, bumped and cracked in a landlocked lagoon; iceberg sculptures washed up on a volcanic beach, a black sand beach made of tiny shells. He was back on Shell Beach, under a thin veil of fog, in the eerie moonlight. She was there again, clothed in white muslin, poking fondly at the shells he'd collected, because she loved them. He reached to touch her hand, but her spectral body seemed to dissolve into the fog, her limbs consumed by tiny swarming crustaceans; the seething blob fused into an armor, and incandescent red armor like the shell of a giant lobster, with its beady eyes and long feelers waving at him. He was trapped in a pot with the other squealing lobsters, tethered behind the *Westward,* twisting and jerking in its wake. He pushed his face upwards and gasped for air, and clawed at the safety line, but it unraveled from its cleat. He got a brief glimpse of Gardie Greene's toothless grin; then he was slipping further down into the depths, just a crust of bread now, enveloped by silvery eels as they flashed back and forth, disintegrating into crumbs for their eel feast. Bars of moonlight imprisoned him beneath the planks of the pier. The weed-covered posts were slippery, and the barnacles ripped his forearms. He broke the surface. The receding waters left him wallowing in a heap of sodden maggots, spilling out on the porch in front of Mug Budro's. He pulled maggots from his nostrils, and out of his eyes and ears. From the bedroom window above Mug's, he heard a slap of female flesh and a squeal. Edith, giggling, poked her head out, her golden hair loosened from under its lace cap. She called to him, clutching her naked breasts; but her hips were yanked back inside by hairy male hands.

Lucía pressed his shoulders down onto the bed. He was drenched in sweat and vomit.

"Shhh... It's okay, *mijo.*"

When his breathing finally slowed, she poured a glass of cold water and tipped it to his lips, tilting his head.

She was perched on the edge of his bed in her silk nightgown, lit only by strips of moonlight from the cracks in the blinds. A little gold crucifix dangled between her breasts. He watched it glinting in the moonlight for a while, as she sponged him off. Then he lapsed back into an uneasy sleep.

An hour before daybreak he finally broke free from the night. The pain had subsided, leaving him with an acute bout of pins and needles in his foot and toes. He rang and rang. It seemed to take forever for the day nurses to come. They changed his sheets and pajamas, propped him up in bed, and gave him his morning medication.

He watched the frost slowly thawing on the window panes. When the sun came up, he reached for a pen and writing paper. Words usually formed easily in Davey's mind, but it was hard to get them down on the page without sounding like a stupid kid. He re-read the letter, tore it up; wrote a second one, decided it was good enough, and sealed it in an envelope. On the front he wrote *To: Mr. Harold Vanderbilt, Rock Cliff, Newport,* along with his return address at the hospital. He propped it on his nightstand.

CHAPTER EIGHT

"This ain't so hard, to be honest," he said.

It was late January, his second day in the gymnasium.

"You're doing so good, Davey!" said Lucía Ortiz. "I know it's hurts, but you need to push yourself."

The winter sunlight was pouring in now through the bay windows. It took a while to get the hang of these parallel bars. He released one hand at a time, but every time he moved his left foot, he had to put his weight painfully on his right. After the first couple of laps, though, he began to lean a little longer and harder with each step.

Lucía was humming to herself. She had a pretty voice.

"So, Lucía. You got lobsters down in Porto Rico?"

"Yes. We call them *langosta*. They're delicious. A bit different from your Maine ones."

"How so?"

"No pincers." She pinched his shoulder through his pajamas. "And by the way, we say Puerto Rico. *Puerto*. You guys tried to changed the name to Porto Rico when you invade us."

"We what?"

She laughed. "*Mijo*, my country had been around for centuries before the Americanos came."

"Oh, that's right," he said. "San Juan was an important port-of-call for silver-laden ships en route from Cadiz to the Spanish West Indies..."

It was weird—since he came off the drugs, he could recite entries he'd read in the Encyclopedia Britannica as if he had the page open in front of him. His memory was more detailed, more vivid now.

He managed twelve laps before the sharp ache in his leg was too much. Lucía helped him over to the massage table.

"It's not just your legs that are weak, is your whole body. At home you are doing physical work every day, fishing, sailing." She was rubbing warm oil into his right calf and ankle. "Here, nothing. We need to keep increasing your activity. In a week or two, I'm going to teach you to use crutches. Ever walk with crutches?"

He shook his head.

Lucía moved around to the top end of the table to work on his neck and shoulders. He liked the way the tips of her hair sometimes brushed his skin.

"So, your home, Davey. Tell me about it. Tell me about where you grew up."

"Ain't much to tell, really, it's just plain old Deer Isle," he said. "There's only one town, Stonington. It's small, a few hundred people, mostly fishermen. There's a bit of trade up and down the coast. I been out on the lobster boats from when I could walk, pretty much. We bait the traps, and haul 'em back in, in any kind of weather. Some years there's plenty for everyone, and the whole town's buzzing. In the lean times, you wonder how you'll eat or make rent, and you have to lay nets as well, for cod and crabs and sea bass."

"Your people were immigrants?"

"Nah. Haskells've been there for generations, along with a few of the other families. I got more cousins than I can count! We have a rare old time, come the fourth of July, or New Year's. Dozens of us, all packed into the Oddfellows, gettin' our knees up. Not a lot of drinkin' in Deer Isle, most times, except when there's holidays we break out a keg or two."

"And music?"

"Ayuh, people bring squeeze boxes and fiddles and banjos, and we all join in and have a sing-song. There's sea shanties, marching songs, old Irish reels, you know."

He doubted she had ever heard an Irish reel. But Lucía was full of surprises.

"I bet you'll have your knees up again before you know it, *corazón*."

"Well, I'm not much one for the dancing." He shifted his numb leg to find a better angle. It was hard to imagine he'd ever feeling like dancing again.

"You got brothers and sisters?" she asked.

There were those butterflies again. When he didn't answer at first, Lucía leaned over him and said, "You okay?"

"I got a brother, Jacob…" he began. "He's five years older."

"What's he like?"

Davey swallowed. "He's a darn good sailor. He's worked on big freighters out on the coast. Stronger than me, I guess. Not that smart though. I reckon I know the wind and tides better, and the shape of the sea beds round our bay."

"No, what he's look like, silly? Is he a handsome blondie like you? I'm always on the lookout for a *papi* for my babies, you know." Her eyes were sparkling.

Davey's stomach turned at the thought of Lucía and Jacob together. *Ugh.* Sometimes you flipped over a squirming female lobster in the bilges of your boat, and you could see the wide fanned tail and the clusters of eggs called berries. He rolled his face to one side, with his eyebrows pinched together.

She said softly, "I'm sorry, *mijo*. Is that too much?" She moved down to his left hand, fanned his fingers out between her own, and began jamming her thumb into his palm. "How's this feel?"

"Feels good," whispered Davey. He closed his eyes and blew out a long breath. "After my accident, Jacob ran off to sea. He promised me he would stay and look after Ma and Pa—he swore to me. But instead, he signed up on a big schooner, bound for England. I fucking hate him for that."

"Oh, Davey." She crossed herself, and brushed the hair back out of his eyes. "This is terrible, to hate your own brother."

"He's a gawmy sod, is what he is. Ma's frail, she's getting on. She can barely cope on her own. Pa had a blood clot in his head, and now he's upstairs in bed. She needs help bad, but I can't do nothing for her, stuck here with my leg busted up. And Jake runs away to fucking England. If he gets hired regular, on a race crew, God knows when he'll be back, if he even *does* come back." His eyes were wide open now, and moist. He gazed straight into hers. "How could he do that? He's a bloody traitor, is what."

His lip was trembling. She gave him a handkerchief from her breast pocket, and he blew his nose.

"I bet you wish you could tell Jacob just how you feel, no?"

He started scratching his neck at the base of his skull, making it red. "I bloody would, an' all. I'd tell him he's a dirty scab. I've never broke a promise, not like that. We ain't even heard a word from him, Ma would have said. How come he ain't sent any money home?"

Lucía went to work on his wrist. When she pushed up the arm of his pajamas, she was shocked by the criss-cross scars on his forearms.

She asked in a soft voice, "How you got these scars?" They looked fresh.

"Oh. That's from hauling up the traps, over the side of our boat," he said. "Sometimes we string 'em thirty or forty in a row. Big heavy wood baskets, and they get all crusted up with barnacles. When you got a full trap, sometimes you're so excited, you don't notice it's ripping up your arms. They can slice you up real good. And they're deadly, too. You get fouled up in the lines, they'll drag you clean overboard. One of my cousins drowned like that when I was little."

"How old were you when your papa got sick?" asked Lucía.

"About seven or eight."

"You think about those times a lot, before his illness?"

"Ayuh. They was good times. But what I been thinking about lately is, is how Pa always liked Jake better than me."

"Oh? Why you say that?"

"Long as I can remember, Jake talked like *he* was Pa's favorite, 'cos he got all Pa's strength, his canny. Said I would never grow up to be like him and Pa."

"That must have hurt a lot."

His eyelids fluttered closed. "In the evenings by the fire, Pa'd be teaching Jake some new knot, or how to bend maple branches into hoops for the pots. Laughing together at some joke they said I was too little to understand. And Jake has to remind me, all the time, now we're older. 'Pa told me this... Pa told me that... You was just a pipsqueak!'"

"I think that would make me feel like *chit*," said Lucía.

"It does. I feel like *chit* alright. He never gives me no credit, Jake. Even when I'm first back to harbor ahead of the fleet. Or one time when I brought in the biggest catch of the day. Never said nothing."

The doors banged shut as the last of the other patients left the gymnasium. They were alone.

"Jake got Pa's fishing knife, right? He got his sea coat, too. All I ever got was the stuff Jake grew out of. Now I'm two inches taller than him, anyway. And I'll tell you something else, Lucía—he's got the smallest nipples I ever seen."

Lucía laughed. She clapped her hands twice. "Okay, *papi*, over on your stomach." He rolled over, awkwardly, trying to favor his good leg.

She went to work on his upper back. "Don't tense up," she whispered, and gave him a little pat between his shoulder blades, resting her palm there until she felt him relax. She placed her other hand on top of the first, and pressed them both deep into his spine. He let out a guttural groan.

"You know what it sound like to me?" she said.

"Mmm?"

"It sound to me like Jacob is better off at sea." She dribbled some oil in the small of his back. "Look, I was no use to my Mama and sister in San Juan, there was no enough work. I had to do what was best for my family. So I came to America for earn my certificate. I was alone in New York City. It was hard, at the beginning. Now I live upstairs rent-free, at the hospital. I make good money. Most of it I send home every month, it's what keep them going. You don't think Jacob wants what's best for his family too?"

"He's never sent Ma squat. She would have told me."

"But you don't know what's in his mind. Maybe he's trying to make something of himself. Look at me, I got big plans."

"Like what?"

"Okay, so I would love to train here as a orthopedic surgeon. What chance do I got, a Puerto Rican woman? No chance. But I will go home to San Juan one day, this I know, and open my own clinic, to help the people of our island. Your brother must has his dreams too."

Davey took all this in. He didn't have much choice: his face was squashed flat on the table.

"Let me ask you this, *mi amigo*. Was it Jacob's fault you broke your leg and nearly drowned?"

"No, obviously," Davey said.

"Is Jacob the reason you're unhappy now?"

"Well… yeah, mainly."

"Is he making you *stay* unhappy?"

Davey thought about this. "No…" he said, without much certainty.

"Jacob's what's keeping you here, at the hospital?"

"No."

"What is, then?" said Lucía. She wiped her hands off on a towel, and with one hand on her hip, she took a long sip from her glass of water.

When he wheeled himself back to his room after dinner, there was a present for him on his pillow, and a handwritten note:

> *Dear Davey, thank you for being a good sport today. I got you something. I think you might like to keep it on your wall. I started it but you should fill it in yourself. Tomorrow's a BIG day! Love, Lucía*

It was a pictorial calendar for 1914, with lithograph prints of famous sailing yachts on the upper page, and a grid of the days of each month on the lower. Davey opened it to the month of March, which featured Kaiser Wilhelm's splendid *Meteor IV*. For each day of the month, Lucía had filled in the number of laps Davey completed on the parallel bars, along with the weight-bearing fractions—1/4, 1/2, 2/3—and abbreviations for the treatments he'd had, which included 'hydro', 'dors.', 'EMS', 'mass.'

and so on. Friday March 6th had a big red star drawn around it. Inside the star was written one word:

¡CRUTCHES!

For the first couple of days his armpits were very sore, but it didn't stop him from getting around the ward in his pajamas, making conversation with everybody he met. By mid-March he was finding the crutches a bit easier; enjoying them, even. When the sun came out briefly, and took the chill out of the air, he put on a dressing gown and took a turn around the gardens.

That was when he received Edith's letter. The nurse from the front desk brought it out to him, a white envelope with his name on it, and a Newport watermark. Excited, he found a bench, leaned his crutches on it, and sat down to read.

Later, in Electrostimulation, he took it from the breast pocket of his pajamas and read it again from the beginning. Lucía had finished setting the dials, and left to attend to another patient. He felt that weird pulsation of electricity, starting with a tingle and rising to a sensation of needles being stuck in his skin. With each jolt his muscles contracted involuntarily, and his toes curled. His leg was getting stronger.

He scanned Edith's words for something he'd maybe missed the first time, some sign of affection; but he gave up and stared blankly at the ceiling, his muscles spasming.

The minutes ticked by until Lucía came back to take off the electrode pads.

"How was that?" she asked.

"Right queer," he said. "Lucía—"

"Yes?"

"I've got to get out of here."

"You just figured that out, *chacho*?"

"Soon as I can walk right. I need to get working again."

"Have you thought how you're gonna earn money? You won't be catching no *langosta* any time soon."

He shrugged. "I'll find a way. Perhaps a desk job at the telegraph office, or the town hall. Or I could train as a cashier at the bank. There's always Mug Budro's bait shop, he'd give me some work."

"Then you got something to look forward to, *mijo*. But take it slow. You're not like Frankie, and Florence, and most of the others here. You're gonna get away. You'll be back on your old boat before you know it."

Back on his old boat. Hauling up the traps. Sailing back into the Harbor with a crate full of fatties. His conscious brain wanted to form a picture of Jacob there alongside him, but his unconscious brain wouldn't let him.

"It's up to Dr. Austin," she said. "Maybe three, four weeks."

He pictured the calendar. "So, end of March, beginning of April?"

"Beginning of April, if you play your cards. You should be able to take the train by then. You might even think about writing your mama and tell her you'll be coming home."

He swung his legs off the table and grabbed his crutches.

"What're we doing next?" he asked brightly.

"Okay, *corazón*, today we're going to try the staircase. It's good for build your stamina. If you're a *very* good boy, I got a nice surprise for you, after." She flashed him a mischievous grin.

He squinted up the first flight of stairs, a little doubtful. They weren't particularly steep; but in the months he'd been here, he'd only ever taken the elevator. It was hard to balance without using both legs. He felt like he was going to trip and fall.

"Steady, Davey. One at a time. I'm right here."

He got in a rhythm, but it was still hard work. When they reached the second floor landing he had to pause to catch his breath.

Lucía tossed her hair back and leaned on the banister. "So I hear you have a sweetheart?"

"Who told you that?"

"Oh, a little birdie. Edith, that's her name?"

Davey blushed. "Well, she's not really my sweetheart. I mean, we've never actually *done* anything. I'm pretty sure she likes me, but..." he trailed off.

"But what?"

"Well, I think she likes Jake more, I dunno. She works for one of the Vanderbilts. She and her dad are on the crew of his yacht, the *Nemesis*. Them and the cook darn near saved my life, near as I can tell, the night of my accident."

"You hear from her since then?"

"Not till today. I got a letter. They're here in Newport, apparently, at Rock Cliffe, getting the house ready for him."

"Davey! What did it say?"

He shrugged. "It didn't really say anything. I mean, it's no surprise, hardly. I'm not exactly a great catch at the moment, am I?"

Lucía eyed the shape of the envelope in his pajama pocket. "Can I see? or it's *privado*?"

"If you want." He handed her the letter.

She read it to the end, then folded and handed it back. A corner of her mouth twitched. "Sometimes when a girl says nothing, you know, it means the world."

He started up the next flight of stairs towards the third floor.

"You think I should write back?"

"Why don't you just telephone to the house?"

"I might get her father—"

"But he's sick, she said. Chances are, Edith answers the telephone. It'll be a surprise, but she'll be impressed too. She's probably lonely there. Ask her to come and visit you! Or better still—" she lowered her voice, "—you could go see *her*."

"Isn't that a bit... forward?" He was almost out of breath.

"I was a young girl once too, yes? We like it when the man is the hunter. You *Americanos*, you never say what you mean. In Puerto Rico, a man is more direct. If you're keen on this *señorita*—"

"Edith's from Ireland."

"Trust me, young girls are the same everywhere."

Davey thought about it. "How do I use the telephone?"

Lucía spoke in a hush. "There's only one line, in the office. Mr. Dubois has an extension on his desk. When Dr. Austin is on his rounds, you tell Dubois you need to call your mother in Deer Isle."

"No, I mean... how do I... *use* it?"

By the time they reached the third floor, he was exhausted. These were the staff quarters, a part of the building he'd never been in. His arms were sore, and he thought he was done for the day. But Lucía beckoned him to follow her along the corridor to a small green baize door in the wall, slightly ajar.

"What's all this, then?" he said, grinning.

It opened on to yet another staircase—this one much narrower and steeper than the main stairs. Lucía flicked on an electric light.

"I told you I had a nice surprise for you!" She pushed him ahead of her.

"Where are we *going*, Lucía?"

She was giggling, and she kept poking his bottom from the step below.

At the top of the stairs was a long, low attic room. It was much warmer up here. They were at the very highest part of the building now, practically in the roof. There were some dusty picture frames covered in a sheet, a stack of folded lawn chairs, a box of croquet mallets. At the far end was a single round window with a view to the west, looking over the gardens and out across Newport Harbor.

And there, silhouetted in the window, was a shiny brass telescope.

Lucía could barely contain her excitement. "You like it? Try it out!"

Davey knew how a refracting telescope worked, but he'd never seen one in person. He found the knob to loosen the tripod head, and stooped to the viewfinder. He was able to pick out a landmark in the harbor, a lighthouse on the tip of a narrow island, and center it in the crosshairs. Then he switched to the main eyepiece, and adjusted the azimuth. The lighthouse came into focus and filled his field of view with enough detail that he could make out the individual panes of glass, and the sea birds perched on the guano-covered rocks beyond.

"I love it!" He laughed. "I just love it!"

There was so much to see: to the south, Newport Cemetery, and the shipyards on Thames Street. Beyond that, Goat Island Naval Base. Clear across Narragansett Bay was Prudence Island to the north, where the ship traffic came in from Bristol and Warwick. Jamestown, to the west, which you could only get to by water; and Rose Island, with its pretty lighthouse. The fishing trawlers in the main channel, heading out to the Grand Banks for the cod. The Block Island Ferry, twice a day like clockwork; even the lobster fleet, in their catboats, laying their traps over by the western shore...

But best of all was the sail racing.

He spotted a fleet of one-design keelboats heading out from the Harbor Yacht Club to the far side of Goat Island. Each had a red star on its sail. He could just make out the men on board, two on each boat, their weight hiked out over the topsides of the square-sided hulls. A "frostbite" race! Their fingers must be freezing, he thought, but he was still envious. He'd never done it himself—aside from trying to beat the other fishing sloops back to Stonington. There was an edition of the *International Rules of Sailboat Racing* in the library. He decided to learn them by heart. He would study the articles in *The Rudder*, and the reports in the New York Times of the big cutter races at Sandy Hook and Brenton Reef. He was determined to use this time to become an expert sail racer. He already knew more about tactics than most of the other Deer Isle lobstermen—and a lot more than his brother.

CHAPTER NINE

He took a deep breath and picked up the receiver. "Hello?"

There was no sound at all. He tried the wind-up handle, giving it a few cranks, which generated a clicking in his ear. Finally an operator's voice came on the line: "Number please?"

"Oh, hello. Could you please connect me with Rock Cliffe in Newport, Mr. Harold Vanderbilt's house?"

"That's Newport 3557. Please hold."

Davey swallowed hard. He pictured Edith, so happy to hear from him she'd drop her feather duster to the tiled floor. Standing there, rigid with excitement, clutching the receiver with both hands, in her dark cotton uniform and white lace apron and cap, flat shoes, and black wool stockings.

A feminine voice answered. It sounded quite proper, but it had that familiar Irish lilt. "Vanderbilt residence, good morning?"

He lit up. "Edith—is that you?"

"I'm sorry, who is this?"

"Edith, it's Davey. Davey Haskell, from Deer Isle."

There was a pause. "Davey?" She instantly muffled her voice. "What are you doing calling here?"

"I got your letter," he said, "and I started to write back, but I reckoned I'd telephone instead."

Edith whispered, "I'm working! I'm not supposed to use the telephone. I can only talk for a minute. Father's in his room, resting."

"Well, I was thinking—I'm here at the rehab clinic, I looked it up and it's only three miles to Bellevue Avenue. There's a trolley service that goes right past the door. Can I come see you?"

"You can't come here! Mr. Vanderbilt arrives tomorrow, and my father wouldn't have it." She sounded agitated. "And can you even walk? On your bad leg?"

He was puzzled that she wasn't more pleased to hear from him. "With crutches, yeah. I get around okay. They say I should be able to go home in a couple more weeks. But I just, er—well, I need to thank you, you and your dad, and Jeb, for taking such good care of me. I could easily have lost the leg. I reckon you saved my life. I owe you."

There was a pause.

"You don't owe us nothing, Davey. I'm just glad you're getting better." She was starting to speak in a calmer voice. "How are they treating you, anyway?"

"Oh, it's pretty good here. Comfy, like. I made some friends, and I've got this great nurse, Lucía. She's been teaching me to walk with crutches. And she even set me up with a telescope, up in the attics!"

"Goodness. A telescope," Edith said, "fancy that."

"I can see the whole harbor. I sit up there and watch the sailboats, and the ferry and freighters coming and going."

"That must be nice for you."

"It's brilliant."

Another silence. Then the echo of a door closing somewhere on a lower floor.

"Look, I gotta go," she said. "I—I can't see you, I'm sorry. It ain't going to work out. Maybe one day."

"Edith," said Davey, "I need to know something."

"Quickly?"

"Just tell me straight. Do you like me, or do you prefer my brother? You ever think about me? Because I haven't stopped thinking about you, ever. If you want me to leave you alone, just say so. But I—I think I'm in love with you. There, now I've said it."

There was nothing but crackling at the end of the line.

"Edith?"

"Oh, Davey," came the response finally. "You're a dear, but I can't *be* with you. It's just not meant to be. I'm sorry. I have to go."

The line clicked dead.

He barely left his lawn chair by the telescope over the next few days, with his sailing books and magazines scattered around. The musty dry smell of the attic was familiar now, comforting. He'd taken to leaving his crutches at the foot of the stairs and hopping up the last flight using the handrails. He had stopped taking the morphine, making do with codeine and aspirin, which Lucía brought him three times a day, with a tray of food. He skipped some meals altogether, and even asked her if a mattress could be brought upstairs for him. Being on his own was good, he kept telling Lucía. She said she wasn't so sure—she wanted him to come back to PT. Davey said he got enough exercise just going up and down those steep stairs.

It was Easter weekend, and the Star boats were out in force. They were circling around an anchored motor launch covered in flags. That had to be the Race Committee boat, getting ready to signal the starting sequence. There were about twenty Stars, reaching back and forth, carving through the chop. From here he was perfectly placed to see the shifts and gusts blowing in from the Bay, in the form of darker patches of water with short steep chop and foamy crests.

View through my telescope

He'd just started to make a sketch when heard footsteps on the staircase behind him. That would be his lunch and his pills.

"Thanks, Lucía," he said. "Just leave it there, please. They're about to start the race."

"Actually, it's me," came an unexpected male voice. Davey spun around in his lawn chair. Standing at the top of the stairs, and stooping a little to avoid the rafters, was Harold Vanderbilt.

"I was told I might find you here," he said, advancing towards the window. "Quite a spot you've got yourself." He was wearing a white linen suit with shirt and tie, and holding a Panama hat. His hair was parted in the middle, and he'd grown a thin mustache over his lip, which made him look a little older. The stem of a pipe was sticking out of his pocket.

"Mr. Vanderbilt! I wasn't..."

"Expecting me?" he laughed. "No, I don't suppose you were. So how are you?"

"Coming along, sir, coming along pretty fine. I can mostly get about on the crutches now, and even a bit without 'em. Did you... come up here just to see me?"

"Well actually, yes, I did. I got your letter, but as I was in Newport for a couple of weeks, I thought I'd wander over and see how you're doing. May I?"

He bent to the telescope's eyepiece, and Davey shifted his deckchair back to make room.

"Ah, I see you're a one-design racing fan?" Vanderbilt adjusted the focus knob. "The Star class are out, eh. Nice fast little boats. Newish design. A bit tippy for my taste; I like to have a good two solid tons under me, at least."

"The way they've set up the start line favors the pin end, see?" said Davey. "But the tide's on the ebb, so you don't want to be too far to the left of the course."

"You may have a point," said Vanderbilt, swiveling the telescope slightly so he could see the buoy that, along with the orange flag on the RC boat, created an imaginary start line. It wasn't quite at right angles to the direction of the wind. "Yes, I see now."

"The way they're all lining up on starboard tack," said Davey, "I reckon they'll be off any second."

Moments later, there was a little puff of smoke from the gun on the R.C. boat that signaled the start of the race. The twenty or so Stars seemed to cross the line almost as one, heeled far over, hard on the wind.

"Number thirty-six got a decent start," said Vanderbilt.

"Right by the committee boat."

"You're right though, the pin end is definitely favored."

"If I was thirty-six I'd tack away onto port early, if it was me," Davey said.

"Why's that?"

"Well, sir, look at those dark patches to the north. There's more wind higher up the Harbor, for sure. And the breeze tends to veer during the early afternoon here, as the mainland heats up. Ain't I right?"

"It does indeed. Good tip. Always sail towards the new wind!" Vanderbilt turned to him and smiled. "I'm glad you've lost none of your sharpness. But you're not even a racer, are you? Where'd you learn all this? From books?"

"I've had plenty of time, stuck in here. But mostly it just stands to reason. Newport Harbor's not a lot different from Penobscot Bay, geographically. Also—" he felt himself blushing a bit, "—I've read what you said yourself, sir, in *The Rudder*. You won the Newport to Bermuda race a couple of years back, didn't you? There was an interview with you, and you let 'em in on a fair few of your secrets. About timed starts, and that."

Vanderbilt shrugged. "Well, the 'flying start' makes the timing quite scientific," he said. "Amusingly, when the *America* won the first-ever Cup in Cowes back in '51, each boat had to start moored to a buoy. You probably knew that."

"Wasn't it Prince Albert himself that invented the flying start?" said Davey, recalling R.W.Biggs' *The Compleat Yachtsman*.

"I think you're right."

The little Star boats spread out over the race course. Vanderbilt swiveled the telescope to the left as far as it would go, moved the tripod forward a couple of inches, lowered it a little, and refocused.

"Aha. Take a look at this."

Davey squinted through the eyepiece. Up on stilts, in a dry dock at one of the boatyards at the far end of Thames Street, was the bare hull of the largest racing yacht he'd ever seen. It had been stripped of all rigging except the main mast, and it resembled a two-hundred-foot long Great White shark that had been beached and skewered with a massive pole. The workers on its deck were like ants.

"Blimey. What's that?" asked Davey.

"That's *Reliance*, or what's left of her," said Vanderbilt, packing his pipe from a pouch of tobacco. "Largest single-masted yacht ever built, and the fastest. Ollie Iselin won his last America's Cup in her, back in '03. Took a crew of sixty-eight to race her. She was loaded with innovations. Under-deck winches, inflatable chamber in her rudder—even a telescoping topmast, though that never really worked. Her hull was so fragile, big waves would put dents in it. Funded in part by a cousin of mine, actually, Neily. She's up for scrap now."

"Bet she fair slaughtered the *Shamrock*, didn't she?"

"That's a fair assessment, yes," chuckled Vanderbilt. "Poor old Lipton, it was a washout. 3-0. No contest, really, because he had to build *Shamrock* to sail across the Atlantic on her own bottom. *Reliance* would have been smashed to smithereens!"

Davey leaned forward to pull open the top pane of the attic window, which was quite stiff. He was conscious he hadn't changed his pajamas in days. He squeezed his arms to his sides. "You think this year's Cup contenders will be faster still?" he asked.

"I don't doubt it. Faster and lighter, stiffer as well. *Resolute* will be the first to splash. I went to view her at Herreshoff's here in Bristol, just the other day. Beautiful lines. Captain Nat assured me she's got a few new tricks up her sleeve, too. His designs are constantly evolving. Though he always has them under a tarpaulin to keep them away from prying eyes."

"What sort of tricks?"

"Oh, the America's Cup is all about how far you can push the innovations, and still stay within the measurement rules. Herreshoff's a genius at it. He and Iselin have won the Cup six times between them. They've revolutionized yacht racing."

"Mr. Iselin must be a heck of a sailor."

"A cunning tactician, and a skilled hand on the wheel," said Vanderbilt. "He grew up racing sandbaggers on Long Island Sound."

"Is he still around?"

"Sadly no, he's pretty reclusive these days. Barely leaves his farm down in New Rochelle. I hear his health is deteriorating. But I think he'd had about enough, anyway, after *Reliance*. He fell out with Herreshoff over the cost of the next generation of yachts."

"Like *Vanitie?*"

"*Vanitie*'s being built in Boston, at Gardner's. Alex Cochran, whom you've met, of course, wanted to go a different route, and save some money. I was against it, frankly. I fancy *Resolute* to edge her out in the trials, but I'll admit the Gardner designs are pretty quick, too."

"You think the Brits have got a shot at the Cup this year, sir?"

"Well, now we have the 'Universal Rule,' which should make it more of an even match. Give old Lipton a sporting chance, eh?"

"Doesn't the New York Yacht Club make up all the rules though, and set the courses?"

"True. That's the defending club's prerogative. Which might be viewed as a slight advantage," Vanderbilt laughed.

"Ever thought about having a crack at it yourself, sir? No disrespect to Mr. Cochran, but you're a much better sailor than him, if you ask me."

"It's complicated," Vanderbilt struck a match on the arm of his lawnchair. He sucked on his pipe until the embers glowed in the bowl. "Until now we've allowed professional skippers on the Cup yachts. But many of us believe in the principal of Corinthian racing, where the boats must only be sailed by amateurs, like myself. The first owner to helm and skipper his own America's Cup yacht to victory will earn a special place in the history books."

"Why can't that be you, sir?"

"Unlikely. There's a pecking order at the Club, you see; always has been. Goes back decades." He blew out a thick cloud of smoke that filled the attic.

"Maybe your time will come?" said Davey.

"Maybe it will," Vanderbilt laughed. "But look, there's something else I need to talk to you about."

CHAPTER TEN

Newport Rehabilitation Center
4ᵗʰ April 1914

Dear Ma,

How are you? I am feeling very emotional writing this because I have to tell you some good news and some bad.

Here goes. First, my leg is doing really well. Dr. Austin asked me to his office and told me they would be discharging me on April 10ᵗʰ, which is next Friday! I am off my crutches, but I will be walking with a cane for another 2 to 3 months probably. After that my leg should be fully healed, but no heavy work for the rest of this year, to avoid going backwards (that's a joke, Ma.) But that means I cannot go out on the sloop, or do any heavy lifting. I was thinking about what other work I can do in Stonington, to earn money, maybe ask at the town hall or if Mug Budro needs help at the bait shop.

Then the other day something amazing happened. You know I told you I figured out it was Mr. Vanderbilt that got me across to the mainland, and as is paying my way at the Center. Well he came to see me in my attic (I'll tell you all about that and my telescope another time) and he said there is a job going in the library at the New York Yacht Club, and did I want him to put in a word? I asked him if he thought *they would really give me the job, and he said actually I am Rear-Commodore there, so I am quite confident they will! He knows I am smart and that I have helped my mate Frank a bit with the library here at the Center, so it seems like a shoo-in. The job pays $30 with room and board, I could have enough to live on still send you and Pa $20 or $25 a month, that would really help, wouldn't it? And you could get Pa more of the pheno-whatsit pills, for his fits.*

So I am wondering if you think that would be all right, for me to go to New York. I feel queer about it, as I've been feeling a bit useless, honestly, since the accident. Have you heard from Jacob by the way? I will not go if you say you need me back home but what use I would be. You would just have another mouth to feed, and who knows if I can even find work with my leg.

Also, some sad news. The little girl here that I liked so much, Florence, died last night. She was only 9. She went in for surgery on her spine, and she did not make it. We are all upset. She was such a brave little girl and an amazing reader too. She read about grownup things she knew she would never have herself. I know some of the patients will end their lives here, like Florence did. I am one of the lucky ones, I am getting out, and I'm determined to make the most of it.

I will miss my friends here, specially Lucia my nurse, and Frank my friend who is blind. They have taught me so much. This has been a strange time of my life, but in some ways it's not all bad.

I love you, and hope you will write back soon care of the New York Yacht Club, 44ᵗʰ St, New York City.

Your loving son,
Davey

The *Boston Flyer* sped through the grim warehouses at the outskirts of Port Chester, then New Rochelle, then the Bronx. It slowed, banking around a steep bend, and crossed the Harlem River. The sound of the locomotive's wheels on the iron bridge woke Davey from a daydream. His forehead was resting on the window, and his breath had formed droplets on the glass. His left hand was draped across the canvas kit bag on the third class bench seat next to him. The contents didn't amount to much: a change of clothes, his wool cap, his wash things; and in the front flap, a small leather-bound volume of *Moby-Dick,* with a hand-written inscription.

The first tall buildings of New York City hauled into view, their glistening tops silhouetted by the last of the afternoon sun. Davey sucked in his breath. It was his first sight of that jagged skyline.

He briefly caught sight of his reflection in the window. He had to admit he looked pretty smart in the coat, rounded shirt collar, and short necktie Frank had "loaned" him. His chest and shoulders were looking more developed all the time, from the crutches. His new center-parting would take some getting used to. It made his face look leaner, and older, too. He wondered if he ought to have shaved; the ridge of fur on his upper lip had taken weeks to grow. At least his acne was finally clearing up. If he'd told Lucía the truth, she might have delayed his trip, and he'd have to say his goodbyes all over again. But the fact was, he was still painfully aware of the metal rods in his leg. Perhaps this dull ache in his tibia was just from the anticipation of his trip; and he'd been sitting still for three hours. With his cane, the few blocks from the station to the New York Yacht Club had better be as easy a walk as they looked on the map.

He flicked open his skimpy canvas wallet and fingered the contents: a five dollar bill, two singles, and loose change. He'd started the day with a crisp ten, advanced to him "on account" by Dr. Austin, who made sure he signed the ledger. Did "on account" mean the generosity of Mr. Vanderbilt? He chuckled as he remembered Vanderbilt probably owned this train, these tracks, and the whole damn New York Central Railroad—he could spare ten bucks.

As the train approached the city with its brakes screeching, it began the descent into a great stone trough where the New Haven and Hartford Line gouged deep into the volcanic rock beneath Manhattan. The clang of the couplings was muffled by the sooty walls of the tunnel. Before long the sky disappeared altogether. Steam swirled outside the windows, lit at intervals by fireman's lanterns on the tunnel walls. Davey's half-empty compartment was plunged into total darkness. The tunnel system here broadened into a maze of dimly lit sidings that twisted off into nothingness.

A long, empty platform came into view. The conductor walked through the carriages with a handbell, calling out: "Ladies and gentlemen, this is your final stop—New York Grand Central Terminal." The wheels ground to a halt with one last massive blast of steam, swiftly followed by the clank of fifty doors flying open. Davey picked up his cane and kit bag. All of humanity poured onto the platform and up the ramp to the magnificent terminal plaza. It was the start of the evening rush hour, and people were hurrying everywhere—businessmen in top hats and suits, fine ladies laden with shopping boxes, porters with trolleys of luggage, immigrant families and their small children. Gazing up at the cavernous expanse of the ceiling, he made his way towards the centerpiece of the plaza, a gleaming gold and marble clock surrounded by construction scaffolding. He pulled out the map he'd sketched for himself on the back of an envelope, and plotted his route: up the double staircase to the western exit, on to Vanderbilt Avenue (he had to laugh), and then a block north to 44th Street.

It was dusk now, and the gas streetlights were just coming on. The air in the city was several degrees warmer than in Rhode Island. Jacob's description had prepared him for the crowds, the grandeur of the architecture, and the constant noise of revving engines, policemen's whistles and honking horns. What surprised him was the *smell* of New York that now invaded his nostrils. Sacks of garbage were piled up on every street corner; the gutters were scattered with horse dung and squashed vegetables fallen from carts on their way to market. Plumes of rank steam poured out of ventilation shafts from the subway. Omnibuses and motor cars rattled past and choked him, spewing gasoline vapors. The place fairly reeked, in a way he'd never imagined. But his body was quivering. He was finally here, staring up at the floodlit skyscrapers of New York City.

It wasn't hard to recognize the Clubhouse from across West 44ᵗʰ Street. He'd seen a lithograph of it, and he recalled the description, word for word: "The façade is designed to bring to mind the stern of an old Dutch galleon, with a trio of angled beaux-arts windows and ornate limestone carvings, a massive doorway topped with a frieze of King Neptune, and a third storey balustrade that resembles a ship's quarterdeck."

There was only one obvious way in to the building, no alley or side road. A doorman stood in front of the imposing main entrance. He was a Black man with a whistle round his neck, in a top hat and long embroidered tailcoat. Davey waited for an omnibus to rattle past, then crossed the street, stopping at the velvet rope by the red carpet.

He cleared his throat. "Good evening!" Davey said, wishing as ever that his voice was deeper.

"Can I help you?" The doorman looked him up and down. He had grown a couple of inches since he was last in Deer Isle, and his shoulders were broader. But this man still towered over him.

"I'm here for a job," he said. "I'm the new assistant librarian. I have this, from Mr. Harold Vanderbilt." He fumbled in his kit bag, and produced the hand-written letter.

The doorman tilted his head and glanced briefly at it, then back at Davey. "And who would you be?"

"Davey Haskell. It's right here, see?"

An automobile pulled up. The doorman rushed to hold the door open for two gentlemen. He bade them a good evening, addressing each by name, and ushered them into the Club. Then he turned back to Davey through a cloud of their cigar smoke and, lowering his voice, said, "I *see* where you're pointing alright, young fella, but that don't make you no *Davey Haskell*. Go on, git the hell outta here."

Davey froze, unsure what to do. But he stood his ground.

The doorman paused for moment, deadly serious; then he broke into a broad, toothy grin. "I'm just yankin' your chain, little brother. You'll find the staff entrance round the block, in the alley on 43ʳᵈ Street. Go down the basement steps and knock. Ask for Mr. Royston, the head butler. He'll get you settled. And I'm Sam, by the way. Welcome to the New York Yacht Club."

He extended his enormous gloved hand. Davey thanked him and made his way back along the street, then a block south to 43rd.

As it turned out, Royston, head butler and barman, was almost the opposite of Sam. About fifty, he was shorter and slighter than Davey, and carried himself with the airs and graces of an aristocrat. The buttons on his striped waistcoat were polished to a high shine, as were his patent leather shoes. His hair was waxed flat to his head in fingerwaves. He led Davey up the back stairs to the top floor, where the male staff quarters were located. In the corridor he turned and glanced over his shoulder. He spoke with a slight lisp.

"What's the matter with your leg?"

"I mashed it up in an accident."

"Any problem sharing a room with a Negro?"

Davey thought about this, then shook his head. "No sir."

"You'll be in here with Sam then. You get the top bunk." Royston led him into a small dormitory with a low vaulted ceiling, and pointed to a bunk bed with a ladder. He glanced doubtfully at Davey's cane, and his bad leg.

"This'll be fine," Davey said, and he threw his kit bag up on the top bunk.

"Alright then, listen carefully. We've got rules here. You stick to the rules, you'll be alright. The Club opens every day at ten, luncheon's served from noon, dinner's at six, and the bar closes when the last member leaves." He was pacing slowly as he spoke.

"You address the fine gentlemen as 'Sir,' and you address me as *Mister* Royston. The librarian, your boss, that's Mr. Squigley. He's... indisposed, presently. You'll meet him tomorrow. You can call the other staff by their first names, long as it's in private. We sit down to eat at 11am and 5pm in the scullery. You get your own breakfast in the kitchen—just stay out of Chef's way. Bathroom's down the corridor on the left, before you get to the main stairs."

He stretched out the fingers of one hand to check his cuticles.

"Now, there's places in this building you've no business going, and that's the Card Room, the Billiards Room, and Mr. Phelps' barbershop on the second floor landing. Don't be seen where you're not needed. You can come and go in the library and the Chart Room as your job requires, and the Model Room, but stay out of the Grill Room and the Palm Café. And don't bring any alcohol in your room, and *never* accept a drink from the gentlemen, neither, because they'll try and get a fella drunk."

Royston flared his nostrils and shook his head.

"Tips, on the other hand, that's another matter. We share 'em, see? Gentleman gives you a tip, you hand it to me for safekeeping. I divide them up at the end of the week. Go on down and see Peggy in the morning for your uniform. Laundry and shoe cleaning and the female staff are all on the floor below this one. But you are *never* allowed in the maids' quarters, on no account, is that clear?"

Davey nodded, and broke briefly into a mischievous smile. It was not returned.

"Payday's Friday. Stop by the purser's office off the scullery to pick up your wages. You can figure out your break times and your day off with Mr. Squigley. Only don't be staying out late, 'cause the 43rd Street door is locked at midnight every night. And no visitors. *Ever.*"

Not much chance of that, Davey thought.

"The last fella was too meddlesome by half. Stuck his nose in where he shouldn't. So let's be clear, you and me..." Royston was buffing his fingernails with a stick. "Just 'cause you're here on the Rear Commodore's recommendation, don't mean you got no silver spoon in your mouth. I'm Head Butler round here, and if I take a distaste to you, you're out on your ass. Understood?"

"Yes sir, Mister Royston," replied Davey. "Only..."

"What?"

"...I thought the head librarian's name was Quigley?"

Royston laughed. "Arthur S. Quigley Jr., but we call him 'Squigley.' You'll see why, soon enough."

"Yes, sir."

He left Davey alone in the dormitory. As his footsteps faded down the back stairs, an outburst of raucous male laughter floated up from the main stairwell, and the chinking of glasses. Davey peaked round the door. The corridor was empty, so he crept to the top of the stairwell and peered over the banister. It was the tallest atrium he had ever been in. Six dizzying storeys below, a uniformed servant crossed the marble floor of the lobby with a decanter on a silver tray. This place was amazing. He had some serious exploring to do in the morning.

Back in his room, he transferred his minimal belongings into the empty bottom drawer of a tall chest, and jammed his kit bag underneath. He felt the mattress: it was squeaky but soft. There was a gentle cooing of pigeons from the ledge outside the dormitory window, and a partial view down to the street. So this was to be his new home! He took out the pictorial calendar Lucía gave him and pinned it on a nail above his bunk. April was a lithograph of *Reliance* under clouds of sail. He smiled as he remembered the stripped and battered hull on the dock in Newport, and his conversation with Harold Vanderbilt.

The ceiling was lit up by the gaslights and passing traffic from 44th St way below. He took his small volume of *Moby-Dick* and climbed the ladder to the top bunk, which was awkward with his leg; after a few pages he began to doodle in the back cover with a pencil, a sketch of Edith that he was rather proud of. Before long he fell asleep.

Around one o'clock in the morning Sam the doorman stumbled into the darkened dorm, bumped his head on a beam, and flopped down on the bottom bunk in his full uniform, rattling the frame.

"Hello, Sam."

"Hey there, little brother," was the muffled response from the bunk below. "Lord... I'm beat."

Within ten seconds, the air was bubbling out from between Sam's lips.

The smell of fresh bread wafted up from the kitchens a little before 7am. He dressed, eager to do a bit of sneaking around before breakfast. Almost no-one was about. He descended the main staircase, pausing to lean on his cane and gaze at each of the maritime landscapes, and the recessed marble busts of prominent New York Yacht Club members. On the oak-paneled half-landing, he stopped to admire a massive canvas depicting the schooner *America*'s 1851 victory in the 100 Guinea Cup— the trophy that became known as the America's Cup. He peeked into the plush Card Room, and over the lace curtains into the barbershop, its walls lined with framed photographs of the barber Mr. Phelps with his famous customers.

On the landing opposite, he noticed that one of the oak panels was actually a sort of false door, with a recessed handle. It was slightly ajar, and threw off a shaft of light. He approached it cautiously—it might have led to one of the places Mr. Royston warned him he was not to go. But he opened it a few inches and slipped inside.

He found himself on a lofty gallery, with a view down the full length of the New York Yacht Club's famous Model Room. He'd never seen anything as astonishing in his life. It was two majestic stories tall, and half a city block long. The far end was dominated by the three massive galleon windows he had seen from 44th Street. There were rows of couches upholstered in plush green leather, and separated by potted palms. The cavernous wood-carved ceiling was crowned with clouds of lightning bolts, mottled with the colors that spilled from a central stained glass skylight. Sea monsters and leviathans scowled down from the balcony. In the center of the room was an immense stone fireplace dripping with seaweed, dolphins and seashells, and topped with an oil painting depicting a vintage schooner race.

And there on a plinth, encased in glass, was the America's Cup itself, where it had resided for over sixty years. Glinting in the morning sunlight, it was a piece of history. Davey shook his head and smiled: it was a pig-ugly thing, in all honesty. That was what all the fuss was over? Still, a lot of beautiful boats had fought for it.

All around him were half-models of the hulls of yachts, scores of them, hundreds even. Their wooden hulls lined every square foot of wall space, like dinosaur ribs in a clay cliff-face. He walked the perimeter of the three-sided gallery, running his hand along the smooth lines of each model, reading its brass plaque with the name and length of the yacht and its designer. He recognized famous past Cup winners like *Mischief* and *Vigilant*; and he halted, wide-eyed, at one vessel he knew all too well: *Westward, 135', N.G.Herreshoff*—the very same yacht he'd crewed on last October as a sixteen-year-old; the same yacht whose martingale had smashed his lower leg. He felt a pang of enormous pride, coupled with a fierce pain that shot down his tibia and made him grimace.

"I'm an early riser, Haskell, as you will discover," said Arthur S. Quigley Jr, peering at Davey over his half-moon spectacles. He had one lazy eye that wandered independently towards the tip of his nose. Hence the name, Davey thought.

"I like to be here no later than eight-thirty, to get a head start on sorting and filing before the Club gets busy. I expect you to be here promptly at ten, and you'll stay till seven in the evening to lock up, assuming no members are still using the library."

Squigley was a small portly man, with wild, thinning hair and eyebrow dandruff. He was buttoned into a brown tweed suit and a waistcoat that needed some adjustment by his tailor. He told Davey he'd been head librarian at the N.Y.Y.C. since taking over the position from his father in 1903.

"You will dust the glass cabinets, wind the clocks, and re-shelve the returns. You must familiarize yourself with our layout and classification, in order to assist members with their enquiries; and generally relieve me of the more menial duties, so I can concentrate on my archiving, which is very important to me." Squigley gestured towards a large flat file cabinet next to his desk, stacked high with papers, dusty nautical charts, and curling news clippings, all looking as if they hadn't been touched in years.

Squigley walked slowly to the far end of the library, pointing out each alcove and section of leather-bound volumes, and reciting the provenance of various paintings and antique clocks on the pedestals and mantels. "You'll have to memorize all this too," he said, "in case a member or guest asks."

Piece of cake, Davey thought, it's already dialed in.

The last alcove on the left had a heavy velvet curtain drawn across it. Squigley pulled it abruptly back and said: "Here is your desk. You'll find stationary in the drawer, and cleaning supplies in that closet."

The space was messy and cramped, with a metal table, desk lamp, and swiveling office chair. There were piles of unsorted books. Pinned to the cork noticeboard was a torn magazine advertisement depicting two young ladies in lingerie. Squigley ripped the page down and threw it in the bin.

"My last assistant was wholly unsatisfactory," he said, fiddling with the wires of his spectacles. "He... overstepped. I hope you'll be an improvement. Get settled in, then come and find me, and we'll make a start on the card filing system." Squigley left him alone in his alcove.

There wasn't much settling in to do. He felt a bit useless and out of place. Yet here he was, with his very own desk at the New York Yacht Club. It beat the heck out of of a leaky lobster boat. He tried his chair for size, spun around in it a couple of times. In one of the desk drawers he found some pencils, a sharpener, a few loose toffees, and an old yellowed copy? of a Sears mail-order catalog with a page torn out. He wondered what his predecessor must have got up to? He'd have to be careful not to 'overstep'—whatever that meant.

He let a decent amount of time pass, and made his way slowly back through the library, his nostrils filled with the musty atmosphere of old books, magazines and maps. It smelled a bit like the library in Stonington, but on a much grander scale—this was the finest maritime library on the planet.

Shafts of sunlight flooded in the windows on to the chart table, and dust particles settled on the ornate Persian carpets. The only sound was the ticking of the clocks. He decided he'd make himself a daily routine: first thing every morning he'd wind those clocks, and dust the bookshelves; he'd spend the day familiarizing himself with the books and filing system, and he'd have the evenings to do some reading of his own. He scanned the headers for each section, and drew a mental map: Voyages. Meteorology. Navigation. Boatbuilding. History. Officers. Racing Rules. Etiquette. Flags. Everything was orderly, predictable; not like the weather in Maine, not like the winter lobster migrations. He glanced around with great satisfaction. He was going to enjoy soaking it all up—and no interruptions from the Deer Isle women's sewing circle. But he felt a little homesick, all the same.

He found Squigley at his desk, fiddling with the ribbon of a large and elaborate typewriter. He briefly glanced up.

"Ah, there you are, Haskell. Pull up a chair. I'm still coming to grips with this confounded machine. It was a gift from a member, Mr. Underwood—he owns the company. Lord knows, a library is no place for a typewriter, even if it's supposed to be noiseless. It has more of a 'clack' than a 'click', don't you think?" He hit a couple of keys. "Do you type?"

"I do not, sir. I'm sure I could learn."

Quigley sat back in his chair and regarded Davey through pinched eyebrows, waiting for his wandering eye to settle.

"I understand you're knowledgeable about yacht racing, and meteorology?"

"New England weather, for sure, and the ways of the ocean. I know sailing boats inside and out, and I've crewed on a big racing schooner before now."

"Yes, with Mr. Vanderbilt—who speaks highly of you, by the way. Well, if you come to know these books as well as you know your reef knots and shackles, you will get along just fine. Always be polite and civil to the members, and don't overwind the clocks. This is the world's foremost maritime library, and it's a place for reading and contemplation. But as you will find out, certain of the gentlemen tend to treat it as their private conference room."

Squigley wriggled out of his desk chair and led Davey on a tour of his cleaning duties: the steel filing cabinet housing the elaborate twin index card system—devised by Arthur S. Quigley *Senior*, it was emphasized. The stone owls carved into the fireplace, lucky racing mascots of a notable former Commodore. A brass-cylindered barograph on the windowsill, with a built-in drawer for fresh graph paper and ink. Shelves containing thousands of magazine back issues: *The Rudder*, *Sporting Life*, and *Illustrated London News*. And the clocks! Davey counted eleven of them around the library. Some were antique with gold detailing, others were more modern and sporty-looking. All had their chimes silenced.

"What's that thing?" asked Davey, pointing to a complicated contraption bristling with spools and lenses.

"Ah. That," said Squigley, his voice brimming with pride, "is an Otlet and Goldschmidt micrograph machine. It is used to view miniaturized photographic copies of important news articles and documents. Allow me to demonstrate." He flicked on a brass toggle switch. A noisy electric fan whirred into life, and as the bulb warmed up, a faint rectangle with fluffy edges appeared, as if by magic, projected onto a diagonal pane of glass. Squigley opened a compartmental drawer containing dozens of reels of celluloid film. He picked a reel at random, clipped it onto a spool arm, and fed it into the viewer. It slid into focus and its contents were projected on the glass: the *New York Times'* report on the 1898 Astor Gold Cup race, won by C. Oliver Iselin.

There was that name again.

"We have every *Times* clipping about our yachts and members, going right back to 1897," said Squigley, lifting his heels. He flicked off the switch. "The reels are indexed on these cards. But you are not to touch this machine, Haskell. It has a very sophisticated mechanism. Perhaps at some point I'll teach you how it works."

Next stop on the tour was the large Victor hobnail safe behind his desk, containing, as he explained, "the Club's most precious and confidential documents, such as handicap ratings and measurements, design specifications for future yacht classes, and"—he peered gravely over his wire spectacles—"the Deed of Gift of the America's Cup itself." He cleared his throat officiously and tapped the tip of his finger to his temple. "The safe's combination is a number known only to the current flag officers and to myself."

He made sure Davey looked suitably impressed.

"…but none of that need concern you. For now, I will require you to learn your duties and free up my time for my archiving, which…" (a slightly puzzled look crossed his face as he realized he was repeating himself) "…is very important to me."

The first few days of the new job passed without incident. He polished the display cases, wound the clocks, and memorized the different sections of the library. During Squigley's long naps, he pulled random books off the shelves, and settled into an armchair, learning all he could about New York City, the N.Y.Y.C.'s seventy-year history, and the celebrated yacht racing regattas and cruises. On weekdays, a smattering of members came to the Club to dine and play cards or billiards. Only a few made use of the library. The bars, on the other hand, seemed to be busy most nights, with a handful of resident members keeping the cocktails flowing until the early hours, before retiring to their lodgings on the fourth and fifth floors. It seemed to have little to do with sailing. It was a peculiar place, on so many levels—a landlocked yacht club in the middle of a big city, many blocks from the water, done up to look like a Dutch galleon.

He liked his roommate, Sam. They carried on conversations bunk-to-bunk, sometimes well after midnight. Davey was fascinated to hear about a life so different to his own. Sam was the son of a freed slave couple who had traveled north from Carolina after Proclamation 95, when he was still swaddled in his mother's arms. His older brothers terrified him with stories about their passage through the border states where slavery had not yet been outlawed. The family made it to Staten Island in '64, where they settled on a small piece of land, and set about planting their own crop, milking their goats, and bringing up their family to a better life. Sam left school at fifteen and got a job sweeping the ferries that crossed to New Jersey and Manhattan. He gazed at the brightly lit hotels along the waterfront, and decided New York City was the place for him. He saved up enough for evening classes in Domestic Science, applying for a job in the kitchens at the old NYYC clubhouse when it was still at Rosebank. From there he worked his way up to become head doorman here at the new location on 44th Street in Manhattan, after the turn of the century. Sam was in his mid-forties, secure, and very happy with his life. He was making a decent wage, plus a little extra in tips; enough to rent a small apartment on the West Side with his family. His wife worked in a millinery store, and their elder daughter Phoebe was engaged to be married to a young man from the City Council.

"You got sisters?" Sam asked.

"Nah."

"A sweetheart?"

Davey flushed a little. "I do. Her name's Edith. She's Irish. Works as a maid on a motor yacht. But I think she likes my brother more. I hate my brother's guts."

Sam's eyebrow shot up. "Where's he at? Deer Isle?"

"He's *supposed* to be in Deer Isle."

"What's his name?"

"Jacob. He's a bastard shit. And I'll tell you what, Sam—he's got the smallest nipples I ever seen."

Sam almost choked. "Damn. How small?"

"Little pin-holes."

Sam snapped his suspenders on his shoulders. "Can't trust a fella with pin-hole teets." He pulled on his red tail coat, and brushed himself down in the mirror, ready for the early shift at the front doors. There was a big luncheon event, he said, and he'd have a busy morning taking care of the members and their guests. Personally, he had no problem with the "swells," as he called them—but never to their face—they were either kind to him, or ignored him completely.

"We know a lot more than they think we know!" Sam said. He had his personal favorites, like Captain Woodbury Kane and old Mr. Temple Bowdoin, who always arrived together. As their chauffeured automobile pulled up, Sam would rush to take their coats and hats, so they didn't have to queue for the coat check room. They'd ask after his family. He'd pick up little snippets of idle chatter and gossip; and more often than not, a hot tip on a racehorse.

"But I get the best stuff when the members're drunk!" Sam joked. "Right when they're leaving for another club or a cocktail party, or to visit their mistresses. I just pour 'em into the back of their cabs and hope they don't pass out. The next day I look for their names in the Obituary pages, just to be sure."

"It doesn't make you sick?"

"Nah. I let 'em do their thing."

Sam said they weren't supposed to talk business or politics on Club premises, according to the bylaws, but many of the members did anyway. He knew all about John 'Junior' Rockefeller's labor troubles in Lubbock, where scores of miners and their innocent wives and children were slaughtered by militiamen while they hid in tents. And about Isaac Harris' tensions with the machinists following the Triangle Shirtwaist factory fire, when a hundred and twenty-three seamstresses were burned alive because the doors were locked. And he was something of a *de facto* expert on the subject of yacht racing, even though he had never set foot on a sailboat himself. He knew which members were considered the helmsmen to beat, and which were the "marshmallows." He had all the scoop on their wives and lovers, and what went on in the guest cabins of their fancy yachts.

There was a great deal to talk about. But Davey had to watch his step. When Sam mentioned Alexander Cochran and his affair with a Russian stage actress, Davey just grunted. He was still new and unproven at the Club, and he didn't want to get sucked into anything.

Plus, the thought of Rula reminded him of Edith, and that made him think of Jacob; and there again was the old pain in his gut.

CHAPTER ELEVEN

"Jolly good. Well, I'll be getting on with my archiving," said Squigley, and he shuffled off to the big oak desk in his alcove.

Davey was dusting a small sculpture of Poseidon on a marble plinth. It was the middle of his second week at the library, and he was coming to understand what "archiving" actually meant. For the umpteenth time that afternoon, he heard the bottom drawer of Squigley's desk slide open, followed by the muted pop of a cork and the clink of a sherry glass. He finished dusting, and moved on to rearranging some Admiralty charts on the chart table. A few minutes later, the snoring started. He peeked around the corner. His boss was slumped in his chair, mouth hanging open, out for the count.

The afternoon light was fading. He headed back to his own alcove. He was still limping a bit, though recently he'd been getting by without his stick, trying to put more weight on his leg. He drew the curtain behind him and flicked on the desk lamp, so he could re-read Jacob's letter.

Kingston Wharf, East Cowes February 26th

Dear Davey,

It has took me an age to write to you. Sorry bout that. It was our cuz, Jim Dawson from the telegraph office as gave me your address at the hospital. A lot happened after they took you away that night in Stonington and I was dead worried. I don't know if you remember much, you was in a load of pain, and I tried to come on the Nemesis with you to the main land, but you said no. Heck of a storm, that was! They told me you was going to make it, but your leg was all stove to hell and they might have it off, and that made me sick to the stomach. I saw Doc Noyes and he said the hospital fixed you up and you were keeping it, what a relief. How is it now, still crook? Look mate. I know you wanted me to stay and look after Ma, but I was offered a job crewing as a topman on Westward, for decent money, I figured that'd be more use to Ma than me sticking around, and her with one more mouth to feed. So I sailed across the Atlantic all the way to Southampton, and Lord that was real sailing Davey, the finest kind. Waves over your head. But wicked cold! There was a few other Deer Islers on the barky too to keep company with, Coo Bray, Cyrus, and that gawmy fucker Gardie Green, but he didn't make it, he's dead now, long story. Uriah Rhodes was skippering, but I got to know him a bit on the crossing and he ain't so bad. He told me Westward's up for sale now, seeing as Cochran only cares about Vanitie and the Cup.

Anyway England is pretty queer. They talk funny and the food is foul! and it's pissing with rain half the time. I got a job in the docks in Southampton for a few weeks trying to save up for a frayter or a steamer back home, then I ran into Coo and he says there hiring for the new Shamrock, so him and me took a chance and got the ferry across to Cowes and we tells em we was on Westward and training for the Cup, before. We said we was Deer Isle men they said, ho ho ho, we could use a bit of that Yankee luck on the Shamrock. So they signed us both on and we'll be training here in the Solent then sailing for New York in July. And ain't that fine and dandy, cause Shamrock'll be in the Cup either way, as I see it, meaning I'm sure to be in it. And maybe I'll even get a ring like Pa's, on me own finger.

So now I have my own set of white canvas ducks, Davey, can you believe it? Me in ducks and a peaked cap with Lipton's Tea printed right on the front. There's cunning fillies here right along the waterfront and they laugh at the way I talk but seem to fancy me anyway. You buy em a couple of gins, they're easy as apple pie. Even a scrawny bugger like you might get yer leg over in England! Oh, yeah well I don't meant to kid you about your leg. I guess we won't be sailing together any time soon, will we Dave. When I think of it I miss home a lot and I just wish it was you and me out on the bay again in Pa's sloop, hauling up the bug baskets. When are they gonna they let you go out? You'll likely be back home before me, specially as I'll be training for the Cup racing in the spring. I bet Ma will be glad to have us back eh. I wonder if Pa's doing any better, I sometimes say a prayer for him for what it's worth, but I ain't holding my breath.

Your brother,
Jacob

It was all he could do not to rip the letter into tiny pieces. He stared deep into the filament of the electric light bulb, and thought of Ma in her cold, unlit kitchen. He was going to send her money as soon as he got his first pay packet, along with his share of the tips. He was nothing like his brother. Jake would come back across the pond with a plum job on a yacht—on *Shamrock IV*, for the Brits, the enemy! And he was stuck here at this desk, with a leg full of nails, no use for anything.

Jacob was going to race in the America's Cup. He wanted to spit.

His jaw was sore from clenching, and now his ankle was aching again, too. What did Lucía tell him? Stretch it out, relax, take a deep breath. Find something to distract you. Lucía was always full of good advice. He wiggled his toes. He pulled open a desk drawer, and set about sharpening his pencils, dropping the shavings into his empty tea mug.

Just then something *really* distracted him: muffled laughter, just the other side of his curtain. He was conscious of two men, two distinct voices. Tweed backsides squeaked into leather armchairs, and ice cubes chinked in crystal glasses. He froze rigid.

"Oh, I wouldn't worry about Quigley, old sport, he's been at the Oloroso again. Shhh, listen…"

The sound of snoring carried from the far end of the library. The two men cackled, then resumed their conversation, without a clue Davey was so close behind his curtain.

"So what's this I hear about Cochran?"

"Yes… he wants to skipper *Vanitie* himself, if she's selected. Which most of us think is a lousy idea. But it's going to be put to the membership. He'd be the first amateur skipper in America's Cup history."

"I hear he's been scooping up quite a few trophies in the Med; seems to believe he's a top helm now…"

"Pah! He's a neophyte, at best. He'd be lost without his professional help—and he goes through them by the dozen."

"You didn't push back?"

"With that fool helming, I fancy Charles Adams on *Resolute* to beat him easily, over the course of the trials. And there goes our whole investment, up in smoke."

More ice clinked into tumblers. "Have you spent any time with him, Fish? I mean, he's a decent enough chap, on land. Kind to his employees. Collects antiquarian books and maps, that sort of thing. Gifted an endowment to Yale to start the Elizabethan Club. But on the water, he seems to turn into some sort of… wild man."

"Between you and me, I never trusted Al Cochran. He's conceited. Inherited forty million from his family, and he's burning through that. His factories are in trouble. Can't keep the unions under control. Can't keep his pecker in his pants, either."

"Ho ho, don't you have problems of your own in that department, Fish?"

"You're referring to the Railroad Union strike?" The older man's voice had a trace of irritation. "Not the same thing. We've had outside agitators, from the I.W.W."

"Unions. Such a nuisance!"

"Did you see the *Times* yesterday? Johnny Rockefeller knows how to deal with disgruntled workers. Send in a bit of muscle!"

"Teach those Wobblies their place, what?"

The older man lowered his voice to a whisper. "Seventy-six strikers dead in Ludlow, unofficially. That'll give 'em pause."

"Pause indeed. But look here, we'd better not talk business. You know the rules."

"I should do, I helped write 'em, ha ha. Well then… how's that frightful Gertrude of yours?"

The younger man sighed. "She's a louche, as ever, old chap. We have a fine arrangement, I must say. I drop her off at the Algonquin, and come here to get plastered. She'll probably be out all night, with those… *unusual* friends of hers. What about your Mamie, where's she this evening?"

"At her card club, as usual. I tell you, Whitney, that woman will be the ruin of me. This morning she had one of her coughing fits. 'Can I get you something, darling?' I inquire kindly. 'Oh, Stuyvey, thank you—that diamond and pearl necklace I saw yesterday at Tiffany's.'"

They both cracked up laughing.

Davey parted the curtain a little. The younger man, Whitney, was facing away from him, with an arm slung across the back of his leather armchair. Opposite sat an older gentleman, ruddy-faced, perhaps in his seventies, with a bald pate and remarkable mutton chop sideburns.

Mutton Chops was the next to speak, in a slow, confidential tone. "Did Cochran take care of that little business matter with the girl?"

Had he heard it right? He parted the curtain another couple of inches.

"As far as I know," replied Whitney, under his breath.

"We can't have anything leak out. Not during a Cup campaign."

"Ugh. I can't abide blackmail."

"I'll tell you, this nation is being overrun with gold-diggers, socialists and radicals. And it's not just the workers. It goes right to the very core of Government. Take this Sixteenth Amendment the Democrats have passed—this 'income tax'?"

"Ludicrous. And unconstitutional. You should declare residency in Rhode Island, Fish, like me. I don't pay a penny."

"And now this nonsense with the Suffragists..."

"Oh! Don't get me started."

"I told Mamie, a woman doesn't need the vote! Either she'll go along with her husband, or vote the other way and cancel him out. Whole thing's utterly pointless."

"Quite."

At the far end of the library, Squigley gave a snort in his sleep.

"Look, about this *Vanitie* thing," said Mutton Chops. "Before the general meeting on Friday, I want to make sure you and I are on the same page."

"Hear, hear."

"I talked to J.P. this morning, and he agrees with me: we just can't let Cochran helm in the trials. The man's too much of a loose cannon. The three of us need to step in, before he damages our investment, or gets somebody hurt."

"We're already trailing *Resolute* in the fundraising stakes. Cochran will have to settle for the afterguard."

"The question is, who else would drive? Charlie Barr?"

"Long dead, old chap." Whitney leaned forward in his chair. "Look... I know he's my brother-in-law, but there's really no doubt in my mind. It should be Harold."

"Harold Vanderbilt? Interesting... I can certainly see that. He's a heck of a talent."

Davey's ears pricked up.

"I've followed a few of *Vanitie*'s early test runs," said Whitney. "Harold's been helming for short spells, and whenever he's driving, she looks like a real demon, especially upwind. He's got the racing pedigree—and the form, too. Won the Astor Cup last month by a country mile."

"He's only, what, twenty-eight? You're right. Maybe this is Harold's time to shine." Mutton Chops clipped the end off a fat cigar.

"Why don't we pitch it to J.P. in private?"

"Good," said Mutton Chops decisively. "If J.P.'s with us, it'll be three against one. Alex will just have to fall in. Harold drives, otherwise we withdraw our funding. What do you say?"

"I'm all for it. But Alex is not going to like it. Not one bit."

"He can't do it without our money."

"What'll we do about... you know who?" There was an awkward pause. "You know Cochran's his favorite. Cross that bridge when we come to it?"

"Agreed."

"We'd better drink up and head down to dinner. Won't they miss us?"

"Not if they aim carefully!" Mutton Chops gave a hearty guffaw and clapped Whitney on the shoulder. Setting down their tumblers, the gentlemen got to their feet and headed for the doorway. They strolled past the comatose Squigley, and disappeared onto the landing, gabbing about polo.

As soon as the doors clicked shut, Davey crept out of his alcove. The library was silent aside from Squigley's snoring and the ticking of the clocks. It was a few minutes to seven. He could knock off work soon. He tidied away his cleaning supplies, straightened up a few magazines, and picked up the tray with the two empty glasses.

He was glowing inside. Harold Vanderbilt was going to helm *Vanitie* in the America's Cup trials, and he was the first to know about it! He couldn't wait to get upstairs and share the gossip with Sam. One by one, the clocks started their muted clunking. Seven o'clock. He thumped deliberately past Squigley's alcove, calling out loudly: "Goodnight now, Mr. Quigley! See you in the morning."

Squigley woke with a start, felt for his spectacles in the pockets of his waistcoat, grunted something unintelligible, and fell back to sleep.

Sam didn't come in till around midnight at the end of his shift.

"Hey, I hear there's some kind of do going on this Friday," said Davey from the top bunk, setting down his copy of *Moby-Dick*. "Would that be in the Model Room?"

"Yeah, there's a Flag Officers' meeting. How'd you know about that?"

Davey started telling him about the conversation he'd overheard in the library, relaying a few of the choicest comments about the Unions, the Suffragists, and the income tax. He was about to mention the blackmail thing.

"Hush—keep your voice down, little brother. Bylaws say nobody's supposed to discuss business and politics on Club premises. But the swells do it anyways. Million-dollar deals get done, all the time. 'Specially when they're eatin' lunch! That old guy with the sideburns you heard, that's Stuyvesant Fish, he's one of the big wheeler-dealers here. Used to be Governor of New York. You know Jeremiah, the head waiter in the Grill Room? He says Fish made a deal to purchase the Illinois Central Railroad, all in about the time it took him to eat a quail egg salad. He tells Jeremiah his new diesel locomotives'll have a separate compartment for freed Negroes headin' north. We gets a whole train compartment all to ourselves, Davey, imagine that!"

"What did Jeremiah say?"

"Jeremiah stoops real low and says, that's mighty Christian of you, Mr. Fish, mighty Christian."

The bunk shook with their laughter.

"Guess you don't get that rich by passing up a business opportunity," said Davey.

"And I'll tell you somethin' else. They sell their daughters!"

"They *what*?"

"Hell yes. To barons and arch-dukes and earls, from Europe and England. Sure as my name's Sam Robinson. Them 'ristocrats, in Luxemborg, places like that, it costs 'em a bundle to keep up their castles and lakes—so when they run short of money, they come to New York to find a wife with a rich daddy. Fritz gets the dowry money, Missy gets a title in front of her name, and Daddy's happy as a hog."

Davey sat up in his bunk. "You're messing with me!"

"I ain't messing. There's this one gentleman here, young Mr. Vanderbilt. Nice enough fella. But his poor sister, Miss Consuelo, their mama brung her up from a little girl to be a real-life princess. Mama used to make her sit still for hours with a steel rod up her spine, so's she'd look like a lady. First chance they got, they married her off to the Duke of Malbarrow. Now she lives in a big palace in England. My Loretta told me, she read it in the Society pages."

Something told Davey to keep his mouth shut about *Vanitie,* and who would helm her in the trials. He'd yet to see Mr. Vanderbilt at the Club. Surely that was just a matter of time? Would he be the kind, studious man he'd discussed racing tactics with, in the attic in Newport? Or, let loose among his polo-playing railroad tycoon friends, would he turn out to be just another liquor-soaked snob?

"Does Mr. Vanderbilt come in much?" he asked Sam.

"Time to time. He'll be there Friday night, I shouldn't wonder, for the meeting. Why d'you ask?"

"Sam, could I get a little extra work, taking snacks around or working the bar or something? Friday night?"

"You really wanna work the extra shift?"

Davey thought for a moment. "Well, you know I'm pretty keen on anything to do with boats and racing. And I could really use the overtime, to send home to my family."

"Reckon you can stand for that long, with your gammy leg?"

"I'll cope."

"Hmm. I can put in a word with Royston for you, if you like." Sam chuckled. "Pete Royston seems like a crusty sonofabitch, but when you get to know him, he's... still a crusty sonofabitch."

Davey was buttoned into a starched white shirt, collar and necktie. The shirt label was making him crazy. Just like that time at school when Jacob put itching powder down his neck. But he was brimming with pride: the Flag Officers were about to announce the name of *Vanitie*'s new helmsman. And he'd be in the Model Room to hear it.

He and Mr. Royston stood on either side of the enormous double doors, each with a tray of drinks and a napkin over one arm. Royston's was loaded with sponsored Mumm champagne in tall flutes, Davey's with ginger ale in crystal tumblers. Royston's tray was the more popular. Members in full dinner dress trickled past them in twos and threes, deep in conversation. There were even a few visiting British Navy officers in their stiff blue uniforms. He caught snippets of their nautical chatter, about some newly commissioned destroyer, or the bookies' odds for the upcoming America's Cup trials, or the merits of Herreshoff's design for the Club's affordable NY50 racing fleet.

A long committee table had been set up under the Model Room's ornate fireplace. There were six place settings, each with a blank pad and pencil, a tumbler, and a carafe of drinking water. Thirty or forty members took their seats in rows facing the fireplace, deep in conversation. The room was already thick with cigar smoke. The talking subsided as the six Flag Officers entered the room, in a neat single file of blue blazers, shiny brass buttons and peaked caps. Davey recognized August Belmont Jr., the present Vice-Commodore, from his portrait in the lobby. Most of the others he couldn't name: but at the tail end was the familiar figure of Harold S. Vanderbilt. As he passed, Mr. Vanderbilt helped himself to a glass of ginger ale, and gave Davey a friendly nod.

"Congratulations, sir," Davey said quietly. Vanderbilt just looked puzzled. Was it possible he didn't know?

The doors banged closed, and the officers took their seats behind the table. Davey followed Royston along the back wall to take his place behind the bar. After a few moments, August Belmont Jr. brought down his gavel, and the room fell completely silent.

"Gentlemen of the New York Yacht Club, the meeting shall come to order. The Race Committee has set the dates and wind limits for the nine-race trials in Newport this summer to select the yacht that will represent the Club in defense of the 14th America's Cup. The contest itself will take place in late September, at Sandy Hook, against the challenger from the Royal Ulster Yacht Squadron, *Shamrock IV.* The Honorable Secretary will fill you in with the details. Also—" He shuffled his papers and cleared his throat, "—we need to address a key piece of business regarding the *Vanitie* syndicate." He passed the gavel to Herbert Sears.

Davey was polishing glasses behind the bar, under the close watch of Royston, but he glanced up from time to time at Mr. Vanderbilt, at the far end of the table, calm as ever. The pipe smoldered in his ashtray.

"Regarding the *Vanitie* syndicate," Sears said.

Davey grinned. This was it!

"Mr. Alexander Cochran—who is currently away in Europe, and sends his apologies—has informed us that, subject to the approval of the membership, he will become the sole financial backer of the campaign, and *Vanitie*'s primary helmsman. The remaining backers, Messrs. J.P.Morgan Jr., Stuyvesant Fish and Harry Payne Whitney, have agreed to dissolve the Syndicate, their financial investments being returned in full."

You could have heard a pin drop.

"Gentlemen, there has never, in the history of the Cup, been a defender that is solely owned and helmed by an individual member," Sears continued. "I bring this to your attention because the issue of Club tradition and protocol has been raised by some members. It must be strictly observed, above all things; yet even we must move with the times. It will usher in a new era of Corinthian yachting in the America's Cup, in which owners may captain their own yachts, instead of relying on paid professional skippers. Therefore, we have decided to present the motion to the general membership, for a vote from which the Flag Officers will necessarily recuse ourselves, as I and others participate in the rival *Resolute* syndicate. So I now ask the honorable members on the floor: all those in *favor* of Mr. Cochran's proposal, that he becomes the sole backer and primary helmsman of the *Vanitie* campaign, please raise your hands."

Without so much as a brief murmur, almost every hand went up. Davey felt the color drain from his face. The champagne flute he was drying cracked in his hands. Royston rolled his eyes.

There was no debate, no dissent. It was as if the members had already been primed about this, and their minds made up; they voted as if in a trance. Harold Vanderbilt merely sat tall in his chair to count the raised hands, and wrote down the number on his pad.

"Thank you," said Belmont. "Any objections?"

One ancient member began to feebly raise his hand, then seemed to think better of it.

"Abstentions?"

Now the elderly member's hand went up. Stuyvesant Fish and Harry Whitney also abstained.

"In which case," continued August Belmont Jnr., "Mr. Cochran's proposal is hereby approved. We wish him luck, and may the best boat win. The meeting is adjourned." He banged the gavel.

Davey was baffled. Had he somehow misunderstood what he'd overheard in the library? He glanced at Fish and Whitney, seated close together in the second row. The blank expressions on their faces gave nothing away. It was as if something, or someone, had scared them off.

The members broke into clusters. Some stood in discussion, while others made their way to the bar to top up their glasses from magnums of chilled Mumm. Davey tried to maintain a professional smile, but his thoughts were awash.

A petite, well-tailored gentleman with a wave of ginger hair and a tartan waistcoat approached Davey's end of the bar and set his glass down on the counter. "Got anything stronger, barman?"

"It's just champagne or soft drinks tonight, sir. There's a full bar in the lobby."

"Just give me a tumbler with some ice then, would you, my dear."

Davey reached for a glass from below the counter, and chinked in three ice cubes with the tongs. The quoiffed customer uncapped a silver flask he'd slyly pulled from his breast pocket, and poured its contents over the ice. Then he swiveled around to face the room, leaning both elbows back on the bar.

"You must be new here."

It took Davey a moment to work out who the customer was addressing. "Yes, sir. It's my second week. I mainly work in the library assisting Mr. Quigley."

"In the belly of the beast, eh?" he grinned. "Probably don't know all these characters by name yet, I imagine."

"I'm gradually learning, sir."

"You can call me Ogden, for a start. Ogden Blum, like the flowers. I write features for *The Rudder*, and under a pseudonym for the *Post*. As a non-voting member I'm not very welcome at an event like this. There again, most of the New York clubs won't have my kind at all." He laughed and smoothed his hair. "The press, that is."

"I see."

"And who might you be?"

"My name is David Haskell, sir."

Blum flashed a coy glance over his shoulder. "So formal!"

"Davey, if you prefer."

"Well, young Davey, let's review the talent on show tonight at the N.Y.Y.C." Blum adjusted his bow tie. "See the gentleman by the palm tree with the combed-over hair? That's Hamilton Twombly. He made a fortune with the Union Sulphur Company, and married an heiress. Big time gambler; bets on polo mainly, $1000 a chukka. Maintains a penthouse apartment in the Woolworth building for his fifteen-year-old 'ward.'"

Davey's shirt label was itching his neck.

"And over by the display case, that's Charles Francis Adams III. Captain of the *Resolute* syndicate, and a champion helmsman. No less than *two* of his ancestors were U.S. Presidents. Adams has an interesting scheme for treating the Harlem water supply with chemicals to sterilize Negroes and Semitics and stop them breeding. He bankrolls a mysterious medical research center up the river. Over there, see the pallid young man cradling his pocket watch? That's Vincent Astor. Due to be married next week, and as you can see, it's making him ill. His old man John J. earned his pile from trading furs to China in return for opium; went down with the Titanic in '12, and left young Vincent seventy million dollars and the world's fastest steam yacht, the *Noma*. Want me to go on?"

"I'm still here," Davey said, feeling a little giddy.

"The handsome devil talking to the Vice-Commodore is Charlie Schwab, chairman of Bethlehem Steel. I like Charlie. Pretty much single-handedly revolutionized the construction industry. Risk-taker; master hustler; made a $200,000 'gift' to the mistress of the Grand Duke of Russia, who then hired him to construct the Trans-Siberian Express—"

Davey tried not to stare too obviously. "And they're all yachtsmen?"

"A handful of the members are true sailors. Charlie Adams, he's the real thing. Harold Vanderbilt, too. Most of them, shall we say, just like a bit of a flutter now and then. They tend to be more comfortable on large motor yachts. Putter around the Harbor at weekends, betting big on the sail racing. They all follow the fleet up the coast on the Club's annual cruise. It's an excuse for a party, really. They certainly know how to have a good time."

"I see."

"So there you have it," said Blum, grinning. "The New York Yacht Club. There's more wealth in this room than the Federal Reserve; more power than the U.S. Congress. Look at the phallic trophies on these walls. The yachts are just a manifestation of their collective egos. And the America's Cup there, on its plinth, that's the very pinnacle. They'll do whatever it takes to keep their grip on it..."

Blum swilled the ice in his brandy and downed the dregs.

"And you know the funniest thing? The one that's *really* pulling the strings—the puppetmaster—isn't even here tonight..."

Just then a severe voice boomed out: "Who let you in, Blum?" It was Stuyvesant Fish. He sauntered up to the bar, clearly a little the worse for wear. "I saw your column in the *Post* last week about the Rail Union strike. The usual drivel, man. Do you just make it up as you go along?"

"Ah, Governor Fish!" said Blum cordially. "I was just leaving. Sorry to hear Al Cochran's kicking you off his campaign. *Quel dommage*! And with *Vanitie* odds-on to win the trials? You must be distraught."

Fish's cheeks flushed. Blum smacked his empty tumbler on the bar. He slipped a five dollar bill into Davey's breast pocket and gave it a pat. "Good luck in the new job!" He winked and strode away.

Harry Whitney approached the bar with his glass empty. Davey ducked below the counter for a fresh bottle. Whitney said: "Ah, there you are, Fish, old chap. Was that Ogden Blum I saw you talking to?"

"Yes. Vile little Hebrew," grunted Fish. "Probably here to dig dirt for his gossip column. We ought to see to it he's permanently banned."

"Queer as a coot, I've heard?"

"Meaning he'll have a friend or two on the Committee, sadly..." Sniggering, they ambled off towards dinner.

It was bizarre. A few days ago they were dead set on replacing Cochran with Vanderbilt—now that decision was reversed, and they were hardly fazed. The whole voting membership seemed to just glaze over and put their support behind Cochran.

Mr. Royston grumbled under his breath: "You're daydreaming, Haskell. Grab a tray and go pick up some empty glasses. And you can hand over that five bucks in your shirt pocket. You'll get your share later."

The Model Room started to empty out as the gentlemen dispersed to the lobby or upstairs bar, or down to the Grill Room, where the dinner gong had sounded. Davey spotted Harold Vanderbilt on a couch at the far side of the room, deep in conference with August Belmont and Herbert Sears. He had been rehearsing in his mind what to say if he got the chance; but he didn't want to get too close. He cleared away some empties from one of the display cases, working his way across the room, and caught the tail end of their conversation.

Belmont was doing the talking. "Very well, it's settled. *Nemesis* as Race Committee Boat for the July trials, and Harold to serve as Regatta Director." The men raised their glasses.

"They'll be lucky to have you as R.D., Harold, with your knowledge of the rules," said Sears. "Decent of you to commit to this. I'm sure your turn at the helm will come too, in due course."

Vanderbilt shrugged and took the pipe out of his mouth. "I find one can often learn more from the bridge of the Committee Boat than from the deck of a competing yacht—"

He was cut short by a loud commotion from the lobby, and a rushing of feet outside on 44th Street. All heads swiveled to the windows, where the echo of a raucous and unruly crowd was getting louder by the moment.

"What the devil—?" exclaimed Belmont. The three Flag Officers jumped to their feet and rushed to the the galleon windows, with several other members bringing up the rear. Royston was frozen behind the bar with his tea towel stuffed in a tumbler, so Davey followed the gentlemen to the windows, keeping a few paces behind. He stopped at the far window and peered down into the street.

A parade of demonstrators had swarmed around the corner of 44th Street, chanting and waving placards and banners. At the head of the column, a tall slender man and a woman in a red beret were egging on the crowd. The man was shouting into a brass speaking horn. Davey could make out a few of the placards: "BREAD OR REVOLUTION— WHICH?" and "WE WANT JOBS NOT CHARITY" and "ONE STRIKE—ONE UNION."

As the crowd passed the Clubhouse, their faces seemed to turn as one, staring up at the sky above 44th St. Their cries grew more intense, and some shook their fists in the air, yelling obscenities. He realized what they were staring at: a group of the Club members had made their way out on the fourth floor balcony. They were jeering and taunting the protestors below. The protestors in turn were screaming back as they pushed and shoved below the windows. Three young policemen watched awkwardly from across the street, lacking a sergeant, unsure what to do.

Then, with a shocking crash, a large red brick clattered through the central stained glass window. It didn't just break one pane—it pulverized the entire twenty-foot high window, which collapsed onto the floorboards with a deafening din, amplifying the cheers of the mob in the street. At the same moment, all the Model Room lights went out.

One of the gentlemen backed up in a panic and knocked over a pedestal, shattering a marble bust of Ulysses S. Grant.

"Time to beat a hasty retreat!" bellowed Herbert Sears through cupped hands. "Let us cross over the river and rest under the shade of the trees!" He imitated a bugle call with his mouth, and led several of the gentlemen skipping across the shards of broken glass towards the exit.

Davey caught the flash of Mr. Vanderbilt's steely blue eyes in the shadows. He was there to the other side of the windows, motionless, surveying the scene below. Some in the crowd were shaking their fists, and a man was brandishing a baseball bat. Vanderbilt caught Davey's eye and said calmly: "Let's you and me get out of the firing line too, eh, Davey?"

In the street, two policemen tried to push their way into the crowd to apprehend the brick thrower. But the cops were caught up in the shoving, and wafted away along 44th with the cheering crowd, who turned the corner down Sixth Avenue and disappeared as a mass.

"Good to see the leg's healing up, old sport," Vanderbilt said over his shoulder as he took off towards the lobby, silhouetted in the light from the double doors.

Davey almost tried to catch up him. He wanted so much to thank him, for everything; and he was aching to ask why he'd just been passed over as *Vanitie*'s helmsman. How come he wasn't more angry, or upset? Was it possible he didn't even realize how close he came?

The man was such an enigma. The rest of them—they were easier to figure out. Davey just wasn't sure where he truly belonged: in the Club with the "swells", or down in the street with the rabble.

Pete Royston roused the entire staff at 6am for the cleanup in the Model Room. Some weren't too happy about it. They stood in a circle in the kitchen, grumbling, looking sullen.

Davey rubbed the sleep from his eyes, and poured himself a mug of steaming coffee. He edged his way into the circle, trying to think of something cheerful to say. He was still the new kid around here, and he felt invisible to some of his co-workers—the lanky barber Thom Phelps, for one, who talked Cockney and smelled of hair oil. And the voluptuous coat check girl, Millie. He had spotted her behind the counter in the lobby once or twice. She always seemed busy. Close up, she had pretty freckles, and reddish hair, tied back with a clip. He smiled at her, and to his surprise she said good morning to him by name, in a honey-sweet southern accent. He was pleased someone had noticed him.

Sam the Doorman was perched on a corner of the kitchen table with the morning edition of the *New York Post*. "Hey, listen to this…" He put on a racetrack announcer's high voice: "'At the swanky New York Yacht Club bar, a cluster of exclusive members, railroad magnates and mining tycoons, sipped Mumm champagne as an angry mob of commoners threw bricks through the windows. It resembled a scene from the French Revolution…'"

"Ho-*rreur*!" said Millie, her dainty hands clutched to her cheeks. She locked her hazel eyes with Davey's. "Roll out the *gill-o-teen*!"

"Sounds a lot like Ogden Blum," remarked Thom Phelps. The way he said 'Blum', it rhymed with 'plum.'

Sam went on: "…there's gonna be a big labor rally in Times Square on Friday evening. 'Factions are coming to the City from all five boroughs— garment workers, longshoremen, streetcar drivers, suffragists…'"

"Does this mean we could get attacked again?" Davey asked Phelps next to him, trying to break the ice.

"I don't *fink* so, sunshine," Phelps said. "But if we're lucky, them upstairs'll decide to keep the Club closed Friday, just to be safe, and we'll get the day *awf.*"

"Enough!" Mr. Royston cut him short. "You all have a job to do. Get on with it."

Grabbing a last mouthful of his fresh bread roll, Davey followed the others up the steps to the lobby, and past the Palm Café, where a handful of resident members in morning suits were poring silently over their newspapers. A team of glaziers arrived with their ladders to make temporary repairs to the galleon window. An armed policeman was posted outside the barred front doors. The Club would stay closed for as long as was required to make it secure.

It took until mid-morning for the domestic staff to sweep up the mess and mop the floors. Davey and Millie spent the morning on their hands and knees picking shards of glass out of the sprawling oriental carpet. At one point he got within a few feet of her.

"Royston's got us working like dogs, don't he?" he said cheerfully, trying to keep his eyes off her cleavage.

Millie wiped her brow with the back of her hand. "Sugar, that man thinks the sun comes up just to hear him crow." She had a charming kind of sing-song to her voice.

"Were you scared, at all, last night, Millie?"

"Hell yeah. I could hear them shouting right outside the front door. I hid under the counter, like a prairie dog with my *tay*-il between my legs."

"You thought they might bust right in the building?"

"You bet. It could have turned real ugly. But I was ready for 'em."

"Ready? How d'you mean?"

She lowered her voice to a whisper. "Some of the members here pack firearms. They check 'em in with me when they arrive, and pick 'em up when they leave. I keep them in a drawer under the counter." She gave him a big wink.

"Firearms?" Davey echoed.

Darn it, there I go again, repeating everything. "You're kidding."

"They have this awkward way of handing me their coat, all folded, and I know there's a holster inside. Usually comes with a big tip, though. And I ain't about to share it with no Pete Royston."

Davey's elbows buckled. He'd never seen a handgun in real life. Only a hog rifle, once, on his cousin's farm. And he'd never fired a weapon, or even held one. He sized Millie up. Was she the kind of girl that could fire a gun, if rioters stormed the Club? She had that sweet accent, all right. But she was poor white trash from the South, and could probably look after herself.

He took two buckets of broken glass down to the service door of the basement, and out into the stairwell off 44th. A row of bins overflowed with the NYYC's trash and refuse, and the air stank of rotten meat and fruit. A rodent scurried away into a downpipe. One bin was heaped with melon skins and shrimp tails, and two whole red lobsters, untouched, that would have fetched a buck apiece back in Maine. He found an empty bin and heaved in the contents of his buckets. The glass smashed and reverberated around the stairwell, hurting his ears.

What was more troubling was the meeting itself. He couldn't stop thinking about the oddly rigid atmosphere, the members's glazed expressions, the way they just rolled over. And Cochran dissolving the Syndicate. If his factories were supposed to be struggling, how could he afford to bankroll *Vanitie* himself? He had to be getting outside help. Maybe from a non-member. Or someone who wanted to stay anonymous.

Something Ogden Blum said stuck with him:

"…you know what the funniest thing is? The one that's *really* pulling the strings—the puppetmaster—he isn't even here…"

Was he talking about Cochran? Or Ledyard Blair, the absent Commodore? Maybe 'Junior' Rockefeller, who knew how to 'put those Wobblies in their place'? Or J.P.Morgan, the wealthy financier that had gifted this slice of mid-Manhattan real estate for the N.Y.Y.C.'s clubhouse? The membership was entirely made up of powerful politicians, bankers, industrialists and their sons—and no women. Was it some sort of bizarre brotherhood, passed on from generation to generation—an old boys' society? All those marble busts in the stairwell, the Astors, Belmonts and Carnegies. They must have had their secrets and rivalries—just like the original families of Deer Isle. Scores were settled out on the water. The names of the victors were engraved on the trophies in the Model Room, and below the photographs that lined the walls of the barbershop…

The barbershop! This might be the perfect moment to talk to Thom Phelps, the bald-headed barber. He looked like a man that would know where the bodies were buried. Royston told him he had no business going there—but Royston was busy now, with the glaziers.

Mr. Phelps' barbershop was on the third floor landing. It had one of those revolving red-striped signs, and a glass storefront with a chequered half-curtain, like a Parisian café. At first he thought there was no-one around. He poked his head through the doorway and peered in.

"Hello?"

The air smelled strongly of pomade. Steel combs soaked in jars. There were loose piles of hair on the tiled floor, and various sporting journals dotted around in racks. A row of three barber's chairs faced the wall-to-wall mirror. Reclining in the center chair, with a copy of *Racing Form* over his face, was Thom Phelps.

"I'm sorry to bother you, sir," said Davey. "Mind if I come in?"

Phelps lowered the magazine as far as the bridge of his nose. "'Allo, Davey. Come to get a trim for that country-boy haircut?"

He took one look at Mr. Phelps' greasy comb-over, and said: "Thanks, I'm good for now. I wondered if I could have a quick look at your photographs. I'm keen on the history of the Club."

Phelps pulled the magazine back up over his eyes. "Be my guest, son."

"You must've cut some pretty famous heads of hair in your time, Mr Phelps!"

The walls were lined with framed photographs of Phelps' clients. Some he recognized—Jay Gould, the railroad magnate; Herbert Sears and August Belmont Jnr, the Flag Officers; John D. Astor, shaking hands with the Kaiser; Stuyvesant Fish with his remarkable sideburns. He paused in front of a familiar figure in a blazer, pictured at the helm of a fast racing yacht.

"Is this Harold Vanderbilt?" Davey asked.

Phelps answered from under his *Racing Form*. "At the wheel of *Reliance*? Nah, that's Cornelius, his cousin. Neily. Quite a family resemblance, eh? He did a spell as Commodore a few years back. Bit of an inventor, too. Told me all about his idea for a mechanical pedestrian walkway under Manhattan, once, while I was giving 'im a shave."

"Whatever happened to that?"

"I told 'im he was off his rocker, didn't I."

"And the chap behind him? With the droopy mustache?"

"That's Oliver Iselin," Phelps said, sitting up. He adjusted his tie. "I'm sure you know who he is."

"No, never heard of him..." Davey shuffled on his feet.

"Legendary yachtsman. Won the America's Cup four times, all in his own boats. The newspapers loved 'im. First great gentleman champion of the sport."

"Oh. And I bet you're his barber, aren't you, Mr. Phelps! What's he like?"

"I used to be, yeah. Cut his hair, trimmed his whiskers too. Ain't seen 'im in years, though. He's sorely missed round here. A fine gent. Bit of a temper, though."

"Oh, really?"

Phelps swiveled in his chair so he could see Davey in the mirror. His Cockney accent got stronger. "He's sat in my shop one day, right, in this very chair. I'm giving 'im a short back and sides. And Mr. Herreshoff, he was sat in that one—Nat Herreshoff, the yacht designer. They get in an argument—goin' on about hull profiles and displacement and whatnot. Big old squabble, they was having! Captain Nat says, look, you can't have it both ways Ollie, if what you want's a soap dish with sails I can build it for you, but it *won't point!* Then Mr. Iselin, he rips the sheet off and storms out of the shop, all red in the face. A soap dish with sails!" he chuckled. "Fuck me sideways."

"Jeezum, Mr. Phelps, you've got some stories."

"I remember it clear as day. He was all lopsided." He stood and brushed down his cotton coat.

"This was when?"

"Oh, ten, twelve years back. The year *Columbia* won the Cup for the second time. Mr. Iselin pulled out of the Syndicate. Claimed it was for health reasons. The two of 'em made nice again, and they won the next one, with *Reliance*, in '03. But Ollie never went back to racing."

"How come?"

Phelps wiped off the blade of a straight razor, and began sharpening it on a wetted leather strap. "You'd have to ask him. Maybe the other gents felt he'd done enough. Maybe they thought he should step aside and let someone else have a go, I dunno. Then again, he had problems at home, too."

"Such as…?"

"I don't recall offhand. Something unpleasant happened on his property, and the coppers were called in. It was in the papers for a while, then it all blew over."

Davey leaned closer to examine the photograph. He was strangely captivated by the icy, determined expression. "Mr. Iselin must have been a heck of a sailor?"

"The dog's bollocks, mate, to be fair."

Just then Mr. Royston burst in from the landing. He saw Davey in front of Iselin's photograph. The veins were bulging on his neck, and the voice that came out of it was a screech. "Haskell! Why in heck are you up here? You ain't done in the Model Room yet."

Davey was at a loss for words. He tried to look innocent and starry-eyed.

"Ah, the kid's just keen on yachting, Pete," said Phelps. "Cut him some slack, why don't ya?"

Royston glared at Davey. "I told you before, sonny Jim, I don't want you snooping around where you got no business being. Don't matter who put you in this job, or why—I can still kick you out on the street. You better shape up, kid. I got my eye on you now." He stretched down the wrinkled skin under one bloodshot eyeball, which was not a sight you could easily forget.

The library was all quiet, aside from Squigley's customary snoring. His boss was in his alcove, out cold. Davey crept over to the micrograph machine and flipped on the power switch. Then he thumbed through the index cards for all references to C. Oliver Iselin. Most of the articles he found related to the N.Y.Y.C. cruises, and his last two victorious America's Cup campaigns; but there were several news clippings mentioning his life *off* the water.

Born into a wealthy family, Iselin had amassed a fortune of his own as one of the foremost bankers in the U.S. He married into yet another fortune when he wed the heiress Hope Goddard. Together they owned a sizeable estate on a peninsula at Glen Cove, and he built a breakwater to protect the bay in front of the residence so he could moor his former America's Cup winning boats there—*Vigilant, Defender,* and *Columbia.* The fourth, *Reliance,* was sent to Newport to be scrapped, after winning the Cup in 1903. Iselin had a long-running dispute with the City of Glen Cove about the sewage washed up on his beach. But these days he seemed to have retired from yacht racing altogether, due to his poor respiratory health, and a family tragedy—the death of their twelve-year-old son, on a European vacation. In 1905 there was a terrible fire that destroyed the shed where he housed the sails and spare equipment from his yachts.

This all struck Davey as little more than odd. But as he read on, the story took a sinister turn. On December 27th 1907 the New York Times reported an unfortunate event on the Glen Cove property. The body of a young man was discovered in one of Iselin's barns, with a .38 bullet hole behind the left ear. The weapon was found nearby. The only clue to the victim's identity was the initials *H.B.*, monogrammed in the rim of his hat. Curiously, his pockets were turned inside out, and the soles of his boots were missing—even though there were shoe prints nearby in the dirt. After a short enquiry, the police and the local coroner certified the death as the suicide of an unnamed vagrant who had wandered onto the property.

Davey pinched his eyebrows together. He was halfway through re-reading the article when Squigley woke abruptly, with a snort, behind the partition.

"Haskell? Is that you?" he called.

Davey flicked off the lamp switch on the micrograph machine, disguising the click by clearing his throat. "Yes, Mr. Quigley. I was just finishing up some tidying." He hastily replaced the reels of microfilm in their drawer.

"Is the Club open yet?" Squigley rasped.

"I believe so. I heard the front doors a few minutes ago."

Squigley appeared from around the corner, staggering a little, with one hand pressed into the small of his back. Davey straightened up some magazines on the chart table, humming the first few notes of *Claire de Lune.*

For one awful moment he thought Squigley was going to rest his hand on the poker-hot grille of the micrograph machine to steady himself; but he grabbed the edge of the chart table instead.

"I'm getting too old for this," Squigley mumbled. "Never get old, Haskell, I don't recommend it. Bad idea altogether."

In the confusion of the previous night, it felt like the right decision to hold off on approaching Mr. Vanderbilt. If Davey could find out more about what was really going on around here, it might prove of value to him; perhaps he could begin to repay the many kindnesses Vanderbilt had shown him. So he was quite surprised when, later that afternoon after Squigley had left, Millie stopped by his alcove in the library with a hand-delivered envelope addressed to him directly, containing a note from none other than the man himself. She stuck around and waited for Davey to read it.

> *660 Fifth Avenue, NY*
> *June 25th*
>
> *Dear Davey,*
>
> *Well, that was quite a lot of excitement! Sorry I did not get a chance to talk to you about how you're enjoying New York, and your job in the library. You certainly seem to be getting around better on that leg.*
>
> *I had a thought: with the America's Cup trials coming up in three weeks, would you like to join us on board the Race Committee boat (my own Nemesis) to help out with signal flags and timekeeping? We depart the morning of July 16th. She's currently docked in Chelsea at Pier 45. Reply to me at the above address to let me know, unless I see you at the Club.*
>
> *Yours,*
> *H.S.V.*
>
> *P.S. I can arrange for Mr. Quigley to give you the time off.*

Davey folded the note and beamed at Millie.

"He wants me on the *Nemesis* for the Cup trials!"

She perched on the edge of his desk. "Who's that?"

He gestured with for her to keep her voice down, though she was already whispering. "Mr. Vanderbilt. He's running the America's Cup trial series next month, *Vanitie* versus *Resolute*, and he wants me to help out with signals and timekeeping."

"I don't know what that means, sweet pea."

"It means I'll be out on the water six or eight hours a day on the Committee boat, flying flags and working the stopwatch." He stuffed the note in his breast pocket, and gazed out the open sash window at the blue Manhattan sky, sniffing the wind.

"My my, you sure have friends in high places! Barely here a month, and you already got a promotion," she said, moving closer. "Well, I'm happy for you, hun. Maybe a little of your luck will rub off on me."

Davy edged his chair away. "You ever been to the yacht races, Millie? It's the most beautiful, graceful thing."

"Oh Lordy, you won't catch me near one of them tippy little sailboats. I can't even swim! No sirree, I'm keeping my pretty feet on dry land."

"Hey listen, do you know how I'd get to Pier 45 from here?"

"Hmm. It's on the Lower West Side. Down past where the ocean liners dock. You can take the El train downtown, then walk to the river. Why?"

"Can you show me on a map? I want to go there Friday afternoon, when the Club's closed for the rally. See if I can find the *Nemesis*."

"What's the rush? Trials ain't till next month, you said?"

He closed his eyes, and his mind formed a picture that made him very happy. "There's someone works on that boat I really want to see."

Millie tut-tutted him and waggled a finger. "You ain't still pining for your little Irish maid, are you now, Davey? You sure it's a good idea?"

He spun in his chair. "How'd you even know about her?"

"Word travels fast in this joint, sweet pea." She stroked the back of his hand with the tips of two fingers. "Way I hear it, the meaner she is to you, the more you lap it up."

He felt the blood rush to his face. It was the first time Millie… the first time *any* girl had touched him like that.

"Millie…"

"What, hun?"

"You remember a gent called Oliver Iselin?"

"Mr. Iselin? 'Course I do. Big wheel of cheese around here, a few years back. His face was always in the papers. Folks used to hang around outside the front door of the Club, hoping to shake his hand."

"Did he pack a gun?"

Millie looked surprised. "Sure did. A snub-nose .38."

"Sounds pretty lethal."

She put her hands on her hips and pouted her plump mouth. "Honey, if you ain't prepared to use it, a .38's about as much good as tits on a bull."

CHAPTER TWELVE

Davey climbed the rickety wooden steps to the 42nd Street station platform. The structure of the Ninth Avenue Elevated Railroad was barely forty years old, but being built mainly out of lumber reclaimed from dismantled ships, it was comically creaky. One banked section of the El was known to locals as Suicide Curve, after a derailment in 1905 that killed or maimed thirty-seven victims. Every month the papers reported another desperate soul that had leapt from the guardrail of its 110-foot towers.

He was fascinated by New York's transportation system. The rail cars on the El were once pulled by horses, but that proved unpopular with pedestrians on Ninth Avenue below. Even with the switch to steam, local residents complained about the clouds of soot raining down on their rooftops and balconies. These days propulsion was electric, though the carriage interiors were still lit by oil candles. To conserve oil and electricity, the line closed every day from 8pm until 5.30am, and all day Sunday.

His first fortnight's wages went straight to Ma in Deer Isle, but he still had his share of the tips from the Model Room bar shift. The El had a fixed ticket price of five cents a ride, well within his means, and the ride gave him a chance to see a real slice of New York life. The cheap single fare brought all sorts of characters into the city from the boroughs—street traders, dock workers, seamstresses, prostitutes—mainly poor people, some of them ravaged by poverty and disease. Every tired and pockmarked face seemed to tell a story.

He was dressed in his best shirt and coat, and his hair was neatly combed. Edith would be so happy to see him. He planned to show her the little sketch he'd made of her in his bunk. This was just a social visit, to surprise her, but his plan was to ask her out on a proper date another day. He had a flyer for Coney Island in his other back pocket. He pictured himself and Edith there, laughing on the rides, eating water ices on the boardwalk, holding hands in the queue for tickets to see Madame Ruby the Mesmerist, the Two-Headed Snake, and Smoko the Human Volcano.

He got off the El at Christopher Street, feeling nervous but excited. It was good to smell the salt in the air, after all this time, and he took in a deep lungful. The high, open platform offered a fabulous view of New York Harbor: the massive ocean liners docked along the Hudson, the forest of the masts and spars, and the smoking chimneys of the factories on the Jersey side. He could see to the rocky Palisades up the river; and off in the haze to the south, Ellis Island and the Statue of Liberty.

It was only a short walk to the water. He crossed the wide, dusty West Street, dodging automobiles, trolley cars, and horse-drawn carts laden with sacks of coal, coffee and manure. Beyond stood the pink granite frontage of Chelsea Piers and the wharfs. Most were occupied by sooty freighters or rakish transatlantic ocean liners. Pier 45 was reserved for private vessels only. The swankiest-looking yachts were docked at the far end, and it wasn't hard to spot the *Nemesis*. She was clearly the most luxurious vessel on the whole wharf, with her gleaming white hull and brasswork, and a N.Y.Y.C. burgee flying from her radio mast. A private gated entrance barred the way to her gangplank. He peered through the slats of the gate, and rang the bronze bell. No response: he rang it a second time.

The main saloon door slid open and a pinched face peered out. It was Mr. Armitage, Edith's father. He felt a tremor in his stomach.

"Yes?" he called out. "Have you got a delivery?"

"It's Davey Haskell, Mr. Armitage. From Deer Isle." He leaned around the gatepost so he could be seen more clearly.

Armitage didn't react.

"A friend of your daughter's. I'm the one as smashed up my leg."

"Davey?" Armitage emerged into the light, still looking a little bewildered, and crossed the afterdeck to the gangway. He was slower and more stooped than Davey remembered, but his snow-white hair set off his tanned skin, giving him a youthful glow.

He unbolted the gate and took Davey warmly by the hand. "Davey! What are you doing here? And how on earth are are you? Come in, come in. We don't get many visitors." He ushered Davey up to the deck.

"Are you feeling better, Mr. Armitage? I heard you hadn't been well."

"Thank you for asking. Yes, I'm perfectly recovered. And you're looking very sprightly yourself! How's the leg?"

Davey stopped at the companionway and gazed around. It was strange to be back on a boat after all this time—especially the *Nemesis*. The last time he came aboard, he was being carried on a gurney. The time before that, he was clambering over her transom like a pirate.

He followed Armitage into the opulent main saloon. The evening sunlight slanted in through lace curtains, illuminating the trophy cabinet, and the carved paneling of satinwood and bird's-eye maple. He squinted, remembering it as if from a dream. *Nemesis* looked very different in this light, all calm and serene.

"I'm working at the New York Yacht Club now, Mr. Armitage. I got a job in the library."

"Yes, we heard. And you came all the way down here to see us!— *Hey, Jeb!* We've a visitor!" There was a banging of pots and pans from the galley. "You gave us quite a scare that night, Davey. But you probably don't remember much about it, do you?"

Jeb Livingstone appeared, ducking his head under the doorway, his face beaming. He crushed Davey's hand in his. "Yeah, we thought for a while we was going to lose you there! What's occurrin', little fisherman?"

"What's occurin', Jeb?" Davey grinned broadly, and glanced past Jeb's shoulder. "I was just wondering—is Edith here? Or..."

Jeb pulled off his hat and undid his apron, exchanging a look with Armitage.

"Come on through to the scullery, young fellow," Armitage said. "I'm sure you could use a cup of tea. Look, I'm afraid you've had a wasted trip—Edith hasn't been on the *Nemesis* in over a month now. She's with my sister and her husband, on their farm in Ohio. She won't be back this summer. I'm sure she'll be sorry she missed you."

"But… I spoke to her on the telephone, just a few weeks ago, in Newport, when you all were at Rock Cliffe. And she wrote me. Never said nothing about Ohio though…"

"Ah yes, we were so relieved. But no, she had to go away for a while. She… well, her aunt and uncle, they really needed some help with the lambing."

"But she's well?"

"She's in fine form, Davey, fine form."

"Don't it leave you shorthanded on the *Nemesis*?"

"We get by. We divide up the tasks, isn't that right, Jeb?"

"In a blind man country, one-eyed man a king," mumbled Jeb enigmatically as he filled the kettle.

"Look, I'm sorry you came all the way down here," Armitage said. "I can give you my daughter's address, if you want, you could write to her. But take some tea with us. Sit, sit!"

Davey slid onto a bench in the booth and brushed his hair back. "It really is grand to see you, Mr. Armitage. You too, Jeb. I never got to thank you for what you did, 'cause… I reckon you two saved my bacon that night, you and Edith." He felt his eyes go a little dewy. "But hey, I got some news! Mr. Vanderbilt has asked me to help out on the *Nemesis* for the Trials in July. He wants me up on the bridge, hoisting flags, keeping time and the like. So we're all gonna be shipmates! What d'you think of that?"

"Yeah, bredda!" Jeb set down a silver tea set, and two-thirds of a homemade fruit cake from the larder. "That's peachy, Davey. Shipmates, is it? Maybe we'll make a proper seaman of you, finally." He pulled up a stool.

"No more acting the maggot on the bowsprit, though, you must promise us," added Armitage. "No more of your heroics."

Davey laughed. "I'm just looking forward to getting back out on the water. The wind in me hair, the swell o' the ocean under me feet... It's not right, an old sea tar like me being stuck indoors, is it?"

"Davey, the old sea tar, is it?" Jeb grinned. He poured three cups of tea, and a shot of rum in his own. "So tell us wha' gwan, little fisherman. How you come to be in New York now?"

With a mouth full of fruit cake, Davey told them all about his time with Lucía, and the oddities of his new job at the N.Y.Y.C. They laughed our loud at his tales of Squigley's long afternoons of "archiving." He replayed the bizarre conversations he'd overheard, and the latest scoop on the members, according to the flamboyant Ogden Blum. He relived the whole incident with the rowdy mob: the workers demonstrating in the street, the brick through the window of the Model Room, and the huddle of outraged gents at the bar, sipping their cocktails. Those N.Y.Y.C. swells were a bit of a joke, weren't they?

But Armitage and Jeb's faces had become solemn. He'd talked out of turn. He sipped from his silver tea cup, felt the soft silk cushion under him; he reminded himself whose yacht he was on. Scrambling for something to dig himself out, he paraphrased a quote he'd read: "I mean, in America, working people are suffering, while a handful of industrialists rake it in…"

He was only making it worse. They were well practiced at being discreet, but he could see the conflicting feelings on their faces. He felt completely foolish now. They'd surely both been in service for most of their adult lives, working for the rich bosses; like him, he assumed they'd came from poverty—Armitage in rural Ireland, Jeb on a sugar plantation somewhere. But it was the rich men, like *Nemesis'* owner, their boss, that paid their wages now.

There was an uncomfortable silence. He chewed his lip.

"But Mr. Vanderbilt behaved very well," he continued, brightening his voice. "He's not stuck up like the rest of them. You know it better'n I do. He's been so good to me, right from the start. I don't know how I can ever repay him."

Jeb looked for a moment as if he were going to come out with a wisecrack, or one of his pearls of Caribbean wisdom. A sharp look from Armitage quickly put a stop to that.

"Mr. Vanderbilt appreciates talent and intelligence, Davey. He must see something in you, a talent. He can help you get ahead. As I always tell Edith and Jeb, work hard on your craft, and above all, stay loyal to your employer. Mr. Vanderbilt's a fine man, and an excellent sailor. He's the future of the Club. If you play your cards right, you could be rewarded with a place on his racing crew, one day. Who knows, you might even make a whole career out of it."

"A job on his racing crew! That'd make my Pa right proud. You probably don't know it, but Pa raced in two America's Cups, on *Vigilant* and *Defender*, with the Deer Isle boys. They won it twice for the USA, against the *Valkyries*. He got one of those aluminum rings, and everything. He wasn't much older than I am now."

Armitage looked astonished. "Well, that makes perfect sense, doesn't it? What's your father's name?"

"Ernie. Ernie Haskell. He don't do much racing these days, mind."

"You know, Davey, *Defender* and *Valkyrie* were anchored just 'round the headland here, at Bay Ridge, during the whole lead ballast scandal. Your father was probably on board that night."

"Lead ballast?" Davey was scratching the back of his hand.

"Not familiar, eh? Well, therein lies a tale," said Armitage. He poured them another cup of tea through a little porcelain strainer. He had a beautiful turn of phrase, with a faint trace of a Dublin accent, to match the twinkle in his eye.

"*Valkyrie III,* do you see, was the British challenger in '95, the year your father would have been on the *Defender*. She belonged by the 4th Earl of Dunraven. He had vast tracts of land in County Limerick, not that he was ever there. Ha! What a dandy the fellow was, though! A right fopdoodle. When he arrived on the New York scene he was a figure of admiration. Wore a monocle on a gold chain, and only the finest suits from Savile Row. He'd appear in his box at the Opera in a new floral waistcoat, and the next day all the young men about town would have their own tailors copy the pattern. But the Earl had a bad case of the gout, you see. One night, the story goes, he strides into a ball at the Waldorf with his foot all bandaged up. Shoe on one foot, bedroom slipper on the other, and a bamboo cane with a sparkling ruby in the handle. At the next big Society ball, wouldn't you know, there's a half dozen of his admirers with their foot in a bandage! One shoe and one slipper, and ruby-handled canes, to a man.

"The Earl was keen on yachting. As his stock rose among the New York elite, he was made an honorary member of the Club, and he took it on himself to fund a British challenge for the Cup. He commissioned a big topsail cutter, *Valkyrie II,* and brought her over from Glasgow in '93. It didn't go so well. He lost pretty badly, to *Vigilant*—which was part-owned by William Vanderbilt, our own Mr. Vanderbilt's father. The following summer, Dunraven nearly drowned when *Valkyrie II* got in a collision and sank in the Clyde.

"So the next year he comes back to New York with a new, faster boat, *Valkyrie III,* that's swept all the trophies at Cowes. Well, it's all over the newspapers that this one's in with a chance, and the betting's pretty fierce. Half of New York turns out on the Harbor to watch the series. First day of the match there isn't a lot of wind, and the party boats are bobbing around on the current. Right before the starting gun, his *Valkyrie III* bumps the American yacht—near brings down her blessed mast!—and Dunraven goes on to win the race, but the Race Committee decides to disqualify him, for causing the collision. Dunraven's fuming, he complains that a spectator boat obstructed him. He wants them to move the rest of the races away from the Harbor, out to sea, but the Committee says no.

"Next day, the breeze is up. The yachts come out to the race course, but the instant the starting gun goes off, what does Dunraven do? He turns his boat around and sails her straight back to the dock, and hops on the next steamer to Liverpool!

"As you can imagine, the press don't take too kindly to this. Everybody's saying, bad sportsman, sour loser. Back in England, he makes matters worse. He gives an interview in the *London Field* and he says on that second morning, his crew noticed the *Defender*—she was anchored alongside the *Valkyrie*, right out here—*Defender*'s waterline was a full foot lower than the day before. He claims during the night some of *Defender*'s crew snuck aboard with pigs of lead ballast, and stowed them in her bilges, to make her lower in the water."

"Because a longer waterline gives you an upwind speed advantage..." Davey was riveted.

"Is that so?" said Armitage. "Indeed. Well, it was strictly against the rules. So now Dunraven's outright insulted the New York Yacht Club's honor, and they don't take it lightly, especially the head of the Yankee syndicate, Oliver Iselin..."

Davey nodded. His lips were tight shut.

"...so the Club decided to launch an inquiry. They set up a tribunal—made up of all their own people, of course—to be held at 44th Street. They invite Dunraven, along with his lawyer, and witnesses. Mr. Iselin sends for a score of his crew from Deer Isle. He charters a special train car to bring them back to New York. Well, at the hearing, one man after another gets on the stand with his hand on the Bible, and swears there was no lead ballast brought on *Defender* that night. After an hour of this, Dunraven gets up and walks out the door and hops on the next steamer back to England."

"Again! Jeezum Crow!"

"So now the press are saying, this fellow Dunraven, he's the blackest cad to ever set foot in New York," laughed Armitage, from the edge of his seat. "So much for the English aristocracy, with their hoity-toity manners and good sportsmanship! The Earl never raced sailboats again after that. He built himself a safari lodge and took up big game hunting, and wrote a book about Ouiji boards and Spiritualism." He slapped his knee and sat back on the bench. "And that's that."

Jeb lit a paraffin lamp and wound down the wick. It fizzed, and the galley was flooded with with a warm glow.

It was all sinking in. Davey exhaled slowly. "My father didn't talk about any of this. He never left Maine again after the Cup races. All's I heard is, after '95, they laid off hiring Deer Islers for the Cup yachts, and went back to mainly Scandinavian crews. That's why we were so pleased when *Nemesis* and *Westward* turned up at Stonington last year."

"Ah well, the Dunraven affair nearly killed off the Cup altogether, you see. The public soured on the whole thing, and the press too. It's a good thing Sir Thomas Lipton came along, with his tea shops and his showgirls. If he hadn't been so bright and cheery about losing, three times in a row, I'm afraid the Dunraven scandal would have put an end to the Cup altogether. The trophy'd have stay nailed to its plinth at the Clubhouse for all eternity!" He had to stifle a cough with his fist. "Of course, it still may."

"Did you work for Mr. Vanderbilt's father back then?" Davey asked.

Armitage ran his fingers through his snowy hair. "No no, I was working for Mr. Iselin, as under-steward on the *Hattie Palmer*, which he used as the tender for the raceboat. The *Defender* race crew came across to eat and sleep, so I got all the gossip. I probably even met your father, or at least watched him working on *Defender*'s deck."

"Oh, I doubt that," said Davey.

"Why so?"

"Well, Pa said he missed most of the racing action, 'cause he was needed down below decks, in the sail locker."

"Really." A thoughtful look spread across Armitage's face. "While you're up there in your library, one day, you might think to have a look into the notes relating to the *Defender* campaign, and the tribunal." He downed the last of his tea, and replaced the cup carefully in its saucer. "I'll say no more than that, Davey. I've said too much already."

He shuffled across the trolley tracks, deep in thought. The last of the sunset dissolved behind the warehouses on the New Jersey riverfront, and the gaslights were starting to come on all along West Street. At the corner of Christopher, he turned and gazed back at the river. Those wharfs must have been Pa's home for two summers, when he bunked down with the whole Deer Isle crew.

A coastal freighter drifted by on the ebbing tide, its topsails limp. It made him think of Jake, working aloft on freighters like that, up and down the Hudson. But the image of Jake brought his mind back to Edith…

Then, in a panic, he turned and bolted along Christopher Street as fast as his leg would carry him. He'd completely forgotten the Ninth Avenue El closed at 8pm. If he missed the last train he'd have to walk all the way home.

He reached the bottom of the steps to the station platform, panting. A uniformed conductor was letting the last passengers out before closing the barrier. He looked up through the tracks to see a red taillight disappearing around the bend.

"Hard luck, fella, you've just missed it," said the conductor, padlocking the gate from the inside. "Come back in the morning. First train's at a quarter of six." He shuffled off into the shadows, swinging his lantern.

"Hey!" Davey called after him. "How do I get to 43rd and 7th?"

"Just follow this street under the tracks, kid, till it becomes Ninth Avenue. Keep going, and make a right on 43rd."

It was getting chilly. Davey glanced up Greenwich Street, then at the dusky sky to the west. He turned up his collar and began the long walk home.

Maybe a walk was just what he needed. It was a lot to take in: being back on the *Nemesis* for the first time since the night of his accident; the disappointment of not seeing Edith; the two men who'd saved his life the night of the storm. At least he'd got to thank them in person. What a strange life they had, waking up each day on a palatial yacht, owned by one of the richest men in America, who was rarely ever there. Of course, they were loyal to their boss and his guests. But what if Mr. Vanderbilt should suddenly decide to give up yachting for Ouija and big game hunting, then what? For that matter, where would it leave *him*?

He walked from one block to the next, lost in his thoughts. An empty streetcar rattled past, heading south. Greenwich Street was mostly devoid of life. The pavement was coated with a thin veil of soot from the elevated railroad above. From time to time he would pass someone on the sidewalk, but these were not the commuters and merchants from the daytime—they kept their eyes down and their coats huddled around them.

Edith. He pictured her soft smile, her flowing hair. Did she care for him, even a bit? He had to be in with a chance, now he was here in New York, with a real job and a wage. He just needed to talk to her, to show her he was sincere. Why hadn't she said she was leaving the *Nemesis* for the summer?

At Gansevoort, under the bend in the El, the street opened up into a wide plaza with a deserted vegetable market. It was almost completely dark now. He cut through the empty stalls, where the morning's prices were still chalked on boards nailed to molasses barrels. A stray dog barked in the distance. The corner of a torn canvas awning flapped in the wind. Under his feet, the cobblestones were matted with rotten vegetables. At the far end of the market, where the road narrowed again and 9th Avenue began, an upturned ash cart with a broken wheel leaned against one wall, next to a heap of dirty rags that looked like something was asleep under them.

Ahead, light poured out on to the sidewalk from he could see the open iron doors of a warehouse. Two men with sharp tongs manhandled a large block of ice from the back of a motor van on to the pavement. There was singing from inside—a rich baritone, with lyrics in Italian, interspersed with bursts of sound from a machine. He peered in as he passed. The room was refrigerated, and long racks of animal carcasses hung there, swaying in the fog. At the rear of the warehouse the rumps of live cattle were packed into a stall. He smelled their mess, and heard the sound of their hooves on the concrete, their occasional nervous bellows. Three men in black rubber aprons hacked at the meat carcasses with gas-powered saws. One looked up briefly, but didn't acknowledge him. He became aware of a stickiness under his feet, and looked down to see blood from the warehouse floor flowing out over the sidewalk and into the dark gutters.

The avenue had many more abattoirs like this one. His impulse was to get away from here, perhaps turn east on 13th Street and find a parallel route. But he was put off by the stench of sulphur and carbolic acid from the glue factories at the edge the meat packing district; so he just kept walking north.

He would write to Edith. Tell her about his new situation. He would find the words to show her how he really felt, and surely she'd agree to give him another chance.

A couple of blocks further on, the neighborhood's character changed again. The El tracks here were flanked by six-story brick tenements, with stoops and half-basements. The smell of drains and body odor was everywhere. He passed by one basement window and saw a large family, maybe two, packed around the dinner table, eating soup and scraps by candlelight. A loud argument was going on between grownups with strange accents.

On the corner of 17th there was a boisterous bar, alive with the strains of fiddle and accordion, and a cluster of men talking outside. A drunken longshoreman in a leather cap staggered out onto the street, stopped in his tracks, bent double, and squinted up at Davey. "Good evenin', your Lordship," he croaked. He fell to his knees and threw up all over the pavement, then collapsed into his own vomit and fell fast asleep.

Davey had almost forgotten he'd dressed up smart for his day out. He'd have felt safer in his gut-spattered overalls, with his hair unkempt and tousled like in the old days. Could he depend on his legs to get him out of trouble? His cane might come in handy, but he wished he had his fish knife with him. He kept to the more brightly lit side of the avenue, crossing over when he needed to, and stared straight ahead, his free arm swinging by his side. He was at 28th Street. Only fifteen blocks to 44th, then a couple of avenues over.

A few of the tenement buildings were completely burned out and boarded up, and most of the gaslights weren't working. The carcass of a cat or a dog had been left to rot in a gutter. Down a narrow side alley, an open fire burned in a bin. Some sort of altercation was going on, punctuated by a woman's yells and the crashing of corrugated iron. A watcher in a bowler hat stood leaning at the corner of the alley, his face lit by the glow of his cigarette.

Would Edith be impressed that he'd braved the wilds of Hell's Kitchen for her? No. She'd probably just say he was a flipping idiot. *I am a flipping idiot*, he thought, *out in a neighborhood like this on my own, after dark.* She was probably safe on her aunt's farm in Ohio right now, warming by a nice fireplace. He pictured her angelic face with the firelight flickering on it, a shawl around her shoulders.

The faintest din of a far-off crowd wafted across the rooftops from many blocks away, somewhere in Midtown. He bent his ear to hear it again—the high-pitched syllables of a man's voice shouting into a megaphone; then the answering roar of a huge horde of people. More oration from the voice in the megaphone; then another, even louder roar. It was a lot bigger, this crowd, than the protest on 44th. The *Post* said there were factions coming from all corners to join the I.W.W. labor rally. The throng must be huge by now, flooding all the streets around Times Square. There was a bright glow in the air to the east, above Broadway. He felt drawn to it; the idea of milling in with a crowd sounded good right now, and he'd never attended a political rally. He could cut through here on 37th St and find his way to Times Square. Or, if it looked like too much of a crush, he could skirt around it and head home, and in twenty minutes he'd be safe and warm in his bunk.

The streets and alleys here were run-down and derelict. In the middle of the block was one flickering street light, hissing with gas. Up ahead there was a dilapidated building with its whole front wall caved in, and rubble scattered across the sidewalk. He was starting across the street to avoid the rubble, when he was distracted by the sound of a single, feeble human cry. He narrowed his eyes to see where in the darkness it was coming from. In the ruined shell of the building, there was a makeshift shelter built from collapsed timbers and an old tarpaulin. He saw now who the voice belonged to: a young girl, no more than six or seven years old. She was squatting in the shelter on a bed of rags, and clutching a small baby to her, perhaps a little brother or sister, that she'd swaddled in a filthy shredded wool blanket. The girl stared at Davey deploringly, her lips forming over and over again the words: "Please... please!" and holding out her hand for change.

She looked so miserable and destitute. He stopped to feel in his pants pocket. His fingers wrapped around the two dollar bills he'd saved from his bartending shift. He took small tentative steps towards the girl. She must have been closer to four than six. She cowered a little as he approached, but her eyes brightened when she saw the money, and he pressed a dollar into her hand, then the second. He gazed into the face of the swaddled infant she was clinging to. It was shockingly pale and undernourished, and moving almost imperceptibly. It was making a suckling shape with its tiny mouth, and the little fingers seemed to be grasping helplessly at thin air. He reached out to touch its pink fingertips.

At the same moment, two menacing shapes moved out from the dark shadows on either side of the shelter. A jolt of adrenalin ran up Davey's spine. He recoiled, lurched backward into the street, and spun around, only to find himself face to face with half a dozen more of them.

It was as if they had appeared from nowhere. His eyes panned around their faces: a loose semicircle of ruffians, street urchins. Muck savages. Their heads were cocked, and hands thrust deep in the pockets of their ragged coats. Nine of them, all told, blocking out the only street light. But as their grubby features came into focus, Davey saw they were all shorter than him, and younger. One looked as young as twelve. The tallest, a pale pimply youth with stringy raven hair, took a couple of steps towards him, and spat a wad of tobacco on the pavement.

"What the feck're you doin' on our street, this time o'night?"

"Yeah, what streeter, spiff?" said another. "Uptown, I bet? You ain't from round here."

Davey tried to make himself tall. He had at least a foot over any of them. "I'm not from the City. I'm from Maine."

"Main Street? Where the bejesus is that? In the boroughs or someplace?"

He was trying to stay calm. But they were circling him now, looking him up and down. "No. Maine, like the state."

"It's way out in the boonies," said the ringleader dismissively. "He's a farm boy! A feckin' culchie!"

"Why's he dressed like a bloody ponce then, Fergal?" squeaked the smallest kid. The rest of them cackled with laughter.

"If you really wanna know, I dressed up smart tonight to go see my girlfriend, down in the wharfs," said Davey.

"Oooh, farm boy's got a piece o' tail, does he?" goaded Fergal.

"Probably got four legs, an' all!" spat another. They all started oinking and mooing, cracking themselves up.

"What's her name then, this filly?"

"Her name's Edith. Edith Armitage."

"Don't know her. English, is she?"

He had to make a quick choice. "No, she's from here."

In an instant, Davey remembered his little sketch of Edith, in his back pocket. He pulled it out and unfolded it in the vague hope it would soften Fergal's demeanor.

"Well she looks like a poxy *hoo-er* to me," Fergal said, grinning at his friends. He snatched it from Davey, scrunched it up and threw it in the gutter. Then he jabbed Davey with four straight fingers to the lower ribs. "Show us what's in yer other pockets then, culchie. C'mon, where d'you keep your wad?"

Davey grimaced with pain, but he knew not to cower. If he did, he was going down. So he composed himself, smiling, and rested his cane casually across his shoulder, with its weighty handle showing.

"Are you boys part of a gang, then?" he said.

"Ain't you never heard o' the Dead Rabbits?"

"You're part of the Dead Rabbits?" said Davey, impressed. He knew about the ill-famed gang from pulp magazines.

"Well, no," said Fergal. "Not the Dead Rabbits. Not exactly."

"We're the *Gophers*!" blurted the littlest kid, stepping forward.

"That was the old name, dumbass," scolded Fergal, and smacked the little one across the head. "We're the Gas House Boys now."

"Yeah! The Gas House Boys!" The rest of them chimed their assent.

"And we're feckin' *hard*, an' all!" shouted a stocky newcomer, pushing his way into the circle. He was bigger than the others, a red-haired ox with a rash of boils on his thick neck. He pulled back the flap of his coat to reveal a pickaxe handle stuffed half into his trousers. On cue, one of his yob cronies let a dangling bicycle chain drop from his wrist, and there was a glint of steel in the night air, possibly a switchblade. Davey's pulse raced, and he felt the blood drain from his face. He'd taken beatings before. But there were no flick knives in Deer Isle.

The circle closed around him. He was massively outnumbered. It was faintly ridiculous that they were all so much smaller than him, but he gripped his cane with both hands, trying to look threatening. Many blocks away, a distant police bell echoed above the buildings; then it faded and tailed off altogether. Fergal grabbed his shirt collar and twisted. "So hand over your feckin' cash, culchie!"

"I gave the little girl my last two bucks," replied Davey, in the calmest voice he could summon. "That's all I got."

"Is that so, now?" Fergal snarled.

The redheaded thug, who had moved round behind him, dropped to all fours. At the same moment Fergal the ringleader shoved him in the chest. He stumbled over backwards and collapsed into the gutter, his cane clattering on the cobblestones out of reach. The gang closed in, yelping like a pack of hyenas, and started rifling through his pockets. When they found nothing but the creased Coney Island brochure, they spat and swore at him, and one little savage started kicking him in the ribs. The others joined in, howling with delight. He covered his face, praying they wouldn't go for his bad leg. They were only kids, but their boots really bloody hurt.

At that moment an unexpected sound from a side-street made the boys swivel their faces as one, and they froze. It was the sound of joyful singing. Davey lifted his head and squinted through his fingers in disbelief, just in time to see the source of the music.

> "Daughters of Freedom, arise in your might!"
> March to the watchwords Justice and Right!
> Yield not the battle till ye have won
> Daughters of Freedom, the truth marches on!"

Coming round the corner was a troupe of middle-aged women, strutting in step with arms linked: a line of them, twelve wide, holding a canvas banner bearing the slogan "THE BALLOT IS OURS!" and singing at the top of their lungs.

"Run, lads! It's bunch of bloody *bull-doikes!*" The littlest kid gave him a last savage boot in the stomach, and the ruffians scattered and disappeared away into the shadows, laughing.

The line of women diverted to his side of the street. "Are you all right, young man?" An older matron stooped towards him. She had a floral hat and enormous bosoms.

Davey's head was spinning. He managed to pick himself up and burst through the line of women. He started to run, ignoring the jolting pain in his ribs and his leg. Around corners, up alleyways, bumping off walls, until he was many blocks away, close to the river. He ran and ran until his lungs gave out and he had to stop running. Where the hell was his cane? Gone. Staggering, he reached out for something to grasp onto, and his body crumpled over a steel construction barrier. He gripped it with his knuckles white and his eyes clenched shut, chest heaving, throat tight. He'd lost his bearings. All he knew was, he was still a long way from 44th St.

When he opened his eyes, he found he was staring down into a trench—a sheer fifty-foot drop to a deep gash in the earth that slanted into the bowels of the city. He pushed his face and arms through the rails, and hung there, trying to slow his breathing. Far below, a team of railroad workers were toiling with shovels and pick-axes at the mouth of a tunnel, lit only by the glare of gas-powered flood lamps. Italians, Blacks, Irish. Some were stripped to the waist, torsos streaked with mud and soot. They splashed through puddles of floodwater and sewage, hefting oak railroad ties. Hammers, swung high above their heads, smashed down on rail spikes, with a rhythmic clang of metal on metal that was deadened and swallowed up by the grimy walls of the trench. A noxious haze rose out of the pit, flaring Davey's nostrils, making his brain a blur. Jeezum, what was that stench? Diesel oil, sewage, scorched timber... a burly welder in an asbestos apron flicked down the visor of his leather mask and lit an acetylene torch, blending the streams from two cylinders strapped to his back, until the flame at the nozzle burned blue. An intense, thousand-degree blue. The shower of sparks seemed to scald Davey's retinae. The ends of two sections of iron rail glowed red— no, white-hot, as their cores melted and fused, like the liquid magma far beneath Manhattan's bedrock.

He lay back on the broken pavement at the edge of the trench, and dug his hands into his pulverized lower back. The welts would heal, but there was an image in his mind he could never erase: that beggar girl with her bloodless infant.

Then a terrible thought came rushing back to him, fully formed:

Edith was pregnant. That's why they'd sent her away.

And in his heart, he knew Jacob was the father.

CHAPTER THIRTEEN

All weekend he felt sick to his stomach. Humiliated, too. He tossed and turned half the night, replaying the whole absurd Gopher Gang ambush in his mind, and wishing he'd had the wits to outsmart the little fuckers on his own. Preparing for the quiz was a welcome distraction, but now he was ready for it to be over with.

It was a bad day for Arthur S. Quigley's eyebrow dandruff. He sat behind his desk, flipping through a slim volume of *Flags and Etiquette*, shielding the illustrations from Davey with one hand. Surely, this late in the afternoon, the man must be wanting to get home and feed his Pomeranians? He drew his chair in close, hoping Squigley wouldn't notice him clutching his lower ribs—because he really didn't want to talk about it.

"How many bells are struck at 6.30am?"

"Five."

"Correct. What are gripes?"

"Gripes... Long strips of canvas passing from the davit ends under the boat to secure it."

"Correct. What is the race starting sequence?"

He could hear Jacob's voice in his ear. *You got your ass rescued by a bunch of Suffragettes, bubba.*

He tried to focus his mind. "Blue Peter for preparation, fifteen minutes before the start. A white ball ten minutes after that. Five minutes later a whistle or gun accompanied by a red ball, and the Blue Peter comes down. Yachts have a two minute window to cross the line and record their start time."

"Or?"

"Or… if they miss the window, their start time shall be recorded at the end of the two minutes." *Would it never end?*

Squigley thumbed through to the later pages. "What is signified by a blue rectangular flag on the starboard spreader of a fore-and-aft rigged vessel?"

"Oh—er… oh wait, I know this," said Davey, his face knotted. "Is it…? No, I'm sorry."

Squigley slammed the volume face down on his desk. "You were supposed to have this by heart, Haskell. Mr. Vanderbilt's instructions were perfectly clear. Why are you wasting my time?"

Davey looked sheepish. "I'm sorry, Mr. Quigley. I'll swot up. I'll have it properly learned in the morning, I promise."

"I suggest you stay until you have it memorized. I should have been home an hour ago. I'm going to leave you my key. Lock up after you, and be here at nine sharp to open up."

"9am it is, yes sir. Good night, Mr. Quigley."

A blue rectangular flag signifies that the Captain is taking his dinner ashore. Davey knew this perfectly well, but he had his reasons to want Squigley gone. He listened to his diminishing footsteps on the staircase. Soon all was quiet, aside from the occasional peals of laughter echoing from the lobby bar below.

The historical records of N.Y.Y.C cruises and trophy races were contained in a wall of glass-fronted cabinets along the south side of the room. For the year 1895, the two tallest and fattest volumes were reports on the America's Cup series between *Defender* and *Valkyrie III*. He pulled them down, and opened the first on a lectern.

The defending American cutter was owned by a syndicate headed by C. Oliver Iselin, while the British challenger belonged to Lord Windham Thomas Wyndham-Quin, the 4th Earl of Dunraven and Mount-Earl. (What kind of man has the same name twice, he thought, but spelled differently?) He ran down the list of crewmen on the American boat, and spotted many he recognized: *Davis, Horace P.*; *Bray, Walter C.*; *Greene, Gardiner S.*… and then his finger stopped on the name *Haskell, Ernest J.*

Pa!

He let out a deep breath of satisfaction and skimmed through the rest of the documents: the Challenge of Record, the N.Y.Y.C. response, the Notice of Race, and finally the section containing reports on the match races themselves.

The second volume detailed Dunraven's allegations in the *London Field* magazine—in which the word "cheat" occurred no less than three times—and the N.Y.Y.C.'s subsequent investigation. According to Dunraven, on the morning of the September 8th race, a boat was sent to row around the *Defender* at anchor, and it was observed that her bobstay bolt, and pipe hole, were out of sight below the waterline. At the time of measurement, they had been clearly visible.

There were no two ways about it: Dunraven was accusing Oliver Iselin of cheating. It was a slap in the face. In the old days it would have been pistols at dawn.

A tribunal was convened. Dunraven and his lawyer cross-examined the official Measurer; the Harbor Pilot; the skipper of the support boat *Mollie Flanders*; and witnesses from *Defender*'s race crew. One by one, under oath, the Deer Islers took the stand, each telling the same story. He overlaid their testimonies in his mind, and they matched almost word for word: the lead ballast in the *Defender* was not touched—not on September 7th or any other night during the racing.

But in this section, Ernie Haskell's name was nowhere to be found. He was not among the witnesses brought to New York City for the hearings. Why was Pa never summoned? When was his first stroke—surely not until well after the *Defender* Cup series? He would have to check it with Ma.

The report referred in several instances to Nathanael Herreshoff's designs for the *Defender*. Davey found these in a separate folder, a hefty leather portfolio tied up with a cord. He took it down from the shelf, spread a wad of the plans on the chart table, and stood back to take them all in.

A gold clock on the mantelpiece behind his head clunked loudly at exactly 11pm. Then all around the library came the clunking sound of other clocks, their chimes muted. He heard footsteps crossing the tiled floor of the lobby below. He hoped it wasn't Royston on the prowl.

There were one hundred and fifty-nine pages of technical drawings on semi-opaque paper, detailing every aspect of the *Defender*'s design: elevations of her hull shape in profile; overhead, and bow and stern views; her spars, rigging and sail plan. He had seen blueprints like these in the library at home in Stonington, and in general they meant very little to him. Someone had circled in crayon the bobstay bolt and the pipe hole, and marked them *A* and *B*, as if presented as evidence at the tribunal. Nothing else leapt out at him.

But when he started to put the plans back in numerical order, he noticed pages nine and ten were on a different grade of paper altogether. It was thinner, and the plans looked as though they'd been traced. These were copies. He checked inside the leather portfolio, and briefly on the floor and behind the chart table. He checked again through the whole stack. The original pages were nowhere to be found. He paused for a second, then straightened up the sheets and replaced them in the portfolio.

Mr. Armitage knew a lot more than he was letting on. Could he have known the whereabouts of the missing pages? Or about Pa's curious absence from the Dunraven tribunal? He would write Ma a note when he sent her his next paycheck, and ask her why he wasn't ever called back to New York.

He replaced the volumes and closed the glass cabinet. Everything was back to normal. He headed for the door and switched off the lights. He turned for a moment, fixing his eyes on the heavy Victor safe behind Squigley's desk, with its three combination dials.

He remembered something Monty Asquith the Gentleman Jewel Thief said, in Issue #5 of Top-Notch magazine, about safe combinations. *People always pick a number they won't easily forget.*

"So if I'm you, Arthur Quigley," he thought out loud...

Probably something simple. His birthday? Too easy to look up. NYYC map co-ordinates? Too many digits. A famous event—4.7.76? No. The dials only went up to 75.

He was on the right track though. What was a date that would annoy the Brits even more than the Declaration of Independence?

CHAPTER FOURTEEN

He woke at dawn and packed his duffle bag. It was a beautiful morning, not yet hot, and the streets were still in shadow. Shopkeepers washed down their piece of the sidewalk, and elderly New Yorkers walked their dogs. He skipped cheerfully across town—avoiding the cracks in the pavement—then south along the river.

Davey's orders were to report to Capt. E.M.Perham aboard the *Nemesis* at the East River Esplanade. Among the sooty barges and lighters, it wasn't hard to spot the flotilla of N.Y.Y.C. motor vessels, all brightly adorned and dressed up for the cruise to Newport for the Trials. The Club ensign flew from *Nemesis'* main mast above the Rear Commodore's private signal—meaning her owner was already on board. Despite her size, even Mr. Vanderbilt's yacht was dwarfed by the flagship, Commodore Ledyard Blair's gargantuan *Diana,* which served as the main spectator boat. A line of carriages and chauffeured automobiles dropped off passengers on the dock. A party of laughing, smartly-dressed guests were embarking via the stern gangplank, followed by porters with their luggage. One lady had a pink parasol and a little yapping dog.

He went straight to his bunk in *Nemesis'* crew quarters, where he changed into his new uniform and combed his hair. There was a full-length mirror on the back of the cabin door. The white cotton and burgundy piping of Mr. Vanderbilt's colors suited him well, and the epaulets showed off his strong, broad shoulders. Ma would be so proud! He practically bounded up the steel staircase to report to the bridge. If there was any discomfort at all in his leg today, he just ignored it.

Capt. Perham seemed a relaxed and level-headed man—definitely not an authoritarian like Uriah Rhodes. He looked Davey up and down. "Well, Mr. Haskell, your reputation precedes you. It's not your first time on this vessel, I hear? You're probably eager to see the crow's-nest where you'll be stationed. You'd better follow me."

Perham led the way up a steep stepladder and through an open hatch onto the flying bridge. It was a full twenty-five feet above water level, with a commanding view of the the *Nemesis* from stem to stern. He explained Davey's duties during the race series.

"This teak cabinet houses all the flags and letter cards. You'll note the four continuous halyards for racing signals, each within easy hand's reach. Here's the dry locker, for binoculars, flares, handheld compass, and so on. Hooks for stopwatch and whistles. Nautical charts, in this flap. And here's the latest code book. You have your signals down by heart, I assume?"

"Reckon I do, sir!"

But he felt more than a little intimidated. He could make a mess of things. What if he muddled his flags at the key moment? He had visions of the priceless racers smashing into each other and crumpling like matchwood.

Capt. Perham put him at ease. "Don't worry, Mr. Haskell," he laughed. "I'll be keeping an eye on you. And if I know Mr. Vanderbilt, he'll want to practice a few starts and finishing sequences before the trials begin proper. You'll soon get the hang of it."

In addition to his racing duties, Davey was to watch for signals from the flagship, and relay any orders from the Commodore, flying *Nemesis'* replies as dictated by the bridge. Capt. Perham reversed down the stepladder, adding: "Oh, and on the way up river, I'll need you to keep a good lookout for ship traffic, flotsam, tree branches, loose railroad ties, that sort of thing. Some of these barges have long tow-lines—deadly! I'd rather too much information than not enough. All right? Good man."

Perham disappeared into the wheelhouse below, leaving Davey alone on the flying bridge.

He stood there, blinking into the low sun over the warehouses, his hands spread on *Nemesis'* bronze railing. He couldn't believe the Captain had addressed him as "Mister Haskell," and he shook his head slowly, saying to himself, "I'm just Davey. Seventeen years old, from Deer Isle, Maine. There must be some mistake..."

The flagship *Diana* sounded a single prolonged blast on her horn. One by one, the resplendent yachts of the N.Y.Y.C. flotilla cast off their lines and idled out into the tidal flow of the East River, with *Diana* at the front, closely followed by *Nemesis* with Capt. Perham at the wheel. A dozen vessels of different sizes fell into a loose formation behind, bobbing on their own wake. Gaily dressed guests began to line the rails, shouting greetings across the water to friends on other yachts. There were steam yachts, twin screw diesels, and various sailboats moving under power, festooned in colorful flags and burgees. Pedestrians all along the esplanade waved or stopped to admire the spectacle.

Not far to the south, the silhouette of the Brooklyn Bridge loomed in the haze over the island of Manhattan. Barges and sailing freighters plied back and forth, and a paddle ferry in mid-channel sounded its bell on the way to the Williamsburg side. Beyond the bridge, a dark grey British dreadnought and two motor torpedo boats loaded supplies from a huge crane at the entrance to the Naval Yard.

The Manhattan skyline was golden in the early morning sun. Davey knew all about its architecture from library books. It was dominated by the Woolworth in TriBeCa—the tallest man-made structure on Earth—and the scaffold-encased edifice of the Municipal, with its half-built dome. The warehouses along the wharfs were topped with billboards and neon signs promoting fountain pens and toothpaste and cruise trips to the Fjords. On the *Nemesis'* semi-circular afterdeck, a small group of Mr. Vanderbilt's guests had come out to enjoy the view—sporting gentlemen, a retired colonel with medals pinned to his coat, a smartly dressed family with an infant and its nurse. Davey thought he spotted Mr. Armitage doing the rounds on the foredeck with cocktails and hors d'oeuvres on a tray, but it was an under-steward he didn't recognize, a younger man with dark oily hair.

"And this is the heart of the action!"

He recognized the voice from the wheelhouse below him. It was Harold Vanderbilt, giving a small group of guests the tour. "During the Trials this is where we'll be taking the official timings, signaling the starts, that sort of thing. Ah, and up the steps there is young Davey Haskell—hello, Davey!—who'll be running up the flags and signals for us. He's my eyes and ears."

Davey knuckled his forehead.

"—and this device here is a *radio telephone*. It has a spark-gap transmitter and an omnidirectional antenna on the mast, installed by my cousin Neily—"

"All so impressive, Harold!" It was the lady with the lapdog and pink parasol.

"Mind if I ask what she set you back?" enquired her distinguished looking companion. "A pretty penny, I shouldn't doubt?"

Vanderbilt laughed, and ushered them over the threshold and down the steps. "Well, you know what they say, Sloan. If you have to ask the price…"

The flotilla picked up speed against the ebb of the East River. Polished brass and fresh white paint glinted everywhere. Each yacht seemed to be getting its own party under way as guests crowded onto the upper decks. Laughter pealed across the water, and a honky-tonk piano on the foredeck of the *Narada* was thumping out ragtime tunes. Two young women attempted a new dance step, champagne spilling from their glasses.

Then, from the direction of the Manhattan skyline, came a deafening boom.

A gasp of surprise rang around the flotilla. The party guests held their breath. It was followed by the clatter of bricks and rubble raining down on slate roofs.

"Happy Fourth of July!" remarked one gentleman sarcastically.

"A little late for that, aren't we?"

Now people started to point: "Look! Oh, look over there!"

"What?"

"There!"

A huge cloud of black smoke spewed out of the top story of an uptown building. The onlookers caught glimpses of the source as they passed the level streets of the Upper East Side. It seemed to be coming from around Park Avenue, or maybe Lexington. At 103rd Street Davey could make it out more clearly: the top three floors of a townhouse had been utterly demolished, and its walls were crumbling onto Lexington Avenue. Startled onlookers ran everywhere.

"What on earth has happened?" asked a lady on *Nemesis'* foredeck.

"Probably a gas explosion, I think," replied her husband. "Something like that."

"Or a bomb..."

"Surely not?"

The frantic clanging of a horse-drawn fire engine was joined by several more from different parts of the city. On many of the yachts, guests still hadn't noticed, or were too busy with their jollity to care.

"Davey," said Captain Perham, "see if you can get the radio telephone working. Ask the operator to connect me to Police Commissioner McKay."

It took forever to get connected to the central police station. Finally the Commissioner came on the line, with preliminary information about the incident. Perham took down details, and made an announcement to *Nemesis'* guests.

"The explosion was indeed a bomb. A group of anarchists, apparently, in an apartment on Lexington Avenue. Darn fools blew themselves up. One survived, and they've got him in custody. No civilian deaths, but lots of innocent people hurt, from what I can tell."

Ripples of alarm and agitation spread through the guests.

"A bomb! In New York?"

"Probably the Wobblies.."

"...Do you think it was meant for Johnny Rockefeller?" a woman asked, fingering her pearls nervously.

"They can't know that yet."

"Goodness. First that archduke in Hungary, now this!"

"...It'll turn out to be some fanatical group or other. The Black Hand, even."

"Really? the *Black Hand*? Here in New York City?"

A little girl tugged on the sleeve of her father's blue blazer.

"When's luncheon, daddy? I'm starving."

The cruise to Newport was spread over four days, with stops in Stonybrook and Sag Harbor. Davey slept badly the first few nights on the *Nemesis*. Despite his time at sea, he was unused to bunking aboard a ship swinging at anchor. One of his three cabin-mates, a portly Ecuadorian boiler engineer named Sanchez, snored like a freight train. And there had been nightly wild parties aboard many of the splendid yachts now anchored around the Harbor, with music and fireworks.

Early on July 23rd—the first day of the Trials—Davey was woken by a horrible grinding noise mere inches above his head. *Nemesis* was lying at anchor, and the crew were holystoning her teak-laid decks. This was a morning ritual ever since the flotilla arrived in Newport. It was Mr. Vanderbilt's polite way of rousing any guests still struggling with hangovers from the previous evening's festivities.

Davey sprung out of his hammock and dressed in his crisp uniform. He helped himself to a bowl of porridge from Jeb's galley stove, and wolfed it down while flipping through the pages of *Flags and Etiquette* for a final refresher ahead of the Skippers' Briefing.

Shortly before 9.30am, *Diana*'s motor launch pulled along the starboard side. Commodore C. Ledyard Blair was piped on board with a bosun's whistle, closely followed by the skippers of *Vanitie* and *Resolute*. Then came the America's Cup Selection Committee: Butler Duncan, Henry Walters, and Robert Emmons. They filed onto the deck, identically dressed in blue blazers, white flannel trousers and peaked caps. Harold Vanderbilt, similarly dressed but at least thirty years their junior, shook each officer's hand and led the party into the saloon. The gentlemen helped themselves to refreshments and took their seats at the table, with Commodore Blair at the head. Davey slipped in quietly with his clipboard, setting himself up on a stool behind the bar and out of the way, ready to take notes.

There was a nautical chart on an easel. Mr. Vanderbilt outlined the day's course with a wooden pointer. The start and finish line would be between the half-mast of the *Nemesis* and a checkered 'pin' buoy southwest of Brenton Reef Lightship. The windward turning mark was a Stars and Stripes buoy nine miles south east of the start line. The preparation signal would be at 11.45am, and the starting gun at noon exactly. The time limit was six hours—if the race could not be completed by then, it would be abandoned.

Vanderbilt reminded the skippers that the nine-race series would be sailed under the America's Cup Racing Protocol of 1903. "The international right-of-way rules apply: port gives way to starboard, windward gives way to leeward, and the yacht closest to a turning mark must be allowed room to round it in a seamanlike fashion. If there's a collision, repair costs are paid for by the owner of the port-tack, windward, or trailing boat. In the event of a protest by either boat, she must immediately fly a red flag. The Committee will hear the protest at the end of the race, and may disqualify the offender from that race, or from the entire series. And regardless of the results, gentlemen, the final selection of the yacht to defend the America's Cup may occur at any time, at the sole discretion of Mr. Butler Duncan and the Selection Committee." He looked around the table. "Any questions?"

Charles Adams of the *Resolute* spoke up. "What's the penalty if a boat touches a mark?"

"A full 360-degree turn, as soon as it is safe to do so."

"And the spectator fleet has been well briefed about keeping clear of the starting area?"

"Indeed," said Commodore Blair. "There will be two marshals' launches to keep the general public at a safe distance. And our own members know better than to interfere."

"Will you clarify the 'man overboard' procedure?" asked *Vanitie*'s Alexander Cochran, with a touch of distaste.

Vanderbilt said, "Glad you brought that up, Alex. The America's Cup protocol is a little different from a regular Club race. You're not obliged to stop racing, as long as there is help close by. But if either boat has to go to the aid of a man in the water, the race will be declared void."

Cochran folded his arms across his chest. "Just try not to drown anyone, will you, Charles," he muttered through the side of his mouth. "And let's agree not to dent our nice shiny hulls on the first day out. Not that you'll be getting near enough to *Vanitie* for that to be a danger, ha ha." No one else was laughing.

Commodore Blair got to his feet. "Gentlemen, I am looking forward to some fabulous racing this week. I wish you fair winds and good fortune."

Nemesis dropped her anchor off Brenton Reef. A marshal's launch was dispatched to lay the Stars and Stripes buoy nine miles to the south east. Davey watched its disappearing wake through his binoculars. He panned across the Eastern horizon, where a wind line was building. On the low cliffs at Newport Neck, he could just make out a few parties of tiny spectators setting out picnic blankets.

And there, further to the north, cutting through the haze, were the towering masts of the two Cup contenders in tow behind their tugs. It was a thrilling sight. On the left, the brilliant white *Resolute* with her pine-colored mast. To the right, the unmistakable gleaming bronze hull of the *Vanitie* with her mast of gun-metal grey. The racers sliced though the chop, and every time their bows lifted they gleamed in the early morning sun like new pennies. Davey felt a jolt of excitement in his stomach. How he wished Edith could see him now, in his smart uniform—a race official at an America's Cup trial!

A peaked yachting cap appeared through the hatch, and Harold Vanderbilt stepped up onto the flybridge beside him. "Ah, here come our competitors. Quite a vision, aren't they?"

They both raised their binoculars to watch the yachts' approach. The mainsail began to break out on *Vanitie*, followed moments later by *Resolute*'s. Davey counted the line of sailors—a mixture of Scandinavians,

Brits and Americans, but looking more like Lilliputians under those giant sails—a dozen hauling on each throat halyard, another dozen on each peak. Every crewman was dressed in their syndicate's colors, and they hauled together in perfect synchronization, like a rowing team at its oars. By the time their distant shouts of 'heaf! *heaf! HEAF!*' reached Davey's ears, it was clear the two boats were already in a contest just to raise their sails.

Resolute's gaff was the first to reach the top of her mainmast, closely followed by that of her rival. The yachts were still under tow, and traveling at over five knots into the headwind. Enormous expanses of Egyptian cotton flapped in long undulating bubbles. Next came the jackyard topsails, which had to be hoisted as a single unit, along with their top and bottom spars. Davey could just make out two or three men aloft in *Vanitie*'s rigging, lacing the luff of the topsail to the mast. One, unmistakable with his long pony tail... was *Cyrus!* Cyrus Thompson, who he hadn't seen since he busted up his leg. Finally, the foredeck crews hoisted jibs and staysails. Each boat raised a baby jibtopsail high on her outer forestay, still tied in wool stops, ready to be broken out a few moments before the start.

The tugs' tow lines were cast off and, using their momentum, the yachts split and bore away on opposite tacks. Their sails smoothed, filled, and separated, a mirror image of each other. It was breathtaking.

The magnificent cutters gathered speed, powered only by the wind. Davey gasped at the expanse of their sails, the creak of their taut rigging as it took up the strain. He didn't need his binoculars now: *Vanitie*'s bow thundered towards him on starboard tack, barely a hundred feet away, her nine-storey high mast throwing a shadow across the sun. Alexander Cochran was at the helm, easily distinguished by his Kaiser mustache, legs apart and foot braced against the heel of the boat. Next to him stood his professional skipper Captain Dennis. Among the busy crew he spotted Jerker, the red-haired Dane. And squatting right behind them by the backstays was a short, beefy sailor he knew very well. Davey waved excitedly, and blurted out: *"Rob! Robbie Sellars!!"*

He turned to Vanderbilt. "That's Robbie, from Deer Isle! I've sailed with him, on my dad's sloop… ayuh, and there's Jem Staples! And Willie Bishop—so Willie made the crew, an' all!"

Vanderbilt didn't react. Davey felt foolish, and vowed to keep his excitement to himself from now on. As *Vanitie* sped past them towards the open water, Cochran and Vanderbilt locked eyes. Cochran made a curious gesture: he took his hands momentarily off the wheel and tapped both index fingers to his temples. Vanderbilt, impassive, disappeared down the steps to the wheelhouse.

The two cutters stayed within a half mile of the start line, plying back and forth across the race area on different angles of sail, making small adjustments to their trim and rigging. Spectator vessels, large and small, were milling around the area, jockeying for a good viewing position, while the two marshals' launches puffed among them, trying to corral them off to the sides of the course. The black-funneled *Diana*, with a crowd of NYYC members and guests of the Commodore along her upper deck, was positioned a hundred yards to the east where her monumental length wouldn't cast a wind shadow or throw off a wake that might upset the racers. And now, with the spectator fleet fanning out from the start line, the sparkling open water was beginning to actually look like a race course. Davey's heart thumped in his chest.

With nearly fifteen minutes to go, the officers of the Selection Committee emerged from the saloon and took up their viewing positions in a row of canvas chairs along *Nemesis'* foredeck. Davey gripped the halyard, ready to hoist the preparation signal, with the whistle between his lips. Vanderbilt gave him a loud countdown from ten seconds. On the word "zero," he blew and hoisted simultaneously, exactly the way he'd practiced it. To his relief, the blue ball went cleanly up the short main mast, right to the cross trees, and he made its halyard off on a cleat. So far, so good.

Resolute sped past them on a broad reach. Alongside Adams in her afterguard, dressed in tweeds, was a figure Davey recognized from magazines: it was none other than Nathanael Herreshoff, her famous designer. He saluted the Race Committee. Meanwhile *Vanitie* was close to the middle of the start line, head-to-wind, her sails flapping. *They're taking a wind shot!* Davey thought. Racers did this to judge which end of the start line would be favored.

"Cochran's taking a wind shot," he heard Butler Duncan say on the foredeck. "He's deciding where he wants to be at the gun."

"Port tack's favored, surely, up at this end?" replied Robert Emmons.

"That seems to be *Resolute*'s plan too."

"Adams'll be in a spot if *Vanitie* attacks him on starboard, though."

"Wait, now he's putting her about."

"Only seven minutes to go. Isn't he too far downwind, still?"

"Come on, Adams! What are you up to, man?" snarled Henry Walters.

"No rush yet," said Butler Duncan. "You're forgetting how damn fast these things are."

At 11.55am, Davey blew his whistle for the last time and hoisted the white ball to the crosstrees. Vanderbilt loaded a Webley revolver with blanks, spun the barrel, and laid it in the open case alongside its twin. The yachts continued their intricate ballet: at about two minutes before the gun, *Vanitie* began a slow turn that would set her up for a starboard tack approach, close to Davey's line-of-sight. Her jibtopsail broke out of its wool stops, which fluttered down to the water. *Resolute* was still several hundred yards away from the line, and gathering speed on port tack. If they converged, *Vanitie* would have the right of way. But as the clock ran down, it was clear that Cochran had timed his approach well, while his rival Charles Adams had been too conservative.

A crescendo of applause spread among the spectator boats. Vanderbilt reached his hand out of the wheelhouse window. "Four... three... two... one..."

The Webley fired with a loud crack, and a puff of smoke blew away on the breeze, cueing a cacophony of whistles and hoots from the spectator fleet. Davey yanked the red ball to the crosstrees and immediately lowered the blue and the white. He pulled his clipboard from the locker, grabbing its pencil on a string to record the time. They were away.

Vanitie was a boat's length behind the line as the gun fired, near to the Committee Boat. She was first to cross, but her sails weren't properly in trim, and she still looked sluggish. Vanderbilt called out "*Vanitie* over at 12.0.9." Davey noted it down. *Resolute* was still a distance back from the line, on port tack; at full speed, with all sails perfectly trimmed, she was an impressive sight. She thundered past at twenty-one seconds after the gun.

With the race underway, Davey took a deep breath and put away his clipboard. Now he could settle back and enjoy the action.

"Beautifully judged start by *Vanitie*," said Emmons.

"Yes. And if she tacks now, she'll be perfectly positioned to take *Resolute*'s wind."

But *Vanitie* didn't tack. She held her course, and the two racers started to draw apart in opposite directions.

"Why isn't he tacking to cover?" said Walters with a frown. "Surely that would be the smart move?"

"Just playing it safe, perhaps, on the first day?"

"I doubt that. 'Safe' is not really Al Cochran's style," quipped Butler Duncan.

"Perhaps the current is more favorable closer inshore?"

From high up on the flybridge, Davey could see why Cochran and Dennis had opted to remain on starboard: so as to be first to catch the more favorable wind. As the mainland heated up, the Atlantic sea breeze tended to back from southeast to east. For a short while *Vanitie* would be headed; but once she turned on to the longer port tack, she would be steadily lifted all the way to the mark. *Resolute* would have to sail a farther distance in less wind. "Always sail towards the *new* wind," Vanderbilt had once told him. A diagram formed in his mind of the arcs of both boats, and *Vanitie*'s was the shorter course to the mark. He doubted Cochran was capable of that kind of strategic thinking—but his skipper Capt. Dennis was no fool.

Nemesis picked up her anchor and motored up the course at ten knots, leaving a small orange marker buoy behind. *Diana* and most of the spectator boats fell in behind; some had seen enough, and returned towards Newport or their home ports.

"The test will be when they come back together," said Butler Duncan. "If *Vanitie*'s not well ahead, it would suggest that *Resolute* has the edge on her upwind, in this breeze at least."

The under-steward brought the officers a tray of gin and tonics and a bucket of ice. Robert Emmons lit a fat Havana cigar. Vanderbilt came out to join them, one hand sliding firmly along the railing. "Swell's picked up a bit, hasn't it?" he said.

After an hour of working to windward, the yachts' courses converged a mile from the Stars and Stripes buoy. The Selectors were well positioned to observe the maneuvers, a little to the east, where Capt. Perham had *Nemesis'* engines idling. It was clear there wasn't much to choose between the two. *Resolute* was coming in on starboard tack, with the right of way, on course to fetch the mark. It looked as though *Vanitie,* on port tack, was far enough ahead to cross in front of *Resolute*, then tack for the mark, perhaps stealing her rival's wind in the process. But the wind had some big shifts and lulls in it now. This would be a close shave.

Davey could see Cochran and Dennis in an animated discussion on *Vanitie*'s afterdeck. Dennis, holding on to the peak of his cap, bent down to sight under the boom toward *Resolute*, still a quarter mile away, his brow knitted in concentration. He glanced up at the luff of *Vanitie*'s mainsail. It was visibly soft, with a few wrinkles close to the mast.

Just then a new slant of wind seemed to reach *Resolute* first, enabling her to lift her bow. It made the closing angle even less favorable for *Vanitie*. The boats were three hundred yards apart, converging fast. Cochran tried to pinch a few degrees higher, but the leading edges of his sails began to flutter, and *Vanitie* flattened out, losing speed.

Capt. Dennis shook his head and raised his speaking trumpet. "All hands to the sheets! Prepare to bear away!"

Alexander Cochran was visibly flustered. Mouthing some profanity, he spun the wheel down several spokes. *Vanitie*'s bow slewed off the wind until her bowsprit was aimed midway along *Resolute*'s sleek hull. He stretched on tiptoes, watching anxiously for *Resolute*'s stern to clear, his temples hardening.

Resolute tore past at full speed, well heeled over, right on course for the mark. As soon as Cochran was able, he steered *Vanitie*'s bow back up into the wind and broke through *Resolute*'s wake. The sails were sheeted taut again; but wind and water were disturbed, and he had turned too sharply, bouncing *Vanitie* through the turn with her rudder churning up a cauldron of bubbles. She stalled and straightened up, sails shivering, losing all her momentum. For a horrible moment, Davey flashed back to a similar incident on Cochran's schooner—the one that nearly cost him his right leg.

"Fall off! Fall off!" Even at a distance of a hundred yards, Davey could hear Dennis yelling as he rushed to take over the helm. Cochran had miscalculated, right in front of the Selectors. Emmons and Walters had a good chortle. Butler Duncan failed to see the joke.

After a painfully long delay, Dennis was able to regain some steerage way by putting *Vanitie* back on her original port tack. He started a slow turn, and her sails flopped across to the new side. They had overstood the lay line by a fair distance, wasting valuable time. *Resolute* flew past the Stars and Stripes buoy and bore away onto her downwind run. *Vanitie* eventually followed her around the mark, and Davey took note of the time: 1.34.47.

"Cochran made a right pig's ear of that one, eh?" said Walters.

"A complete botch-up!" replied Emmons.

"It was an easy mistake to make in this flukey wind," countered Butler Duncan.

Vanderbilt had rejoined them on the foredeck, binoculars around his neck. "No damage done, that's the main thing," he said. "And this is only the first mark."

Davey wondered what was going through Mr. Vanderbilt's head right now. Wasn't Alex Cochran his friend? And why did Butler Duncan seem so intent on defending him?

Resolute's massive boom swung out over the water, and her enormous balloon jib was hoisted to the topmast like a string of sausages; five crewmen yanked on the sheet, the wool stops broke open, and it filled and set beautifully. *Vanitie* followed suit, and began the chase with a deficit of four hundred yards. The boats were on a nine-mile northerly reach back to the finish line in a bloom of white canvas.

"Now for a true test of their relative speed," said Emmons.

"*Vanitie*'s got some catching up to do," added Walters.

Cochran took over again at the wheel, and began the chase. A subtle game of cat-and-mouse ensued. Every time he brought *Vanitie*'s bow a few degrees to starboard, *Resolute* matched it, as if Adams was saying, "Don't try that, chum!" Cochran would then bear away a little to port; each time he did so, he gained a few feet. This continued for a good three-quarters of an hour, with the gap steadily closing.

The gentlemen of the Selection Committee enjoyed a hearty luncheon of brisket and roast potatoes in the aft cockpit. Davey didn't want to miss any of the action, but he was famished. Below in the galley, he found Jeb Livingstone hunched over the stove.

"Lobsterboy! Bin doin' some busy work up top, is it? You must be starved."

"Can I bring a sandwich up on deck with me?"

"No, man. Sit yourself down, eat a food."

He tried not to scarf down his lunch—the delicious burnt ends of the brisket, in a pool of gravy, and a big hunk of white bread. He was truly grateful, as he knew Jeb was short-handed. "Any word on how Mr. Armitage is bearing up?"

"Last I heard, he was still feelin' poorly."

"I reckon if he ain't better soon, you could be in line for a promotion."

Jeb scowled. "Wash ya mout' out with soap, badmind. He's my friend."

Blushing, Davey stared into his coffee mug.

"So, lobsterboy," Jeb said, more kindly, "who's winning this? I ain't been paying attention."

"*Resolute*'s ahead for now, but I reckon the bronze beauty is gonna catch up to her afore the day's out."

"Mr. Cochran's got himself a nice boat aright. He likes to collect pretty things."

"Are you a betting man yourself, Jeb?"

"I've got a couple of bucks ridin' on this," said Jeb, pulling the coffee pot off the stove. "So you make sure *Resolute* get the checka flag today, little fisherman, yeah?"

"The checkered flag is for the motor cars, Jeb, as you well know," laughed Davey, and he shook his head. "You let us think you're some sort of Simple Simon, but you're actually genius-clever. I hear you got a university degree—chemistry, was it?"

"Fluid dynamics." Jeb shrugged, and put on an old-lady voice: "Every hoe have dem stick a bush."

"There's no arguing with that," Davey wiped his mouth on a napkin. "Isn't Mr. Vanderbilt involved in auto racing too? There's a Vanderbilt Cup, I've read somewhere?"

Jeb lowered his voice. "That'd be his older brother, William. But Mr. Harold keeps a whole stable of race cars too, at Rock Cliffe. He can't drive them, on account he had his license revoked, back in his Harvard days. Now he lets his girlfriend do the driving, isn't it?" He loaded up a tray with the coffee pot and a silver creamer. "An' she's no slouch, neither. Last month the cops pulled her over doing fifty on a country lane, ha ha!"

"He's got himself a girl?" asked Davey, surprised.

"Sure. A young lady named Eleonora Sears. She's a family friend, from Boston. A top-ranking tennis player, and she wins a lot of horsey trophies, too."

"Is she his fiancé?"

"More of what you might call a *smoke screen*," Jeb whispered.

He wasn't sure he got Jeb's drift. But the talk of trophies set his mind back on to the race. Peering through a porthole, he was amazed to see how the gap between the yachts had closed up. He stuffed his face with a last bite of lunch, and thanked Jeb profusely.

"Man got to eat," Jeb said. He shooed Davey out of his galley. "Galang 'bout your business now, mi bredda."

"Mate, half the time I don't know what the heck you're talking about," Davey called back over his shoulder.

He hurried up to the fly bridge, just in time to see *Vanitie* steal *Resolute*'s wind and overhaul her on the starboard side. The white boat visibly slowed as her mainsail wrinkled, and her balloon jib collapsed like a sack. The Selectors nodded, clearly impressed.

Nemesis steamed north to pick up her marker buoy and reset the finish line. In the final minutes, a ripple of applause spread around the spectator boats, followed by a crescendo of sirens, claxons and steam whistles. Harold Vanderbilt once again leaned out of the wheelhouse window, fired his Webley revolver, and clicked his stopwatch as the tip of *Vanitie*'s bowsprit broke the line first.

"Two fifty-seven and fourteen seconds," he shouted. Davey confirmed it and jotted it down. *Vanitie* turned broadside-on, letting her sails flap. The noise from the spectator boats was now deafening. *Resolute* crossed the line only two boat lengths behind, and also got a gun.

Alexander Cochran stretched his shoulders and shook out his wrists, looking highly satisfied with *Vanitie*'s debut performance. But his face darkened considerably back in Newport Harbor an hour later when the Race Committee confirmed that, on corrected time, *Resolute* had won the first race of the Series by sixteen seconds.

CHAPTER FIFTEEN

"*Thwack!*" Silence, a faint distant "*plop*"; then a brief "*swish*" and another "*thwack.*" The sequence repeated, over and over.

After eight races in light to moderate winds, the score was even: *Vanitie* and *Resolute* had won four apiece. The morning of the final day of the Trials dawned drab and overcast, with barely a breath of wind ruffling the waters of Newport Harbor. Patches of heavy fog had settled on the docks. Aboard the flotilla of yachts anchored around the club pier, NYYC members were nursing hangovers from the previous night's festivities. Davey wandered up on deck, curious about the odd repetitive sound coming from the bow.

There on the foredeck, in his striped pajamas and dressing gown, was Harold Vanderbilt. He was barefoot, astride a small Persian rug, whacking golf balls into the still, grey waters of the harbor with a heavy wooden driver. His hair was wild, and he hadn't shaved.

"Excuse me, sir?"

Barely looking up, Vanderbilt caressed another ball with the head of his driver.

"Ah, good morning, Davey."

"Sir, I was wonderin'... what with no wind and all..."

Thwack! Vanderbilt jettisoned the ball into the deep waters of the harbor, watching its path intently until it fell with a *plop!*

"Yes?"

"Is there likely to be any racing today?"

Vanderbilt leaned his club on the rail. He reached into the pocket of his dressing gown and pulled out his toothbrush and a tin of powder.

"We'll probably make that determination at nine o'clock. We may postpone until after lunch, or call it off altogether for today. Depends on what the meteorological office has to say about this stalled front." He dabbed the tip in the tooth powder and began to brush, leaning over the rail.

"Well, sir, if the racing's off, is there any chance of an advance on what's due to me? Ten dollars would do it, and I could go ashore and send a wire home."

Vanderbilt smiled and spat out his tooth powder, then picked up his driver and toyed with a golf ball. He shuffled his weight from foot to foot, the wooden head of his club teasing the ball.

"Better stay put till noon. If the sea breeze kicks in, we might still get a race off mid-afternoon. But yes, go in and see Capt. Perham, by all means. Of course you must have your wages. You've done well! Very well, in fact."

He drew back the club and smashed the ball far out over the slack waters. Davey watched its low trajectory. It skimmed the surface and disappeared.

Across the foggy harbor were the two Cup contenders, anchored near the tip of Goat Island. The white-hulled *Resolute* was lying peacefully on her mooring; but there was a great deal of activity aboard *Vanitie*. Her motor tender was alongside. A spar was being replaced. It took around a dozen shoremen, in addition to a score of *Vanitie*'s racing crew. The hefty pole was nearly forty feet long. With the shoremen and the extra spar on board, her bronze hull was visibly lower in the water, and wallowing in the oily calm. *Extra weight*, he thought. *Bad in a light wind—good in a blow*.

He sat on the edge of the coach roof, and suddenly flashed on the Earl of What's-his-name, complaining that the Americans had loaded *Defender* with extra pig ballast. All for the sake of lengthening her waterline by a few inches! On a Cup boat, he knew, even a small advantage could determine the outcome. Yet the Deer Isle men denied that *Defender* had brought aboard any pig lead... all except one, his Pa, Ernie Haskell. It was curious, a puzzle that didn't add up.

The tide was beginning to turn. *Nemesis* was swinging on her mooring, and the pale outline of the sun was faintly visible through the fog over the town. On the steps to the wheelhouse he heard the radio telephone ring. Capt. Perham answered it: "Yes, sir... I'd say it's definitely lifting, but there's still hardly a breath... *Vanitie*'s swaying up a new topmast... Very well then, Mr. Iselin, I'll let them know."

On August 3rd, the late edition of the *Newport Daily News* reported that more wind was expected for the following day—much more, in fact. An Atlantic storm system was forecast to make landfall off Cape Cod, bringing gale-force northwesterlies and squalls. Dark clouds were already forming over the mainland by nightfall, and during the early hours of the night a long swell began sweeping into Newport Harbor. By breakfast time, Davey had the distinct feeling he would soon be wishing he'd brought his lobsterman's oilskins.

Mr. Vanderbilt wanted to get the deciding race done and dusted before the worst of the gale blew in. When the Selection Committee came aboard at 9am, *Nemesis*' engines were already fired up. At the mouth of the Harbor, it was already gusting seventeen knots off the land, and whipping the tops off the waves, with an intermittent drizzle. In the open sea, the swell was from two different directions. Only *Diana* and one of the larger steam yachts had ventured out. Most of *Diana*'s guests were probably below in the saloon, wondering if they'd made the right choice.

Butler Duncan sat at the table, both hands wrapped around a mug of cocoa. "Tell us what you're thinking, Harold? A more challenging course for the final day, perhaps?"

Vanderbilt sucked on his pipe and studied the chart. "Five legs of a figure-of-eight. Then we can always shorten course, if the weather gets too rough. We'll lay the start line south-west of Brenton Reef... here. A beat to windward, and leave the lightship to starboard. Two laps, finishing at the lightship; nearly thirty miles in all."

"Shouldn't take long in this wind," said Emmons.

"And those big spinnakers will get a proper workout."

"Good show, Harold. It'll give us a sense of these crews' abilities under fresher conditions," said Butler Duncan. The selectors all nodded their approval.

Davey was taking it all down on his clipboard. With the skippers not on board, he would have to signal the course from the mainmast. He was already visualizing the flag combination in his mind: BL green RC x2, BL, NNW, 7... The old-fashioned NYYC racing signals were gospel. He borrowed a hooded oilskin jacket from Sanchez the engineer, and climbed to the flybridge. Signaling was going to be tricky today, with the *Nemesis* tossing in the swell, and the spray sloshing across the deck underfoot.

The competitors cast off from their tows with a roar of flapping canvas. Both had made changes from the previous race: *Vanitie* had stepped a new steel topmast, and *Resolute* was experimenting with a little more rake. After a dominant start to the series, *Resolute* had lost the last two races. Alexander Cochran appeared to have the momentum. His aggression was beginning to pay off.

The sailors were in their heavy weather gear. Charles Adams wore a long sea-coat, alongside Nat Herreshoff at *Resolute*'s helm, with oilskins over his tweed suit. No doubt he was keen to observe how his latest design would perform in these fresher winds.

A Webley revolver would scarcely be heard on a day like this, let alone Davey's little whistle, but he blew it anyway at 10.45am, hoisting the preparation signal. The racers split and took off in opposite directions, making final adjustments to their sails. At the five-minute warning, *Vanitie* bore away onto a broad reach.

Looking to pull off a 'Vanderbilt start', eh, Cochran? Davey thought. *How did that go for you last time?*

Sure enough, at two and a half minutes before the gun, the bronze-hulled *Vanitie* made a wide right turn into a gybe—just as Cochran practiced it in Penobscot Bay. He retraced his own wake, steering to hit the line tightly close-hauled on starboard. *Resolute* had sailed further before her turn, but was now angled towards the anchored *Nemesis* on a blistering beam reach, her bow shooting out a wide flat sheet of spray.

Davey eyeballed the gap between the yachts. At the rate they were converging, they would come together at, or close to, the Race Committee boat. The numbers and angles were dancing in his head. With thirty seconds to go, they were around two hundred yards apart. The white-hulled *Resolute* was perhaps a little nearer, and at top speed; both boats were on starboard tack, but *Vanitie*, in the leeward position, had the right of way.

The window below slid open and Vanderbilt leaned out ready to fire the starting gun. Davey prepared his red signal ball. When he turned to look at the racers, it was suddenly clear how precarious the situation was. If *Vanitie* held her close-hauled course, there would be no room for *Resolute* to squeeze inside the Committee boat's stern. An emergency tack at such short notice would put *Resolute* in grave danger of ramming right into the anchored motor yacht; yet there was barely time to ease her mainsail and duck behind.

Cochran was within his rights. Was he really going to risk a major collision at the start of a Trials race? A look of alarm crossed Adams' and Herreshoff's faces: surely *Vanitie* would give them room. They began to wave, and shout "HEY! WATER! WATER *PLEASE!*" at the top of their lungs. Several of the prone seamen anxiously sat upright, gripping the rail. But *Vanitie's* sails were strapped in hard, and Cochran just stared straight ahead, his eyes fixed on the luff of his jib.

Then everything happened very quickly: Vanderbilt counted down to the start... *Resolute's* men scampered down her deck to ease the sheets... the gun cracked, and Davey hoisted the red ball in place of the white... *Resolute* let her mainsail go, and her bow carved a wide swathe downwind in a deluge of wake and foam, only narrowly missing *Vanitie's* drum-tight backstay thanks to a lucky swell that lifted the tip of her bowsprit. There was an audible gasp of horror from the spectators on the deck of the motor yacht *Diana*.

"*Vanitie* started, 12.0.7," Vanderbilt called calmly from the wheelhouse, as if this kind of near-catastrophe was an everyday occurrence.

Davey was stunned. It took him a moment to come to his senses, grab his clipboard and record the time. *Resolute* had stalled out, and was now parallel to the start line with her crew working to get her flogging sails hauled back in. She limped across the middle of the line at 12.0.48. Adams finally steadied her back on course, a hundred and fifty yards behind, well to leeward of her rival, and coaxed her back up to speed.

The gentlemen of the Selection Committee had watched the start in utter disbelief. "Bloody Cochran!" exclaimed Robert Emmons. "He nearly caused a major collision!"

"Pure foolishness, if you ask me," said Henry Walters. "*Resolute* could have lost her bowsprit."

"Quite so—or the whole damn rig!"

Butler Duncan was following *Vanitie*'s vanishing wake through his field glasses as she thundered off up the race course, with *Resolute* a sad second. "Tell you what, though, it was dashed fine timing by Cochran, again. That's three races in a row."

"And strictly speaking, he did have the right of way."

"He'll argue Adams should have anticipated it sooner. What did you make of it, Harold?"

Vanderbilt wasn't about to be drawn into the debate. *Nemesis*' anchor was hauling up, and it was hard to make out the selectors' conversation over the sound of the capstan: something along the lines of "irresponsible… obstacle… possible protest…" Davey knew there was nothing in the rules to say *Resolute* was entitled to barge in like that, next to the RC boat. Still, Cochran had some balls to hold his course so stubbornly, with his million-dollar investment at stake. And it was odd that Butler Duncan persisted in praising him.

The wind had increased to over twenty knots, and the racers were heeled well over, waves spilling along their lee scuppers, each with around thirty crewmen lying along the windward rail. *Nemesis* followed the racers up the course at a respectful distance.

It was a giant game of tic-tac-toe. *Resolute* was stuck in *Vanitie*'s wind shadow, could not live there, and tacked over onto port. But no sooner had *Resolute*'s bow passed through the eye of the wind than *Vanitie* matched her turn, giving her dirty air on the new tack. Each time Adams tacked, Cochran covered, keeping his bronze boat between *Resolute* and the windward mark.

"He's doing a pretty good job," said Butler Duncan. "Hard to see how Adams'll get past him on this beat."

"Just have to see how they stack up on the spinnaker run, eh?" said Emmons.

Davey had never seen a spinnaker in real life. It was the largest sail they carried. In a tight race, the spinnaker leg offered better passing opportunities as one boat tried to blanket the other's wind with her enormous spread of canvas.

On *Nemesis*' foredeck, the gentlemen were well sheltered from the rain by the canvas awning, but forced to dodge the occasional wave that spewed over the rail. They decided to withdraw to the wheelhouse for the remainder of the race, although Henry Walters said he was feeling queasy and might go below for a lie-down.

It all came down to this, and Davey wasn't going to miss a minute. He bit into a sardine sandwich; his Thermos of hot tea in the slot of his canvas chair would keep him warm. He imagined the sailors smarting from the wet ropes slipping though their hands, and the bruises all over their bodies. And yet, he'd have given anything to be on the deck of one of those slick racers right now, hauling on the lines, right in the thick of the excitement. Perhaps somewhere, thousands of miles away, his brother was up the mast of the *Shamrock IV* right now, staring out across the Atlantic rollers and wondering which boat would get picked as *Shamrock*'s opponent for the trophy itself. Either way, he thought, Jake would get to race in the actual America's Cup finals.

Lucky sod...

The wind was beginning to slice the tops off the swells, throwing white horses' manes down their faces. Half a mile from the lightship, *Resolute* tacked onto starboard, the tip of her bowsprit only fifty feet behind *Vanitie*'s shiny bronze stern. But this time *Vanitie* did not cover: her crew were looking distinctly weary, and Cochran surely knew his lead was under threat.

Davey spotted a big gust on the water's surface, from a new direction. Charles Adams must have seen it too. He took full advantage of the lift, which held just long enough for *Resolute* to reach the lay line. One last tack would fetch her all the way to the bright red Brenton Reef Lightship; whereas *Vanitie* had two tacks left to complete, and would round the mark a minute behind at best.

The lightship's crew were out on the gantry to cheer the yachts past. *Resolute* rounded first, and gybed, her massive spinnaker boom thrusting far out past her forestay. The enormous spinnaker was dragged forward to be hoisted for the long run downwind. Cochran, still a distance from the lightship, tacked *Vanitie* on to starboard; but Davey noticed that he oversteered, and bore off the wind, putting himself on course to converge directly with *Resolute*. Being the downwind boat, he had every right to do so. Adams responded to the attack by altering course to starboard also, shouting to his men to hurry with the spinnaker.

At this point, Cochran could have comfortably passed upwind; but instead he bore away yet again, forcing Adams to respond and turn even further off his natural course. Cochran then squeezed his rival up and up by degrees, until the two racers were reaching in parallel, with *Vanitie* in the leeward position. *Resolute*'s crew seemed confused as to what to do with her giant spinnaker, still only halfway up the mast. Then, with a crack, it broke out of half of its wool stops, flapping wildly. Cochran luffed again, pushing his bowsprit perilously close to *Resolute*'s stern, and yelled at the top of his lungs "COME UP! COME UP!" Charles Adams, with little power left in his sails, could only keep turning feebly upwind, away from his destination. At forty-five degrees to the wind, his massive cotton parachute flopped between the forestay and shrouds like a punctured zeppelin, and its long sheets dragged in the ocean, almost fouling *Vanitie*'s keel.

With his boat immobilized, Adams froze rigid at *Resolute*'s wheel. He could do nothing but watch as *Vanitie* creamed past his lee at full speed, with Cochran screaming obscenities at him, and a red protest flag running up the shroud. *Vanitie* reached the layline, executing a perfect tack. and Cochran heeled her over on a blazing final approach to the lightship, her crew already preparing the spinnaker for the downwind leg.

On the flagship *Diana*, the few spectators still on the deck knew they had witnessed something astonishing; they were cheering and shouting enthusiastically. But there were more than a few boos as well. Later, Davey documented Cochran's aggressive maneuver in his sketchbook:

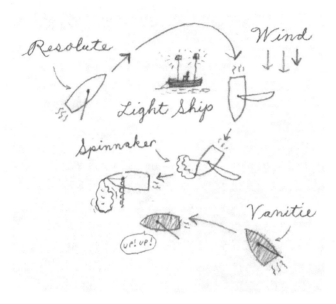

"Can he *do* that?" blurted Henry Walters, emerging from the saloon, swaying and evidently a little tipsy.

"Perfectly legal, I'm afraid," said Vanderbilt. "He had every right to luff Adams all the way to the moon. If he really wants to protest, it will have to be upheld."

"Yes, but it's not very sporting, is it? Yachting is supposed to be a sport for gentlemen—"

"—and gentlemen, Henry, are *not* to be trusted," Butler Duncan said with a smirk.

In a cloud of white canvas, *Vanitie* powered off towards the southern mark while *Resolute* wallowed in her wake, with a dozen men still trying to retrieve her flailing spinnaker. Cochran looked back at his crippled opponent just in time to see the sorry sail rip clean in half as *Resolute's* men hauled it back on board, cueing curses from her afterdeck.

Resolute was finally able to round the mark and hoist her balloon jib; but it was a poor substitute for her torn spinnaker. *Vanitie* was pulling away at thirteen knots, her gleaming bronze hull surfing cleanly over the Atlantic swells, every mile adding half a minute's gap between her and her rival. From the windows of *Nemesis'* wheelhouse, Emmons and Walters watched with grudging appreciation. *Resolute* was so far behind, she was barely a smudge on the northern horizon, where the clouds were lowering, and the rain starting down in visible sheets.

Emmons shook his head. "We still can't tell which is the faster boat downwind," he remarked, "when only *Vanitie's* flying a spinnaker."

"Al Cochran certainly has the edge in the dirty tricks department," interjected Emmons.

"That he does!" said Butler Duncan.

"Strange how some men become obsessed with winning," said Emmons."I don't really *get* Cochran. On the helm, he seems to turn into a... a feral beast."

"More like a paper tiger, if you ask me," said Walters.

"Give him his due," said Butler Duncan. "His sailing's come on a long way in a short space of time, wouldn't you agree? He will be a formidable opponent for the British."

The gentlemen had moved on from hot tea to single malt whisky— all aside from Vanderbilt, who was collating times in his notebook. The weather was worsening, and with many of *Diana's* passengers probably seasick or drunk, she turned to head back to Newport. Butler Duncan gripped a handrail as the *Nemesis* bucked on a high wave. "What do you say we shorten course, Harold? We can end it at the lightship after the next leg."

Vanderbilt agreed. "Little sense in risking more damage." He shouted the order up the stepladder.

Davey, by now quite cold and wet, was happy to spring into action and shorten the course. He found the *S* flag in the basket, a blue square on white, which he hoisted on a halyard. As it reached the masthead Capt. Perham sounded two blasts on *Nemesis'* steam horn, signaling that the next leg would be the last.

The rain was starting to slant horizontally, with little rivulets forming on the windscreen and down the side of the hatch. Vanderbilt called up the steps: "Davey! Come on down! And slide the hatch closed behind you, will you?"

He slid down the ladder, cheerful but soaked. "The wind's picking up, sir. Getting more gusty, too."

As *Vanitie* rounded the last mark with a substantial lead, Cochran raised a hand to acknowledge the Committee, jutting his chin, confident of the win. His crew looked tired, though. They were slower to sheet the sails home this time, like a weary Maine trawler crew returning from a long spell on the Grand Banks. With her foresail still flapping, the bronze racer heeled far over on her new closehauled course, and her bow plunged into the steepening waves. The wind was howling in her rigging. She was clearly overpowered, and top-heavy.

Capt. Dennis shouted something in Cochran's ear. He squinted doubtfully up at the shivering jackyard topsail, and nodded his assent.

I'd get that bugger down, if I were you, Davey said to himself.

Dennis raised his speaking-trumpet to give the orders. Two sailors began to scurry up the mast on either side. Dennis turned to Cochran again and motioned for him to feather up into the wind.

A streak of lightning lit up the black sky, followed by a clap of thunder that was surprisingly close. Cochran brought *Vanitie*'s bow up, and Dennis gave the order to drop the jackyard; its halyards were let fly, and four men yanked on its downhaul to bring it under control. But Cochran had turned too far into the wind, and as the huge topsail filled on the wrong side, *Vanitie* heeled way over to port. The clew flew out over the water, its sheet thrashing around wildly on the deck.

Rob Sellars and Willie Bishop dropped down *Vanitie*'s slick floorboards to get hold of the flogging rope. As they reached the rail, a fierce gust of wind laid *Vanitie* over almost flat. Her bow plunged into a steep wave, and a powerful torrent of water washed over the lower side of the deck. When it cleared out of the scuppers, a spluttering Rob Sellars was there hanging onto the chainplates for dear life—but little Willie Bishop was nowhere to be seen.

Capt. Dennis slid down the afterdeck, scouring the waves for his crewman. But he was gone.

"MAN OVERBOARD!" he screamed, just as Willie Bishop's head bobbed to the surface in *Vanitie*'s foaming wake. Several of the sailors rushed to the stern of the boat. One grabbed a lifebuoy, managed to prize it free, and hurled if off the stern. But within moments they had left both the lifebuoy and the struggling Bishop hundreds of feet behind.

Davey's heart was in his throat. He flashed on Willie's little brother, who was in his bible study class.

"Good Lord," said Emmons, "did a man go in?"

"They'll need to heave to, surely!" said Walters.

Cochran, rigid at *Vanitie*'s wheel, glared over his shoulder at the floundering seaman, and then at the proximity of the marshal, the *Nemesis,* and the Bristol tug. They were a thousand feet away, but changing course towards to the spot where the floundering Bishop was waving his arms. Cochran just tossed his head back and held his course. He braced one foot on a strut, and the giant cutter ploughed off across the sea through the vortex of her own wake, with all sails pulling.

"Steer towards him," Vanderbilt yelled to Perham, "but don't get too close, in this sea. We can launch the skiff for him."

Davey had witnessed all this from the wheelhouse, aghast. His eyes were glued to where he last saw Willie Bishop's head, and he kept pointing to the spot as Capt. Perham steered towards it. But Willie was only visible at the peaks of the waves, flailing to reach the lifebuoy and clearly struggling to stay above the surface in his heavy oilskins. In each trough, they lost sight of him altogether. Vanderbilt sent three seamen aft to ready the *Nemesis'* rowing skiff. The Bristol tug was heading towards them too, but still far off, making slow headway in the steep sea.

Charles Adams, being the closest to the unfortunate Willie Bishop, opted to turn his vessel to the aid of the man overboard rather than continue with the race. He brought *Resolute* up onto a close reach, and the sails were eased to shed her speed. With a fix on Bishop, he feathered the bow up into the wind, heaving-to. Willie was kicking desperately, trying to reach the lifebuoy. *Resolute*'s men prepared to throw coils of rope.

The *Nemesis* arrived on the scene, closely followed by the marshal's launch. There was no need to launch the skiff: *Resolute*'s rails were lower to the water, and her men retrieved the exhausted sailor and haul him on board. Willie Bishop was promptly wrapped in a blanket, and transferred to the warmth of the marshal's launch.

"Davey, I want you to signal '*race abandoned*'," said Vanderbilt. "You know the one?"

"*N* flag, blue and white checks, sir," said Davey. He ran up the ladder and hoisted it to the mainmast. As it reached the peak, Capt. Perham sounded three blasts on the horn.

Resolute doused her sails, picking up a tow from the Bristol tug, and *Nemesis* motored behind. About half way back to the lightship they caught up with *Vanitie* and steamed past her lee. Vanderbilt stood on the flybridge and pointed to his masthead to make sure they had seen the abandonment signal. But Cochran and Dennis stuck doggedly to their course, beating hard into the wind with the cold and weary crew still lying along the windward rail in their racing positions.

It was not until 5.30pm that *Vanitie* was finally towed into Newport Harbor behind her own motor tender. The exhausted sailors had already stowed the sails, eager to drop anchor and transfer to the tender to warm up. But Cochran demanded to be conveyed immediately to the *Nemesis*, moored alongside the NYYC pier. He marched up the gangplank, irate, still dripping in his sea clothes.

In the saloon, a group of gentlemen were circled round the wood stove, dry and comfortable and sipping hot toddies. Cochran burst in through the companionway doors, red in the face, and immediately singled out Charles Adams, who was deep in a leather armchair in dry clothes, warming his hands on an Irish Coffee.

"What the hell kind of horseshit move was that, Adams?" Cochran yelled. "Any fool could see the man was perfectly safe. There were three boats on their way to pick him up! You only went to his aid because you knew it would mean the race would be void. You're a sneaky—"

He took a step towards Adams, but Harold Vanderbilt stood and cut him off. At six foot two, Vanderbilt towered over the sodden and bedraggled Cochran. "Alex," he said, "you need to calm down. You obviously won't have heard the news."

Cochran's eyes were fierce and swollen. He took a deep breath. "And what news would that be?" he unbuttoned his sopping sea coat.

"It's been all over the radio since this morning," said Vanderbilt. "England has declared war on Germany. The Kaiser has crossed into Belgium. He's gathering his forces on the border with France."

Cochran flopped down into an armchair, dumbstruck. He gazed around the room. Almost the entire Board of the NYYC was present. Ledyard Blair cleared his throat and spoke gravely. "We've received word that *Erin* and *Shamrock IV* have been ordered to report to the nearest British naval base, at St. George's, Bermuda. I'm afraid there will be no America's Cup match next month, Alex. Possibly not even this year."

Vanderbilt sucked on his pipe. "Europe is at war, old chap."

PART III

CHAPTER SIXTEEN

LEDYARD Blair slid the cablegram into the middle of the table, and raised his voice above the din, trying to call the others to order. "Gentlemen! If we agree to Sir Thomas Lipton's request, it will render the prospect of a proper Cup series impossible, unless by some miracle the war blows over in the next few weeks."

A quorum of NYYC board members were seated around the makeshift conference table in *Diana's* saloon: Harry Payne Whitney, Stuyvesant Fish, Hamilton Twombly, August Belmont, J.P.Morgan Jr., and the three members of the Selection Committee. Several heated conversations had broken out simultaneously. Harold Vanderbilt, the Rear Commodore, was seated at the far end of the table. He was dressed in a tuxedo and white bow tie. He was already late for a gala ball in the marquee on his mother's front lawn at Marble House.

Davey, as usual, had made himself invisible. He was perched on a stool behind the bar with his clipboard. He was actually doodling a new sketch of Edith, and struggling to remember details of her face. No one took the slightest bit of notice of him.

"It's simply out of the question," protested Stuyvesant Fish. He tapped a copy of the Deed of Gift with his meaty index finger. "The wording is very specific: *"...Vessels selected for this Cup must proceed under sail on their own bottoms to the port where the contest is to take place."* Meaning she cannot, and must not be taken under tow!"

"Can't we make an exception, just once?" asked Walters. "There's a bloody war going on, after all."

"Hardly,'" said Fish. "If we waive *this* condition, then how can we ever justify the others?"

"I'm not quite with you…"

"Look, this war in Europe will probably blow over in a month or so," said Butler Duncan. "Lipton's clever. He'll use the down time to neutralize our advantage. He could claim we've already set a precedent by waiving the 'own bottom' rule."

"Make further modifications to *Shamrock IV* in New York, you mean?"

"Or hire and train a local crew, that know our waters."

"No no, it just won't do," said Commodore Blair. "It's against the protocol. The Cup contenders must all be isolated in dry dock, in New York, until things settle down."

Henry Walters disagreed. "We can't expect *Shamrock* to sail here from Bermuda without her motor tender. As I understand it, all she has is a jury rig. The rest of her gear is on the steam ship *Erin*, and *Erin's* been recalled to Europe."

"She's got no engine, for Pete's sake!" exclaimed Twombly. "You can't let a big sailboat drift around in the Atlantic…"

There was a slight pause. "Do you know how ridiculous you sound, Twombly?"

Harold Vanderbilt cleared his throat. He had stayed out of the discussion until now, but he leaned forward on his elbows, fingers laced. The older members along both sides of the table turned to hear what he had to say.

"Gentlemen, I think I have a solution."

The room fell silent.

"My new schooner *Vagrant II* just splashed last week at Herreshoff's. She's a hundred and thirty foot on deck—larger than her predecessor, with nearly twice the sail area. Twin forty-five horsepower auxiliary diesels, and sub-aqua signaling equipment. So here's my plan, Mr Commodore: I will sail to Bermuda to rendezvous with *Shamrock*, and escort her back to New York. If these nor 'westerlies hold, we can be in

Bermuda in five or six days. We should arrive around the same time as Lipton, or shortly after."

The other board members exchanged glances. Vanderbilt added, with a pleasant smile: "And with the trials postponed, I find myself with more than a little time on my hands."

"Seems ambitious," said Fish after a few moments. "First time out in a brand new boat, and all the rest?"

"Lest we forget," said Henry Walters, adjusting the knot in his club tie, "Harold knows those waters pretty well. You won the Newport to Bermuda race in the original *Vagrant* in... when was it?"

"In 1910," said Vanderbilt, "but I've made the passage on several occasions, actually. It's under seven hundred miles. I'll bring my crew over from the *Nemesis,* plus a couple of carpenters and sailmakers from Herreshoff's, and we can help *Shamrock* out with whatever she needs. And we'll have a nice sail back, in company." He glanced around the table. "I think it's the decent thing to do, don't you?"

"I say we put it to the vote," said Butler Duncan.

"All in favor?" said Commodore Blair.

The gentlemen approved unanimously.

"Very well. I'll wire Sir Thomas right away."

CHAPTER SEVENTEEN

He loved watching the way Harold Vanderbilt drove *Vagrant II* down the faces of waves at twelve knots, gouging a white wake into the darkening ocean, as the last sight of land faded behind them. New, immaculate, and a mere thirty feet shorter than *Westward*, she was designed to be sailed short-handed by a crew of only six. He admired the way her owner spoke easily to Captain Perham and the three or four within earshot.

"She's a larger, steel-hulled version of the old *Vagrant*. I told Nat Herreshoff I wanted accommodation for half a dozen guests, and a limited crew. She's as fast as any luxury cruiser-racer yet built, with all the latest maritime advances, sourced from the best suppliers."

There was nothing condescending about his attitude, nothing boastful about his description of his new prize. He was merely stating facts. He listed the schooner's innovations: a cabin refrigeration system, dual-geared winches, a true wind indicator, a radio telephone, and even an experimental sub-aqua detection/communication/navigation system called a Fessenden Oscillator—though the Admiralty had advised him not to deploy it, because of U-boats.

By 9pm the sunset was only a faint glimmer on the western horizon. The advantage of a schooner rig was that it offered several ways to reduce sail. The preferred plan for night passages was reefed mainsail, foresail, staysail and jib. With all hands on deck, her owner and expert helmsman carved a gentle turn up into the wind.

Vanderbilt feathered the schooner into the oncoming rollers just long enough for six men to winch up her boom, ease the halyards, bowse down the reefing tackle, and flake the bottom six feet of canvas with a row of reefing points. Then he bore away again, keeping his eye on his compass until the needle came to rest on the desired heading. *Vagrant II* settled onto a comfortable nine-knot broad reach, with six hundred nautical miles of empty ocean between her and Kitchen Shoals, Bermuda.

She was a stunning vessel. Similar in style to *Westward,* Davey reflected, sharing as she did the same Herreshoff design pedigree, though more efficient, with her ropes and rigging set up so she could be trimmed from the cockpit. Herreshoff's latest refinements included the flush-mounted brass fittings in the deck, with finely-carved channels on the coachroof to feed the sheets to within easy reach of the helm. The dual-speed winches, in themselves, were a marvel. They made hoisting and trimming the sails so much faster, with effortless communication between helmsman and crew.

Davey helped flake the topsail into its canvas bag. The cotton sails were still crisp to the touch, and had the smell of 'brand new' about them. If he had to choose one vessel to own himself, he would definitely pick *Vagrant* ahead of any of the larger, more opulent yachts he'd seen in Newport Harbor. But when he had thoughts like that, he heard Jacob's coarse laughter in his head: "Forget it, kid. They're not for the likes of you'n me."

This was the farthest Davey had ever been from land. It was a moonless night, and across the lonely expanse of the Atlantic, only the occasional crests of waves were visible. The long curve of *Vagrant*'s teak laid deck was lit by a row of small electric lamps, and the luffs of her enormous spectral sails were dimly illuminated by lanterns so the helmsman could call the trim.

A little before ten, Mr. Vanderbilt handed the wheel to Capt. Perham. They were still north of the Gulf Stream, and there was a slight chill in the air. Perham called for the lights to be doused until the next change of sails; all except the compass binnacle. With no navigation lights showing, *Vagrant II* was as good as invisible. The idea of hostile German predators seemed far-fetched, but such were the instructions of the British Admiralty.

Even with her reduced sail plan, *Vagrant II* still made nine or ten knots on a beam reach, her fastest point of sail. The peaks of the rollers were well over head height. Every trough felt like a lull, and every peak a gust, but she never veered from her course. The strong northwesterly breeze continued into the early hours, when it freshened and backed to the west. At 4am the second watch came back up on deck. Perham sent hands forward to douse the staysail and jib. Davey busied himself on the afterdeck. He didn't feel ready to go back out on the bowsprit—not yet.

The others in his watch went below and retired to their hammocks, or stayed up playing cards. But this was his first night in the open Atlantic, and he was too excited to sleep; so he headed to the galley to warm up with a belly full of Jeb Livingstone's delicious ham and pea soup, washed down with hunks of homemade brown bread.

"Jeb," he said, "that crossing to the mainland on the *Nemesis*, after my leg got stove in. Musta been quite a storm?"

Jeb slid in next to him on the bench, in his plaid pajamas. "Ah, lobsterboy, it was one of the worst I ever seen, and I seen a few. We was gettin' tossed around in the ocean like a drowned rat! I thought we was gonna lose you, as the Lord's my witness."

"Was I awake for any of it?"

"You were sorta *half* awake, Davey, but you were screamin' like a wild banshee, on account of your leg was strapped into this sorta metal contraption, and you were bleeding out. We were tryin' to put the ether mask on you, that the doc gave us in Deer Isle, but you kept yankin' it off. When the storm got real bad, you got thrown off your gurney, and you were thrashin' around in all the broken glass, with the sea water swillin' around the floor. You wouldn't even let us touch you."

Davey nodded. "And who was steering the *Nemesis*? Uriah Rhodes? Captain Perham?"

Jeb laughed. "*Mi back foot!* No man, it was Mr. Vanderbilt. Wouldn't let no-one else do it. And he did a masterful job, like always. The way he brought her up round the mole in Belfast Harbor in that tempest, and slid her gently alongside the dock like she wouldn't crack an egg—I never seen nothin' like it."

Four days later, the wind deserted them altogether.

An hour after he'd finished his watch and finally got his head down in his bunk, Davey was awoken by a leathery hand on his shoulder. It was Dag Coates, the burly Bristol sailmaker who looked after *Vagrant*'s sail locker.

"Up you get, matey! There's a dungeon of fog, and it's mighty thin pokin'. Cap'n wants the sails down. He's firing up the engines."

Davey pulled on his canvas smock and joined the rest of the bleary-eyed sailors on deck, barefooted. It was starting to get light, with no visible horizon, only a grey blur. The swell had flattened, and there was barely a cat's-paw of wind to ripple the waves. A lookout had been posted at the top of the main mast, which was already obscured by the fog. The brand new twin 45hp diesels fired up with a throb. Capt. Perham kicked the engines into gear, the crew took down the sails, and the schooner surged forward for the first time that day.

Under power, there wasn't much to do or see. Davey's mind started to wander. Gill fishing was boring like this, on foggy winter days in Maine. He was better off than his mates back in Deer Isle. They'd be out of a job now, he thought, what with the war in Europe, and the Trials cancelled. They'll probably be out on the Bay, hauling traps for ten hours a day, while I'm getting paid for sitting around on a mahogany coach roof doing nothing…

"Davey!" It was Mr. Vanderbilt, calling him through the hatch from the pilot house. "Come on down here for a moment, will you?"

This was his first time in *Vagrant*'s splendid pilot house. It was even better than the descriptions in brochures. The windows offered three hundred and sixty degree visibility through thick panes of beveled glass. The ceiling was of tongue-in-groove Oregon pine. The cabinet doors, framed in burled walnut, opened to wide drawers stacked with charts and plans. A matching brass chronograph and barometer were mounted on the bulkhead, and an array of fine meteorological instruments that he couldn't name, but *longed* to tinker with.

Capt. Perham was leaning over a nautical chart with a pencil and a protractor. Vanderbilt was perched on a canvas high chair, dressed in a smoking jacket, unshaven, his hair unbrushed. The air was filled with the aroma of his pipe. He gestured at the chart.

"Take a look, Davey. Here's Bermuda. Shaped a bit like a scorpion, isn't it? Sort of Cape Cod, in reverse. And see how it's completely surrounded by reefs? The whole thing is really a line of rocky sand dunes sitting on top of an extinct volcano. There's only one way in through the reefs, from the east, and you have to stick to the deeper channel. We're about here, seventeen miles north of Kitchen Shoals." He indicated the position with the tip of his pipe. "Capt. Perham managed to get a good fix with the sextant before the fog set in. We're heading for the naval base at St. George's, here, at the eastern end of the island. Normally we'd be there in four or five hours, but now there's this blasted pea soup of a fog. If it doesn't lift soon, we have a couple of choices. We could head for the shallow waters inside Breaker Ledge, drop anchor and wait till it clears. Trouble is, then we're a sitting duck. If there are any hostile German ships out there, a motor torpedo boat, a destroyer—even a sub—could pick us off like a fish in a barrel, before we got underway. You see?"

Davey nodded gravely.

"Or," Vanderbilt continued, "we could chance it, and feel our way in though the reefs in the fog. Odds are the Admiralty'll have knocked out the nav beacons to confuse the Germans, and the channel buoys'll all be gone, too. Without a local pilot, we'd risk running onto a shoal and getting smashed to pieces."

"You really think there are German ships out there?" said Davey, eyeing the oily surface of the ocean.

"Truthfully, I don't know. The war's only a few days old. I was hoping to use the Fessenden Oscillator, but it's not a good idea when there are subs about."

Davey blew out through his lips. "There's one thing I know, sir. If a German submarine gets in a fight with a wooden sailboat…"

"…there's only going to be one winner," Vanderbilt laughed. "Yes. My thoughts entirely. And I'm already rather fond of *Vagrant II.*" He tapped his pipe on the ashtray. "So the question is, with your Penobscot Bay savvy, do you think you can help us feel our way in through the reefs? Can we send you out on the bowsprit?"

They both glanced down at Davey's bad leg. Vanderbilt quickly looked away, and began to repack his pipe from a tobacco pouch. "I don't want to insist, of course," he added.

"I'll do it, sir," replied Davey brightly. "May I ask what *Vagrant* draws?"

"Fifteen foot nine," said Perham. "You should take a lead line with you. You'll have to cast it to the side, or we'll run it over. And keep your eyes and ears open. These reefs come up out of nowhere. We'll have to feel our way around the perimeter, and hope we can find the entrance."

Vanderbilt was studying the chart. "It's a tricky one. The tide's going to be on the ebb, and we have to allow for a bit of swell, too. Twenty-five feet of depth is the safe limit, I'd say. Anything less than that, you holler. We'll slow down to just a couple of knots; that way we'll hear your calls better as well. The moment you see four fathoms on the lead line, we'll throw her in reverse."

"Mind if I copy a quick sketch from the chart, sir?" Perham gave him a sheet of paper.

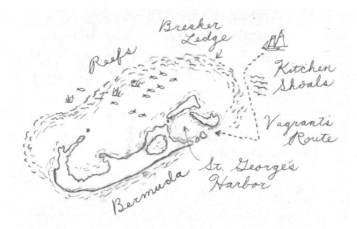

Davey searched in the starboard locker for the ten fathom lead line—a sixty-foot coiled rope with a knot every six feet and a lead weight on the end—and threw it over his shoulder. Still barefooted, he strode up to the bow. His white duck shirt was open, and he could feel the fog on his neck and chest. His pulse was elevated. The rest of the crew spread out behind him at intervals along both rails, with orders to listen and watching intently. He paused for a moment at the bowsprit and glanced back through the fog, where he could barely see Vanderbilt and Perham in the cockpit. The first mate was at the helm. Then he took a deep breath and stepped up on the thirty-five foot bowsprit, trying not to think about the last time he did this. At least *Vagrant II* had skeleton safety netting. He walked pigeon-toed the full length of the bowsprit, balancing with his arms, until he was able to perch at its narrowest point.

He sat and waited. The engines slowed to a barely audible chug. The schooner's foamy bow wave became a gentle silver stream. He began to unwind his line, and cast the lead weight into the water ahead and off to the side, until it sunk to its full extent..

"No bottom with this line!" he shouted. His voice seemed strangely deadened by the fog all around. It was as if he was in a white room with no windows and a mirrored floor.

"No bottom," came the helmsman's muffled response from the cockpit. The rest of the crew was silent as the schooner crept forward through the swirling fog. Occasionally it thinned for a moment; but the sun was never more than a lighter splodge that quickly darkened again. They were sailing in a dense cloud. He trailed his sounding line, alert to any sort of contact, as if he was feeling for a bite from a crab; but all he felt was the subtle vibration of the rope, and the weight moving through the water.

Vanderbilt had his stopwatch out, and was marking the chart at intervals with a pencil and ruler. An hour seemed to pass very slowly. For a while, a pair of graceful long-tailed birds with orange beaks wheeled above them in clear air.

There was a sudden hail from the lookout at the masthead: "On deck there! Breakers at two o'clock!"

"Helm half left, engine to idle," Capt. Perham ordered the helmsman. "See 'em, or hear 'em?" he shouted up to the lookout.

"I hear 'em, sir."

Moments later, Davey felt his fully extended line touch bottom. He swiftly wound it up, counting the knots in the rope, until he felt it run clear of the seabed.

"Eight fathoms with this line," he called out.

"Good," said Vanderbilt calmly, marking his chart. "That'll be the start of Kitchen Shoals. So we're... *here*." He pointed to the chart. "The new heading should be 142°."

The helmsman adjusted his heading to the compass, and set both throttles on low revs.

"Breakers at two o'clock now," called the lookout.

Davey ran out his line again. "Seven fathoms with this line!"

He could hear the breakers too, off to starboard. He looked in their direction: all he could see was a wall of fog. But the throb of the engine had a slightly different timbre to it now. As *Vagrant* crept down the northeastern perimeter of the unseen reefs, he flared his nostrils and sniffed the air towards the port bow. He'd learned from an early age to pick out the scent of guano—and there it was. The excrement of seabirds.

"Sir! I think there's a rock or a sandbar at ten o'clock. Maybe a quarter mile off?" Davey called.

"You're sure? What's your depth now?" said Vanderbilt.

Davey ran out his line. "Five and a half fathoms, sir."

"If he's right, that's Sea Venture Shoal." Vanderbilt showed Capt. Perham the location on the chart. "It's a drying reef marking the entrance to The Narrows. There's usually a beacon there, but they're sure to have removed it. We need to keep it on the port bow, and once it's directly due west of us, we can turn right to two-sixty-three. But we need to get close enough to the shoal that we're confident it's dead astern."

"Lookout, you're to listen for more breakers to port," called Perham to the masthead.

Vagrant's engines were barely above idle, and she was making less than two knots. After ten minutes, the lookout confirmed there were breakers to the east.

"I hear 'em, and see 'em now too, sir!" he called down, pointing.

"Hard a-starboard!" ordered Perham. "Set course to 263˚."

It was a crucial moment. If Vanderbilt had miscalculated, they would run hard aground on the reef. But the impact never came, and Davey was getting a steady five fathoms.

"We should be within range of St. George's. I think we can break radio silence," said Vanderbilt. "I'll make one quick call. They'll have had the dispatches from New York, they'll be expecting us." He went below to the pilot house and powered up the short-wave radio. It hissed with static for a few seconds, and then went dead.

"So much for that, then," muttered Vanderbilt.

The fog was still thick, but just as *Vagrant* settled on her westerly course, a double flash of lightning lit the cloud all around. Afterwards the sky seemed somehow darker; and seconds later, a long boom of thunder rolled across the northern sky. As they crept in through what they hoped was Bermuda's eastern channel, a two-foot swell picked up under *Vagrant*'s stern that seemed to push her towards the unseen land. A few ghostly fingers of wind started to appear on the water's surface.

"I've seen this before down here," said Capt. Perham to the helmsman, "when a tropical airmass meets an unseasonably cool sea temperature.

This breeze ought to clear away the fog soon enough, but there can be pretty fierce squalls and downpours. The sooner we're into St. George's, the better."

They became conscious of a shrill whistling sound. It seemed to be surrounding them in the swirling fog, like the squeaking of a thousand rusty door hinges.

"Hear that?" rasped Dagger Combs at the rail. "*Frogs*! Bloomin' millions of the buggers! Land ain't far off now, lads." Warm laughter peeled round the sailors.

Just then, standing on the bowsprit, Davey caught a new scent on the air. He knew you could sometimes catch the scent of flowers and shrubs before you reached a tropical island. But that wasn't it.

"Sir!" he called aft, "I think I smell cooking!"

Vanderbilt came back on deck, and turned to where Davey was pointing, off the starboard bow. Others smelled it too, and they nodded. Then the masthead lookout shouted: "Land ho!" With the fog starting to clear a little, two lines of breakers were clearly visible off to the left and the right of the bow, at the foot of a pair of low wooded headlands with a narrow gap between them. *Vagrant* was heading straight towards the gap. The headland on the left had a small unlit beacon atop it; the right-hand one had a fortified gun emplacement carved into the rock. Its 8-inch breech-loading gun was trained in their direction. The Union Jack was flying from its flagstaff, and two uniformed British soldiers stood on the observation platform behind a low wall of sandbags. One had binoculars trained on the US ensign on *Vagrant*'s masthead; he lowered them, and rotated a shuttered signal lamp towards them. Capt. Perham read the signal out loud, a letter at a time: '*V-A-G-R-A-N-T P-R-O-C-E-E-D*.' A cheer went up from the crew.

"Congratulations, sir," said Capt. Perham. "A very fine landfall!"

"Finest kind…!" Davey said to himself from his perch, grinning up at the rocky cliffs on either side of the channel. It was the first time he'd seen a foreign country, and it looked a lot like the coast of Maine. He felt a few drops of rain on his head, and held out the palm of his hand.

Vanderbilt shrugged, but he was clearly happy. He took over the wheel himself, to bring his schooner proudly through the cut.

"You can come on back now, Davey," called Capt. Perham through cupped hands. It echoed off the cliffs on either side. "Ready the anchor and boats! We'll be in port in ten minutes."

Another flash of lightning lit up the cliffs, followed by a long grumble of thunder. *Vagrant* cleared the cut where the channel opened out into St. George's Harbor. It was a beautiful, wide lagoon of calm turquoise water. Now the fog was mostly blown away, and he could see a line of cranes and warehouses along the waterfront to the northwest, interspersed with brightly-colored colonial mansions and Royal Navy buildings with their white roofs. A naval launch had just set out from the dock to intersect their course.

Jeb Livingstone came up on deck to see St. George's, and joined Davey and several of the crew on the foredeck. "Quite a sight, eh, lobsterboy?"

"Oldest British naval base in the New World, I've read," replied Davey. "Brits have been here since sixteen-something."

Then he caught his breath. "Look, Jeb! That's got to be Lipton's steamer *Erin*! And there's the *Shamrock*!"

Moored alongside the long stone pier was the huge and imperious steam yacht *Erin* and, just beyond, the unmistakable sight of the pea-green America's Cup challenger *Shamrock IV*, with sails stacked on her stripped-down deck, and a stumpy jury mast.

A squally wind was picking up, and the gusts seemed to be coming from multiple directions at once, throwing dark patches across the water and making *Vagrant*'s approach to her intended anchorage hard to judge. About three hundred yards off the land, Vanderbilt throttled back and brought her up until she was close to a standstill, her bow pointing directly at the white customs house on Ordinance Island; then he gave the command to drop anchor. It broke the water with a loud *ploof*, and the chain ran out a few fathoms and stopped. Vanderbilt put her gently into reverse until he felt the anchor bite into the harbor bed; he waited for her to settle on her chain, and powered down the engines.

Minutes later, the British naval launch drew alongside, standing off by a boat's length. A young officer in blue uniform stepped out onto the launch's foredeck with a clipboard in his hand. He was flanked by two marines with rifles. Davey had to remind himself that the Brits were on the same side.

The officer saluted, and hailed the cockpit in a booming voice: "Good afternoon, *Vagrant II*. Would Captain Perham identify himself?"

"I am Capt. E.M.Perham, United States civilian. This is *Vagrant II*'s owner, Mr. Harold Vanderbilt."

"Lieutenant William Harris of the Royal Navy, sir. Welcome to Bermuda."

Vanderbilt tipped the peak of his cap. "Please come aboard, Lieutenant."

The launch tied up alongside *Vagrant*'s gangplank, and the officer stepped onto the deck. "We'll need to search the vessel and see your identity papers, gentlemen," he said, "along with a full crew list."

Later that evening, Davey found some of the *Shamrock IV* crew in the White Horse pub on King's Square. A gang of them were standing around the bar. As his eyes adjusted to the light, he quickly scanned their faces, but the only familiar one was that of Coo Bray, his old mate, from Deer Isle. He was perched on a high stool at the far end, chugging ale from a pewter mug. He looked like he'd already chugged a few. He sprang up, spilling his beer on the counter, and wrapped Davey in a bear hug.

"Davey bloody Haskell! From Deer Isle! What're you doing all the way out here in the middle of the Atlantic? Barman, get this lad a drink!"

"Coo, where's Jacob?" said Davey, fixing him in the eye. "Where's my brother?"

Swaying a bit, Coo glanced around and pulled Davey in close to his face, so he could speak confidentially. His body odor was terrible.

"The Royal Navy Reserves have been here. They're signing up a bunch of our *Shamrock* lads. I'm alright, I got a U.S. passport, but Jacob's got no papers, see, and he's worried they'll try to press him into the service. So he took off, a couple of hours ago, on his own."

"Where was he going?"

Coo wiped his mouth on his sleeve. "There's an old gunnery up on top of the hill, Fort Albert. Jake took off up there with a bottle. I reckon that's where you'll find him, if you go looking."

The sky had darkened. He rushed up the wet cobblestones through the town, past the ruins of a half-built church, until the road was nothing more than a muddy track. It was little-used, with a shabby granite wall on one side and overgrown shrubs on the other. The wind was whipping the tops of the palm trees, and the rain was coming hard now, forming into rivulets that flowed downhill under his feet. The track had become steep and slippery, making it hard to keep his footing. He felt his heart pumping, and for the first time in many weeks, there was a sharp jab of pain in his lower leg.

He stooped to catch his breath, with his hands on his knees. In the harbor far below, a black squall touched down on the water, flattening an expanse of the steep chop. He could see *Vagrant* swinging on her anchor, her prow dipping in the swell.

The track leveled out and opened to a dark clearing under a canopy of wind-blown palm fronds that provided little shelter from the rain. Beyond it, Davey saw a line of grey limestone battlements. There was a moat of sorts, but it was stuffed full of flowering vines and rotten beams. He tiptoed across the slats of a rickety wooden drawbridge, through a gate that was half off its hinges. A metal plaque read: 'Fort Albert— Royal Garrison Artillery, 1865.'

Davey paused between the gateposts, and yelled: "JACOB!"

His voice reverberated around the grimy granite slabs of the forecourt. The fort was flanked by several desolate buildings: a row of dormitories and latrines, a workshop, and various munitions sheds with stoved-in corrugated roofs. Most of the windowpanes were smashed, and creepers were growing up out of the frames, enveloping the walls of the buildings, as if the jungle was trying to swallow the encampment whole.

"JACOB! Jacob Haskell!" he called again. He took a few steps across the slick paving stones.

He heard a voice, above and behind him. He spun around. The rain was slanting down, stinging his eyes.

"Jeezum Crow. Hello, little brother!"

Jacob was sitting with his legs swung over the battlement wall, twelve feet up. A yellow oilskin jacket was slung over his head and shoulders, but he was drenched to the skin anyway. He had an almost-empty bottle of whisky in one hand and a harmonica in the other.

Davey swelled to his full height. "Get down here, you fucker!" he shouted.

"Well, it's nice to see you too, little brother. What the heck are you doing in Bermuda? And how in the Sam Hill did you find me all the way up here?" Jacob hopped down onto what was left of a stone spiral staircase. Halfway down the steps he lost his footing, and slid the rest of the way on his arse. He landed at the bottom, laughing, and checked his bottle was intact.

"Get over here, pipsqueak. How the heck are you? How's the leg? My little Davey. Gimme a kiss."

Davey backed off a few steps, leaving Jacob with his arms swinging. When he spoke it was through clenched teeth.

"You and me have a few things to get straight. You made me a promise, remember? The night I busted my leg. You swore you was gonna stay and look after Ma, and I believed you, but you ran off like a fucking coward, didn't you."

"Hold on," said Jacob. "Hold your horses. I said a lot of weird shite that night; I wasn't thinking straight. I was worried sick about you. They said you might lose the leg, and that would be *if* you was lucky. I never swore to nothing though! I'd a told you any kind of crap just to keep you cheerful. I was just praying they'd get you to the mainland in time to save your life."

"So you just fucked off to England without even waiting to find out?"

"It wasn't like that." Jacob took a slug of his whisky. "By the time I got my head straight, I realized I was no use to Ma. The fishing was all gone to shit last season, and I was just one more mouth to feed. So yeah,

I took a job on *Westward*, so I could get out of her hair, make myself useful. I reckon you'd a done the same, in my shoes."

The rain was gushing down Davey's face and into the neck of his shirt. His hair was plastered to his head. "You're a fucking bastard," he said. "You shoulda stayed behind like you promised. Ma needed us around, she needed the help. Pa's sick and I was stuck in the hospital. She musta been worried to death, with winter coming on and all."

Jacob parked his backside on the rusty shell of an upturned wheelbarrow and tried to rest all his weight on the wheel, which spun. He caught himself, but the oilskin fell away from his shoulders.

"She mighta been worried about *you*, pee wee, not me. Looks like the hospital fixed up your leg pretty good though. So when they let you out, what did you do? Go straight back to Deer Isle to take care of Ma?"

Davey flipped over a fallen palm frond with his foot.

"Figure that's a *no*." Jacob smirked. "You ran off to the city, didn't you? Ayuh, c'mon Dave. You're full of shit, same as me."

"That was different. I couldn't lift nothing, or pull on a rope. If there'd a been work for me in Deer Isle, I'd have gone back in a heartbeat."

"Yeah? How'd you get to Bermuda, then? First class cabin on a luxury liner?"

"Mr. Vanderbilt's been helping me out. Got me a job at the Yacht Club library. Now I'm crewing for him too, on his schooner. Been doing the timekeeping in the Cup trials, stuff like that. But when they called it off for the War, we sailed down here to rendezvous with the *Shamrock*."

"Oh. Vanderbilt, I get it. Uh-huh."

"You coulda worked for him too, Jake, if you hadn't a buggered off to England."

"Yeah, but *Shamrock*'ll be in the Cup, whenever that happens, won't she."

Jacob swigged the last dregs of his whisky bottle, screwed up one eye to check it was really empty, then sent it spinning across the paving stones. After a moment he shook the raindrops out of his harmonica, put it to his lips, and began to play. It was a tune from home.

"You were always crap at that." Davey spoke in a tremor, forcing out the next words. "Now, you're gonna tell me the truth about Edith."

Jake stopped blowing. There was only the splatter of the rain on the paving stones, and the tail end of a distant thunder clap, miles away.

"Who?"

He turned and glared at his brother. "*Edith.*"

Jacob narrowed his eyes, as if flipping through the list of girls from his past. "The little Irish filly from the *Nemesis*?"

"Don't pretend you don't remember, you gawmy sod."

"Oh yeah," chuckled Jacob, "the one you was all soft on. Ha ha, 'course I remember! Lovely little squishy tits, that one had. What about her?"

"You *fucked* her, didn't you?" He took two steps straight towards Jacob, staring him down.

"Jeezum, Davey, you're still thinking about that little tart?" Jacob avoided his gaze, grinning. "Well, maybe I did, maybe I didn't."

Jake didn't see the rugby tackle coming. It hit him in the midriff, with the full weight of Davey's right shoulder behind it, knocking the breath clean out of him. He grimaced in pain and fell sideways onto the wet paving stones, clutching his ribs, with Davey on top of him.

"You fucking bastard! I'll kill you!" Davey's fists were clenched, and he was trying to land punches in his brother's face. But Jacob's strong arms were raised to protect himself, and his elbows deflected the blows. He managed to bring a knee up in Davey's groin and throw him off to the side so he could wriggle out from underneath.

"What the hell's got into you?" Jacob yelled, starting to pull himself up.

"*I'll fucking kill you!*" Davey screamed again, lunging at Jacob's legs. Jacob tried to take a step sideways, but his knees were wrapped in Davey's death grip, and he stumbled back on the wet stones again. He tried to crawl away, dragging Davey with him.

"Get the fuck *off* me, you little squirt!" said Jacob. He kicked out, the heel of his boot landing square on the bridge of Davey's nose. Davey yelped and let go, and Jacob managed to crawl a yard away, shouting: "I ain't gonna fight a fucking cripple!"

The two of them lay there in the rain, a few feet apart, panting. Davey rolled over onto his back, blood pouring from his nose, and waited for his breath to slow.

"Edith's pregnant, you cunt, didn't you know?"

Jacob sat up on his elbows, his eyes blinking from the rain and sweat running down his face. "How do you know that? You been seeing her?"

"No. But her dad told me. Armitage, sorta."

Jacob swallowed hard. "Lemme tell you, if Edith's knocked up, it sure as heck ain't mine. All we ever did that night was talk. I might of kissed her on the cheek. That was it. I didn't lay a finger on her. I swear to you, little brother. I couldn't do that to her. Not after..."

"Not after what?"

"She made me promise never to tell a living soul."

Davey knew all about his brother's promises. "About what?" he said, though his teeth.

"About that shit Cochran."

"Alex Cochran? The ponce with the mustache? What's he got to do with it?"

Jacob shook his head. "Something bad sure's hell happened on the *Nemesis*, during the tryouts. She tried to tell me, but she couldn't get the words out, an' I wasn't gonna push it. I couldn't figure what she was saying. Someone forced her to... do things for them; she didn't say what, exactly. I reckon it was Cochran, for sure. Said she had to keep it secret, or Vanderbilt would sack her, and her dad would think she was a little tart."

"Oh, so what, now you're saying the baby's Cochran's?"

"What did I just tell you?"

"You didn't even *try* to poke her?"

Jacob said, "No, on my life."

Davey's eyes were pinched shut. He took several deep breaths through his nose. "She was talking about Rula, making her do things, not Cochran. And anyway, you're talking out your ass. What would he even want with Edith, when he had his mistress on board?"

"That woman was too drunk to fuck, mostly, far as I could make out."

"You expect me to believe your horseshit?"

"Cross my heart."

They lay there, drenched and breathless, for several minutes. The chorus of frogs had started up again. Around and above them, palm fronds were swaying. Davey stared past the trees into the clearing sky. A handful of fading stars were still visible. He sniffed, and wiped his face with the sleeve of his sodden shirt, tasting the blood in his nose. He could hear the rain trickling away in the gaps between the paving stones. There was a strong smell of earth. He rolled over on his side and scanned Jacob's profile.

Jake's long hair was matted with mud, and his eyes were closed. His shirt was ripped, and his hands were crossed on his heaving stomach. He mumbled something that sounded like: "Shouldn'a called you a cripple, kid..." Then he turned his face away, and started to snore.

Davey slowly pulled himself to his feet. It had stopped raining, but he was shivering. He stared down at his brother, out cold. He wiped his nose, took off his sodden pea jacket, and laid it over Jacob's sleeping body.

It was starting to get light. He turned and limped up the steps to the ramparts, resting his weight on the rusty barrel of a cannon. The cold rain pooled around his feet. On the horizon to the east, the purple clouds were lit by occasional spidery bolts of lightning as the storm moved away across the Atlantic.

"Jacob, you're a lying shit," he said.

CHAPTER EIGHTEEN

That was a surprisingly large glass of brandy that Sir Thomas Lipton was cradling; especially for a man who made his fortune from tea and cakes.

"So, Harold," he enquired from under his outrageous whiskers, "What news from our pals at the N.Y.Y.C.?"

Davey and one of the Swedes had rowed the gentlemen from *Vagrant II* across to Lipton's steamship *Erin*. Both Davey's eyes were purple from the swollen welt on the bridge of his nose. He leaned against the coachroof, next to an open porthole, occasionally peeking inside.

Erin's chart room was splendidly lit by the low morning sunlight, with its maritime oil paintings of various *Shamrocks* from the past, and the barley-twist detailing around the oval table. Sir Thomas was seated in the middle of a semicircular red velvet bench. To his right sat Harold Vanderbilt and Capt. Perham. To his left was William P. Burton, the wealthy businessman and racing manager of *Shamrock IV.* Across the table was Lt. Bill Harris, the uniformed officer from the Royal Navy launch of the previous day, with his cap under his arm.

Vanderbilt pushed his spectacles up the bridge of his nose and unfolded a piece of paper. "This came from the Commodore an hour ago… I'll just read it, shall I? 'SLIGHT CHANCE CAN STILL RUN CUP SERIES THIS YEAR IF WAR IN EUROPE OVER NEXT FEW WEEKS STOP LATEST POSSIBLE START TO SERIES FIRST WEEK OCTOBER ELSE RECOMMEND YOU LAY UP BROOKLYN DRY DOCK PENDING RESCHEDULE IN 1915.'"

"Well. That sounds like the best one could hope for, in the circumstances," said Sir Thomas. "The Navy has requisitioned *Erin* for use as a hospital ship. I will return with her to Plymouth. From there, she'll continue on to the Mediterranean, the Baltic, or wherever she is needed…"

"Quite right," Burton said gravely. "One must do what one can to support the war effort."

"…but I see no reason why *Shamrock IV* should not continue to New York. She didn't make it this far across the pond to turn back now! Let's hope we still get some racing in, when that infernal Kaiser comes to his senses. Nobody in England wanted this war. Not even me, and I'm a Scot."

A muffled laugh went around the room.

"It'll be my honor to escort *Shamrock* to New York," said Vanderbilt. "We might be the last two civilian vessels allowed back into the Harbor. The US Coast Guard are closing down all recreational boating beyond the Verrazano Narrows."

"You really think we can be there in five or six days, under sail alone?" asked Burton.

"A week, at the outside, so long as we don't run into any Germans," said Vanderbilt calmly. "How many crew do you have available at this point?"

"Half of them must return with *Erin* to England, with a couple of question marks. The remainder are either too young or too old to enlist, or they're foreign nationals. Which leaves roughly seventeen, plus three Scandinavians from *Erin*'s regular crew."

"And that's enough to sail *Shamrock* to New York?"

"Yes, plenty," said Burton. "We're jury-rigged for the crossing. The topmast and boom are lashed down on deck. We'll need to transfer the rest of her racing gear across from *Erin*."

"There's room for a few extra sails and spars on *Vagrant*, if it would help," offered Vanderbilt. "And of course, Sir Thomas, there's a very comfortable cabin for you on *Vagrant*, if you change your mind."

"I'm terribly grateful to you, old boy, but I'd better put in an appearance back in England. I won't forget this, though!" Sir Thomas clapped Vanderbilt on the shoulder. "And by golly—I was impressed with the way you brought that pretty schooner of yours in through the reefs yesterday. We were watching for you from the headland. That fog came down like a ton of bricks! Quite a feat of seamanship."

"I have my New England fishermen to thank for that."

"Is that so?" Lipton took a sip of his brandy.

Lt. Harris, a little impatient, interjected: "Gentlemen, if you'll forgive me, there is urgent business with regard to *Erin*'s requisition. As soon as refueling and provisioning are complete, she will depart for Plymouth under the flag of the Red Cross, transporting a company from the Bermuda Garrison. The Admiralty has provisionally granted Sir Lipton the naval rank of Commander until you reach England. I have your commission here, sir..."

Harris produced a document on Royal Navy letterhead, and continued. "We are concerned that two of *Erin*'s crewmen are unaccounted for since she docked in St. George's. If caught, they may be charged with failure to report. A third sailor was apprehended in the town square this morning, somewhat inebriated. He says his name is Jacob Haskell. He has no papers with him, but he claims to be an American national; says his younger brother is in *your* employment, Mr. Vanderbilt—one David Haskell? Can you verify this?"

Vanderbilt raised his eyebrows. "Well, yes—as it happens the lad came across with us on our skiff, you can talk to him yourself." He turned to Capt. Perham. "Would you fetch him in, please?"

Perham stepped out on deck, returning with Davey moments later. In his shabby white canvas ducks, it must have been clear to Lt. Harris that he had no identity papers on him either. He didn't bother to ask.

"State your full name and nationality?"

"David Haskell, sir. Born in Maine, USA." He looked sidelong at Harold Vanderbilt, as if to say, *am I in trouble?*

"Have you an older brother, Haskell?" questioned the Lieutenant.

Davey bit his lip, but did not reply.

After a moment Vanderbilt said, quietly: "Davey…?"

He cleared his throat. "I do have an older brother, yes, sir. Jacob."

Two hours after sunset on August 17th, a full moon had risen above the Eastern horizon to bathe the ocean in silver. A ridge of low cloud was clinging to the Gulf Stream, making it as clearly visible as the white cliffs of Dover from the English Channel. The moderate breeze that had blown from the Northeast all day had veered a little, and *Vagrant II* was sailing free under outer jib, foresail, and main. She was making barely six knots though the water; but the conveyor belt of currents was doubling her true speed towards her destination. At this rate, the skyscrapers of New York City could be within sight before the end of the following day.

Half a mile off *Vagrant*'s starboard quarter, swaying in the moonlit ocean, was *Shamrock IV*—a proud racing machine strangely hobbled by her cut-down mast, and her decks laden with spare sails and spars. The two yachts had sailed in company all the way from Bermuda, maintaining radio silence per the instructions of the Admiralty, and communicating only with flags.

Davey was on the first watch of the night. There was not much work to do, and he was joined on the foredeck by the topmastman, Aksel, who made him laugh with a long story about his mad granny and her pig farm in Norrbotten. A loose halyard was smacking against the gaff, and Aksel went aloft to make it fast.

Then, silence. As *Vagrant* carved into each successive swell, the blanket of her bow wave hissed out behind and disappeared in blackness. Looking aft, Davey could see the silhouette of Harold Vanderbilt, with one hand on a spoke of the wheel, his face lit by the glow of his pipe. His legs were slightly astride to ride the roll of the deck, and his gaze was fixed on the compass, with an occasional glance around the horizon or up at the trim of the sails.

The bell rang for nine o'clock. Jeb the cook appeared in the gangway with a tray of hot cocoa, and Vanderbilt called the sailors of the night watch back to the helm. Davey took a mug and warmed his hands on it. "Wind's dying, Jeb," he said. "We're slowing down."

Jeb gazed out across the dark water to the West. "Pay-shunt man, him ride dankey," said Jeb.

"You're a right fountain of wisdom tonight," quipped Davey.

"What you so uptight about now, little fisherman?"

Davey said nothing. Jeb scratched a sideburn and jutted out his chin. "Ya get nuttin' from a pig but a grunt!" He turned and ducked his head down into the companionway.

Davey crossed to the starboard shrouds. The moon was high overhead now. Across the expanse of silver ocean, there was *Shamrock IV.* He studied her intently, wondering if his lying brother was on deck, or halfway up in the rigging, staring back at him through the darkness.

The swells flattened a little as *Vagrant* neared the center of the Gulf Stream's powerful northerly current, where a broken line of clouds was throwing dappled moonlight onto the water. The wind had come aft of the beam, and Vanderbilt called to the crew for the mainsheet to be eased.

"Davey," he said, as the other sailors moved away forward. "Come here and take the wheel."

Davey tried to keep his face impassive, as if steering a luxury schooner was an everyday occurrence for him. He stepped up to the wheel in his bare feet, and gripped the spokes, elbows and knees rigid. He peered over the coachroof on tiptoes, as if there were obstacles in the ocean he would need to swerve to avoid.

Vanderbilt laughed. "You can relax your grip a little," he said. "Fall in with the rhythm, and don't over-correct. Keep an eye on the luff of the main. The moment it softens, bear away a touch and keep it full. There, see? You don't need me to tell you how to sail. It's really no different from your little sloop—the same principles apply. Things just happen more slowly, and with greater force."

Davey took a deep breath, and gave himself over to the roll of the swells, until he began to feel it. He could sense Vanderbilt's eyes on him. He glanced down at the compass in its illuminated brass binnacle.

"Your course is three-fifty-five, but don't feel you have to be glued to the compass. Look, up there, to the right of the mast? The bright star?"

"It's Arcturus, isn't it?"

"Correct. Keep Arcturus between the foremast and shrouds, and you'll be bang on course."

The way the Polynesians did it, Davey thought. Vanderbilt settled into the cockpit bench, adjusted the cushion and leaned back. He reached into his pocket for a slim silver whisky flask, and tipped a small shot into his cocoa.

Davey could feel Vanderbilt watching the way he handled the wheel. He paid close attention to his steering. Sometimes a little more wind pressure would heel the schooner more and dip her lee rail, and his natural reflex was to ease her head up to level her off. In the lull that followed, he would gently bear away again, setting her back on course. Was he doing it right? He'd learned to sail at an early age, on his Pa's clinker-built fifteen-footer. Vanderbilt also learned as a boy. But Vanderbilt had surely learned to steer big racing yachts like this as soon as he was tall enough to hold the wheel.

"You ever miss your home?" asked Vanderbilt.

Davey flicked the salt-encrusted hair away from his face. "Deer Isle? Not much to miss, really. Same routine, day in day out, whatever the weather, dropping lobster pots and pulling 'em back up. Some gill fishing, as well, though the cod's close to fished out. We're down to about twenty-five boats in the East Bay fleet now. Used to be a lot more in my Pa's time."

"Pretty hard to make a living, I would imagine?"

"No one's getting rich off it, that's for certain," Davey laughed. "We get by though, I guess."

He was telling this to a man who'd never needed to "get by" in his life. Why did he feel ashamed?

"What's it like for you?" Davey asked.

"What's what like?"

"*Being* you. I mean... your family's got everything, right? Railroads, polo fields, racing cars. Big palaces. Cripes, your sister's a duchess!" He shook his head. "I just can't imagine it. All the same..." he moved to the side, steering with one hand so he could turn around and have a conversation.

"Yes?" Vanderbilt was smiling at him, as if waiting for him to trip himself up.

"Well, you've always been kind to me, and generous. It's like, you know I'm smart, and you know I can sail all right. You're not what I expected, is all. You're sorta... *normal*."

Vanderbilt pushed his spectacles up his nose. When he finally spoke, it was just audible over the bubbling wake behind *Vagrant's* rudder.

"Actually, Davey, the fact is you're a breath of fresh air, compared to the people I usually hang around with. You have no idea how stuffy and boring my life can be. I'm on the boards of five different companies. I have to sit through meetings of the shareholders, mergers and acquisitions, audits, government depositions—interminable business negotiations. I'm surrounded by sycophants.... gossip columnists, society matrons and matchmakers; gold-digging debutantes. It drives me out of my mind. I wake up some mornings and can't be bothered to dress, or go into the office. I prefer to just go sailing, in my pajamas. Out here, we're hundreds of miles away from all that... that rubbish. Just us, and the wind and the waves."

Davey nodded.

He relit his pipe and took a long draw. "Look at this schooner, will you? Total mastery of nature and the elements. The culmination of all Nat Herreshoff's design genius. The sweat and skill and craftsmanship went into this boat, resulting in a thing of utter beauty, like a... Leonardo, or a Schubert aria. Only a handful of yachts on this scale are completed in a year, anywhere in the world. How come *I* get to be the one to enjoy her? How did I deserve this? Just because my father, and his father, and *his* father had..."

"Big piles of cash?" quipped Davey.

"...considerable business acumen." Vanderbilt threw a loose cushion, which hit Davey between the shoulder blades. "*And* big piles of cash. But my father hated what he inherited, all that responsibility he was lumped with. And he took it out on his kids—when we saw him, which was not often. Most of the time we were alone with our governess, in a big drafty mansion on Fifth Avenue. Long dark corridors, and scary gargoyles on the roof. I don't recall any real affection between him and my mother, either. She hated the family business more than he did. Know what she said?"

"What?"

"She said: 'the railroads enable the working classes to move around more than they ought.' Ha! Father was more interested in racehorses. When I was eighteen he ran away to his château in France, leaving me and my brother to run the businesses. I think I loathe it even more than Willy does. I'll tell you, Davey, there are times when I'd happily swap it all for a fishing sloop in Deer Isle."

"No you wouldn't, mate."

They both got the giggles. They triggered each other, until Davey had to hold his stomach to stop his sides from splitting.

"It's a bloody shite life, if you really want to know!" he managed to say. "You'd freeze your balls off up there. No no, Mr. Vanderbilt—you should enjoy this, because you can. You have to enjoy it enough for all of us."

"Harold."

"Beg your pardon?"

Vanderbilt composed himself. "I'm 'Harold,' to my close friends. And I'd like to think of you that way. Not in front of the other men—but please feel free to call me Harold, when we're alone."

Davey shrugged, carelessly, but he felt a warm glow of pride.

"Harold, then. Okay." He shifted his weight to the other foot and glanced over his other shoulder. "Hmm, *Shamrock*'s caught up just a dite in the last hour, looks like?"

"Yes, I've been watching. It's these smoother seas. See the way she seems to accelerate in the puffs? Impressive really, given how little canvas she's flying, with that jury rig. That's one slippery hull. Did you get a good look at the shape of it?"

"I did. Different to our American boats, that's for sure," said Davey. "Her bow's sorta stunted, isn't it? And that weird beamy tumbledown."

"Well, Lipton's got nothing to lose at this point. He encouraged Charles Nicholson to take a whole new approach. Triple-skinned mahogany on a steel frame, massive sail area, and a flatter bottom. Retractable centerboard. Boxy stern. Quite a departure from the other *Shamrocks*."

"It'll add up to better hull speed?"

"Theoretically, a boat's maximum speed is a factor of waterline length and displacement. But if you can design a hull that rises up as the boat gathers speed, like a power boat, that equation may not apply any more. The sky's the limit, really."

"So you think Nicholson may be onto something?"

"He's a pretty smart designer. He built a schooner called *Margherita* that kicked the pants off *Westward*. Which gave Captain Nat pause for thought! *Shamrock IV*'s no looker, that's for sure, but she'll be damn fast, I reckon. Might give *Vanitie* a real run for her money. If we ever get a Cup series—"

"Oh, so it's definitely *Vanitie*, not *Resolute*, then?"

Vanderbilt checked himself. "You didn't hear it from me. Agreed?"

"I was pretty sure the Board was gonna give it to *Resolute* after the trials," he said. "There wasn't much between them, speed-wise. But... all due respect, because I know he's your friend—Mr. Cochran's a bloody disaster when he's on the helm, if you ask me."

"That's what you think?"

"I can't lie. He acts like it's all in the name of the sport, but he'll cause a serious collision one day, or a sinking even, if you was to let him loose on the Brits."

"Confidentially, I wouldn't call Alex Cochran a friend, not these days. We had a bit of a falling-out. A big one, actually."

"Over the way he sails?"

"And some personal stuff. Nothing I care to talk about. Fair to say, I don't think we'll be sailing together going forward."

Personal stuff. His mind turned to Jacob—Jacob, who might be watching him right now, for all he knew, across the water. His brow tightened into a frown, and he gripped the wheel until his knuckles were white.

"What's the story with you and your brother?" Vanderbilt asked. It was as if he was telepathic. "You practically disowned him, back there in St. George's."

Davey's head dropped, and he felt a sourness in the pit of his stomach. Rapid images flashed through his mind—Jake running off to sea, Ma hunched over her stove; Edith, innocent lovely Edith, in her shame—his lips pursed tight, and he turned his face away in case his eyes misted over. He chose not to answer.

"Here, let me show you." Vanderbilt stepped forward alongside him at the helm, placing his left hand on a spoke of the wheel, and the right on top of Davey's left. "I'll teach you how to sail this boat *fast*. See, every stronger puff you get, I can tell your instinct is to head up to meet it—which works in a smaller boat. In a big schooner like this, though, on a reach, you want to head up a touch during the *lulls*, not the puffs— that'll get you to up the next puff sooner. Watch the color of the water to windward. You can even see it at night. Where it's shiny, that's a lull, so ease her up to punch through it. Just as the next puff hits, *that's* when you bear away, and you stay in it for as long as you can. The darker the water, the stronger the puff."

With his hand on Davey's, Vanderbilt eased *Vagrant* up to meet the next puff, then bore away, riding it downwind with the bonus of an ocean swell underneath him. He had a gentle touch. "Feel that? Go easy on the helm. Let *it* steer you. Keep water flowing smoothly over the planes of the rudder and the hull—you don't want it to turn to bubbles. Disrupt the flow, it's like putting on the hand brake. Oh— you've probably never driven an automobile, have you? Well, maybe I'll teach you that one day, as well."

"I'd look a right ponce rolling into Stonington in one of those things."

Vanderbilt chuckled. "I expect you would. Tell me, the older sailors in Deer Isle, do they still talk about the Cup campaigns of the nineties, ever? *Defender, Vigilant?*"

"All the time. It makes our town so proud," he said. "But it's as if those was the... golden years, and we're nothing, me and my brother's generation, 'cos we missed it. That's why we was all so excited when you turned up, you and Mr. Cochran in the *Nemesis*."

"Must have felt like your chance to prove yourselves. To your dad, to the others?"

"Ayuh. But I'm not under any illusions about that. 'Specially the *Defender* boys."

"Oh?"

Davey flicked the hair out of his eyes. "You probably know more than I do, being from the Club and all. About Iselin, and Herreshoff, and everything."

"What do you mean?"

The stars were behind a thick layer of cloud now, and Davey switched his gaze to the compass in the binnacle. 355 degrees, on the nose. He had to choose his words carefully.

"You told me how Mr. Herreshoff's a genius. Always trying out new innovations, isn't he? Every new yacht he designs?"

"An absolute genius." Vanderbilt slid his hand down the column beside the wheel, where he flicked on a panel light that illuminated the streamlined electrical console, and its dazzling array of gauges.

"Look at these gauges. Engine oil, temperature, revolutions. This one's a true wind indicator—links to an anemometer at the top of the foremast. Right now, you see, we've got around eleven knots, and eighty-five degrees. Most instruments can only tell you the *apparent* wind, of course, as that's all the sails know about. The *apparent* wind's usually a bit stronger, and more on your nose. But this one gives you the *true* wind, factoring in your speed through the water. It's a first, in yacht navigation. All Herreshoff's idea, of course."

He was changing the subject, but Davey went along with it.

"The dial goes up to fifty knots?"

"Yes. In that kind of wind, the instruments wouldn't be much help, would they?" Vanderbilt joked. "Actually, I need to get Herreshoff's people to re-position it in the console so I can read it more easily."

"And this one?"

"That's the Fessenden Oscillator. Might be all the rage soon, but it's quite experimental, for now. The antenna's under the waterline."

"How does it work?"

"The same way fish communicate, oddly enough. My cousin Neily is an investor. Fessenden's building a network of U.S. lightships and buoys that transmit long distance sub-aqua radio signals. It's mainly funded by the White Star Line—they've been pressing hard for it since the *Titanic* went down in '12—it'll detect icebergs, apparently. Even submarines. But the rollout was put on hold this year due to the threat of war, and the U-boats in the Atlantic."

"It can really hear *submarines*?" asked Davey, glancing around the horizon.

"Even the shape of the seabed, one day, they claim."

"Jeezum Crow. We coulda used that, getting in to Bermuda last week, in that dungeon o' fog."

Vanderbilt smiled. "Well, at this point I'd put more faith in your traditional Deer Isle methods, frankly. But all these innovations will come into their own one day."

"Like pumping water in to *Defender* for extra ballast?" said Davey.

"Oh." Vanderbilt let go the wheel and took a step back. They both stared straight ahead in silence. A moment passed, and he said, "You'd better tell me what you know."

"I know what went on below decks. Jake told me."

"I see." Vanderbilt stuttered over his words: "They were… experimenting with all sorts of new ideas, looking for an extra half knot of boat speed—"

"It was illegal under the Cup rules, wasn't it?"

"That's a very serious accusation, Davey."

"But it's true, isn't it!" He was reaching, hoping Vanderbilt would fall for his bluff. "After all, Mr. Iselin grew up racing sandbaggers, you said? I'm sure he knew all about the benefits of movable ballast."

"It was before my time. My father was head of the *Defender* syndicate. He told me the whole story years later, after all the squabbling had died down."

"What *was* the story?" Davey was staring at Arcturus, and concentrating on the steering, but he could feel Vanderbilt was scanning his profile.

"You'll keep it to yourself?"

Davey shrugged again. "I'm just interested in how yacht design has changed since back then. It was twenty years ago. Before I was even born."

"Well, in the trials, *Defender* had a hollow rudder. You could flood it with something like eleven tonnes of sea water. It was an early prototype for the one that ended up in *Reliance*—but by then it was approved by the Committee. In '95 it was pretty revolutionary. Herreshoff wanted to patent the idea, and maybe offer it as an option on all his yachts. The idea was that you flood the bladder for the upwind leg, which lowers the center of gravity and trims the helm. Then for the downwind leg you expel the water with a foot pump."

Davey nodded. "Makes sense. Did it work?"

"Over the course of the trials, it didn't really seem to give *Defender* a speed advantage, so they never declared it to the measurers. Herreshoff said the bladder should be sealed up, so there'd be no controversy over the rules."

"But that never happened?"

"Well, according to my father, when *Defender* was beaten on the second day of the Cup series—albeit because *Valkyrie* fouled her and was disqualified—the Syndicate got nervous. Iselin had never lost a Cup race before. There was a strong blow forecast for the third day, and Iselin called for the bladder to be flooded overnight. He didn't tell Herreshoff, of course, because Herreshoff would have insisted Iselin declare it to the measurers. It was only an advantage if no-one else knew about it. But next morning Dunraven spotted *Defender* sitting lower in the water. He jumped to the conclusion that Iselin ordered pig lead be brought on board during the night. So he quit the series, and all hell broke loose—"

"Why couldn't Iselin just come clean?" Davey said. "About the bladder?"

"It was a grey area. The *Racing Rules of Sailing* state that you can't have movable ballast. He could have declared it—arguing that nothing in the rules specifically defined sea water as ballast. But that would have been to risk getting disqualified altogether. And he'd have gone down in history as the man that lost the America's Cup."

"But if he covered it up and then got... exposed, he'd be branded as a cheat—"

"Exactly," said Vanderbilt. "It wasn't only his reputation at stake: it was the honor of the N.Y.Y.C, and the integrity of the America's Cup itself. My father told Iselin it was all on him, and if the truth ever came out, the Syndicate would deny all knowledge of it."

Davey whistled through his lips. "He'd backed himself into a corner."

"Yes. But then he got lucky. Dunraven had made a stink about the New York spectator fleet, saying he was being deliberately impeded. Iselin used his influence, and the New York papers started saying Dunraven was just a sore loser—I mean, he broke Iselin's topmast, and whined about it! Then Dunraven got back to London and went out on a limb with some wild claim about pig ballast and, well, the public didn't believe him. He became an international laughing stock, and the N.Y.Y.C. expelled him."

Davey let it sink in. So that's what Armitage was hinting at! He must have known his boss bent the rules, and the whole *Defender* crew was in on the trickery. But Pa was the one on the pumps. The mere idea of it filled Davey with revulsion. Pa was an honest, God-fearing man. How could he have let himself get roped in to that? No wonder he got sick.

He had one last chance to eke the truth out of Vanderbilt. "You're saying, Iselin won the Cup—but only if he could make the Deer Islers shut up about the bladder?"

Vanderbilt's face grew very long. He took a couple of breaths. "Look, I don't know about that. Truly, I don't. I was ten years old. My father told me about it much later, when I joined the Club and started getting interested in racing. He never mentioned anything about... witness tampering, if that's what you're suggesting."

"Of course not. I'm just saying Iselin must have found some way to keep the crew quiet—"

"Or maybe just waited for the heat to die down. After a while the newspapers lost interest in poor old Dunraven. The public forgot all about him, and moved on. Readers were more interested in how many millions *Reliance* cost, and Tommy Lipton's mustache, his showgirls and his tea houses."

"And there's no… evidence, no proof of any of this anywhere, I bet?"

"Oh, locked away in the safe at 44th Street, perhaps." Vanderbilt downed the dregs of his cocoa, staring at Davey intently. "Or not."

Best not to dwell on it, he thought. He would do some more digging when he got home. Not that anyone in Deer Isle would likely tell him the truth. Who could? John Armitage—that was who. He was *there*. He would go see Mr. Armitage, ask some questions, find out what really went on below *Defender*'s decks and what, if anything, Pa had to do with it.

"So how do *you* feel about all this, Harold?" Davey said quietly. It felt odd to use his Christian name.

"Well. I don't like it, not a bit. But it's all part of the Club's legacy. As a younger member, you're an heir apparent. You climb the rungs of the ladder, you inherit the legacy, the good and the bad. It's the same with my family. I look at some of what we've done, and there are things I'm not proud of. But we do a lot of good in the world, too. It evens out."

They stood in silence for a few moments, swaying with *Vagrant*'s gentle motion. The stars were starting to fade. Vanderbilt pulled out the nautical chart, glanced at his timepiece, and pointed out their rough position.

"Captain Perham should be up in a few minutes for the second watch. You're done a fine job on the helm, Davey. Very nice work. I'll head below now to rest. My cabin's right under here. Just thump on the deck if you need me."

He disappeared down the companionway steps, leaving Davey alone at the helm.

Seventeen, and helming of one of the most beautiful wooden schooners on the planet. He could feel her pulse: it flowed through the bare soles of his feet, and the spokes in his hands. How he hoped Jacob was watching him right now, somewhere high in the rigging of *Shamrock IV*, steering this 130ft beauty like a veteran. He gazed up at the billowing sails, then off towards the eastern horizon, and took in a deep lungful of the pristine Atlantic air. It was all a lot to process.

A quarter-mile away, in the silver corridor of moonlight, something massive breached the surface. It swayed there for a second, the salt water gushing off its barnacled flukes; then with barely a ripple it plunged back into the ocean, a thousand feet down into the depths.

His heartbeat slowed. Had he really just seen that? He'd heard of strange hallucinations, at sea. He checked over his shoulder at *Shamrock*—if Jacob was on watch, surely he must have seen it too. But when he stared back at the same spot, the pool of empty moonlight was unbroken.

At 4am, the ship's bell broke in to his trance. Capt. Perham stepped out onto the deck with the five bleary-eyed sailors of the second watch in tow. The breeze was dying; Perham called for topsails, and the sleepy topmastmen went aloft. Davey showed him their position on the chart, and gave him the compass bearing: 355 degrees, and a hundred and ten miles of ocean between them and New York City.

The sky was paling now, the stars all but extinguished. He turned to go below, with a last glance at the corridor of glassy moonlight to the northeast; then back over the starboard quarter at *Shamrock IV*. Maybe Jacob was there, watching him. But he didn't need his brother to tell him what he'd just seen.

At the foot of the darkened stairway, he hesitated for a moment by the door of the master suite. There was a faint aroma of tobacco. Shafts of light crept across the planks of the floorboards from the louvered blinds, moving from side to side with the sway of the boat. He felt physically unable to step on them. He listened. All he could hear was the rushing of water under the hull, and the sound of his own breathing. After a few moments he hopped over the shafts of light and tiptoed forward to his bunk in the crew quarters.

CHAPTER NINETEEN

As the two yachts sailed through the Verrazzano Narrows, a motor torpedo boat departing for the Atlantic fired a triple salute from its bow gun, with a dozen uniformed seamen waving from its stern rail. The moderate southerly wind had held through the day, and the yachts were making a brisk ten knots on the flood tide. It was a drab, grey evening with no sunset, and Davey saw the famous first view of the Statue of Liberty looming in the haze, and the skyscrapers of lower Manhattan, where the lights were just coming on.

They were able to use the radio now, to alert New York of the yachts' imminent arrival. He imagined tomorrow's newspaper headlines: Lipton's Ugly Duckling Arrives in New York... *Shamrock IV* Braves U-boat Infested Waters... Great Personal Risk to Heroic Harold Vanderbilt...

At Bay Ridge, a Harbor pilot's launch pulled alongside to escort *Shamrock* and *Vagrant* to their berths in the East River. The pilot, a ruddy-faced man in a peaked cap, hailed *Vagrant* through a brass speaking trumpet and saluted Capt. Perham. He climbed aboard via the rope ladder.

"I have a telegram here..." he reached in his coat pocket, "...for a Mr. Jebediah Livingstone."

Surprised, Perham took it and said: "Thank you. We'll make sure he gets it."

The pilot told them they were indeed the last two vessels into the Harbor before it was closed to civilian traffic. In the Buttermilk Channel, with dusk falling, a fast motor launch approached from the

City. On its deck were a gaggle of excited news reporters, in Homburg hats and overcoats; with their flashbulbs popping, they made several foamy circles around the two sailboats. Then the first of the spectator boats arrived on the scene, amid hoots and whistles. By the time the yachts finally dropped their sails near the eastern span of the Brooklyn Bridge, and *Vagrant* fired up her diesel engines, the noisy flotilla had swelled to twenty vessels. The two yachts were surrounded, bathed in a pool of searchlights. A Harbor tug towed *Shamrock* into her berth at Dock 72. *Vagrant* tied up at the next open berth, tucked in behind the stern of a rusting hulk of a Confederate ironclad.

It was fully dark now, but Brooklyn Navy Yard was buzzing with activity. Heavy cranes loaded supplies and ammunition onto two British warships, and the relentless hammering of construction echoed round the dry docks. The air was thick with soot and smoke. A few dozen onlookers jostled for a peek at Sir Thomas Lipton's pea-green challenger as she moored alongside the wharf. Reporters crowded the quay with notepads open, shouting to the sailors, hungry for a quote. There was even a Pathé newsman cranking a box camera.

Harold Vanderbilt, in white flannels and a cricket sweater, watched demurely from *Vagrant*'s cockpit as the gangway was lowered. He stepped ashore with his attaché case under his arm, and hair perfectly kempt, to meet his limousine. The gaggle of reporters that had rushed along the dock encircled him, peppering him with questions; he waved them away, regally. A chauffeured Rolls-Royce Silver Ghost edged forward, parting the crowd, and the driver sprung round to hold open the door. Vanderbilt took a last proud glance back at *Vagrant II* before settling into the back seat. Then the Rolls pulled away, flashing cameras pressed to its windows.

Davey was coiling ropes on *Vagrant*'s foredeck. He watched the Rolls drive the length of the wharf to where *Shamrock IV* was moored. It slowed there momentarily, tailpipe panting in the night air. He spotted a lone figure, climbing from *Shamrock*'s deck up the steps to the dock.

It was his brother Jacob, with his kit bag over his shoulder. An icy jolt ran up Davey's spine.

The rear window wound down, and Jacob leaned in. Words were exchanged. Then he got in, and the door closed behind him. The Silver Ghost rolled away along the damp cobblestones, lit only by the sparks from the torches of acetylene welders on the side of a British destroyer.

Davey found Jeb at the table in the galley. His face was buried in his hands, the open telegram beside him. Davey said kindly: "What's occurin', Jeb?"

The big man didn't speak, at first. He kept his face hidden. Finally he sat up, and his almond eyes were full of tears. "It's from Mary Armitage, John's sister in Ohio," he said, cradling the telegram. "John died, on Monday. At Bellevue Hospital. It was pneumonia. The funeral's next week."

He could see Jeb was trying to compose himself, but it must have felt like a dagger in his heart.

"He'd been sick for a while, hadn't he? Oh Lord, I'm so sorry, Jeb. I know you and Mr. Armitage were close." He flashed on his own Pa, and imagined never seeing him again.

"There was so much I wanted to say to him. We never had a chance to say goodbye. Him and me were together on the *Nemesis* for twelve years."

Davey put an arm around Jeb's burly shoulder. He was trying to keep his own emotions together for Jeb's sake, but they were shot to shreds. He was barely treading water. Poor Edith. Her father—gone. And all the memories lost, that died along with him!

Memories. Evidence. Secrets.

"Jeb, what would you have said?"

"That I appreciate all he's done for me. That I promise to take good care of his daughter." Jeb wiped his nose on his sleeve. "That I'll be a good father to his grandson."

The low clouds above 44th St. were criss-crossed with floodlights, and the whole front of the Clubhouse was brilliantly illuminated for the gala reception. The crowd milling outside was a friendly crowd, this time, packed with sports fans and autograph hunters, chattering excitedly about the brave *Shamrock IV* sailors had sailed across the U-boat infested waters of the Atlantic; and about Harold Vanderbilt and his gallant American crew, who had risked all to sail to Bermuda and guide the British challenger safely in to New York.

From an unlit doorway on the far side of 44th, Davey surveyed the scene, unnoticed. Motor cars were pulling up to drop off celebrity guests at the red carpet. Sam the Doorman was on duty next to the velvet rope, unclipping it for members and their wives, with a whistle round his neck to direct traffic. A police officer was posted either side of the front door, prepared for any crowd trouble; but it was a joyous occasion.

He watched the library on the third floor, waiting patiently for the lights to go out, which would tell him Squigley had finally left to go home to his dogs. He was still in his *Vagrant II* ducks, in the Vanderbilt colors, unwashed. He'd slept in them; or tossed in his bunk, rather. Sleep eluded him. The news of Mr. Armitage's death was deeply worrying. How would he ever know the truth now, about his Pa? What went on beneath the decks of the *Defender*—and what really happened between Oliver Iselin and the Deer Isle boys? If there were answers, they were locked in that safe, up there in the library.

And if his hunch was right, he reckoned he had a shot at guessing the combination.

A man's silhouette appeared at the last window and briefly parted the curtains. Davey ducked back into the shadows. The lights went out in rapid succession. Soon, his moment would come.

He crossed the street and weaved through the crowd, making a beeline for the red carpet. Sam looked resplendent in his top hat and tailcoat. He beamed a big smile. "Davey! I barely recognized you. What, you growin' a beard now?" He unclipped the velvet rope. "Hey, the party's already started, you oughta be in there celebrating with the *Shamrock* boys."

"Sam, have you seen my brother, Jacob?"

"Long black hair, built like a brick shithouse? Yeah, reckon I seen him. Nearly didn't let him in, he was already three sheets to the wind."

Davey nodded. "That's him. Who else is here?"

"Lemme see—all the *Shamrocks*—most of your buddies from *Vagrant*—bunch of the flag officers, Fish, Harry Whitney, Schwab, Butler Duncan. Ogden Blum. Alex Cochran too. You lookin' for someone in particular?"

"Squigley still here?"

Sam glanced up over his shoulder to the fourth floor. "Gone home."

"How about Harold Vanderbilt?"

"Mr. Vanderbilt? Nah, we ain't expectin' him tonight. Heard he was headed out to Long Island for the polo tomorrow."

"You're a pal, Sam. Listen, I have to run up and get something from the library. If Mr. Vanderbilt does pull up, give me three blasts on your whistle, okay?"

Sam looked dubious. "What are you up to, Davey?"

"Thanks. It's important. I'll catch up with you later." He smacked Sam playfully on the arm and strode past into the lobby.

It was brightly lit, and crowded with merry people clamoring to get to the free bar—members and guests, Navy officers, and several bewildered-looking English sailors. Davey had to push his way through. He spotted his favorite Southern coat check girl behind the cloak room counter, and smiled at her from across the lobby. She beckoned him over.

"Well hello, sailor boy. Don't you look handsome, though!"

"Hello Millie. How the heck are you?"

"Finer than frog hair split four ways. Hey, Pete Royston's looking for you. Said to go see him right away if you showed up."

"Do me a favor, Millie—don't let Royston know I'm here."

"Whatever you say. Speaking of favors, sweet cheeks—" she gave her chest a little jiggle—"when am I gonna get me some of that good Deer Isle lovin'?"

He laughed awkwardly. "Remind me to introduce you to my brother Jake."

"Oh, I'm pretty sure I already met your hounddog of a brother. He's up there now, drunker'n Cooter Brown."

The Model Room party in was in full swing, with music, laughter, and the chinking of glasses. But he peeled off and hared up the staircase.

"Take your sweet time, why don't ya, sailor boy?" Millie called after him, leaning over her counter.

Just as he reached the first floor landing, the din from the party changed in timbre.

"Gentlemen!" he heard a muffled voice boom out. It sounded familiar, and loud enough to still the chatter in the crowd. He paused by the faux panel door, conflicted, and bit his lip. Then he slipped through the door and out on to the darkened gallery that looked down on the Model Room. He crept round the perimeter to where he could peer down through the carved stone above the fireplace.

The room was packed. Alexander Cochran, swaying visibly, was standing on a table with a half-empty bottle of Moët and Chandon in his fist. His tie was undone, and his mustache—formerly an homage to the Kaiser's—was these days styled in a more acceptable chevron. He slammed the heel of a leather riding boot on the tabletop. It echoed around the crowded room, reverberating off the half-hulls of the model yachts. A hush fell.

"Gentlemen, I would like to offer a warm Yankee toast to our good friends from the other side of the pond. To the brave crew of *Shamrock IV*."

"*Shamrock IV!*"

Fifty members in black tie raised their glasses and toasted a group of rather dazed-looking British and Swedish seamen. And there, in the midst of them, was Jacob, with flushed cheeks and a stupid grin on his face. Davey stayed hidden in the shadows.

Cochran launched into his speech, gesticulating with his bottle in between slugs. "What fine sailors you fellows must be, to have made it across the Atlantic under sail alone, during a time of open hostilities! What fine sailors, indeed, to have made it across the Atlantic... at *all*, in that..." (he paused, as if searching for the right word) "... in that... *ugly* fucking green abomination of a sailboat..."

An explosion of guffaws and mock-outrage filled the room. He went on: "... an abomination that certain people—who shall remain nameless, but you know who you are, Ogden Blum—*scandalously* claim is the fastest racing yacht ever built!"

Rosy faces turned to the bar, where the diminutive Ogden Blum—decked out in a dark burgundy velvet suit and yellow gingham waistcoat—gave a half-smile and raised his Martini glass to the room.

Cochran continued: "Now, I have it on very good authority—my *own*—that such a title rightly belongs to one boat, and one boat alone—a certain bronze-hulled beauty of an *American* racer by the name of *Vanitie*."

The members cheered this enthusiastically. *Shamrock*'s men weren't applauding. They looked uncomfortable, trying to take it in good humor.

"What a shame, then—what a damned shame that this idiot war in Europe has denied us the chance to prove, once and for all, that *American* designs and *American* seamanship are the finest on the high seas. So—" He wiped his mouth on his sleeve, pausing for effect. "The America's Cup shall remain bolted to its plinth in the alcove there, where it's been since '51. But tonight I issue a challenge,"—he turned to the oil painting above the fireplace, and his booming voice cranked up another notch—"to Sir Thomas Lipton, across the water. I challenge you to a race, sir! A private match race—my *Vanitie* against your *Shamrock IV*…"

In an instant, the crowd seemed to sober up.

"… a race around the Island of Manhattan, for a purse of one million dollars, in cash, to the winner."

There was a collective intake of breath as it sank in. Then a slow crescendo of applause swelled, until it reached a deafening ovation. Glasses were hastily refilled. Debate spread like wildfire.

Davey caught snippets of excited quarreling: a race around Manhattan—such an original idea! But madness, surely, in yachts of this size? The current… the shallows on the Jersey side… the narrow bends of the Harlem River… and what about overhead clearances—the Queensboro, the Williamsburg, the Brooklyn Bridge? It couldn't be done with topsails or spinnakers, that was for certain. Could these cutters even sail with no topmast? Certainly. *Shamrock* had crossed the Atlantic with hers lashed down on her deck…

More than a few of the members seemed to be shaking hands on private side bets. The Champagne flowed, and a jazz record blasted from the gramophone. The party was hopping.

The *Shamrock IV* boys were now mixing merrily with the Club members and visiting British Navy officers. Jacob was there, in a circle of gents clearly charmed with his down east wit. Even as he held court, Jake kept scanning the flushed faces around him like he was expecting someone. He pushed his way through the throng, working the room. Eventually he seemed to give up the search, and sauntered over to the bar, where Pete Royston began to refill his champagne glass. Jake snatched the freshly opened bottle of Moët out of his hands, and joined on the end of a passing conga line.

Davey withdrew into the shadows and ducked back along the gallery, towards the stairwell. He would have to work fast now, before word got back to Royston that he was in the building.

On the deserted half-landing, he found what he was looking for.

It was a giant painting commemorating the famous yacht race off the Isle of Wight, and the celebrated schooner *America* that stole the trophy away from under the Royal Yacht Squadron's nose. He squinted to read the inscription in the bottom corner of the canvas. There it was, in fine black strokes, right above the artist's signature: *100 Guinea Cup, IoW 22.8.51.*

Of course. The painter was English. He had the numbers the wrong way around in his mind. He just hoped his gut feeling was correct.

He raced up the remaining flight of stairs to the library, muffling his steps as best he could. The merriment from the party was still echoing up the stairwell, but the upper floors of the building were silent. The domestic staff must have gone to bed. Squigley would be warm at home by now, tucked up with his Pomeranians. He felt in his pocket for his key.

To his surprise, the door was not locked. He turned the handle, slipped inside the darkened library, and closed it carefully behind him, shutting out the sound of the party. The familiar musty book smell filled his nostrils. His heart was beating like a drum, and he could feel rivers of perspiration on his neck. The library was illuminated only by the gaslight from 44th Street, three stories below, where he could hear the murmur of the crowd. Occasionally a motor car or omnibus passed, lighting up the ceiling. He crossed the rug and crept into the alcove behind Squigley's desk; and there, in the shadows, was the massive Victor safe, with its three brass dials.

Kneeling on the hard floorboards, he clicked the first dial to the number 22. He spun the next one to 8, and the third to 51. He flexed his fingers, took a breath, and grabbed the hefty steel handle.

Yes!

The heavy door unlatched with a loud ka-*chunk*, and swung open on its sturdy hinges. The interior was entirely dark. He fumbled in his pocket for a match. To the left were two shelves, to the right a vertical partition. The top shelf held a stack of scrolled documents and a couple of large ledger books. The entire lower shelf was occupied by a shallow glass display case containing a hand-inscribed letter, on parchment, with four signatures and a wax seal. It was the Deed of Gift itself.

In the vertical partition were three leather portfolios. He lit a second match to check the labels, and found the one he wanted. It was marked '*Defender* vs *Valkyrie III* addendum, Nov. 1895.' He set the portfolio down on the desk and undid the string. It fell open easily, with a cloud of dust.

At first he thought it was empty. Damn! He was half-expecting to find the missing original pages from the plans. But as his eyes adjusted, he noticed a small, unsealed vellum envelope. Puzzled, he opened the envelope and took out its contents:

A narrow strip of celluloid film.

He took it carefully between his thumb and forefinger, holding it up to the light from the window. Made on Squigley's precious micrograph machine, evidently. With a nervous glance back at the library doors, he stepped over to the machine, and flipped on the brass toggle switch. The noisy fan came on. It took forever for the bulb to warm up; then he slipped the microfilm under the lens, projecting its spectral images on the crude screen. He swiveled a knob until it came in focus.

A handwritten caption on the side-strip read '*Defender*, February 1895.' The film showed the two original pages from the blueprints—a series of sectional diagrams of the yacht's hull, marked Page 9, and a more detailed view, marked Page 10, showing the yacht's keel from the side. The lower part of the keel was solid lead; but the upper part was hollow. And it had a visible inner membrane.

The bladder wasn't in *Defender*'s rudder—it was in her *keel*.

A tube led from the bladder to the hull, below the waterline; another led to a pump. Written on the blueprints, by hand, were the words: *+18 tonnes of water.*

Eighteen tonnes! With all that additional ballast pumped into the keel, the yacht's waterline would be considerably extended, and her maximum speed increased. She could fly more canvas, and the lowered center of gravity would help keep her upright to the wind, with all the power thrusting forward. No wonder it took two men to operate the pumps.

It was ingenious—and totally illegal.

Bringing his eyes closer to the screen, he noticed there was a crude depiction of two sailors in the rear of the hull, each with a foot on a pump. Davey pursed his lips and blew out. One of those men had to be his Pa.

A quiet voice from the shadows made Davey jump half out of his skin. "You might be interested in this little book, as well."

He spun around.

The man was relaxing in a leather armchair a few feet across the library. He was a tall figure, almost completely in darkness, aside from two diagonal bars of light across his neck and shoulder from the streetlamps outside.

"Hello, Davey."

An omnibus rattled past on 44th St, and for a moment the beams of its headlights lit up the ceiling. His heart was thumping as he tried to focus on the man's face.

A tumbler of whisky rested on the arm of the chair. The glare from the street seemed to pick up the crystal rim, and the frames of the man's wire spectacles, scorching Davey's eyes. In his other, outstretched hand, was a small black notebook.

It was Harold Vanderbilt.

The ceiling went dark again. Davey cleared his throat, and motioned to the book. "What is that?"

"It's a list of the witnesses at the *Dunraven* tribunal. Each man's first and last name, and alongside it, the amount he was paid to appear before the panel." Vanderbilt placed the notebook softly in his lap, and took a sip of his whisky. "I would imagine a hundred and fifty dollars was a lot of money to a working fisherman from Maine, back in '95? Half a year's wages, at least?"

Davey was speechless.

Vanderbilt tapped his fingernails on the cover. "It belonged to Oliver Iselin." He packed down the bowl of his pipe with his thumb, and struck a match on the side table, without ever taking his eyes off Davey. "But now you've seen the original blueprints, anyway. So you know the truth."

"You lied to me. It wasn't the rudder they were flooding—it was the keel. Eighteen tonnes of extra ballast."

"And a good few feet of additional waterline. A huge advantage, in a blow."

"Good old Captain Nat, eh?" said Davey sardonically. "Always one step ahead."

"What was your plan, exactly? Were you going to the press? Publish a pamphlet, maybe, like Dunraven? That didn't turn out so well for him."

Davey let out a long exhale. "There's no plan. I just—wanted to know for sure. I want Ma to know the truth, and Jacob."

"Well, they'll be relieved about one thing. There's no Ernie Haskell in this book," Vanderbilt said. "Looks like your dad was clean."

"But the rest of them... not so much?" He searched for a sign of warmth in Vanderbilt's expression, any sign, but it was cold and hard.

"So. What now?" Vanderbilt said. "I presume you're going to expose Iselin, and the Syndicate, and the Club?"

Davey slowly put the microfilm back in its envelope, closed the portfolio, and re-tied it.

"When did you know?" Davey asked. "When did you figure I was gonna come looking for this, tonight? I thought you were driving to Long Island."

"I turned the car around. I knew the gala reception would be your best opportunity." He blew out a cloud of smoke. "The other night, when you were helming *Vagrant*, something wasn't right. You were altogether too interested in the *Defender* story—too serious, by far. I've seen you get excited about the America's Cup before. You get all smiley and twitchy, like a little boy. It's very endearing, actually. But when you were asking me about *Defender*, I could tell something else was at stake for you, something darker. You'd got a sniff of something. And I realized later I'd completely put my foot in it by mentioning the safe."

Davey eyed his escape route to the door.

"When we docked in Brooklyn," Vanderbilt went on calmly, "why didn't you head over to see your brother? He was right there, flaking sails on *Shamrock's* foredeck, one pier over. I stopped the car. Jacob and I got chatting. I told him he had you to thank for vouching for him in St. George's. And I told him his little brother was a pretty fine sailor. He said, 'Well, we come from good stock, don't we?' I offered him a ride over the bridge. Of course, he was all eager to tell me about his time as a masthead man on the coal barges, and about your dad, how he raced on *Defender*. How come you never told me he worked down under the decks?"

"Our dad's none of anyone's business," whispered Davey. His eyes were glazed over. The thought that Jacob had ridden in the back of Vanderbilt's limousine was repulsive, and he wasn't sure why. "What else did Jake tell you?"

"Not much. But I put two and two together. There's clearly bad blood between the two of you. And I had a feeling you weren't just going to let it drop. I had to get to the safe first. I came in through the kitchens, and up the back stairs."

"You needed me to open it?"

Vanderbilt chuckled. "Oh for Christ's sake, I'm a Flag Officer; it's not as if I don't know the combination. How'd you think I got the book?"

"All the lights were out..." Davey said.

"I spotted you lurking across 44th street, and I knew I'd hit the jackpot. I turned out the lights and waited for you to show up. I opened the safe, and grabbed Iselin's book. But frankly, I didn't even know about the microfilm. You found the envelope—and you know how to work the machine. Those pages in the blueprints, they were obvious fakes. Someone got rid of the originals a long time ago. Maybe even Herreshoff. He wouldn't have wanted any trace."

Davey was wide-eyed. "You knew about this whole swindle?"

"I'm ashamed to say I did," Vanderbilt said. "But it was ancient history, until you dredged it up."

"Then… this microfilm… it's the only existing copy of the original blueprints?"

"Exactly. So it's good you found it before someone else did. Because now I can destroy that too, along with the notebook. Then none of this ever happened. But you'll want to see the book, first."

He tossed the notebook across Squigley's desk. It skidded to a stop. Davey opened it to a random page. There were the familiar names of the sailors, and in the margin, the bribes they took. In curiously slanted left-handed handwriting he'd seen once before. It was Uriah Rhodes' writing.

Davey's blood was pumping in his veins. *Can I make it to the door before he blocks my way?*

Vanderbilt rubbed his steely blue eyes under his spectacles. His words were calm but firm. "No, don't bolt, old chap. All I have to do is call down to those policemen at the front door. I'll have you arrested and charged as a thief. Nobody will back up your story—not even your friend Sam. They'll drag you out of here in handcuffs, past all the reporters. And neither of us wants that. Come on Davey, take a seat, talk to me."

"I'll stand, thanks."

"All right. Now you're in possession of all the facts, but you need to think this through, sensibly. You don't want to be starting something you can't undo."

Davey's voice quivered. "I can't undo what they did to my dad. But I'm not gonna let them get away with it, neither. Iselin is a bloody cheat. All of them—the Syndicate. Your own father, too; he knew. This club, I'm sorry, Harold, but you're a bunch of hypocrites. You talk about sporting this, and fair play that. And the public suck it up, don't they?"

"Listen to me. Of course you feel hurt. You want justice for your dad. That's only natural. So, say you talk, you go to the newspapers, or the police, and blow the lid off it. Even if they believe you—what happens when you show your face at home, after it all comes out?"

His shoulders sagged, and he shook his head. "The whole world'll know the Deer Isle sailors took Iselin's dirty money."

"Exactly. All that Cup glory, up in smoke. And for what?"

Davey took three steps to the window, and stared into the streetlights below. He pictured Ma, stooped over her chores, and thought of how she'd be treated around town, if it all blew up. He felt his heart tighten.

"So now you're just gonna take care of your own people?" Davey's tongue tasted salty from the sweat on his upper lip, and his voice was a dull monotone.

Vanderbilt swirled the ice cubes in his glass. It sounded deafening. "Look, my friend. There's a lot you don't know about this club. This is not the first time there's been a blood-letting. You heard that racket downstairs? That'll be Cochran, laying down this crazy challenge, a million dollar race round the island. But it's all a set-up. Lipton's accepted already, they've agreed the terms. They exchanged telegrams this morning."

"So the race is on?"

"Lipton already accepted the bet. Why wouldn't he? He's more popular in New York than ever, even when he loses. But he's a British subject. He can't be seen to be taking part in the America's Cup, with his country at war. And nor can the Club. So this race round Manhattan is even better, don't you see, because it'll look like a personal grudge match—a cockfight between two millionaires. But only if it seems it was *leaked*. Cochran blurts it out, tonight, at a private NYYC reception, as if he's throwing down the gauntlet—knowing Ogden Blum will scoop it in tomorrow's *Post*. Then Sir Thomas can make a big hoo-hah of accepting the challenge, in front of the press and photographers, flanked by Lipton's Tea banners. And it'll run for a full news cycle."

"The race isn't real, then?" Davey perched himself on the edge of the desk.

"Oh, the race is real, all right. And the million dollars, too. Which is not chump change, even to Cochran. Whereas Sir Thomas, he can afford it; he'll make it all back in publicity. But Cochran desperately wants to win it, to recoup what he's invested in the campaign. I reckon Ollie Iselin's bankrolling him. He's probably got huge side bets on, too. And there's something else." He took a deep slug of his single malt. "Lipton's asked me to helm *Shamrock IV.*"

Davey was astonished. "You'd helm a British boat?"

"It's just one racing yacht versus another. And as Lipton knows, these are my home waters."

"You must believe *Shamrock*'s got a chance then?"

"You've seen how slippery she is."

"She looks pretty quick. But even if she's slower, I'd back you in a match race against Cochran, any day."

"Go on..."

"*Vanitie*'ll be the clear favorite," said Davey, thinking out loud. "Everyone'll be expecting her to win."

"Aha..."

"But if *Shamrock* wins, it'll look like it's you that's made the difference."

"And you should join me, old sport. You can do your talking on the water. After all, there's more than one way to skin a cat." Vanderbilt was smiling. "So. Are you in? Or are you still fretting about something that happened in 1895?"

Davey stared at Iselin's notebook.

"This is the way the world turns, Davey. The old men, they all die, eventually. But the New York Yacht Club will be here in a hundred years. The America's Cup must go on. *I* need the Cup to go on... so that you can help me win it, one day, you and your brother."

He thought of his Ma, and his father's pale blue eyes, and the shame it would bring. After a moment he picked up the book, the portfolio and the vellum envelope, and placed them back in the safe. Then the heavy door swung closed with a clang, and he spun the dials.

CHAPTER TWENTY

It was late morning on August 28th, 1914. From the observation platform in the Statue of Liberty's torch, New York Harbor must have looked like a children's boating pond. As far as the eye could see in every direction, there were spectator boats of different sizes: steamers and ferries, sailing yachts, motor launches, even rowboats and canoes, jostling for a favorable viewing position for the start of the race. Many appeared to be in the hands of 'fair weather' boating enthusiasts.

But the weather today was not exactly fair. The clouds were heavy and threatening, and the breeze had built to a fresh four or five on the Beaufort scale. As the tide slackened and the ebb picked up, the wind blew the Harbor chop flat; by noon, the surface waters around Ellis and Liberty Islands were swirling with confused eddies and frothy wake. A pair of marshal's launches sped back and forth with bullhorns, trying to keep the spectators to the south of the start line. An anxious freighter towing a coal barge—heading upriver with *real* business to do—let out a long blast of its foghorn, and dozens of vessels had to scatter to let it through. Then the flotilla rapidly reformed, in a cacophony of hoots, whistles and expletives.

New York's most sumptuous private yachts pushed to the front, their rigging festooned with multicolored flags and burgees. Members of the City's exclusive clubs packed their decks, easily identifiable in their ubiquitous blue blazers and white flannel trousers. Commodore Ledyard Blair's gargantuan *Diana* was laden with passengers, mainly non-sailing members and their wives and children. They lined *Diana*'s rails under the fluttering "N.Y.Y.C. Official" ensign. Liquor flowed, and an eight-piece brass band played jaunty marches on her afterdeck.

There was a surge of applause as the two splendid America's Cup racing yachts came into sight, towing behind their steam tenders. Their mainsails were still flaked on the massive booms. Among the sailors on the foredeck of the pea-green *Shamrock IV* was Davey Haskell, enjoying the closeup view of the Statue of Liberty and the bristling southern end of Manhattan Island. *Shamrock*'s entire 35-man crew was attired in Sir Thomas Lipton's cotton ducks, with a four-leaf clover insignia on the breast.

Harold Vanderbilt stood at the helm, looking distinguished in a cricket jumper, slacks and peaked cap, with a silver stopwatch slung round his neck. He smiled and waved to the crowds lining the Battery Park railings.

William P. Burton, Sir Thomas Lipton's personal representative, called *Shamrock*'s crew around the helm. They formed into a huddle: twenty-three men from Sweden, ten from Britain, and two from Deer Isle. Davey scanned the faces in the circle, careful to avoid eye contact with his brother. They were a raggle-taggle crew, short of match racing practice. Many of their shipmates had been called away to the war in Europe. Their starched white uniforms did little to disguise that their hands were soft, and they had never raced together as a team.

Capt. Burton looked uncomfortable, and he wasn't hiding it. The order had come down from Sir Thomas Lipton himself: he was to relinquish *Shamrock*'s helm to Vanderbilt, the young New Yorker. Today, Burton would be calling tactics instead. This sounded like a demotion. But, after a single afternoon's practice with their new helmsman, the *Shamrock* sailors were won over. Vanderbilt was a skilled leader. The sailing master Tom Diaper said it best when he muttered under his breath: "Who pays the ferryman, boys?" Sir Thomas had promised a hefty bonus to every man if they won. And after all, better to be hauling ropes, than digging trenches in northeastern France.

Burton reached into his blazer pocket, unfolded a printed copy of the Sailing Instructions, and read them aloud one last time. They had appeared in the morning edition of the *New York Times,* and Davey had them memorized: "Start at the Statue of Liberty; north around the Spuyten Duyvil lightship and back to the start, leaving Manhattan entirely to starboard. America's Cup protocol; no protests; no handicaps."

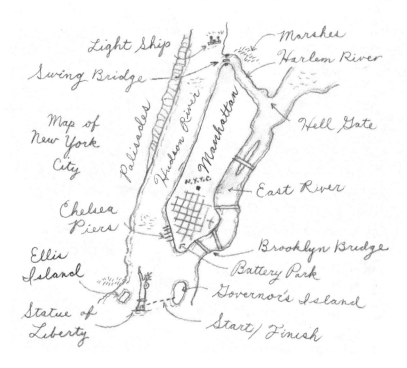

"And a million dollar prize to the victor!" called Vanderbilt, to loud applause from the circled crew. "Very well, Mr. Diaper—let's hoist the main."

Tom Diaper sent *Shamrock*'s deckhands to the halyards. A hundred yards away on *Vanitie*, his counterpart Uriah Rhodes made the same call. A line of fifteen men clapped on to each throat halyard, and a dozen more on each peak, bracing a taut leg against the deck. They heaved and hauled, and the leathered hoops rose around the mast, as the great folds of canvas began to catch the wind.

Viewed from Battery Park, the two racers spreading their wings must have been a tremendous sight. *Vanitie*'s mainsail was first to fill. She cast off her tow and began to bear away with her staysail backed. A bigger cheer went up along the harbor front when *Shamrock IV*'s main flattened and filled: it was emblazoned with a three-storey high advertisement for *Lipton's Tea*. Flashbulbs popped. A cluster of N.Y.Y.C. members aboard the flagship tutted and shook their heads.

At 1.15pm the Race Committee boat *Cristobel* raised the fifteen minute warning. The two cutters were reaching across the river on opposite tacks, their bow waves creaming out beside them. They passed within a mere hundred feet of each other, at a combined speed of twenty knots. There were many Deer Islers in *Vanitie*'s crew—Davey briefly caught sight of Bill Otley's lank black hair among the mast men. And there at her helm stood Alexander Cochran, legs astride, eyes fixed straight ahead, impassive behind his tinted eyeglasses. He had his afterguard gathered around him: his newest professional skipper Harry Haff; *Vanitie*'s designer, William Gardner; and, strutting the deck with his sea-coat, bullhorn and beard, the unmistakable figure of Uriah Rhodes.

There was another man, an older gentleman in a cap and an ankle-length trench coat. As *Shamrock* crossed her wake, Vanderbilt turned to Burton and said under his breath, "*Vanitie*'s got an extra set of eyes on board today, did you see? That was Oliver Iselin."

"Iselin!" said Burton. "The four-time America's Cup winner? He's still around?"

"Ollie doesn't tend to race these days. Can't be much under seventy. Bad asthma, I'm told."

Davey recognized the old man's icy and intense expression from the photograph on Phelps' wall. He was sail racing legend, with more experience than the rest of them put together. And a cheat. But there was no time to dwell on that. Davey was one of ten on *Shamrock*'s thick mainsheet, which controlled the angle of her boom via an array of heavy blocks. As Vanderbilt edged the boat closer to the wind, Tom Diaper called out small adjustments, gazing up at the massive mainsail: "Trim in six feet… three more… How's she feel now, sir?"

Vanderbilt eyed the camber of the sail. "I'm happy with the main. We'll ease the staysail a touch, and break out the jib, if you please, Mr. Diaper."

A gust hit, and *Shamrock* knifed through the wind, heeling far over.

The breeze was picking up. Vanderbilt bore up into the pressure to level off. He glanced over his shoulder and said: "In two minutes, we'll go into a slow tack and begin our reach back to the line." His diction was clear and calm as ever.

With the ebb under them, it would not take long to get back there. "Davey," Vanderbilt called, "come back here and keep time." He gave Davey his stopwatch and pointed to a clipboard and pencil hanging from the binnacle. "You remember the formula, yes?"

"I do."

Vanitie was now beam-reaching along the start line on port. Vanderbilt steered a course to cross her wake. When the five-minute gun sounded, a red ball went up on the RC boat's flagstaff, and Davey started the countdown. Cochran gradually bore away to match *Shamrock*'s course and speed.

Vanderbilt had picked a transit between *Cristobel*'s flagstaff and Fort Jay on Governor's Island. When they lined up, he shouted: "Mark it!"

Davey clicked.

"Time?"

"Four minutes forty-six," replied Davey, and he scribbled it down. Half the time, plus twenty... "So we tack at two forty-three?" he said confidently.

Vanderbilt had already done the math in his head. "We need to adjust for the current. We'll tack at *t* minus three minutes."

"Got it."

The racers were speeding towards the south end of Governor's Island. *Vanitie* was a hundred yards upwind; her course was converging steadily with *Shamrock*'s. The gap was closing fast.

"Dammit!" said Burton. "Cochran's looking to block you."

Vanderbilt said firmly, "This will have to be a gybe, not a tack. Let the boys know."

He's using your own starting formula against you, Davey thought.

Tom Diaper passed the order around the foredeck crew. "This will be a gybe, not a tack! Get ready!"

Four sailors scrambled down the deck to the jib and staysail sheets.

Three more rushed to the backstays, ready to take up the strain as the boom slammed across to the new side.

"Get ready!" called Vanderbilt.

Vanitie was now only a boat's length off their port quarter.

"Three ten…. Three-oh-five…" called Davey.

"Gybe-*ho!*" shouted Vanderbilt, and he swung the wheel down. Davey joined the others on the tail of the mainsheet. *Shamrock IV* began to make a wide carve to the right. The boom lurched across, the mainsail filled on the new side; the headsails followed. It was all a little rushed and ragged, with the men still unsure of their positions.

Across the water, *Vanitie* mirrored the turn, carving smoothly to her left and up into the wind. The two boats' sterns came startlingly close, in a maelstrom of froth and foam. But *Vanitie*'s disciplined American crew trimmed her sails perfectly, keeping them powered up all the way. They'd had plenty of recent practice in the trials, so they'd surely have stamina too. Davey wondered if *Shamrock*'s mixed bag of sailors could really go the distance?

Vanitie flew head-to-wind and bore away onto her new tack; a few seconds later, *Shamrock IV* settled on a parallel course. This was the yachts' final, close-hauled approach to the line before the start gun. They gathered speed, two boat-lengths apart, the waves streaming along their leeward rails. A chorus of honks, steam whistles and clanging bells rose among the spectator boats.

"Time now?" shouted Vanderbilt.

Davey called, "A minute and ten." He swiveled to sight past *Vanitie*'s stern, at the tower of flags on the Race Committee boat, just in time to see the Blue Peter come down. "One minute!"

The transit was still a way off. *Vanitie* looked early, though. She was three hundred feet off their beam, and well to windward—not far enough ahead to be blanketing their wind, but surely too close to the line, with fifty seconds still to go? Cochran obviously knew it too. He altered course to the west, quickly bearing down on *Shamrock*.

"Hold your course," said Burton. "You can luff him as high as you want. Push him over the line early!"

But Vanderbilt opted to bear off a few degrees instead, avoiding a confrontation. "It's not worth it, Burton," he called. "Let's just sail fast."

"Twenty seconds!" called Davey, gripping the stopwatch. His heart was thumping now. From ten to zero, he counted down each second. Vanderbilt craned his neck to look back at the flagstaff, watching closely for his transit. There was a puff of smoke, followed by the report of a brass cannon, barely audible over the racket from the spectators. That was the start gun: both yachts were behind the line. They rounded up in unison until they were speeding neck and neck, hard on the wind.

"A very fine start, sir," said Burton.

"Every last man to the rail!" Thirty-two crewmen rushed up to the windward side. In their white uniforms and caps, they lay on their elbows on the canvas deck like sardines in a pan. *Shamrock* was at full power, with *Vanitie* two boat lengths to windward.

Davey fixed his eyes on their adversary. It was the first time he was able to directly compare their speeds—and so far they looked dead even.

Burton scanned the river upwind. "Port will be the longer tack, once we're through the river mouth. We'll have to put her about before Ellis Island there. We may to need to hail *Vanitie* for room."

Squatting on the afterdeck, with a hand on the backstay, Davey had a moment to catch his breath. Among the crew on the windward rail he spotted his brother, lying flat on his stomach. Jacob turned his face and raised his head, peeking out from under his cap, and caught Davey's eye. Before Davey had a chance to look away, Jake gave him a big wink, then grinned, as if to say, "Got you!"

As the racers came within a quarter mile of Ellis Island, the racers were close enough that Burton was able to hail across the water: "*Vanitie*, we will need water to tack!"

No response.

"*Vanitie*! We need room, for the shallows. Come about, please!" Burton repeated at the top of his voice, pointing to Ellis Island. It sounded English, quaint and pompous.

Perhaps Cochran, who was in the windward position and required to give way, never heard the call over the rushing of the wake and the groaning of *Vanitie*'s fully loaded stays. Perhaps he just wanted to intimidate them. But the yachts were getting closer to the island—too close. Davey could see the architectural details of the buildings in frightful clarity. Capt. Burton snatched the speaking trumpet from Diaper, leaned over the windward rail and yelled at the top of his lungs: "WATER! Give us room please, NOW!"

At that moment, Jacob came running back to the cockpit and said, "Mr. Vanderbilt, sir! There's a marked channel behind Ellis Island—we cut through there all the time in the coasters. And a decent back eddy too, flowing north, during the ebb."

Burton looked affronted, but Vanderbilt pushed the chart at him. "What's the depth in the channel?"

He held the chart close to his face, squinting, and traced the route with his finger. "Never less than forty feet, if you keep to the middle. But it's narrow."

"All right. Crack off the sails a touch! We're going in."

"Are you certain? Looks like Cochran's getting ready to go about."

"Hands to the centerboard, in case we touch."

Diaper sent two men below. *Shamrock*'s draft was about twenty-four feet with the centerboard down, and fourteen with it up. Burton stared again at the chart, a concerned look on his face. "But there's no room for error..."

They passed within a hundred feet of the lower end of the island, just as *Vanitie* rounded up into a tack. The Ellis Island channel was well marked. Just beyond were the reedy marshes of the New Jersey shore. They could afford to sail about another five hundred yards before they'd be forced to tack through the channel to avoid running aground.

Right after *Shamrock* flopped over onto port, Davey caught sight of the covered wooden walkway at the back side of the island; the dormitories, the hospital, the water tower and incinerator. Long queues of immigrant families were huddled there out of the wind with their luggage. He imagined their amazement at the massive racing yacht as it ploughed through the channel, its wake washing along the Jersey mudflats. It was their very first glimpse of the American Dream.

Shamrock IV had the eddy under her now. When they emerged from behind the north side of the island, Davey bent down for a clearer view under the mainsail: via the detour, they had gained considerably. He thought, *Jacob'll be mighty pleased with himself.* He spotted Jake halfway up the mast, hanging off a spreader with one hand. The usual crap.

Both racers were now on the longer port tack over to the Manhattan side; but *Shamrock IV* had made more progress upwind. The first crossing was going to be interesting. With her larger sail area, *Shamrock* seemed as fast, or even slightly faster than her rival, though perhaps not able to point as high. *Vanitie* was farther across the river, and would be the first to go about. Vanderbilt's choice would then be whether to carry on, or tack on top of her and try to take her wind. If he judged it right, he could initiate a tacking duel, with his own *Shamrock* in the controlling position.

"What do you think, Captain Burton?" He said. "Tack on top of him, or stand on?"

"The fewer maneuvers the better. Let's stay as we are, and keep our speed up."

Davey eyed the situation. *Vanitie* had just tacked on to starboard near the Battery Park shore, and was pointing at their stern. "Wind's come ahead a bit, sir..." he said quietly, not wanting to contradict anyone.

"And it's a header. Good for Cochran, bad for us," Vanderbilt said. "We should go now or never."

All Burton could do was purse his lips. Vanderbilt called to Diaper for the tack.

The crew worked the lines smoothly through the turn, and *Shamrock* came out of it perfectly placed to give *Vanitie* some bad air. Davey looked back and saw a few wrinkles appearing in the luffs of the bronze boat's sails. Cochran would be forced to bear away a few degrees to maintain his speed.

Twice more they criss-crossed the river, making their way north, with *Shamrock* firmly in control. The fleet of spectator boats followed in midstream, at a respectful distance. Davey's heart rate slowed somewhat. He was able to take in the whole vista of southern Manhattan. He recognized the pink façade of Chelsea Piers, where he'd once tried to pay a visit to Edith Armitage on the *Nemesis*. Behind the wharfs, he could see the wooden towers of the Ninth Avenue El, where he'd missed his train. It all seemed an eternity ago. On West Street, he spotted a line of motor cars heading northwards, some of them open-topped, with cheering passengers leaning out to wave their handkerchiefs and flags.

They were still three hundred yards from the Jersey bank. Over *Shamrock*'s stern, Davey was surprised to hear Uriah Rhodes call for an early tack. Vanderbilt must have heard it too, and he immediately gave Diaper the order to tack to cover. Both boats flew head to wind at the same moment. But while *Shamrock* completed her tack and set her sails on the new side, *Vanitie* checked herself mid-turn, and bore away again onto starboard, quickly regaining speed. Their courses were now split. Cochran—or his afterguard—must have spotted a patch of dark water blowing down the western shore, indicating a gust and a favorable wind shift; Burton had completely missed it.

Jacob was only half a dozen bodies forward of the cockpit. "Cochran's a clever bastard," he said out loud. "That was a *fack*."

Several of the crew around him burst out laughing. Capt. Burton was within hearing distance. "*What*?"

"He did a *fack*, sir. Instead of a *tack*. It's an old Deer Isle move," shouted Jacob.

"An old Wivenhoe move, more like!" grunted Tom Diaper. The British sailors agreed with him.

"What does the '*F*' stand for?" asked Burton, bewildered.

"Best leave that to your imagination, sir," said Jacob.

The wind was shiftier now, as the terrain to the west rose up and the New Jersey Palisades upset its flow. When the boats crossed again, the roles were reversed, and *Vanitie* had retaken the lead. With her superior pointing ability, the American boat was able to draw away from her rival with each tack, positioning herself between *Shamrock* and the wind. Davey knew that getting lucky with a wind shift could hand the advantage first to one boat, then the other; spotting it early could lead to major gains. Capt. Burton seemed to be oblivious to this.

At one point, *Vanitie* tacked a hundred yards ahead, close to shore below the wooded hillside of Hudson Heights. Davey spotted a small gang of feral boys running alongside the railroad tracks, whooping and hollering. One of them picked up a stone and hurled it at the gleaming bronze yacht. It fell far short of her stern, but it cued his friends to stop and pick up rocks and bricks as well, and hurl them at the yachts, laughing and cheering.

It was the Gas House Boys!

A half-brick smashed onto *Vanitie*'s afterdeck, and the fragments scattered across the teak floorboards. Alex Cochran swiveled round in disgust and glared at the ruffian gang.

Rhodes screamed into his bullhorn, in his broadest Glaswegian. "OY, YOU! PACK THAT *IN!*" As one, the boys stood tall and gave him the finger, then cracked up laughing and ran off across the tracks.

As the British boat reached the northern limits of the island, it was clear that they were no match for *Vanitie* over a long beat to windward. Davey used his stopwatch to time the deficit as they passed a navigation buoy: they were trailing Cochran by two and a half minutes.

"This looks bad," said Vanderbilt. "What do you make of it, Burton?"

"I don't see a way past her before the windward mark," he said. "But with our larger sail area, we may have an edge on the downwind. Is there a place to overtake?"

"Not once we're in the Creek, no, at least before the East River…"

"You know these rivers better than I do, Vanderbilt."

"It's the far side of the tracks, though," he laughed. "Hey, Jacob. Jacob Haskell! Come on back here for a moment, will you?"

Jake sprung up on the sloping deck and balanced his way back to the cockpit. It was the closest Davey had been to his big brother all day. He busied himself with a loose line, trying to act nonchalant.

"Take a look at the chart," said Vanderbilt. "Once we're in the Harlem River, where's the first place we might be able to get past *Vanitie*?"

"Here," Jake said, after a beat. "Hell Gate. Where the two rivers converge. The current can be a bastard, but see the shallows here, inside Mill Rock? We used to ignore the channel markers, in the coal barges, even when we was heavy. There must be a good fifteen foot of water at mid-tide."

"We'll be on a run," Davey said. "What if we pull up the centerboard at the corner, and slide right across?"

"That could work," said Vanderbilt. "Or it could be a disaster."

Burton looked grave. "If it'll get us close enough to take her wind, it might be our only chance to pass her."

"I think that's right," said Vanderbilt. "Let's at least try to stay on their heels, in the meantime."

But Davey could see *Shamrock*'s crew were weary from the relentless rope handling. *Vanitie* had pulled a good half mile ahead now, with the city well behind them. The north end of Manhattan Island was a rocky, wooded wilderness, aside from the railroad tracks running along the river. He caught his first sight of the entrance to Spuyten Duyvil Creek, with its iron swing bridge, the center section of which was swiveled in the open position, leaving room on either side for shipping to pass in and out of the Harlem River.

Captain Burton pointed at the towering spans of the bridge. "One of yours, I assume?"

Vanderbilt shrugged. "The Central Railroad Company's, actually, so yes."

The two harbor pilot launches had been instructed to hold the spectator fleet a mile south of the lightship, giving the yachts maneuvering room at the windward mark. *Shamrock* had one more long tack to make onto the port layline. Half a mile up the river, *Vanitie* was already preparing to bear away around the lightship towards the entrance of the creek. Her lead looked to have doubled to four or five minutes. As she gybed at the mark, men bustled around her decks, easing sheets and backstays, Rhodes barking orders at them through his bullhorn. *Vanitie*'s boom swung out over the water, and as she sped back towards *Shamrock*, with the tide under her, Davey got a good look at the faces of her afterguard around the helm. Harry Haff was squinting up at the sails, passing instructions to Rhodes, who relayed them through his bullhorn to the trimmers. Oliver Iselin had his cap pulled down over his forehead, hands thrust deep in the pockets of his trench coat. He seemed to be the one calling tactics. Cochran, at the wheel, was rigid as always. As the yachts drew close, Cochran turned and glared directly at *Shamrock's* afterguard with a sour grin on his face. He cupped a hand to his mouth, and shouted across the water: "Checked the train schedule recently, Vanderbilt?"

Haff and Iselin were clearly amused by this.

Burton said quietly, "Some sort of private joke?"

Vanitie sped through the open swing bridge just as *Shamrock* tacked over for the last time before the lightship.

Moments later, they understood. It was Jacob who spotted it, as they rounded the lightship. He did a double-take, and yelled, "Jeezum Crow! I think the bridge is closing!"

Seconds later, they heard the metallic creaking of the bridge, and saw the little waves it made in the water as it turned. The central section of the bridge was swiveling, the gaps on either side shrinking fast.

Capt. Burton searched Vanderbilt's face. "What on earth…?"

Vanderbilt let out a deep breath. "Iselin!" he groaned. "This is his doing. He's on our Board. I should have known."

The railroad bridge closed behind *Vanitie* with an almighty clang.

For a while, *Shamrock's* seamen and officers were speechless, staring in disbelief at the huge rusty structure that barred their way.

"So what the hell do we do now?" said Burton at last, flushing visibly. "Wait for it to open again?"

"Ease the sails," muttered Vanderbilt, shaking his head. "Might as well. The race is over." He let go the wheel, and reached for his tobacco pouch.

Tom Diaper reluctantly gave the order. With her sheets eased, *Shamrock's* speed fell off rapidly. She began to drift sideways down the river, sails flapping. The crew looked shell-shocked. Some were arguing and pointing; others just flopped down on the deck or the coachroof, shoulders slumped, hands blistered and raw.

"Ruddy Yank bastards," muttered Tom Diaper. Then he swiveled back to the helm and knuckled his cap. "No disrespect, sir."

Davey's eyes followed the name on *Vanitie's* transom as she took off on a broad reach towards the first bend of Spuyten Duyvil Creek, where it narrowed and became the Harlem River. They had to be making eleven knots on a dead run. The wind in the creek was shifty, blowing over the uninhabited wooded slopes at the north end of Manhattan Island and swirling among the moored barges and empty boathouses. With her massive mainsail all the way out, the bronze cutter seemed to take up half the width of the river. The groaning of her backstays echoed eerily off the cliffs, and her white wake spewed noisily behind her, breaking onto the muddy river banks on the Bronx side. Along the right bank, there was a row of run-down single-storey warehouses; on the left, the reed beds in the low-lying marsh gave way to a rambling shanty town of huts and rusty corrugated iron dwellings. Some of the inhabitants were scattered along the bank, washing clothes or huddled around bonfires. Few had noticed the opulent yacht creaming down the Harlem river, with its massive sails, gleaming bronze hull and polished woodwork. *Vanitie*'s crew ran about the deck in their white cotton uniforms, preparing for the inevitable gybe.

Cochran spun the wheel, but before the boom was halfway to the centerline, a shifty gust of wind caught the wrong side of the sail, lifting it four feet in the air. With enormous force it crashed over onto the new side, causing *Vanitie* to heel abruptly to port. The jolt shook the entire mast. The mainsheet men managed to get a single turn around the surging bollard; but it was not enough to stop the rope from tearing painfully through their hands, the friction scorching them. Two of them dropped to the deck in agony, nursing their rope burns.

As *Vanitie* spun to the right, the end of her boom swept across the bank, scything through the row of corrugated iron huts. The roofs of the immigrant dwellings shattered like matchwood. A woman in a Hijab screamed in terror and ran, dragging her two toddlers behind her. The bronze racer rocked a few times and leveled off, the boom and the wash from her stern wave leaving a trail of destruction along the river bank.

It was a shocking display of seamanship. Adrift on the Hudson River side of the swing bridge, all *Shamrock*'s men could do was stare helplessly, too exhausted even to crack jokes. Tom Diaper was slumped on the coach roof. Burton stood with his hands on his hips. Vanderbilt just frowned and puffed on his pipe, downcast.

But Davey's face was knotted in concentration. He glanced towards the lightship to the north, then back down the Hudson. He took a step towards Capt. Burton and said, "Can I see the Sailing Instructions a minute, sir?"

Burton pulled the printed sheet from his coat pocket. "The time limit is six hours, in case you're wondering. It's barely 4pm now. It would take a bloody miracle for the race to be abandoned before they circumnavigate the island."

He handed the sheet to Davey, who shut his eyes for a moment, as he reached deep into his memory. A broad grin spread across his face from ear to ear: he had found exactly what he was looking for.

"Right here! It doesn't say we have to *circumnavigate* the island... it only says '...the island of Manhattan is to be left *entirely to starboard.*'"

"So?" Said Burton.

"We can sail backwards!"

Burton and Diaper looked mystified. "*Backwards?*"

"Hey Jake! Get over here!" Davey called.

Jacob approached the afterdeck. "What is it, shorty?"

Vanderbilt was the first to catch on. "And leave Manhattan entirely... to *starboard?*" He glanced down the river, then up at the sails. "For God's sake... that's so... stupid, it's brilliant."

"It is, isn't it? And Jake'n me know how. We do it all the time, back home."

The distant Statue of Liberty was barely a dot on the southern horizon. Burton waved the back of his hand dismissively. "Bah. In some clinker-built fishing tub? Oh, Spare me. We're sixteen blasted miles from the finish."

"No, really, we can do it!" Davey turned to Vanderbilt. "You said it yourself, sir. All the same principles apply, you said; only the forces are greater, and things happen more slowly."

"There's certainly nothing in the rulebook that says you can't sail backwards," said Vanderbilt. "So we'll be leaving Manhattan to starboard—a straight shot back down the Hudson, and the first boat over the line's the winner!"

Burton took off his cap and ran his hand over his balding head. "But surely sailing backwards would mean a vessel's port and starboard side are reversed?"

Vanderbilt said: "I think not. Starboard is starboard. They can argue it all they like, but they'll find there's no nautical precedent." He blew out a mouthful of smoke. "All right, you Haskell brothers, I'm all ears. How do we go about this?"

"Tell 'em, Jake!"

Jacob was grinning too now. "All right. We'll need to get some way on, just two or three knots. Bring her up into the wind, sir, and as she slows, we push the boom all the way out on the port side—as many men as can reach it, and a "preventer" run forward to the windlass…"

"…and we can use the staysail to help steer," added Davey. "Back it if we need to, to keep her head-to-wind."

"There's gotta be enough weight in the bow, so we'll need every available man to the foredeck. And maybe trail something in the water?" Jake said.

Tom Diaper chimed in. "On Thames barges when there's a current running, we drag a bit of anchor chain in the water to keep 'em straight. We calls it 'drudging'."

"Yeah, drudging!" nodded a couple of the English sailors.

"Just the ticket," said Vanderbilt.

"The rudder'll be working in reverse, mind," said Jacob. "You'll want two on the helm, like as not, 'cos the stern will try to yaw towards the wind—"

Capt. Burton interrupted. His face and neck were flushed, and he was straining to keep his voice lowered. "Look here, Vanderbilt, I'm still responsible for this vessel! I have to be accountable to the owner. What if we lose control and wreck her on the rocks? This could be a blasted catastrophe."

But Vanderbilt was smiling from ear to ear. "Then you can pin it on me, old man. I'll cover any loss or damage myself." He tore off his cricket sweater. "And if I know Sir Thomas, he'd want us to have a go."

Some of the Swedes were a little bewildered, but for the most part, the men understood the drill. Diaper divided up the tasks, and Jacob made the call to the cockpit.

"All set, gents. Let's sheet in and get moving—slow, like—then gently bring her up." He hurried to the foredeck to organize the other sailors.

Shamrock was still three hundred yards from the river bank, and close to the creek entrance. Vanderbilt was on the wheel with Capt. Burton, Davey close beside him. Tom Diaper had a dozen of the tallest men ready to push the boom out—which was not going to be easy, even with the extra leverage of a "preventer" led forward from the tip of the boom. The challenge would be to get all the forces in balance and keep them there. The timing was critical.

A complete hush fell about the deck. Vanderbilt waited until the yacht was barely moving forward at walking pace, then gently spun the helm to round up in a smooth curve. Davey watched the way he handled the wheel, recalling how expertly he'd done it in *Vagrant* when they anchored in St. George's Harbor. Once again, his judgement was impeccable. With the boat dead into the wind, Davey picked his moment, and signaled to Jacob on the foredeck.

"Boom out—GO!"

A dozen seamen reached up to push on the boom, while the broad-shouldered Jacob and two more cranked on the windlass. *Shamrock's* huge mainsail swung slowly out over the river. The wind pressure on its front side steadily increased. At forty-five degrees it was already acting as a brake; and at seventy degrees it was almost touching the shrouds, held there by the thick preventer.

Davey leaned over the rail near the helm to watch the swirling eddies in the water. For a moment the cutter seemed to be completely stationary; then, ripples of a new wake began to form. He grinned. She was starting to move backwards. It was magic.

He called intently over his shoulder. "How's it feel, sir?"

Vanderbilt stood beside the helm, with each hand on a spoke of the wheel, legs slightly apart, his gaze fixed down the river. "So far, so good."

Davey eyed the rocky river bank. With the ebb underneath them, they had to be moving downriver at four or five knots already. They left the mouth of the creek behind, off their starboard beam, and the iron swing bridge disappeared behind the point.

"She feels pretty heavy," said Vanderbilt. "Davey, help me out here."

Davey took a grip with both hands and felt the forces on the rudder. "I think she needs more weight in the bow, sir."

"You know what?—you take her, old sport. You've clearly got a good feel for this." Vanderbilt took a step to the side and folded his arms. Davey took a deep breath and licked his lips, taking control of the wheel.

Diaper sent more Brits and Scandinavians to the foredeck. They were a cluster of about twenty now, around the windlass; this was a new sensation, and they were not quite sure what to do with themselves. Three sailors gripped the clew of the staysail, ready to back it at short notice. But the forces were delicately in balance, and *Shamrock* was picking up straight-line speed.

"Jacob!" called Vanderbilt, "take my binoculars and hike up the mast. See if you can spot *Vanitie*." He handed Jacob his powerful Abbe-König field glasses.

Jake slung them over his shoulder and went running up the leathered hoops, ape-like, as the crew on the foredeck watched, mesmerized. He climbed until he reached the gaff, eighty feet above the deck. He swung his legs over and gazed across the headland towards the eastern horizon.

He didn't need the binoculars. "I see her, skipper! She's almost to the East River."

Davey's knuckles were white from gripping *Shamrock's* wheel. She felt continually on the point of veering off course. But with a swift call to the foredeck, the staysail could be backed momentarily to press on her bow and balance the angle of attack. He evolved a hand signal: a raised arm with a cupped palm meant "back the staysail." The universal "slit your throat" sign meant "let it flap." He used the signals the moment he felt her start to yaw one way or the other, careful not to over-correct. Vanderbilt stood watching a yard away, arms folded.

At the city limits, the astonished spectator boats were buzzing in circles, unsure what to do. Some had not made it this far up the river, but those that had were bobbing about in the chop over towards the Jersey palisades, trying not to bump into each other while clearing a space for *Shamrock* to pass unimpeded.

A line of speeding automobiles, chock full of passengers, tore down the waterfront, honking their horns at *Shamrock IV*. Jacob whooped back at them from the top of the mast: there was a Packard Six, a Duesenberg sportster and a Napier T21; a couple of Studebakers, and assorted motorcycles; even a beaten-up Hutchisons Pies flatbed delivery truck. At the head of the snake was a shiny Stutz Bearcat convertible, steered erratically by a striking woman in goggles, with a silk scarf streaming out behind. A pale young gentleman in a top hat appeared to have passed out in her passenger seat, while a red-headed chorus girl teetered on the back sill between a pair of society toffs, slugging from an open champagne bottle. The yellow Stutz screeched to a halt on the Riverside Drive Viaduct. Its rear passengers stood on their seats to cheer and toast the passing *Shamrock* as she ploughed backwards down the Hudson. The sailors waved back enthusiastically, especially Jacob, who was astride the gaff, with his shirt unbuttoned to his navel. He blew a pretend kiss to the ladies. They blew it right back, and one of them, the driver—no, could it be?—She looked awfully familiar, didn't she?—

"Davey, look," he shouted down towards his brother on the deck, "It's Rula bloody Vanska!"

"In an expensive new automobile," observed Vanderbilt wryly.

From the viaduct down to 72nd St, where Manhattan was mainly flat, they had a clear view along each city street, with occasional glimpses of their adversary. Jacob called out a running commentary on *Vanitie's* progress to the deck below. For a while they caught sight of her sails at the far end of every cross street; but Jacob scratched his head when, beyond the trees of Central Park, her silhouette began to change.

"Sir," he shouted down to the deck, "something's happening. The tip of her topmast's showing now, above the main. It's rising… it's growing! Oh Lord, it's gotta be a full forty foot higher than the mainmast!"

"What the devil?—" said Burton.

"Of course. Cochran's got a new mast!" said Vanderbilt. "Crafty beggar…"

Davey flashed on their conversation in his attic. "With a telescoping topmast, like *Reliance?*"

"Precisely. It probably *is Reliance*'s mast. They saved it till they were past the Queensboro Bridge."

"They'll never have time to sway up a tops'l, though, will they?" asked Butler incredulously, staring off the east.

"They won't need to," called Jacob, lowering his binoculars. "The tops'l's already on it!"

At that moment, *Vanitie*'s club topsail began to unfurl from *inside* her telescopic topmast, wound out towards the tip of the gaff by its own sheet. It filled and set above her main, vastly increasing her sail area.

"Good old Captain Nat," Vanderbilt said. "Always got something new up his sleeve."

"She's drawing ahead!" shouted Jacob.

Capt. Burton was dumbfounded. "How the blazes did they manage that?"

"One of the advantages of a hollow steel mainmast," said Vanderbilt, "is that you can engineer a narrower topmast to fit *inside* it…":

"… and a furling topsail inside that!" said Davey.

"…if your name's Nathanael Herreshoff, that is," added Vanderbilt.

"Using some sort of a pulley system?"

"Foot-operated, I would imagine, from belowdecks." Vanderbilt and Davey exchanged a brief glance.

"Good Lord, I had no idea," said Burton. "What'll they do about the Brooklyn Bridge, though?"

"Well, that's going to get interesting. The clearance is only 130ft at low water. They'll be around one sixty, one seventy now."

At either end of 57th St, which offered a view clear across Manhattan, the two yachts caught sight of each other once again. *Shamrock* was making a good six knots in reverse, with the advantage of a current running under her. *Vanitie* was moving several knots faster; but she had more distance to cover, and by now the ebb in the East River was surely slackening. The dash to the finish was going to be a close-run thing. Jacob lost sight of *Vanitie* once more as the yachts drew level with the

Woolworth Building; the next time he saw her, she was about to pass under the central span of the Brooklyn Bridge. He relayed the news to the deck.

"Cochran's got her heeled right over! Jeezum, I wouldn't want to be up *Vanitie*'s mast right now." He focused his binoculars. For a moment Davey thought he heard a sickening rending of metal. But *Vanitie* was two miles away, among the docks, and it was hard to hear much over the general noise of the city.

Davey was doing most of the steering. Vanderbilt stood next to him with his right hand occasionally on a spoke, and his pipe wedged between his teeth. The Hudson was wider and choppier here, and the wind had picked up a notch: a cleaner breeze, blowing unobstructed across the tidal wetlands of Hoboken and the industrial Jersey shore. *Shamrock*'s rudder still felt delicately balanced, but ready to struggle free at any moment. Davey caught a glimpse of the tip of *Vanitie*'s topmast over the streets of lower Manhattan. They must have managed to clear the Brooklyn Bridge, heeled way over. Everything now would hinge on how the two boats stood as they came together off the south end of the island.

"When we come together we'll both be on starboard tack, won't we?" said Davey, as if reading Vanderbilt's mind. "What does the rulebook say about right of way when one boat is sailing backwards?"

"I don't believe the rules ever anticipated a race quite like this one," replied Vanderbilt.

Burton said, "But we're the windward boat, no question. The onus is on us to keep clear."

Vanderbilt nodded. "What I'm wondering is, once the island's behind us, do we keep on like this to the finish, or do we spin her around and cross the line pointy-end first, like normal people?"

"I say we just leave well enough alone, don't you?" said Burton. The Englishman strutted across the afterdeck, starting to look quite pleased with himself, Davey thought, and his performance as *Shamrock*'s tactician; probably beginning to formulate the exact words for his race report to Sir Thomas.

Jacob had shinned down a halyard, and he came back to the helm to hand Vanderbilt his binoculars. "Keep on like this, gents, and I reckon we've got the beating of 'em," he enthused. He grabbed Davey's shoulder and shook it vigorously. "Right, shortass?"

But Davey kept his gaze fixed downwind, his hands on the spokes.

"What, you gonna get all spleeny on me now, you little squirt?" said Jacob, smirking at a pair of the other seamen on the afterdeck.

Davey was concentrating on the steering. Vanderbilt had walked to the stern rail with the field glasses trained on the Race Committee boat *Cristobel*, now visible off the end of Governor's Island—the finish line. The right hand end of the line was a little closer, in the shadow of the Statue of Liberty.

"You know what, Jake?" Davey said under his breath. "It fucking hurts me when you talk to me like that. We both done good here. I ain't your doormat no more. Show me a little respect, for a change, okay?"

He swiveled and fixed Jacob with his sky blue eyes—their father's eyes. Jacob froze rigid, right where he stood; then, after a beat, his face softened. He reached out and touched Davey's arm, and said: "I'm sorry, Dave. You're right, I can be a gawmy sod sometimes. You deserve better. Listen—"

"You don't gotta say nothing. Not now. Let's just win this, eh?"

Jacob nodded solemnly, and Davey focused his eyes on the finish line.

The colorful flotilla of spectators boats in the Harbor had re-materialized, joined by those that had followed *Shamrock IV* down the river. The fleet was forming into a wide semi-circle below the finish, between Liberty Island and the steam yacht *Cristobel,* bedecked with colorful flags. On board, about now, the Race Officer would be readying a small brass cannon.

At Battery Park, a huge crowd had gathered to see the grand finale. It was as if Coney Island had come to Manhattan. Thousands of people lined the railing, dressed for the occasion—men in linen suits and Panama hats, women in their finery clutching lapdogs or small children, street merchants selling pretzels and balloons, and newsmen cranking box cameras. There were bookies on soap boxes yelling odds and exchanging fistfuls of cash. A handful of uniformed policemen bustled around the waterfront, trying to keep things in order. Some of the revelers were dancing on the steps of the rotunda to the strains of a ragtime band.

A young boy screamed from atop his father's shoulders: "Here they come!" Almost simultaneously the two yachts hauled into each other's view from opposite sides of Battery Point, greeted by an excited roar. It was a bizarre sight: to the west was *Shamrock IV,* her vast mainsail emblazoned with the *Lipton's Tea* logo, her pea-green hull ploughing backwards through the water. To the east was *Vanitie*, with her upper rigging a tangled mess of broken spars and ropes. Children were running and laughing. Mothers waved their handkerchiefs. There were *ooh*s and *aah*s when *Vanitie* caught a gust of the new wind from around the point and heeled way over on a beam reach, with the imperious Oliver Iselin now astride the helm. The bow of her bronze-plated hull sliced through the chop, gleaming like a diamond drill. The general ruckus swelled to a circus atmosphere.

About a thousand yards still separated the yachts, with the gap closing fast. *Shamrock* was perceptibly closer to the finish, perhaps only a minute from the line. But *Vanitie* was gaining, still a clear threat, the spray from her bows like smoke. Davey felt his heart pumping. If there was any risk of a collision, *Shamrock* would be required to give way, or *Vanitie* could claim the victory. They were shaving it close. Davey feared *Shamrock* had zero chance of making a seamanlike maneuver while traveling backwards at upwards of eight knots.

Two hundred yards from the finish line, he could see Oliver Iselin gesturing at *Vanitie*'s trimmers to haul the sails tighter, trying to eke every last drop of speed out of the bronze racer. Cochran, clutching a shattered wrist, was barking in his ear. But then his face took on a look of total despair: there was a thunderous crack, and *Vanitie*'s peak halyard parted. The throat tore away from the mast, and the massive gaff spar fell away to leeward, rending a long, wide rip most of the way down her cotton mainsail, until the head dangled helplessly with its peak trailing in the river. The crippled vessel skewed into the wind and slowed to a near standstill, in full view of a score of NYYC members and their wives lining the deck of the Commodore's steam yacht.

Moments later, *Shamrock IV*'s transom crossed the finishing line. The brass cannon fired from the bow of the Race Committee boat with a puff of smoke, its report drowned out by the ear-splitting chorus of horns and bells and claxons from the spectator fleet. The *Shamrock* sailors, with wide grins on their faces, cast off the preventer and let the mainsail flop in the breeze. One or two dropped to their knees. They stretched out their aching spines, and rubbed their raw, shredded hands. Some hugged and slapped each other on the back.

"Come here, little brother," said Jacob, grinning.

Harold Vanderbilt steered the victorious *Shamrock IV* slowly back past the Race Committee boat. The NYYC Flag Officers saluted and applauded him from the bridge. He tipped his cap in reply, and pointed the bow towards Battery Park. His happy but depleted crew spread out along the deck, waving to the spectator boats.

Davey and Jacob curled their bare toes over the bowsprit and soaked up the applause from the cheering crowds. *Shamrock IV* came alongside the embankment and turned east towards Brooklyn, only a hundred feet from the wall. Packed along the railing, each ecstatic face came into focus: to his delight, Davey spotted Sam from the Club, with his family. And Millie, too, his favorite coat check girl. And there was a whole posse from Deer Isle—Rollie Staples, Mug Budro, and Mr. Wilkinson among them—that had made it down to the City to watch the race.

"Davey! Look!"

There was their Ma, with Dr. Noyes. Their own Ma! She was crying into her handkerchief. Davey couldn't believe it. He yelled out to her, but it was lost in the hubbub. She managed a smile, and waved to her boys. She looked so pretty, and so well.

And there, in the midst of the crowd, was Edith Armitage, holding a baby. Alongside her, with his arm tight around her shoulder, stood Jeb Livingstone, the baby's proud father.

CHAPTER TWENTY-ONE

"You talked to her?"

"She walked me to the station this morning." Davey sighed. "Jeb Livingstone, ayuh. Who'd a thunk it?"

The pair of them were leaning back on a blanched log on Shell Beach, watching the last fading rays of the sunset that reddened the roofs of the huts on Powder House Island.

"It won't be easy," Jacob said.

"I reckon they'll be taken care of," Davey said. "Her old man left her his life savings. And Mr. Vanderbilt's giving Jeb a raise to stay on."

"Edith can get her old job back?"

"Yep. When the baby's old enough. They'll both miss her dad, though," said Davey. "So will I."

"He seemed like a good old bird."

"He was." Davey kicked a piece of driftwood, thrusting his hands deeper in his pockets. He saw Jacob watching his face, concerned. "I'm okay. There's other fish in the sea."

"You got that right, mate!" Jacob said. "I'm fixed up with a pretty pair of fish at McGinty's later. You should come."

"I might just do that." But Davey's mind was elsewhere. "Soon as we've got Ma's roof fixed up, I'm heading back to New York. Last thing she needs is one more mouth to feed. I'll be sending her half my paycheck every month, from the Library."

"Huh! You should be running that place. That geezer Squigley'll have to croak sooner or later."

"How will I know?" Davey laughed. "And, what about you?"

Jacob moved to the water's edge. "I kinda liked it in Europe. If we join the war, I might even sign up." He pulled out his tobacco tin and began to roll a smoke. The first faint star appeared above the eastern horizon. "I never told you the truth about why I sailed off on the *Westward,* after your accident, did I?"

Davey shook his head.

"See, there's a lot you don't know. Pa said to keep you out of it, for your own good. But I reckon you need to hear it now." He struck a match to light his smoke, and for a moment the glow lit up his face. He took a deep drag.

"When Pa and the boys got back from New York, they was all stoked up about winning the Cup. They walked round the town like lords o' the manor, showing off their winner's rings, melted down from *Defender*'s plates. A few weeks went by. One day Gardie Greene calls the crew together in the back room at the Oddfellows, and Uriah Rhodes is sitting there, all secret like. Rhodes says they're calling for witnesses to go on the stand at a hearing at the Yacht Club, to testify against Dunraven. They're gonna send a special train car, and they'll each get paid a pretty bundle—more than they ever made from the sailing. Only there's a catch. They have to follow a script. And there's to be no mention of what Pa was doin' down below decks, pumpin' out the bilges."

"Pumping air into the *bladders,* you mean."

"Well, yeah, but no one was sayin' that out loud, 'cos it was against the rules. All the boys are ready to take the money—they don't even have to lie, just swear there was never any extra pig lead brought on board. All except Pa, that is, and a bloke called Herb Bray, Coo's little brother—"

"Coo Bray has a brother?"

"—but he scarpered. Quit Deer Isle and never came back. Rumor was he was running an automobile showroom in Larchmont—then he vanished altogether."

Those initials, H.B... why did they sound so familiar?

"What about Pa?"

"He wouldn't have nothing to do with it. Flat refused to take Rhodes's dirty money, and he tried to talk the others out of it. He said any questions he was asked, he would tell the plain truth, nothing more, nothing less. That was what the Bible told him to do, and he would follow the Word of the Lord and his conscience. But when New York got wind that a couple of the Deer Islers weren't playing the game, they threatened to change their mind and not bring 'em to the tribunal at all, and no hush money neither."

"Not Rhodes' dirty money. *Iselin's*."

"Iselin's, yeah. So those West Bay bastards, led by Gardie, they sent Pa to Coventry. They blocked him, jostled him at the market. He'd find holes in his nets, or the bungs pulled out of his bilges. They cut his floats, and set his traps adrift. Anything to get him to take the money and shut the fuck up. Well, this goes on day after day, but Pa's not giving an inch, he's too proud.

"Then one day, right before the tribunal, Pa's on Rollie Staples' pier stacking his pots. He gets an 'accidental' nudge from that fucker Greene, and he trips on the edge of the dock and goes for a dive. It's low tide and only a couple of foot of water there, and the rocks and all. He was unconscious when they pulled him out. His head was bleeding, he had a belly full of sea water, but they was all laughing like hyenas. They got him to Doc Noyes, and the Doc fixed him up and sent him to bed. The rest of 'em traipsed off to New York, and came home with pockets o'cash—and not a cent for Pa, not even to pay his doctor's bill.

"Pa was never right after that. His eyes were all blurry, he couldn't make out his own floats in the water. He was getting headaches and sweats at night, and spitting up. In the end he goes back to the Doc, and Doc says there might be a blood clot in his brain. Told him he might have to think about doing something not so, you know... strenuous. Of course Pa would never quit lobstering, it was all he knew. He just went downhill from there. Every time he took the boat out, we was worried he'd never come home. One day—this was before his second stroke—he told me the whole story. He said, if anything ever happened to him, out on the Bay or whatever, I should *see* to Gardie Greene, Bible or no Bible."

Davey's eyes were squeezed shut, and the back of his head was pressed on the damp tree trunk.

"Oh Christ…"

"And I'll tell you what, Dave—and this is going to be hard for you to hear. When you ran out on that bowsprit, and slipped off and got mashed, it was 'cos someone had loosened the safety lines."

"Greene?"

"You don't need three guesses, mate."

Davey felt a jolt of phantom pain in his leg. Five long months in the hospital flashed by him, like a black hole in his young life.

"So don't hate me, Davey, but I'm going to tell it to you straight. When the *Westward* needed crew to cross the Atlantic, and Gardie Greene signed up, I knew that was my chance. I could never touch him in Deer Isle, with all his West Bay mates around him. We sailed off across the pond, and right when we was close to the end, off the coast of Ireland, there was this freak ice storm. Darker'n the inside o' my pocket, with icicles, an' all. Gardie was on night watch. I come up on deck, I checked no one was about. He was there alone on the foredeck, and I got right in his face. I told him to 'fess to what he done to Pa, or I was gonna bust him up. He just laughed and bared his gold tooth and pulled out that stupid fish knife of his, you know, with the antler handle? He's waving it at me like a daft git. He says, your Da was always a lily liver, he was a scab, he got what was coming to him, an' so did your little shit stain of a brother, too. Then the red mist come down and I went for his legs, and he falls back and cracks his head on the mast. I got the fish knife off him and Davey boy, I stuck that knife in the stupid cunt's gullet, right up to the hilt. He grabs onto a line, but the deck's all icy. He goes down on his knees with the blood pouring out his throat. He's all tangled up in the line, and I watched the life go out of his eyes. I was so frightened, I just left him like that and hid below. I thought, if the law catches up to me, then so be it, but at least I done right by our Pa. And that's God's honest truth. I done right by Pa."

Davey couldn't speak. He stared at his brother, his face contorted with a mixture of disgust and pity. Finally, through the bile rising in his throat, he said: "What happened when you got to port?"

"Oh, no one done a darn thing. In Cork there was this bent customs man, Sargeant Quinn. Uriah Rhodes slipped him a few quid, and he put it down as death by misadventure or whatnot," Jacob laughed. "We give him a Christian burial, which was more than that gawmy fucker deserved. I reckon Rhodes knew what was what, and he done me a solid."

Davey was counting the first dim stars that came out between the clouds. There was a gentle wind now, blowing in over the dark waters of Penobscot Bay. High up behind the beach, a rusty shed roof was creaking against a beam. A hermit crab scuttled under a rock. The air had a chill to it; it would be fall soon. He buttoned the collar of his shirt. Seconds went by, maybe minutes. He lost count.

"You ever seen the Aurora Borealis, Jake?"

His brother licked his fingers and fizzed out the glowing tip of his roll-up. "Ayuh, me and Pa, we seen 'em once, up at Aroostook. Beautiful, they were. Like dancers in the sky."

"I'd have been too young, I suppose."

"Yes, mate. That's about the size of it," Jake said, smiling. "Nobody never tells you stuff when you're the littlest."

Jacob hauled him to his feet. They walked back along the beach towards Ma's cottage, and the solitary light in the upstairs window.

THE END

Harold S. Vanderbilt was Commodore of the N.Y.Y.C from 1922-24. He successfully defended the America's Cup three times, in 1930, 1934 and 1937.

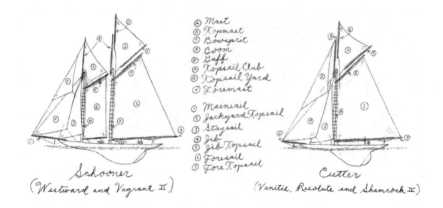

Ⓐ Mast
Ⓑ Topmast
Ⓒ Bowsprit
Ⓓ Boom
Ⓔ Gaff
Ⓕ Topsail Club
Ⓖ Topsail Yard
Ⓗ Foremast

① Mainsail
② Jackyard Topsail
③ Staysail
④ Jib
⑤ Jib Topsail
⑥ Foresail
⑦ Fore Topsail

Schooner
(Westward and Vagrant II)

Cutter
(Vanitie, Resolute and Shamrock IV)

GLOSSARY OF TERMS

'gybe-ho!'	call made when helmsman has started a turn away from the wind; the *boom* is about to swing across to the new side
'helm's a-lee!'	call made when helmsman has started a turn into the *eye of the wind*
'lee-ho!'	*See 'helm's a-lee'*
'ready about!'	call made when the helmsman is about to *tack* through the *eye of the wind*
aft	rear/back part of a boat; towards the *stern*
afterdeck	rear/back deck of a boat; around and behind the *helm*
afterguard	decision-making team on a racing yacht, usually helmsman, tactician, navigator etc.
aloft	up the mast, up in the rigging
amidships	middle part of a boat
AP flag	Answering Pennant (red and white vertical stripes)—'all races not yet started are postponed until further notice'
apparent wind	wind direction and speed experienced in the boat—a combination of *true wind* and that generated by forward motion
baby jibtopsail	small triangular sail usually flown from the forestay above other headsails

backing	deliberately filling a sail with wind from the 'wrong' side, to help turn a boat
backstay	rope or wire running from the top of a mast to the stern of the boat
bad air	temporarily unstable wind due to an obstruction or a competing sailboat that 'steals' another's wind
ballast	weight in the lower part of a vessel's hull to help keep her upright and/or extend the waterline
balloon jib	voluminous, loosely cut triangular headsail used for *reaching* and *running;* predecessor of the *spinnaker*
barky	seaman's familiar term for a yacht or ship
beam reach	sailing with the wind at right angles to the direction of travel
bear off, bear away	turn a boat's bow away from the wind direction eg from *close-hauled* to *reaching*
bearing	angle between the craft's forward direction and the location of another object
belay	tie off or *make fast* a line; cancel an order
belaying pin	wood or metal pin to which ropes and *halyards* are *made fast*
binnacle	waist-high case or stand on the deck of a vessel, generally mounted in front of the helmsman, in which navigational instruments are located
bioluminescence	biochemical emission of light by a living organism. Sometimes seen at night in calm, warm water as a blue or green glow
block	pulley that ropes and lines are pulled through. Multiple blocks add leverage or *purchase*
bobstay	diagonal support wire from the tip of the *bowsprit* down to the stem of a vessel

boom	wood or metal pole supporting and controlling the foot of a sail
bowman	sailor whose position is in the bow of a boat
bows	foremost part of a vessel
bowse	haul by means of a *tackle*
bowsprit	spar extending forward from a vessel's bow, to which *forestays* and *bobstay* are fastened
broad reach	fast point of sailing with the wind blowing over a vessel's *quarter*; ~100 degrees to ~150 degrees to the direction of travel
bulkhead	dividing wall or barrier between compartments in a vessel
burgee	flag bearing the colors or emblem of a sailing club, typically triangular
by the lee	vessel sailing with sails on the wrong side of the boat; poor steering, or a sudden change of wind direction, can cause a vessel to be 'caught by the lee'
catboat	US East Coast fishing vessel with a single sail
capstan	rotating vertical drum for raising an anchor, hauling in a cable etc
cavitate	sudden formation and collapse of low-pressure bubbles in liquid. Causes a keel or rudder to lose its 'grip'
centerboard	an extendable/retractable keel, allowing a vessel to sail in shallower water
clew	the rear corner of a sail
clinker-built	a method of boat building where the edges of hull planks overlap each other
close reach	point of sailing with the wind blowing at ~55 degrees to ~80 degrees to the direction of travel

close-hauled	sailing as close as possible to the wind direction; typically heeled over
companionway	steps or ladder from the deck down into the vessel
corrected time	a vessel's elapsed time to complete a race, adjusted for her *handicap*
covering	keeping your sailboat between the opposition and the next mark to make it harder for them to overtake
crash-tack	a too-rushed *tack*
crash-gybe	a too-rushed *gybe,* also a *Chinese gybe*
cross, cross in front	when boats on opposite *tacks* converge and one passes ahead of the other
crosstrees	horizontal stanchions part way up a mast, supporting *shrouds*
crutch	support for a boom when the main sail is lowered. Usually stowed when moving
displacement	amount of water displaced by a hull, ie a vessel's weight
dolphin smasher/ masher	rigid metal stanchion running from the bowsprit down to the bobstay; also known as a *martingale*
douse	pull down a sail
dredger	vessel for clearing mud from the sea bed
drudging	trailing a rope or anchor behind a vessel in order to control her drift or orientation
duck below	when two vessels converge on opposite tacks and one opts to *bear away* and pass behind the other
bear away, ease away, bear/crack/ fall off	turn away from the wind, eg from *close-hauled* to a *reach*
ebb tide	falling/receding tide, lowering the sea level

eddy, eddies	channel of water moving in opposite direction to general tidal flow
ensign	flag on a vessel denoting nationality or club affiliation
eye of the wind	precise direction from which the wind is blowing
falls	slack part of a rope, coils
fathom	six feet of depth
fetch	course that will allow a boat to round a point or *windward* mark without additional *tacks*
fife rail	also *pin rail*; wooden rail surrounding base of a mast with a number of *belaying* pins to which lines and halyards are made fast
flake	fold a sail horizontally onto a boom or deck
Flood tide	rising/advancing tide, raising the sea level
flying bridge, flybridge	open deck located above the wheelhouse, or bridge on the cabin roof
flying jib	triangular foresail, outermost of two or more jibs, set well above the jib
footrope	rope enabling crew to walk out along a bowsprit or spar
foremast	forward of two or more masts
foresail, fors'l	principal sail on a *foremast*
forward, for'ard	front part of a boat; towards the *bow*
forestay	wire supporting the strain on the front of a mast, attached to the *bow* or *bowsprit*
fouled	rope, line, chain or net that is caught or tangled up; also, a racing boat that has been compromised by a competing boat that has broken a rule of racing
Friendship sloop	small traditional fishing boat design originating in Friendship, Maine
furl	fold a sail

gaff	diagonal *spar* supporting the head of a *mainsail* or *foresail*
gaff-rigged	vessel with a four-sided *mainsail* with a diagonal *gaff* at the head. (As opposed to three-sided Bermudian or Marconi rig)
galley	boat's kitchen
go about	or *tack*; turn through the *eye of the wind*, switching sails to the opposite side
gybe	turn further away from the wind while *running*, switching sails to the opposite side
gunwale, gunnel	upper edge of the side of a boat or ship
halyard	rope or wire attached to the head of a sail or spar, used to haul a sail up the mast
handicap	formula applied to the time of each vessel to complete a race, in order to compensate for differences in size or speed. Can be based on measurement of hull and sails, or past performance
harden sails	haul in or trim sails, eg when turning more into the wind or rounding a *leeward* mark
heading	direction a vessel is pointing
heave-to	bring a sailboat to a halt by *backing* some sails to 'put on the 'brakes'
helm	steering mechanism; can be a wheel or a tiller; also the person steering the vessel
hoist	raise a sail or spar
holystoning	scrubbing the deck with a brittle sandstone
hoops	sliding wood or metal rings, sometimes wrapped in leather, connecting the *luff* or front of a sail to the mast
inboard	closer to the centerline of a vessel

jackyard topsail	large three- or four-sided sail flown above the mainsail with its own upper and lower spars
jib	triangular foresail flown on the forestay
Jibtopsail	triangular foresail flown on the forestay above other headsails
Judas	a loose line
keel	heavy longitudinal metal plate along the centerline of a vessel's hull, extended downward to increase stability
knots	nautical miles per hour (1 nautical mile = 1.1508 statue miles)
lay line	an imaginary line which, if followed while *close-hauled*, would allow a boat to *fetch* a mark without additional *tacks*
launch	naval motor vessel for harbor use
lazarette	sail lock near *stern* of boat
lazy sheets	unused one of a pair of ropes that *sheet in* a headsail
lee	side of a vessel furthest from the *eye of the wind* and therefore usually more sheltered
leeward	furthest from the *eye of the wind*
leeward mark	turning mark in sailboat race that is farthest from the *eye of the wind*
longshoreman	person employed in a port to load and unload ships
luff up	turn towards the *eye of the wind*; when a *leeward right-of-way* boat forces a *windward* boat further up to windward
luffing	a sail that is flapping; the act of forcing a windward boat further up to windward
make fast	tie off or belay a line

mainsheet, main sheet	rope connected to and controlling the end of the boom and therefore the angle of the mainsail
martingale	rigid metal stanchion running from the bowsprit down to the bobstay; also known as a *dolphin masher/smasher*
masthead (man)	highest part of a mast; sailor working *aloft*, or posted as lookout
movable ballast	weight in the lower part of a vessel's hull to help keep her upright (and/or extend the waterline) that can be moved when tacking, sailing downwind etc
new wind	wind coming from a new direction, eg later in the day, as the land heats up, or around a headland
off the wind	away from *the eye of the wind*; pointing lower than optimal due to bad steering
one-design	certain design/rigging restrictions that a class of racing sailboat must conform to in order to assure equality
overpowered	sailing with too much sail area for the current wind conditions; can be slower, and potentially dangerous
overstand	sail too far past the *layline* before *tacking*, therefore covering unnecessary distance
pay off	turn the bow away from the wind to fill the sails and pick up speed
phosphorescence	delayed emission of light
pin rail	also *fife rail*; wooden rail surrounding base of a mast with a number of *belaying pins* to which lines and *halyards* are *made fast*
port tack	with the wind coming over the left side of the boat. A port-tack boat must give way to a starboard-tack boat
port, starboard	left, right

port-light	openable window in the side or deck of a vessel
powered up	with wind filling well-trimmed sails, providing optimal forward motion
prevailing wind	predominant wind direction and force in a given season; predictable, and named for the broad area of the Earth over which it forms
preventer	line attached to the rear end of a boom and hauled forward to prevent it from accidentally flying across the boat
protest	if a racing sailboat believes she has been *fouled* (with or without a collision) she may protest the other boat, which may result in that boat being penalized or disqualified
prow	where the sharp forward end of a hull meets the deck
purchase	gaining mechanical advantage, leverage; a line that adds additional leverage eg to a *mainsheet*
quarter	off the aft 1/4 of a vessel
R.C. boat	Race Committee boat that sets the start/finish line, marks, flags, timing, course, gun etc, usually anchored
rail	the edge of a sailboat's deck; can refer to a safety guardrail to prevent from slipping overboard
rake	the degree to which a mast is angled backwards from the vertical. More rake will tend to cause a boat to steer up into the wind.
ratlines	ladder rungs to enable crew to climb up the *shrouds* of a mast from the *rail*
reef	submerged or exposed rocks; to reduce the exposed sail area in strong winds
reef points	thin ropes attached to the lower portion of a sail allowing its foot to be furled to reduce the exposed sail area in strong winds

reefing tackle	ropes and *blocks* used to reduce sail when *reefing*
right-of-way	when boats meet, one has the right to hold her course and the other must 'give way.' eg the starboard-tack or leeward boat has right-of-way.
rolled	overtaken by another boat, usually because they 'stole' your wind or gave you *bad air*
round up	turn into the wind from a from close-hauled course; bring sailboat to a standstill
rudder	vertical plate in wood or metal that steers the boat by displacing water to either side
run	sail with the wind directly behind
runners, running backstays	rope or wire running from the top of a mast to the stern of the boat—usually in port/starboard pairs, because one will take up the tension on the mast while the other is let go slack
saloon	main living/dining area on a yacht
schooner	a fast yacht with two or more masts
scuppers	hole or gap in the side of sailboat's deck/rail to let water out when heeled over
sheet	rope that pulls in the *clew* or back corner of a sail to fill it with wind
sheet in, sheet, haul in	pull in the clew of back corner of a sail to fill it with wind
shrouds	wire or rope supporting the mast(s) amidships from the rail
skiff	flat-bottomed rowboat typically with a pointed bow and square stern
smack	traditional large fishing sailboat
sounding	measuring or measurement of water depth, usually counted in fathoms (1 fathom=6 feet)
spans	transverse links of a *peak halyard* on a *gaff-rigged* sail, connecting the *gaff* to the main mast

spar	wood or metal pole supporting the head or foot of a sail
spinnaker	parachute-shaped sail for downwind sailing
spreaders	stanchions used to deflect the *shrouds* and allow them to better support the mast
starboard tack	sailing with the wind coming over the right side of the boat. A starboard-tack boat has the *right-of-way* over a port-tack boat
stays	wires or ropes used to support masts
staysail, stays'l	large triangular sail running from the deck towards the tip of the mast, usually with its own *boom*
stern	back or rear of the boat
sternsheets	a boat's aft-most section, or the seating in this section of an open boat
stops	a sail is sometimes hoisted 'in stops' meaning it is tied with wool, like a string of sausages, making it easier to hoist—then 'broken out' by yanking on the *sheets*
bollard	a solid drum bolted to the deck, around which a *sheet* or *halyard* is wound to take the strain
tack	or *go about*; turn through the *eye of the wind*, switching sails to the opposite side
tack line	rope connecting a sail's bottom forward corner to the deck, mast or bowsprit
tackle	mechanism consisting of ropes, pulley blocks, hooks etc, for lifting heavy objects
taffrail	rail around a ship's *stern*, sometimes ornamented
tar	familiar name for a working seaman
telescoping topmast	mast extension that fits inside the mainmast and can be wound up using an interior winch
tender	support vessel for a larger boat

throat	swiveling junction between a *boom* or *gaff* and the mast
thwart	a bench seat across a small boat
tiller	lever/handle controlling the *rudder* in a boat with no steering wheel
topmast	extension to the mainmast, required is flying a topsail
topping lift	lines from the top of the mast to the tip of the *boom* to keep it raised when the sail is down or to help with tacks and gybes
topsail cutter	yacht with a single mast, *gaff-rigged* mainsail, and triangular topsail, eg America's Cup yachts before 1930
topsail, tops'l	triangular sail hoisted above the mainsail
transit	imaginary line extension drawn between two visual points, eg a smokestack and a flagpole, to aid with positioning during a sail race
transom	flat vertical rear side of a vessel
trim	adjust sails for optimum performance
trimmer	sailor whose job it is to *trim* sails, eg jib trimmer, mainsheet trimmer
true wind	actual wind direction and speed, as if a boat were anchored or not moving
upwind/downwind	towards/away from the *eye of the wind*. In a sailboat race, there are usually several *upwind* (tacking, zigzagging) and *downwind* (often with *spinnaker*) legs
veer/back	the compass wind direction moves clockwise (veers) or anti-clockwise (backs)
way	forward momentum through the water
weather mark, windward mark	turning mark on a sailboat race course that is closest to the *eye of the wind*

weather rail/leeward rail	upwind or downwind side of a heeling sailboat. Crew usually line the weather rail to add ballast. The leeward rail is often close to or under the water
wind shot	turning directly into the eye of the wind before the start of a race, with sails flapping, to verify which end of the line is 'favored' ie further upwind
windlass	horizontal turning drum to aid with hauling up an anchor or a line
windward/leeward boat	when two boats sail in parallel on the same tack, the leeward boat (furthest from the *eye of the wind*) has the right-of-way

ACKNOWLEDGMENTS

I have many people to thank for helping me bring this novel to print. Firstly, my grandmother Margery Spring-Rice whose coffee-table book of giant photographs by 'Beken of Cowes' led me, as a young boy, to my love of classic racing yachts. Mark Gabrielson, whose excellent biography 'Deer Isle's Undefeated America's Cup Heroes' inspired me to write my own fictional account of the 1913-14 campaign. The creative writing coaches who convinced me 'it's not that hard' (they were wrong!): Michelle Brafman, Bridget McNulty, and Fiona Ingram. My literary agent Merrilee Heifetz who told me, to my amazement, that she'd spent every summer in Deer Isle for the last thirty years; and the locals she connected me with, including a young waterman who rowed me around Stonington Harbor during his lunch break. Tony Brannon, my guide to the former British naval port of St. Georges, Bermuda. Leslie Wells for her patient editorial advice; Grant Morris for his friendship and support; and Carli Schultz for her project management. On the historical research front, I am grateful to Americas Cup scholar Steve Tsuchiya, and Darien Brahms for their research into the NYYC members' list of the early 1900s. My medical/physical therapy advisors were Jen Millar, Josh Ewen, and Sharon Turban. Finally, my understanding of how to sail and race classic yachts has benefitted from conversations with expert mariners Jim Thom, Ken Read, Bouwe Becking, Andrew Gilmour and Barney Sandeman.

I have tried to make the sail racing as authentic, and the historical and geographical settings as plausible as I can, but there may be inaccuracies. I apologize in advance if I have offended any living descendants of the historical characters named in my book.

Printed in the USA
CPSIA information can be obtained
at www.ICGtesting.com
CBHW021757300724
12430CB00017B/135

9 781665 758314